EX LIBRIS

VINTAGE CLASSICS

THE MERRY-GO-ROUND

William Somerset Maugham was born in 1874 and lived in Paris until he was ten. He was educated at King's School, Canterbury, and at Heidelberg University. He spent some time at St. Thomas' Hospital with the idea of practising medicine, but the success of his first novel, *Liza of Lambeth*, published in 1897, won him over to letters. *Of Human Bondage*, the first of his masterpieces, came out in 1915, and with the publication in 1919 of *The Moon and Sixpence* his reputation as a novelist was established. At the same time his fame as a successful playwright and short story writer was being consolidated with acclaimed productions of various plays and the publication of *The Trembling of a Leaf*, subtitled *Little Stories of the South Sea Islands*, in 1921, which was followed by seven more collections. His other works include travel books, essays, criticism and the autobiographical *The Summing Up* and *A Writer's Notebook*.

In 1927 Somerset Maugham settled in the South of France and lived there until his death in 1965.

OTHER WORKS BY W. SOMERSET MAUGHAM

W. SOMERSET MAUGHAM

The Merry-Go-Round

VINTAGE BOOKS
London

Published by Vintage 2000

6 8 10 9 7

First published in Great Britain by William Heinemann in 1905

Vintage
Random House, 20 Vauxhall Bridge Road,
London SW1V 2SA

www.vintage-classics.info

Addresses for companies within The Random House Group Limited
can be found at: www.randomhouse.co.uk/offices.htm

The Random House Group Limited Reg. No. 954009

A CIP catalogue record for this book
is available from the British Library

ISBN 9780099288701

The Random House Group Limited supports The Forest Stewardship
Council® (FSC®), the leading international forest-certification organisation.
Our books carrying the FSC label are printed on FSC®-certified paper.
FSC is the only forest-certification scheme supported by the leading
environmental organisations, including Greenpeace. Our
paper procurement policy can be found at
www.randomhouse.co.uk/environment

MIX
Paper from
responsible sources
FSC® C016897
www.fsc.org

Printed and bound in Great Britain by Clays Ltd, St Ives plc

TO

HERBERT AND MARGUERITE BUNNING

'I bring not only all I wrought
Into the faltering words of speech,
I dedicate the song I sought,
Yet could not reach.'

1

ALL her life Miss Elizabeth Dwarris had been a sore trial to her relations. A woman of means, she ruled tyrannously over a large number of impecunious cousins, using her bank balance like the scorpions of Rehoboam to chastise them; and, like many another pious creature, for their souls' good making all and sundry excessively miserable. Nurtured in the Evangelical ways current in her youth, she insisted that her connections should seek salvation according to her own lights, and with harsh tongue and bitter gibe made it her constant business to persuade them of their extreme unworthiness. She arranged lives as she thought fit, and ventured not only to order the costume and habits, but even the inner thought, of those about her; the Last Judgement could have no terrors for any that had faced her searching examination. She invited to stay with her in succession various poor ladies who presumed on a distant tie to call her Aunt Eliza, and they accepted her summons, more imperious than a royal command, with gratitude by no means unmixed with fear, bearing the servitude meekly as a cross which in the future would meet due testamentary reward.

Miss Dwarris loved to feel her power. During these long visits – for in a way the old lady was very hospitable – she made it her especial object to break the spirit of her guests, and it entertained her hugely to see the mildness with which were borne her extravagant demands, the humility with which every inclination was crushed. She took a malicious pleasure in publicly affronting persons, ostensibly to bend a sinful pride, or in obliging them to do things which they peculiarly disliked. With a singular quickness for discovering the points on which they were most sensitive, she attacked every weakness with blunt invective till the sufferer writhed before her raw and bleeding; no defect, physical or mental, was protected from her raillery, and she could pardon as little an excess of avoirdupois as a want

7

of memory. Yet with all her heart she despised her victims, she flung in their face insolently their mercenary spirit, vowing that she would never leave a penny to such a pack of weak fools; it delighted her to ask for advice in the distribution of her property among charitable societies, and she heard with unconcealed hilarity their unwilling and confused suggestions.

With one of her relations only Miss Dwarris found it needful to observe a certain restraint – for Miss Ley, perhaps the most distant of her cousins, was as plain-spoken as herself, and had besides a far keener wit, whereby she could turn rash statements to the utter ridicule of the speaker. Nor did Miss Dwarris precisely dislike this independent spirit; she looked upon her, in fact, with a certain degree of affection and not a little fear. Miss Ley, seldom lacking a repartee, appeared really to enjoy the verbal contests, from which, by her greater urbanity, readiness, and knowledge, she usually emerged victorious; it confounded, but at the same time almost amused, the elder lady that a woman so much poorer than herself, with no smaller claim than others to the coveted inheritance, should venture not only to be facetious at her expense, but even to carry war into her very camp. Miss Ley, really not grieved to find someone to whom without prickings of conscience she could speak her whole mind, took a grim pleasure in pointing out to her cousin the poor logic of her observations or the foolish unreason of her acts. No cherished opinion of Miss Dwarris was safe from satire; even her Evangelicism was laughed at, and the rich old woman, unused to argument, was easily driven to self-contradiction; and then – for the victor took no pains to conceal her triumph – she grew pale and speechless with rage. The quarrels were frequent, but Miss Dwarris, though it was a sharp thorn in her flesh that the first advances must be made by her, in the end always forgave. Yet at last it was inevitable that a final breach should occur. The cause thereof, characteristically enough, was very trivial.

Miss Ley, accustomed when she went abroad for the winter to let her little flat in Chelsea, had been obliged by unforeseen circumstances to return to England while her tenants were still in possession, and had asked Miss Dwarris whether she might stay with her in Old Queen Street. The old tyrant, much as she hated her relatives, hated still more to live alone; she needed someone on whom to vent her temper, and through the illness of a niece, due to spend March and April with her, had been forced to pass a month of solitude. She wrote back, in the peremptory fashion which even with Miss Ley she could not refrain from using, that she expected her on such and such a day by such and such a train. It is not clear whether there was in the letter anything to excite in Miss Ley a contradictory spirit, or whether her engagements really prevented it, but at all events she answered that her plans made it more convenient to arrive on the day following and by a different train. Miss Dwarris telegraphed that unless her guest came on the day and at the hour mentioned in her letter she could not send the carriage to meet her, to which the younger lady replied concisely: 'Don't!'

'She's as obstinate as a pig,' muttered Miss Dwarris, reading the telegram, and she saw in her mind's eye the thin smile on her cousin's mouth when she wrote that one indifferent word. 'I suppose she thinks she's very clever.'

Her hostess greeted Miss Ley, notwithstanding, with a certain grim affability reserved only for her; she was at all events the least detestable of her relations, and, though neither docile nor polite, at least was never tedious. Her conversation braced Miss Dwarris, so that with her she was usually at her best, and sometimes, forgetting her overbearing habit, showed herself a sensible and entertaining woman of not altogether unamiable disposition.

'You're growing old, my dear,' said Miss Dwarris when they sat down to dinner, looking at her guest with eyes keen to detect wrinkles and crow's-feet.

'You flatter me,' Miss Ley retorted; 'antiquity is the only excuse for a woman who has determined on a single life.'

'I suppose, like the rest of them, you would have married if anyone had asked you?'

Miss Ley smiled.

'Two months ago an Italian Prince offered me his hand and heart, Eliza.'

9

'A Papist would do anything,' replied Miss Dwarris. 'I suppose you told him your income, and he found he'd misjudged the strength of his affections.'

'I refused him because he was so virtuous.'

'I shouldn't have thought at your age you could afford to pick and choose, Polly.'

'Allow me to observe that you have an amiable faculty for thinking of one subject at one time in two diametrically opposed ways.'

Miss Ley was a slender woman of middle size; her hair, very plainly arranged, beginning to turn grey, and her face, already much wrinkled, by its clear precision of feature indicating a comfortable strength of character; her lips, thin but expressive, mobile, added to this appearance of determination. She was by no means handsome, and had certainly never been pretty, but her carriage was not without grace nor her manner without fascination. Her eyes were very bright, and so shrewd as sometimes to be almost disconcerting: without words they could make pretentiousness absurd; and most affectations, under that searching glance, part contemptuous, part amused, willingly hid themselves. Yet, as Miss Dwarris took care to remind her, she was not without her own especial pose, but it was carried out so admirably, with such a restrained, comely decorum, that few observed it, and such as did found not the heart to condemn: it was the perfect art that concealed itself. To execute this æsthetic gesture, it pleased Miss Ley to dress with the greatest possible simplicity, usually in black, and her only ornament was a Renaissance jewel of such exquisite beauty that no museum would have disdained to possess it: this she wore around her neck attached to a long gold chain, and she fingered it with pleasure, to show, according to her plain-spoken relative, the undoubted beauty of her hands. Her well-fitting shoes and the elaborate open-work of her silk stockings suggested also a not unreasonable pride in a shapely foot, small and high of instep. Thus attired, when she had visitors Miss Ley sat in an Italian straight-backed chair of oak, and delicately carved, which was placed between two windows against the wall; and she cultivated already a certain primness of manner which made very effective the audacious criticism of life wherewith she was used to entertain her friends.

Two mornings after her arrival in Old Queen Street Miss Ley announced her intention to go out. She came downstairs with a very fashionable parasol, a purchase on her way through Paris.

'You're not going out with that thing?' cried Miss Dwarris scornfully.

'I am indeed.'

'Nonsense; you must take an umbrella. It's going to rain.'

'I have a new sunshade and an old umbrella, Eliza. I feel certain it will be fine.'

'My dear, you know nothing about the English climate. I tell you it will pour cats and dogs.'

'Fiddlesticks, Eliza!'

'Polly,' answered Miss Dwarris, her temper rising, 'I wish you to take an umbrella. The barometer is going down, and I have a tingling in my feet which is a sure sign of wet. It's very irreligious of you to presume to say what the weather is going to be.'

'I venture to think that meteorologically I am no less acquainted with the ways of Providence than you.'

'That, I think, is not funny, but blasphemous, Polly. In my house I expect people to do as I tell them, and I insist on your taking an umbrella.'

'Don't be absurd, Eliza!'

Miss Dwarris rang the bell, and when the butler appeared ordered him to fetch her own umbrella for Miss Ley.

'I absolutely refuse to use it,' said the younger lady, smiling.

'Pray remember that you are my guest, Polly.'

'And therefore entitled to do exactly as I like.'

Miss Dwarris rose to her feet, a massive old woman of commanding presence, and stretched out a threatening hand.

'If you leave this house without an umbrella, you shall not come into it again. You shall never cross this threshold so long as I am alive.'

Miss Ley cannot have been in the best of humours that morning, for she pursed her lips in the manner already characteristic of her, and looked at her elderly cousin with a cold scorn most difficult to bear.

'My dear Eliza, you have a singularly exaggerated idea of your importance. Are there no hotels in London? You appear to think I stay with you for pleasure rather than to mortify my flesh. And really the cross is growing too heavy for me, for I think you must have quite the worst cook in the Metropolis.'

'She's been with me for five-and-twenty years,' answered Miss Dwarris, two red spots appearing on her cheeks, 'and no one has ventured to complain of the cooking before. If any of my guests had done so, I should have answered that what was good enough for me was a great deal too good for anyone else. I know that you're obstinate, Polly, and quick-tempered, and this impertinence I am willing to overlook. Do you still refuse to do as I wish?'

'Yes.'

Miss Dwarris rang the bell violently.

'Tell Martha to pack Miss Ley's boxes at once, and call a four-wheeler,' she cried in tones of thunder.

'Very well, madam,' answered the butler, used to his mistress' vagaries.

Then Miss Dwarris turned to her guest, who observed her with irritating good-humour.

'I hope you realize, Polly, that I fully mean what I say.'

'All is over between us,' answered Miss Ley mockingly, 'and shall I return your letters and your photographs?'

Miss Dwarris sat for a while in silent anger, watching her cousin, who took up the *Morning Post* and with great calmness read the fashionable intelligence. Presently the butler announced that the four-wheeler was at the door.

'Well, Polly, so you're really going?'

'I can hardly stay when you've had my boxes packed and sent for a cab,' replied Miss Ley mildly.

'It's your own doing; I don't wish you to go. If you'll confess that you were headstrong and obstinate, and if you'll take an umbrella, I am willing to let bygones be bygones.'

'Look at the sun,' answered Miss Ley.

And, as if actually to annoy the tyrannous old woman, the

shining rays danced into the room and made importunate patterns on the carpet.

'I think I should tell you, Polly, that it was my intention to leave you ten thousand pounds in my will. This intention I shall, of course, not now carry out.'

'You'd far better leave your money to the Dwarris people. Upon my word, considering that they've been related to you for over sixty years, I think they thoroughly deserve it.'

'I shall leave my money to whom I choose,' cried Miss Dwarris, beside herself; 'and if I want to, I shall leave every penny of it in charity. You're very independent because you have a beggarly five hundred a year, but apparently it isn't enough for you to live without letting your flat when you go away. Remember that no one has any claims upon me, and I can make you a rich woman.'

Miss Ley replied with great deliberation.

'My dear, I have a firm conviction that you will live for another thirty years to plague the human race in general, and your relations in particular. It is not worth my while, on the chance of surviving you, to submit to the caprices of a very ignorant old woman, presumptuous and overbearing, dull and pretentious.'

Miss Dwarris gasped and shook with rage, but the other proceeded without mercy.

'You have plenty of poor relations – bully them. Vent your spite and ill-temper on those wretched sycophants, but, pray, in future spare *me* the infinite tediousness of your conversation.'

Miss Ley had ever a discreet passion for the rhetorical, and there was a certain grandiloquence about the phrase which entertained her hugely. She felt that it was unanswerable, and with great dignity walked out. No communication passed between the two ladies, though Miss Dwarris, peremptory, stern, and Evangelical to the end, lived in full possession of her faculties for nearly twenty years. She died at last in a passion occasioned by some trifling misdemeanour of her maid; and, as though a heavy yoke were removed from their shoulders, her family heaved a deep and unanimous sigh of relief.

They attended her funeral with dry eyes, looking still with

13

silent terror at the leaden coffin which contained the remains of that harsh, strong, domineering old woman; then, nervously expectant, begged the family solicitor to disclose her will. Written with her own hand, and witnessed by two servants, it was in these terms:

I, Elizabeth Ann Dwarris, of 79 Old Queen Street, Westminster, spinster, hereby revoke all former wills and testamentary dispositions made by me, and declare this to be my last will and testament. I appoint Mary Ley, of 72 Eliot Mansions, Chelsea, to be the executrix of this my will, and I give all my real and personal property whatsoever to the said Mary Ley. To my great-nephews and great-nieces, to my cousins near and remote, I give my blessing, and I beseech them to bear in mind the example and advice which for many years I have given them. I recommend them to cultivate in future strength of character and an independent spirit. I venture to remind them that the humble will never inherit this earth, for their reward is to be awaited in the life to come, and I desire them to continue the subscriptions which, at my request, they have so long and generously made to the Society for the Conversion of the Jews and to the Additional Curates Fund.

In witness whereof I have set my hand to this my will the 4th day of April, 1883.

ELIZABETH ANN DWARRIS

To her amazement, Miss Ley found herself at the age of fifty-seven in possession of nearly three thousand pounds a year, the lease of a pleasant old house in Westminster, and a great quantity of early Victorian furniture. The will was written two days after her quarrel with the eccentric old woman, and the terms of it certainly achieved the three purposes for which it was designed: it occasioned the utmost surprise to all concerned, heaped coals of fire on Miss Ley's indifferent head, and caused the bitterest disappointment and vexation to all that bore the name of Dwarris.

2

It did not take Miss Ley very long to settle in her house. To its new owner, who hated modernity with all her heart, part of the charm lay in its quaint old fashion: built in the reign of Queen Anne, it had the leisurely, spacious comfort of dwelling-places in that period, with a hood over the door that was a pattern of elegance, wrought-iron railings, and, to Miss Ley's especial delight, extinguishers for the link-boys' torches.

The rooms were large, somewhat low-pitched, with wide windows overlooking the most consciously beautiful of all the London parks. Miss Ley made no great alterations. An epicurean to her finger-tips, for many years the passion for liberty had alone disturbed the equanimity of her indolent temper. But to secure freedom, entire and absolute freedom, she was ever ready to make any sacrifice: ties affected her with a discomfort that seemed really akin to physical pain, and she avoided them – ties of family or of affection, ties of habit or of thought – with all the strenuousness of which she was capable. She had taken care never in the course of her life to cumber herself with chattels, and once, with a courage in which there was surely something heroic, feeling that she became too much attached to her belongings – cabinets and exquisite fans brought from Spain, Florentine frames of gilded wood and English mezzotints, Neapolitan bronzes, tables and settees discovered in out-of-the-way parts of France – she had sold everything. She would not risk to grow so fond of her home that it was a pain to leave it; she preferred to remain a wayfarer, sauntering through life with a heart keen to detect beauty, and a mind, open and unbiassed, ready to laugh at the absurd. So it fitted her humour to move with the few goods which she possessed into her cousin's house as though it were but a furnished lodging, remaining there still unfettered; and when Death came – a pagan youth, twin brother to Sleep, rather

15

than the grim and bony skeleton of Christian faith – ready to depart like a sated reveller, smiling dauntlessly and without regret. A new and personal ordering, the exclusion of many pieces of clumsy taste, gave Miss Ley's drawing-room quickly a more graceful and characteristic air: the *objets d'art* collected since the memorable sale added a certain grave delicacy to the arrangement; and her friends noticed without surprise that, as in her own flat, the straight, carved chair was set between two windows, and the furniture deliberately placed so that from it the mistress of the house, herself part of the aesthetic scheme, could command and manipulate her guests.

No sooner was Miss Ley comfortably settled than she wrote to an old friend and distant cousin, Algernon Langton, Dean of Tercanbury, asking him to bring his daughter to visit her new house; and Miss Langton replied that they would be pleased to come, fixing a certain Thursday morning for their arrival. Miss Ley greeted her relatives without effusion, for it was her whim to discourage manifestations of affection; but notwithstanding the good-humoured, polite contempt with which it was her practice to treat the clergy in general, she looked upon her cousin Algernon with real esteem.

He was a tall old man, spare and bent, with very white hair and a pallid, almost transparent, skin; his eyes were cold and blue, but his expression singularly gentle. There was a dignity in his bearing, and at the same time an infinite graciousness which reminded you of those famous old ecclesiastics whose names have cast for ever a certain magnificent renown upon the English Church; he had a good deal of the polished breeding which made them, whatever their origin, gentlemen and courtiers, and, like theirs, his Biblical erudition was perhaps less noteworthy than his classical attainments. And if he was a little narrow, unwilling to consider seriously modern ways of thought, there was an aesthetic quality about him and a truly Christian urbanity which attracted admiration, and even love. Miss Ley, a student of men, who could observe with interest the most diverse tendencies (for to her sceptical mind no way of life nor method of thought was intrinsically more valuable

16

than another), was pleased with his stately, candid simplicity, and used with him a forbearance which was not customary to her.

'Well, Polly,' said the Dean, 'I suppose now you are a woman of property you will give up your wild-goose chase after the unattainable. You will settle down and become a respectable member of society.'

'You need not insist that my hair is greyer than when last you saw me, and my wrinkles more apparent.'

At this time Miss Ley, who had altered little in the last twenty years, resembled extraordinarily the portrait-statue of Agrippina in the museum at Naples. She had the same lined face, with its look of rather scornful indifference for mundane affairs, and that well-bred distinction of manner which the Empress had acquired through the command of multitudes, but Miss Ley, more finely, through the command of herself.

'But you're right, Algernon,' she added, 'I am growing old, and I doubt whether I should have again the courage to sell all my belongings. I do not think I could face the utter loneliness in which I rejoiced when I felt I had nothing I could call my own but the clothes on my back.'

'You had quite a respectable income.'

'For which the saints be praised! No one can think of freedom who has less than five hundred a year; without that, life is a mere sordid struggle for daily bread.'

The Dean, hearing that luncheon would not be ready till two, went out, and Miss Ley was left alone with his daughter. Bella Langton had reached that age when she could by no stretch of courtesy be described as a girl, and her father but lately, somewhat to her dismay, had composed a set of Latin verses on her fortieth birthday. She was not pretty, nor had she the graceful dignity which made the Dean so becoming a figure in the cathedral chapter: somewhat squarely built, her hair, of a pleasant brown, was severely arranged; her features were too broad and her complexion rather oddly weather-beaten, but her grey eyes were very kindly, and her expression singularly good-humoured. Following provincial fashions in somewhat costly materials, she dressed with the serviceable plain-

17

ness affected by the pious virgins who congregate in cathedral cities, and the result was an impression of very expensive dowdiness. She was obviously a capable woman who could be depended upon in any emergency. Charitable in an unimaginative, practical way, she was a fit and competent leader for the philanthropy of Tercanbury, and, fully conscious of her importance in the ecclesiastical hierarchy, ruled her little clerical circle with a firm but not unkindly hand. Notwithstanding her warm heart and truly Christian humility, Miss Langton had an intimate conviction of her own value; for not only did her father hold a stately office, but he came from good county stock of no small distinction, whereas it was notorious that the Bishop was a man of no family, and his wife had been a governess. Miss Langton would have given her last penny to relieve the sick wife of some poor curate, but would have thought twice before asking her to call at the Deanery; her charitable kindness was bestowed on all and sundry, but the ceremonies of polite society she practised only with persons of quality.

'I've asked various people to meet you at dinner tonight,' said Miss Ley.

'Are they nice?'

'They're not positively disagreeable. Mrs Barlow-Bassett is bringing her son, who pleases me because he's so beautiful. Basil Kent is coming, a barrister; I like him because he has the face of a knight in an early Italian picture.'

'You always had a weakness for good-looking men, Mary,' answered Miss Langton, smiling.

'Beauty is quite the most important thing in the world, my dear. People say that the masculine appearance is immaterial, but that is because they are foolish. I know men who have gained all the honour and glory of the earth merely through a fine pair of eyes or a well-shaped mouth. ... Then I have asked Mr and Mrs Castillyon; he is a member of Parliament and very dull and pompous, but just the sort of creature who would amuse you.'

While Miss Ley spoke a note was brought in.

'How tiresome!' she cried, having read. 'Mr Castillyon writes to say he cannot leave the House tonight till late, I wish they wouldn't have autumn sessions. It's just like him to think such a nonentity as himself is indispensable. Now I must ask someone to take his place.'

She sat down and hurriedly wrote a few words.

MY DEAR FRANK,

I beseech you to come to dinner tonight at eight, and since when you arrive your keen intelligence will probably suggest to you that I have not asked nine people on the spur of the moment, I will confess that I invite you merely because Mr Castillyon has put me off at the last minute. But if you don't come I will never speak to you again.

Yours ever,
MARY LEY

She rang the bell, and told a servant to take the letter immediately to Harley Street.

'I've asked Frank Hurrell,' she explained to Miss Langton. 'He's a nice boy – people remain boys till they're forty now, and he's ten years less than that. He's a doctor, and by way of being rather distinguished; they've lately made him assistant-physician at St Luke's Hospital, and he's set up in Harley Street waiting for patients.'

'Is he handsome?' asked Miss Langton, smiling.

'Not at all, but he's one of the few persons I know who really amuses me. You'll think him very disagreeable, and you'll probably bore him to extinction.'

With this remark, calculated to put the younger woman entirely at her ease, Miss Ley sat down again at the window. The day was warm and sunny, but the trees, yellow and red with the first autumnal glow, were heavy still with the rain that had fallen in the night. There was a grave, sensuous passion about St James's Park, with its cool, smooth water just seen among the heavy foliage, and its well-tended lawns; and Miss Ley observed it in silence, with a vague feeling of self-satisfaction, for prosperity was a comfortable thing.

'What would be a suitable present for a poet?' asked Miss Langton suddenly.

19

'Surely a rhyming dictionary,' answered her friend, smiling. 'Or a Bradshaw's Guide to indicate the aesthetic value of common-sense.'

'Don't be absurd, Mary. I really want your advice. I know a young man in Tercanbury who writes poetry.'

'I never knew a young man who didn't. You're not in love with a pale, passionate curate, Bella?'

'I'm in love with no one,' answered Miss Langton, with the shadow of a blush. 'At my age it would be ridiculous. But I should like to tell you about this boy. He's only twenty, and he's a clerk in the bank there.'

'Bella!' cried Miss Ley, with mock horror. 'Don't tell me you're philandering with a person who isn't *county*. What would the Dean say? And for heaven's sake take care of poetical boys; at your age a woman should offer daily prayers to her Maker to prevent her from falling in love with a man twenty years younger than herself. That is one of the most prevalent diseases of the day.'

'His father was a linen-draper at Blackstable, who sent him to Regis School, Tercanbury. And there he took every possible scholarship. He was going to Cambridge, but his people died, and to earn his living he was obliged to go into the bank. He's had a very hard time.'

'But how on earth did you make his acquaintance? No society is so rigidly exclusive as that of a cathedral town, and I know you refuse to be introduced to anyone till you have looked him out in the *Landed Gentry*.'

Miss Ley, singularly unprejudiced, ridiculed her cousin hugely for this veneration of the county family; and though her own name figured in Burke's portentous volume, she concealed the fact as something rather discreditable. To her mind the only advantage of a respectable ancestry was that with a whole heart she could ridicule the claims of blood.

'He was never introduced to me,' answered Bella unwillingly. 'I made friends with him by accident.'

'My dear, that sounds very improper. I hope at least he rescued you in a carriage accident, which appears to be one of Cupid's favourite devices. He always was an unimaginative god, and his methods are dreadfully commonplace. . . . Don't say the young man accosted you in the street!'

Bella Langton could not have told Miss Ley the whole story of her acquaintance with Herbert Field, for the point of it lay to some extent in her own state of mind, and that she but vaguely understood. She had arrived at that embarrassment which comes to most unmarried women, when youth is already passed and the monotonous length of middle age looms drearily before them. For some time her round of duties had lost its savour, and she seemed to have done everything too often: the days exasperated her in their similarity. She was seized with that restlessness which has sent so many, nameless or renowned, sailing like stout Cortez across unknown seas, and others, no fewer, on hazardous adventures of the spirit. She looked with envy now at the friends, her contemporaries, who were mothers of fair children, and not without difficulty overcame a nascent regret that for her father's sake, alone in the world and in all practical concerns very helpless, she had forgone the natural joys of women. These feelings much distressed her, for she had dwelt always in a world of limited horizon, occupied with piety and with good works; the emotions that tore her heart-strings seemed temptations of the devil, and she turned to her God for a solace that came not. She sought to distract her mind by unceasing labour, and with double zeal administered her benevolent institutions; books left her listless, but setting her teeth with a sort of angry determination, she began to learn Greek. Nothing served. Against her will new thoughts forced themselves upon her; and she was terrified, for it seemed to her no woman had ever been tormented by such wild, unlawful fancies. She reminded herself in vain that the name of which she was so proud constrained her to self-command, and her position in Tercanbury made it a duty, even in her inmost heart, to serve as an example to lesser folk.

And now Miss Langton took no pleasure in the quiet close where before she had delighted to linger; the old cathedral, weather-beaten, grey and lovely, no longer gave its accustomed message of resignation and of hope. She took to walking far into the country, but the meadows, bespangled with butter-cups in spring, the woods, with their autumnal russet, but increased her uneasiness; and most willingly she went to a hill from which at no great distance could be seen the shining sea, and for a moment its immensity comforted her restless heart. Sometimes at sundown over the slate grey of the western clouds was spread a great dust of red gold that swept down upon the silent water like the train of a goddess of fire; and presently, thrusting through sombre cumuli, like a Titan break-ing his prison walls, the sun shone forth, a giant sphere of copper. With almost a material effort it seemed to push aside the thronging darkness, filling the whole sky with brilliancy; and then over the placid sea was stretched a broad roadway of unearthly fire, upon which might travel the mystical, passionate souls of men, endlessly, to the source of the deathless light. Bella Langton turned away with a sob and walked back slowly the way she came. Before her in the valley the grey houses of Tercanbury clustered about the tall cathedral, but its ancient beauty pressed her heart with bands of pain.

Then came the spring: the fields were gay with flowers, a vernal carpet whereon with delicate feet might walk the angels of Messer Perugino, and she could bear the agony no longer; in every hedgerow, on every tree, the birds sang with infinite variety, singing the joy of life and the beauty of the rain and the glorious sunshine. They told her one and all that the world was young and beautiful, but the time of man so short that every hour of it must be lived as though it were the last.

When a friend asked her to spend a month in Brittany, sick of her inaction, she accepted eagerly. To travel might ease her aching heart, and the fatigue of the journey allay that springing of the limbs which made her feel apt for hazardous under-takings. Alone the two ladies wandered along that rugged coast. They stayed at Carnac, but the mysterious antique stones suggested only the nothingness of life; man came and went, with hope and longing, and left the signs of his dim faith to be a mystery to succeeding ages; they went to Le Faouet, where the painted windows of the ruined church of Saint Fiacre gleam like precious stones: but the restful charm of these

22

scenes had no message for a heart thirsting for life and the love that quickens. They passed to the famous calvaries of Plougastel and Saint Thégonnec; and those grim crosses, with their stone processions, (the effort at beauty of a race bowed down by the sense of sin), oppressed her under that grey western sky with dismay: they suggested only death and the grave's despair, but she was full of expectation, of longing for she knew not what. It seemed to her as though, she knew not how, she were sailing on that dark silent sea of which the mystics speak, where the common rules of life availed not. Travel gave her nothing that she sought, but increased rather her unquiet; her hands itched for work to do, and she went back to Tercanbury.

3

At last, one afternoon of that very summer, after the vesper service in the cathedral, Miss Langton, wandering listlessly towards the door, saw a young man seated at the back of the nave; it was late, so that he and she seemed to possess that vast building by themselves. With glowing eyes he stared into vacancy, as though his own thoughts blinded him to the Gothic loveliness about him, and his eyes were singularly dark. His hair was fair, and his face, womanlike in its transparent delicacy of skin, was thin and oval. Presently a verger went to him saying that the cathedral would be closed, and as he rose, paying no other attention to the man's words, he passed within a yard of Bella, but in his abstraction saw her not. She thought no more of him, but on the following Saturday, going, as was her habit, to the afternoon service, she saw the youth again, seated as before in the furthermost part of the nave, well away both from sightseers and from devout. A curiosity she did not understand impelled her to remain there rather than go into the choir, separated from the nave by an elaborate screen, where by right of her dignity a seat was reserved for her not far from her father's decanal stall.

The boy, for he was little more, this time was reading a book, which she noticed was written in verse; now and again, with a smile, he threw back his head, and she imagined he repeated to himself a line that pleased him. The service began, softened by distance so that the well-known forms gained a new mystery; the long notes of the organ pealed reverberating along the vaulted roof, or wailed softly, like the voice of a young child, among the lofty columns. At intervals the choir gave a richer depth to the organ music, and it was so broken and deadened by obstructing stone that it sounded vaguely like the surging of the sea. Presently this ceased, and a tenor's voice, the pride of the cathedral, rang out alone; and as though the magic sound had power over all material obstacles, the melody of the old-fashioned anthem – her father loved the undecorated music of a past age – rose towards heaven in a sobbing prayer. The book fell from the young man's hand, and an eager look came into his face as he drank in the silver harmonies; his face was transfigured with ecstasy so that it resembled the face of some pictured saint glorified by a mystic vision of the celestial light. And then, falling on his knees, he buried his face in his hands, and Bella saw that with all his soul he prayed to a God that gave men ears to hear and eyes to see the beauty of the world. What was there in the sight that made her own heart beat with a new emotion?

And when he sat once more on his chair there was a look in his face of exquisite content, and a smile of happiness trembled on his lips, so that Bella turned sick with envy. What power was there in his soul that gave a magic colour to things that left her, for all her striving, still untouched? She waited till he walked slowly out, and, seeing him nod to the verger at the door, asked who he was.

'I don't know, miss,' was the answer; 'he comes here every Saturday and Sunday regular. But he never goes into the choir. He just sits there in the corner where no one can see him, and reads a book. I don't interfere with him, because he's very quiet and respectful.'

Bella could not tell why she thought so often of the fair-haired youth who had never so much as noticed her presence, nor why, on the Sunday that followed, she went again to the nave awaiting his appearance. Observing him more closely, she noticed the slimness of his figure and the shapely length of his hands, which seemed to touch things with a curious delicacy; once their eyes met, and his were blue like the summer sea in Italy, and deep. A somewhat nervous woman, she would never have ventured to address a stranger, but the candid simplicity of his expression, in which strangely there was also a certain appealing pathos, overcame her shyness, overcame also her sense of the impropriety of making friends with a person about whom she knew nothing. Some hidden intuition told her that she was arrived at a turning-point in her life, and courage now was needed to seize with both hands a new happiness; and as though the very stars were favourable there had occurred to her a way to scrape acquaintance. Excited, for it seemed very adventurous, she waited impatiently for Saturday, and then, asking her favourite verger for his keys, after the service went boldly to the youth whose name even she did not know.

'Would you like me to take you over the cathedral?' she asked without a word of introduction. 'We can go round alone, and it's very pleasant without the chatter of vergers and the hurry of a crowd.'

He blushed to the very roots of his hair when she spoke, but then smiled charmingly.

'It's very kind of you,' he answered; 'I've wanted to do that always.'

His voice was pleasant and low, and he showed no surprise whatever; but all the same Bella, now somewhat startled by her own audacity, thought it needful to explain why she ventured the suggestion.

'I've seen you here very often, and it struck me that you would like to see the cathedral at its best. But I'm afraid you must put up with me.'

He smiled again, and appeared now to take note of her for the first time. Bella, looking straight in front of her, felt his eyes rest thoughtfully on her face, and suddenly she seemed to herself old and lined and dowdy.

'What book is that you have?' she asked, to break the silence.

Without speaking he gave it her, and she saw it was a little collection, evidently much read, for the binding scarcely held the leaves together, of Shelley's lyrical poems.

Bella unlocked the gate that led into the apse, and locked it again behind her.

'Isn't it delightful to feel one's self alone here?' he cried, and with springing step and smiling eyes walked forwards.

At first he was a little shy, but presently the spirit of the place, with its dark chapels and stone knights recumbent, the tracery of its jewelled windows, loosened his tongue, and he poured forth his boyish enthusiasm with a passion that astonished Bella. His delight communicated itself to her so that

26

she found a new enchantment in the things she knew so well; his glowing poetic fervour seemed to gild the old walls with magic sunshine; and, as if those prisoned stones were strangely thrown open to heaven, they gained something of the outer freshness of green lawns and flowers and leafy trees: the warm breath of the west wind stole among the Gothic columns, lending a new splendour to the ancient glass, and to the groinery a more living charm. The boy's cheeks were flushed with excitement, and Bella's heart beat as she listened, enchanted with his pleasure; he gesticulated a good deal, and under the movements of his long exquisite hands (her own, for all her well-bred ancestry, were short, thick-set and ungraceful) the past of the mighty church rose before her, so that she heard the clank of steel when knights in armour marched over the still flags, and saw with vivid eyes that historic scene when the gentlemen of Kent in gally hose and doublet, the ladies with ruff and farthingale, assembled to praise the God of storm and battle because Howard of Effingham had scattered the armada of King Philip.

'Now let's go into the cloister,' he said eagerly.

They sat on a stone parapet looking out on the cool green sward where in time past Augustine monks had wandered meditative; there was a dainty gracefulness about the arcade, with the slender columns, their capitals delicately carved, recalling somewhat the cloisters of Italy, which, notwithstanding their cypress-trees and their crumbling decay, suggest a peaceful happiness rather than the Northern sense of stricken sin. The boy, though he knew the magic of the South only from books and pictures, was quick to catch the impression, and his face expressed a rather pitiful longing. When Bella told him she had travelled in Italy, he questioned her eagerly, and his young enthusiasm gave a warmth to her answers which with any other, fearing to be ridiculous, she would carefully have suppressed. But the scene before them was very lovely; in massive splendour the tall central tower looked down upon them, and its stately beauty entered their souls, so that the youth, though he had never seen the monasteries of Tuscany, was comforted. They sat for a while in silence.

27

'You must be a very important person,' he said at last, turning to her, 'or we should never be allowed to remain here so long.'

'I dare say to a verger I am,' she answered, smiling. 'It must be late.'

'Won't you come and have tea with me?' he asked. 'I have rooms just opposite the cathedral gate.' Then, catching Bella's look, he added with a smile: 'My name is Herbert Field, and I'm eminently respectable.'

She hesitated, for it seemed odd to drink tea with a youth whom she had never seen before, but she was mortally afraid of seeming prudish; and a visit to his rooms, whereby she might learn more about him, would add a finish to the adventure. Finally her sense decided her that living life, not mere existence, for once lay under her hand.

'Do come,' he said; 'I want to show you my books.'

And with a little persuasive motion he touched her hand.

'I should like it very much.'

He took her to a tiny room over a chemist's shop, simply furnished as a study, with a low ceiling and panelled walls: these were decorated with a few photographs of pictures by Pietro Perugino, and there were a good many books.

'It's rather poky, I'm afraid, but I live here, so that I can always see the gateway. I think it's one of the finest things in Tercanbury.'

He made her sit down while he boiled water and cut bread-and-butter. Bella, at first somewhat intimidated by the novelty of the affair, was a little formal; but the boy's manifest delight in her presence affected her so that she became gay and light-hearted. Then he displayed a new side of his character: the rather strenuous passion for the beautiful was momentarily put aside and he showed himself quite absurdly boyish. His laughter rang out joyously, and, feeling less shy now that Miss Langton was his guest, he talked unrestrainedly of a hundred topics that sprang up one after another in his mind.

'Will you have a cigarette?' he asked when they had finished their tea, and, on Bella's laughing refusal: 'You don't mind if I smoke, do you? I can talk better.'

28

He drew their chairs to the open window, so that they could look at the massive masonry before them, and, as though he had known Bella all his life, chattered on. But when at last she rose to go, his eyes grew suddenly grave and sad.

'I shall see you again, shan't I? I don't want to lose you now I've found you so strangely.'

Really he was asking Miss Langton to make an assignation, but by now the Dean's daughter had thrown all caution to the winds.

'I dare say we shall meet sometime in the cathedral.'

Womanlike, though she meant to grant all he desired, she would not give in too quickly.

'Oh, that won't do,' he insisted. 'I can't wait a week before seeing you again.'

Bella smiled at him while he looked eagerly into her eyes, holding her hand very firmly, as though till she made some promise he would never let it go.

'Let's take a walk in the country tomorrow,' he said.

'Very well,' she replied, telling herself that there could be no harm in going with a boy twenty years younger than herself. 'I shall be at the Westgate at half-past five.'

But the evening brought counsels of prudence, and Miss Langton wrote a note to say that she had forgotten an engagement, and was afraid she could not come. Yet it left her irresolute, and more than once she reproached herself because from sheer timidity she would cause Herbert Field the keenest disappointment. She told herself sophistically that perhaps, owing to the Sunday delivery, the letter had not reached him, and, fearing he would go to the Westgate and not understand her absence, persuaded herself that it was needful to go there and explain in person why she could not take the promised walk.

The Westgate was an ancient, handsome pile of masonry which in the old days had marked the outer wall of Tercanbury, and even now, though on one side houses had been built, a road to the left led directly into the country. When Bella arrived, somewhat early, Herbert was already waiting for her, and he looked peculiarly young in his straw hat.

'Didn't you get a note from me?' she asked.

'Yes,' he answered, smiling.

'Then why did you come?'

'Because I thought you might change your mind. I didn't altogether believe in the engagement. I wanted you so badly that I fancied you couldn't help yourself. I felt you must come.'

'And if I hadn't?'

'Well, I should have waited. ... Don't be horrid. Look at the sunshine calling us. Yesterday we had the grey stones of the cathedral; today we've got the green fields and the trees. Don't you feel the west wind murmuring delicious things?'

Bella looked at him, and could not resist the passionate appeal of his eyes.

'I suppose I must do as you choose,' she answered.

And together they set off. Miss Langton, convinced that her interest was no less maternal than when she gave jellies to some motherless child, knew not that Dan Cupid, laughing at her subterfuge, danced gleefully about them and shot his silver arrows. They sauntered by a gentle stream that ran northward to the sea, shaded by leafy willows; and the country on that July afternoon was fresh and scented: the cut hay, drying, gave out an exquisite perfume, and the birds were hushed.

'I'm glad you live in the Deanery,' he said; 'I shall like to think of you seated in that beautiful garden.'

'Have you ever seen it?'

'No; but I can imagine what it is like behind that old red wall, the shady lawns and the roses. There must be masses of roses now.'

The Dean was known as an enthusiast for that royal flower, and his blossoms at the local show were the wonder of the town. They went on, and soon, half unconsciously, as though he sought protection from the hard world, Herbert put his arm in hers. Bella blushed a little, but had not the heart to withdraw; she was strangely flattered at the confidence he showed. Very discreetly she questioned him, and with perfect simplicity he told of his parents' long struggle to give him an education above their state.

'But, after all,' he said, 'I'm not nearly so wretched as I

thought I would be. The bank leaves me plenty of time, and I have my books and I have my hopes.'

'What are they?'

'Sometimes I write verse,' he answered, blushing shyly. 'I suppose it's ridiculous, but it gives me great happiness; and who knows? – someday I may do something that the world will not willingly let die.'

Later on, when Bella rested on a stile and Herbert stood by her side, he looked up at her, hesitating.

'I want to say something to you, Miss Langton, but I'm rather afraid. ... You won't drop me now, will you? Now that I've found a friend, I can't afford to lose her. You don't know what it means to me having someone to talk to, someone who's kind to me. Often I feel so dreadfully alone. And you make all the difference in my life; this last week everything has seemed changed.'

She looked at him earnestly. Did he think he made no difference in hers? She could not tell what stirred her when those blue appealing eyes asked so irresistibly for what she was most willing to give.

'My father is going into Leanham on Wednesday,' she answered presently. 'When your work is over, will you come and have tea in the Deanery garden?'

She felt herself ten times rewarded by the look of pleasure that flashed across his face.

'I shall think of nothing else till then.'

And Miss Langton found that her restless anxiety had strangely vanished; life now was no longer monotonous, but sparkled with magic colour, for an absorbing interest had arisen which made the daily round a pleasure rather than a duty. She repeated to herself all the charming inconsequent things the boy had said, finding his conversation agreeably different from the clerical debates to which she was used. They cultivated a refined taste in the chapter, and the Archdeacon's second wife had written a novel, which only her exalted station and an obvious moral purpose saved from excessive indecency. The Minor Canons talked with gusto of the Royal Academy.

But Herbert spoke of books and pictures as though art were a living thing, needful as bread and water to his existence; and Bella, feeling that her culture, somewhat ostentatiously pursued as an element of polite breeding, was very formal and insipid, listened with complete humility to his simple ardour.

On Wednesday, almost handsome in summer muslin and a large hat, she went into the garden, where the tea-things were laid under a leafy tree. Miss Ley would have smiled cruelly to notice the care with which the Dean's daughter arranged her position to appear at her best. The privacy, the garden's restful beauty, brought out all Herbert's boyishness, and his pleasant laughter rang across the lawns, rang like silver music into Bella's heart. Watching the shadows lengthen, they talked of Italy and Greece, of poets and of flowers; and presently, weary of seriousness, they talked sheer light-hearted nonsense.

'You know, I can't call you Mr Field,' said Bella, smiling. 'I must call you Herbert.'

'If you do I shall call you Bella.'

'I'm not sure if you ought. You see, I'm almost an old fossil, and it's quite natural that I should use your Christian name.'

'But I won't let you assume any airs of superiority over me. I want you to be absolutely a companion, and I don't care twopence if you're older than I am. Besides, I shall always think of you as Bella.'

She smiled again, looking at him with tender eyes.

'Well, I suppose you must do as you like,' she answered.

'Of course.'

Then quickly he took both her hands, and, before she realized what he was about, kissed them.

'Don't be foolish,' cried Bella, withdrawing them hurriedly, and she reddened to her very hair.

When he saw her discomfort, boylike, he burst into a shout of laughter.

'Oh, I've made you blush.'

His blue eyes sparkled, and he was delighted with his little wickedness. He did not know that afterwards, in her room, Bella, the kisses still burning on her hands, wept bitterly as though her heart would break.

4

WHEN Miss Ley entered her drawing-room she found the punctual Dean already dressed for dinner, very distinguished in silk stockings and buckled shoes, and presently Bella appeared, attired with sombre magnificence in black satin.

'I went to Holywell Street this morning to look round the book-shops,' said the Dean, 'but Holywell Street is pulled down. London isn't what it was, Polly. Each time I come I find old buildings gone and old friends scattered.'

With melancholy he thought of the pleasant hours he had spent fingering second-hand books, and the scent of musty volumes rose to his nostrils. The new shops to which the Jewish vendors had removed no longer had the old dusty nonchalance, the shelves were too spick and span, the idle lounger apparently less welcome.

Mrs Barlow-Bassett and her son were announced. She was a tall woman of handsome presence, with fine eyes and a confident step; her grey hair, abundant and curling, recalled in its elaborate arrangement the fashion of the eighteenth century, and her manner of dress, suggested by the modes of that time, gave her somewhat the look of a sitter for Sir Joshua Reynolds. Her movements were characterized by a kind of obstinate decision, and she bore herself with the fine uprightness of a woman bred when deportment was still a part of maidenly education. She was immensely proud of her son, a tall strapping fellow of two-and-twenty, with black hair no less fine than his mother's, and with singularly beautiful features. Big-boned but unmuscular, very dark, his large brown eyes, straight nose and olive skin, his full sensual mouth, made him a person of striking appearance; and of this he was by no means unconscious. He was a good-humoured, lazy creature, languid as an Oriental houri, unscrupulous, untruthful, whom his mother by an exacting adoration had forced into insincerity. Left a widow of means,

Mrs Barlow-Bassett had devoted her life to the upbringing of this only son, and was pleased to think that hitherto she had kept him successfully from all knowledge of evil. She meant him to find in her a friend and confidant as well as a mother, and boasted that from her he had never kept a single action nor a single thought.

'I want to talk to Mr Kent this evening, Mary,' she said. 'He's a barrister, isn't he? And we've just made up our minds that Reggie had better go to the Bar.'

Reggie, who, notwithstanding the attraction of a splendid uniform, had no inclination for the restraints of a military career, and disdained the commercial walk in which his father had earned a handsome fortune, was quite content to put up with the more gentlemanly side of the law. He knew vaguely that a vast number of dinners must be eaten, a prospect to which he looked forward with equanimity; and afterwards saw himself, becomingly attired in wig and gown, haranguing juries to the admiration of the world in general.

'You're going to sit next to Basil,' answered Miss Ley; 'Frank Hurrell is to take you down.'

'I'm sure Reggie will do well at the Bar, and I can keep him with me in London. You know, he's never given me a moment's anxiety, and sometimes I do feel proud that I've kept him so good and pure. But the world is full of temptations, and he's so extraordinarily good-looking.'

'He is very handsome,' returned Miss Ley, pursing her lips.

She thought her knowledge of character must be singularly at fault if Reggie was the virtuous creature his mother imagined. The sensuality of his face suggested no great distaste for the sins of the flesh, and the slyness of his dark eyes no excessive innocence.

Basil Kent and Dr Hurrell, meeting on the doorstep, came in together. It was Frank Hurrell whom Miss Ley, somewhat exacting in these matters, had described as the most amusing person she knew. His breadth of shoulder and solid build were too great for his height, and he had reason to envy Reggie Bassett's length of leg; nor was his face handsome, for his brows were too heavy and his jaw too square, but the eyes were expressive, mocking sometimes or hard, at others very soft, and there was a persuasiveness in his deep resonant voice of which he well knew the power. A small black moustache concealed the play of a well-shaped mouth and the regularity of his excellent teeth. He impressed you as a strong man, of no very easy temper, who held himself in admirable control. Silent with strangers, he disconcerted them by an unwilling frigidity of manner, and though his friends, knowing that at all times he could be depended upon, were eager in his praise, acquaintance often accused him of superciliousness. To be popular with all and sundry he took no sufficient pains to conceal his impatience of stupidity, and though Miss Ley thought his conversation interesting, others to whom for some reason he was not attracted found him absent and taciturn.

An extremely reserved man, few knew that Frank Hurrell's deliberate placidity of expression masked a very emotional temperament. In this he recognized a weakness and had schooled his face carefully to betray no feeling; but the feeling all the same was there, turbulent and overwhelming, and he profoundly mistrusted his judgement, which could be drawn so easily from the narrow path of reason. He kept over himself unceasing watch, as though a dangerous prisoner were in his heart ever on the alert to break his chains. He felt himself the slave of a vivid imagination, and realized that it stood against the enjoyment of life which his philosophy told him was the only end of existence. Yet his passions were of the mind rather than of the body, and his spirit urged his flesh constantly to courses wherein it found nothing but disillusion. His chief endeavour was the search for truth, and somewhat to Miss Ley's scorn (for she rested easily in a condition of satisfied doubt, her attitude towards life indicated by a slight shrug of the shoulders) he strove after certainty with an eagerness which other men reserve for love or fame or opulence. But all his studies were directed at the last to another end; convinced that the present life was final, he sought to make the completest use of its every moment; and yet it seemed preposterous that so much effort, such vast time and strange concurrence of events, the world and man, should tend towards nothing. He could not but think that somewhere a meaning must be discernible, and to find this examined science and philosophy with an anxious passion that to his colleagues at St Luke's, worthy craftsmen who saw no further than the slide on their microscopes, would have seemed extraordinary and almost insane.

But it would have required an imaginative person to discover in Dr Hurrell at that moment trace of a conflict as vehement as any passionate disturbance of more practical people. He was in high good-humour, and while they waited for the remaining guests talked to Miss Ley.

'Isn't it charming of me to come?' he asked.

'Not at all,' she replied; 'it's very much nicer for a greedy person like you to eat my excellent dinner than to nibble an ill-cooked chop in your own rooms.'

'How ungrateful! At all events, as a stopgap I have no duties to my neighbour, and may devote myself entirely to the pleasures of the table.'

'Like a friend of mine – people weren't so polite forty years ago, and much more amusing – who, when his neighbour made some very foolish remark, shouted at her: "Go on with your soup, madam!"'

'Tell me who else is coming,' said Frank.

'Mrs Castillyon, but she'll be monstrously late. She thinks it fashionable, and the *county* in London has to take so many precautions not to seem provincial. Mrs Murray is coming.'

'D'you still want me to marry her?'

'No,' replied Miss Ley, laughing, 'I've given you up. Though it wasn't nice of you to abuse me like a pickpocket because I offered you a handsome widow with five thousand a year.'

'Think of the insufferable bore of marriage, and in any case Heaven save me from an intellectual wife. If I marry at all, I'll marry my cook.'

'I wish you wouldn't make my jokes, Frank. ... But as a matter of fact, unless I'm vastly mistaken, Mrs Murray has made up her mind to marry our friend Basil.'

'Oh!' said Frank.

Miss Ley noticed a shadow cross his eyes, and examined his expression sharply.

'Don't you think it would be a very suitable thing if she did?'

'I have no views on the subject,' returned Frank.

'I wonder what you mean by that. Basil is poor and handsome and clever, and Mrs Murray has always had an inclination for literary men. That's the worst of marrying a cavalryman – it leads you to attach so much importance to brains.'

'Was Captain Murray an absolute fool?'

'My dear Frank, you don't ask if a guardsman has intelligence, but whether he can play polo. Captain Murray did two wise things in his life: he made a will leaving his wife a large fortune, and then promptly departed to a place where stupidity is apparently no disadvantage.'

Miss Ley, for Bella's peculiar edification, had invited also the most fashionable cleric in London, the Rev. Collinson Farley, Vicar of All Souls, Grosvenor Square, and it amused her to see the look of Frank Hurrell, who detested him, when this gentleman was announced. Mr Farley was a man of middle size, with iron-grey hair carefully brushed, and a rather fine head; his well-manicured hands were soft and handsome, adorned with expensive rings. He was an amateur of good society, and could afford, such were his fascinations, to be very careful in his choice of friends; a coronet no' longer dazzled a man who realized how hollow was earthly rank beside earthly riches. Poverty he could excuse only in a duchess, for there is in the strawberry leaves, even when, faded and sere, they wreathe the wrinkled brow of a dowager, something which inspires respect in the most flippant. His suave manner and intelligent conversation had gained him powerful friends when he was but a country rector, and through their influence the opportunity came at last to move to a sphere where his social talents met their due appreciation. Ecclesiastical dignity, like the sins of the fathers, may descend to the third and fourth generation, and obviously a man whose grandfather was a bishop could not lack decorum; something was surely due to a courteous person who had been actually born in an episcopal palace.

Mrs Castillyon, as her hostess predicted last to arrive, at length appeared.

'I hope I'm not late, Miss Ley,' she said, putting out both hands with a pretty little gesture of appeal.

'Not very,' replied her hostess. 'Knowing that you make a point of being unpunctual, I took care to ask you for half an hour earlier than anyone else.'

In solemn procession the company marched down to the dining-room, and Mr Farley surveyed the table with satisfaction.

'I always think a well-dressed table one of the most truly artistic sights of our modern civilization,' he remarked to his neighbour.

And his eyes wandered round the dining-room, in the furniture of which he observed a comforting but discreet opulence. Mr Farley had known the house in Miss Dwarris' lifetime, and noticed now that a portrait of her no longer hung in its accustomed place.

'I see you have removed that excellent picture of the former occupant of this house, Miss Ley,' he said, with a graceful wave of his white and jewelled hand.

'I couldn't bear that she should watch me eat three meals a day,' replied his hostess. 'I have a vivid recollection of her dinners: she fed me on husks and acorns, like the prodigal son, and regaled me with accounts of the torment that awaited me in an after-life.'

The Dean smiled gravely. He looked upon Miss Ley with a kind of affectionate disapproval; and though often he rebuked her for the books she read or for the flippancy of her conversation, took always in good part the irony with which she met his little sermons.

'You're very uncharitable, Polly,' he said. 'Of course Eliza was a difficult person to live with, but she exacted no more from others than she exacted from herself. I always admired her strong sense of duty; it was very striking at the present time when everyone lives entirely for pleasure.'

'We may not be so virtuous as our fathers, Algernon,' answered Miss Ley, 'but we're very much easier to live with. After all, forty years ago people were positively insufferable: they spoke their minds, which is a detestable habit; their tem-

38

per was abominable, and they drank more than was good for them. I always think my father was typical of his period. When he flew into a passion he called it righteous anger, and when I did anything to which he objected he suffered from – virtuous indignation. D'you know that till I was fifteen I was never allowed to taste butter, which was thought bad both for my figure and my soul? I was brought up exclusively on dripping and Jeremy Taylor. The world was a hazardous path beset with gins and snares; and at every turn and corner were immature volcanoes from which arose sulphurous fumes of hell-fire.'

'It was an age of tyranny and vapours,' said Frank, 'of old gentlemen who were overbearing and young ladies who swooned.'

'I'm sure people aren't so good as they used to be,' said Mrs Bassett, glancing at her son, who was much engrossed in a conversation with Mrs Castillyon.

'They never were,' answered Miss Ley.

'The perverseness of men would have made an infidel of me,' added the Dean, in his sweet, grave voice, 'but for the counteracting impression of Divine providence in the works of Nature.'

Meanwhile Reggie Bassett enjoyed his dinner far more than he expected. He found himself next to Mrs Castillyon, and on sitting down proceeded to examine her with some effrontery. A rapid glance had told her that the boy was handsome, and when she saw what he was about, to give him opportunity at his leisure to observe her various graces, she began to talk volubly with her other neighbour. But presently she turned to Reggie.

'Well, is it satisfactory?' she asked.

'What?'

'Your inspection.'

She smiled brightly, flashing a quick, provoking look into his fine dark eyes.

'Quite,' he answered, with a smile, not in the least disconcerted. 'My mother is already thinking that Miss Ley oughtn't to have let me sit by you.'

Mrs Castillyon was a vivacious creature, small and dainty

like a shepherdess in Dresden china, excitable and restless, who spoke with a loud, shrill voice; and with a quick, nervous gesture, constantly threw herself back in her chair to laugh boisterously at what Reggie said. And finding he could venture very far indeed without fear of offence, the model youth told her little scabrous stories in a low, suave voice, staring meanwhile into her eyes with the shameless audacity of a man conscious of his power. It is the fascination-look of the lady-killer, and its very impudence appears to be half its charm; the rake at heart feels that here modest pretences are useless, and with unhidden joy descends from the pedestal upon which the folly of man has insisted on placing her. Mrs Castillyon's face was thin and small, overpowdered, with rather high cheek-bones, her hair, intricately dressed, had an unnatural fairness; but this set Reggie peculiarly at his ease, for he had enough experience of the sex to opine that women who used such artifices were always easier to get on with than the others. He thought his neighbour quite pretty, notwithstanding her five-and-thirty years; and the somewhat faded look of a thin blonde was counterbalanced by the magnificence of her jewels and the splendour of her gown: this was cut so low that Bella from the other side of the table naïvely wondered how on earth it was kept on at all.

When the men were left to smoke, Reggie, helping himself to a third glass of port, drew his chair to Hurrell's.

'I say, Frank,' he exclaimed, 'that was a nice little woman next to me, wasn't it?'

'Had you never met Mrs Castillyon before?'

'Never! Regular ripper, ain't she? By Jove! I thought this dinner would be simply deadly – politics and religion, and all that rot. The mater always makes me come, because she says there's intellectual conversation. My God!'

Frank laughed at the idea of Mrs Barlow-Bassett combining instruction with amusement for her son at Miss Ley's dinner-table.

'But Mrs Castillyon's a bit of all right, I can tell you. Little baggage! And she don't mind what you say to her. ... Why, she isn't like a lady at all.'

'Is that a great recommendation?'

'Well, ladies ain't amusing, are they? You talk to 'em of the Academy and all that sort of rot, and you've got to take care you don't swear. Ladies may be all very well to marry, but, upon my soul, for giving you a good time I prefer them a bit lower in the scale.'

A little later, on the stairs, when they were going up to the drawing-room, Reggie slipped his arm through Frank's.

'I say, old man, don't give me away if my mater thanks you for asking me to dinner on Saturday.'

'But I haven't. Neither have I the least desire that you should dine with me on that day.'

'Good Lord! d'you think I want to come – and talk about bugs and beetles all the evening? Not much! I'm going to dine with a little girl I know – typewriter, my boy, and a real love touch. Stunning little thing, I can tell you.'

'But I don't see why, because you wish to entertain a young person connected with typewriting, I should imperil my immortal soul.'

Reggie laughed.

'Don't be an ass, Frank; you might help me. You don't know how utterly rotten it is to have a mother like mine who wants to keep me tied to her apron-strings. She makes me tell her everything I do, and of course I have to fake up some yarn. The only thing in it is that she'll swallow any damned lie I tell her.'

'You can tell her lies till you're blue in the face,' said Frank, 'but I don't see why the devil I should.'

'Don't be a beast, Frank. You might help me just this once. It won't hurt you to say I'm grubbing with you. The other night, by Jove! I nearly gave the show away. You know she always waits up for me. I told her I should be working late with my crammer, and went to the Empire. Well, I met a lot of chaps there and got a bit squiffy. There would have been a shindy if she'd noticed it, but I managed to pull myself together a bit, and said I'd got the very deuce of a headache. And next day I heard her tell someone that I was next door to a tee-totaller.'

They reached the drawing-room and Frank found himself close to Mrs Bassett.

'Oh, Dr Hurrell,' she said, 'I want to thank you so much for asking Reggie to dinner on Saturday. He's been working so hard that I think a little relaxation will do him good. And his tutor keeps him sometimes till past eleven – it can't be good for him, can it? The night before last he was so tired when he came in that he could scarcely get up the stairs.'

'I'm delighted that Reggie should care to come and dine with me sometimes,' answered Frank, somewhat grimly.

'I'm always glad to think he's with you. It's so important that a young man should have really trustworthy friends, and I feel sure your influence is good for him.'

Reggie, listening to this, gave Frank a very slow and significant wink, then went off with a light heart to resume his conversation with Mrs Castillyon.

5

PRESENTLY all Miss Ley's guests, except Frank Hurrell, bade her good night, and he showed no intention of following their example.

'You don't want to go to bed yet, do you?' she asked the Dean. 'Let us go into the library.'

Here Frank took from a drawer his pipe, and helping himself from a tobacco-jar placed in readiness, sat down. Miss Ley, noticing Bella's slight look of surprise, explained.

'Frank keeps a pipe here and makes me buy his favourite tobacco. It's one of the advantages of old age that you can sit into the small hours of the morning and talk with young men.'

But when he too was gone, Miss Ley, an old-fashioned hostess solicitous for her guests' comfort, accompanied Bella to her room.

'I hope you enjoyed my little party,' she said.

'Very much,' replied Bella. 'But why do you ask Mrs Castillyon? She's dreadfully common, isn't she?'

'My dear,' answered Miss Ley ironically, 'her husband is a most important person – in Dorsetshire, and her own family has a whole page in the *Gentleman's Bible* or the *Landed Gentry*.'

'I shouldn't have thought she was county,' said Bella seriously; 'she seemed to me very vulgar.'

'She is very vulgar,' answered Miss Ley, 'but it's the sort of vulgarity which is a mark of the highest breeding. To talk too loud and to laugh like a bus-driver, to use the commonest slang and to dress outrageously, are all signs of the *grande dame*. Often in Bond Street I see women with painted cheeks and dyed hair dressed in a manner which even a courtesan would think startling, and I recognize the leaders of London fashion. .... Good night. Don't expect to see me at breakfast;

43

that is a meal which only the angels of heaven should eat in company.'

Miss Langton sat down as though she had no wish to go to bed. 'Don't go just yet. I want to know all about Mr Kent.'

Miss Ley, following her friend's example, made herself comfortable in an armchair. Once Miss Dwarris asserted that a virtuous person as a matter of discipline should do every day two things which he disliked, whereupon Miss Ley answered flippantly that then she must be on the direct road to everlasting happiness, for within the twenty-four hours she invariably performed a brace of actions which she thoroughly detested: she got up, and she went to bed. Now, therefore, in no hurry to go to her own room, she proceeded to tell Miss Langton what she knew of Basil Kent. In truth it was not strange that he had attracted Bella's attention, for his appearance was unusual; he managed to wear the conventional evening dress of an Englishman with becoming grace, but one felt, such was his romantic air, he should by rights have borne the armour of a Florentine knight. His limbs were slender and well made, his hands white and comely, and his brown curly hair, worn somewhat long, set off the fine colour of his face; the dark eyes, thin cheeks, and full sensual mouth were set into a passionate wistfulness of expression which recalled again those faces in early Italian pictures wherein the spirit and the flesh seem ever to fight a restless battle – to them the earth is always beautiful, rich with love and warfare, with poetry and deep blue skies, but yet everywhere is disillusion also, and the dark silence of the cloister, even amid the painted turbulence of court or camp, whispers its irresistible appeal. None looking at Basil Kent could imagine that any great ease of life awaited him; through his brown eyes appeared a soul at the same time sensual and ascetic, impulsive and chivalrous, yet so sensitive that the storms and buffets of the world, to which inevitably he exposed himself, must assault him with double violence.

'Well, he's the son of Lady Vizard,' said Miss Ley.

'What?' cried Bella, 'you don't mean the woman about whom there was that dreadful case five years ago?'

44

'Yes. He was then at Oxford, where Frank and he were bosom friends. It was through Frank that I first knew him. His father, a cousin of the present Kent of Ouseley, died when he was a child, and Basil was brought up by his grandmother, for his mother married Lord Vizard very shortly after her husband's death. Even now she's a beautiful woman. In those days she was perfectly gorgeous; her photograph was in all the shop-windows – her prime coincided with the fashion for young men to buy the portraits of celebrated beauties they did not know, and the chastest women thought it no shame for their pictures to be exposed in every stationer's shop or to decorate the chimney-piece of a platonic counter-jumper. At that time Lady Vizard's doings were minutely chronicled in the papers that concern themselves with such things, and her parties were thronged with all the fashion of London. She was to be seen at every race-meeting surrounded by admirers; of course she had a box at the opera, and at Homburg attracted the most august attention.'

'Did Mr Kent ever see her?' asked Bella.

'He used to spend part of his holidays with her, and she dazzled him as she dazzled everyone else. Frank told me that Basil simply worshipped his mother; he has always had a passion for beauty, and was immensely proud of her magnificent appearance. I used at one time occasionally to meet her at parties, and she struck me as one of the most splendid, majestic women I ever saw; one felt that something like that must have looked Madame de Montespan.'

'Was she fond of her son?'

'In her way. Naturally she didn't want him bothering around her. She kept her youth marvellously. Lord Vizard was younger than herself, and she didn't much care to produce a boy who was very nearly grown up. So she was quite pleased that old Mrs Kent, whom she detested, should look after him. But when he came to stay she filled his pockets with money, took him to the play every night and thoroughly amused him. I dare say she too was pleased with his good looks, for at sixteen he must have been more beautiful than a Greek ephebe. But if ever he showed any signs of inconvenient attachment, I

45

doubt whether Lady Vizard encouraged him. From Harrow he went to Oxford, and Frank, who is a very acute observer, told me that then Basil was a peculiarly innocent boy, absurdly open and frank, who never kept a secret from anybody, and said without thinking, ingenuously, everything that came into his head. Of course scandal for a good many years had been busy with Lady Vizard; her extravagance was notorious, and Vizard was known to be neither rich nor generous; but his wife did everything that cost a great deal of money, and her emeralds were obviously worth a fortune. Even Basil cannot have helped seeing how many masculine friends she had, though perhaps, when he was spending with her the occasional week to which he looked forward so intensely, she took pains that nothing too flaunting should come to his eyes; and when strange gentlemen slipped sovereigns into his hand he pocketed them under the impression that his own merit had earned them. And now I must go to bed.'

Miss Ley, with a tantalizing smile, rose from her chair, but Bella stopped her.

'Don't be cattish, Mary. You know I want to hear the rest of the story.'

'Are you aware that it's past one o'clock?'

'I don't care, you must finish it now.'

Miss Ley, having created this small diversion, sat down again, proceeding, not at all against her will, with the recital.

'Basil's only vanity was his mother, and he talked of her incessantly, taking a manifest pride in her social success and the admiration which everywhere she excited; he would have staked his life on her immaculate character, and when the crash came he was simply overwhelmed. You remember the case; it was one of those in which a prudish English public takes keen delight. Every placard announced in huge letters that for the especial delectation of the middle classes a divorce in high life was being fought at the Law Courts in which there were no less than four co-respondents. It appeared that Lord Vizard, chiefly because he was frightened of his wife's extravagance, had at last filed a petition in which he named Lord Ernest Torrens, Colonel Roome, Mr Norman Wynne and somebody else. The pair evidently had not for some time enjoyed great connubial felicity, for Lady Vizard brought a counter-petition, accusing her husband of philandering with her own maid and with a certain Mrs Platter, a lady who inhabited a flat in Shaftesbury Avenue. The case was fought on both sides with the greatest acrimony, and a crowd of witnesses testified to behaviour which one at least hopes is unusual in the houses of the great. But of course you read the details in the *Church Times*, Bella.'

'I remember it was reported in the *Standard*,' answered Miss Langton, 'but I read nothing.'

'Virtuous creature!' said Miss Ley, with a thin smile. 'The average Englishman would never keep his respect for titled persons if the reports of proceedings in the Divorce Court did not periodically give him some insight into their private life. ... Anyhow, the things of which Lord and Lady Vizard accused one another were enough to make the hair of a suburban paterfamilias stand right on end.'

Miss Ley paused for a moment, and then with calm deliberation, as though she had given this matter the attention of a lifetime and carefully weighed all sorts, proceeded.

'A divorce, you know, can be managed in two ways – respectably, when both parties are indifferent or afraid and no more is said than is essential for the non-intervention at a subsequent stage of that absurd gentleman, the King's Proctor; and vindictively, when in their eagerness to bespatter the person whom at some previous period they solemnly vowed to love to the end of their days, they care not how much mud is thrown at themselves. Lady Vizard made a practice of detesting her husbands, and she loathed the second far more because he had not the grace to die, like the first, four years after the marriage. His penuriousness, ill-temper, insobriety were dragged into the light of day; and he brought servants to testify to his wife's most private habits, produced letters which he had intercepted, and subpoenaed tradesmen to swear by whom accounts for jewellery and clothes had been settled. Lord Vizard engaged the cleverest criminal lawyer of the time, and for two days his wife with unparalleled wit, courage, and resource bore a cross-examination which would have ruined a weaker woman. It was partly on this account, because they admired the good fight she made, partly because it seemed impossible that such an imposing creature should have done the quite odious things of which the husband accused her, but still more because they thought there was precious little to choose between kettle and pot, that the jury found the charges not proven; and Lady Vizard in a manner remained mistress of the position. The rest you can guess for yourself.'

'No, I can't, Mary. Go on.'

'No word had reached Basil that proceedings were to be taken, and his first knowledge of the affair came with the morning paper and his eggs and bacon. He could scarcely believe his eyes, and he read the report with incredulity changing quickly to dismay and horror. The news dazed and crushed him. A hundred trifles he had seen but never noticed came to his mind, and he knew that his mother was no better than the painted harlot who sells her body for a five-pound note.'

'But how d'you know all this, Mary?' asked Bella doubtfully. 'You're not inventing it, are you?'

'I read the papers,' answered Miss Ley, with some asperity. 'Frank told me a good deal, and my common sense the rest. I flatter myself I have a certain knowledge of human nature, and if Basil didn't feel what I tell you, he should have. But I shall never finish my story if you keep on interrupting me.'

'I beg your pardon,' said Bella humbly. 'Pray go on.'

'Frank, you know, is somewhat older than Basil, and at that time was in Oxford, taking his M.B. He found the poor boy overcome with shame, anxious like a stricken beast to hide himself from all strange eyes. But Frank is made of sterner stuff; he persuaded him to go about as though nothing had happened, and even to dine in hall as usual. What for the one would not have been so very difficult to the other was unendurable. Basil imagined that everyone stared at him as though he were a thing unclean; he had bragged a good deal of his wonderful parent, and he thought now that all his words must be scornfully repeated. The papers continued their edifying story; witnesses told shameful things; and Basil, haggard and sleepless, could not conceal his torment. Frank had set him an ordeal beyond his strength, and without a word to anyone he fled to London. After the trial he went to see Lady Vizard, but what happened then I do not know. He never returned to Oxford. At that time they were recruiting for the Imperial Yeomanry, and Basil, passing by chance through St James's Park, saw the men drilling. He wished to get out of England, where everyone seemed to point at him with scorn, and here was an opportunity; he enlisted, and a month later sailed for South Africa.'

'As a trooper?' asked Miss Langton.

'Yes. I believe he distinguished himself, for they offered him a commission, but this he refused and was given instead the Medal for Distinguished Conduct in the Field. He remained there three years, and did not return to England till the last batch of Yeomanry was brought home. Then he settled down to read for the Bar, and was called last year.'

'Does he ever see his mother, d'you know?'

'I believe never. He has a small income, about three hundred a year, and on that in a modest way is able to live. I think he has only gone to the Bar as a sort of form, for he means to write. You probably never saw the little book of South African sketches which he brought out last year – impressions of scenery and studies of character. It had no particular success, but to my mind showed a good deal of promise; I remember an account of some battle about which there was an uncommon swing and dash. He's working at a novel now, and I dare say some day will write a very clever book.'

'D'you think he'll ever be famous?'

Miss Ley shrugged her shoulders.

'You know, to achieve great success in literature you must have a certain coarseness in your composition, and that I don't think Basil has. Really to move and influence men you must have complete understanding, and you can only get that if you have in you something of the common clay of humanity. ... But now I really must go to bed. You're such a chatterbox, Bella, I believe you would keep me up all night.'

This was somewhat hard on Miss Langton, who for an hour had barely opened her mouth.

6

BUT while the two ladies thus discussed him, Basil Kent stood on the bridge over the ornamental water in St James's Park, and looked thoughtfully at that scene than which perhaps there is none more beautiful in the most beautiful of all cities, London: the still water, silvered by the moon, the fine massing of the trees, and the Foreign Office, pompous and sedate, formed a composition as perfect and no less formally elaborate than any painted by Claude Lorrain. The night was warm and balmy, the sky clear; and the quiet was so delightful, notwithstanding the busy hum of Piccadilly, where, at that hour, all was gaiety and frolic, that it reminded Basil of some restful, old-fashioned town in France. His heart beat with a strange elation, for he knew at last, without possibility of doubt, that Mrs Murray loved him. Before, though he could not be unaware that she saw him with pleasure and listened to his conversation with interest, he had not the audacity to suppose a warmer feeling; but when they met that evening he surprised a blush while she gave her hand, and this had sent the blood running to his own cheeks. He took her down to dinner, and the touch of her fingers on his arm burnt him like fire. She spoke but little, yet listened to his words with a peculiar intensity as though she sought in them some hidden meaning, and when his eyes met hers seemed to shrink back almost in fear. But at the same time her look had a strange, expectant eagerness, as though she had heard the promise of some excellent thing, and awaited it vehemently, yet half afraid.

Basil recalled Mrs Murray's entrance into the drawing-room, and his admiration for the grace of her bearing and the fine sweep of her long dress. She was a tall woman, as tall as himself, with a certain boyishness of figure that lent itself to a sinuous distinction of line; her hair was neither dark nor fair, the eyes grey and tender, but her smile was very noticeable for a peculiar sweetness that marked an attractive nature. And if there was no precise beauty in her face, its winsome expression, the pallor of her skin, gave it a fascinating grave sadness reminiscent of the women of Sandro Botticelli: there was that same inscrutable look of melancholy eyes which suggested a passionate torment repressed and hidden, and she had that very grace of gesture which one is certain was theirs. But to Basil Mrs Murray's greatest charm was the protecting fondness, as though she were ready to shield him from all the world's trouble, which he felt in her; it made him at once grateful, proud, and humble. He longed to take in his own those caressing hands and to kiss her lips; he felt already round his neck the long white arms as she drew him to her heart with an affection half maternal.

Mrs Murray had never looked handsomer than that night when she stood in the hall, holding herself very erect, and spoke with Basil while waiting for her carriage. Her cloak was so beautiful that the young man remarked on it, and she, flushing slightly with pleasure because he noticed, looked down at the heavy brocade as splendid as some material of the eighteenth century.

'I bought the stuff in Venice,' she said, 'but I feel almost unworthy to wear it. I couldn't resist it because it's exactly like a gown worn by Catherine Cornaro in a picture in one of the galleries.'

'Only you could wear it,' answered Basil, with flashing eyes. 'It would overwhelm anyone else.'

She smiled and blushed and bade him good night.

Basil Kent was much changed from the light-hearted youth whom Frank had known at Oxford, for at that time he gave himself carelessly, like a leaf to the wind, to every emotion; and a quick depression at the failure of something in which he was interested would be soon followed by a boisterous joy. Life seemed very good then, and without after-thought he could rejoice in its various colour, in its ceaseless changing beauty; it was already his ambition to write books, and with the fertile, rather thin invention of youth, he scribbled incessantly. But when he learned with shame and with dismay that the world was sordid and vile, for his very mother was unchaste, he felt he could never hold up his head again. Yet, after the first nausea of disgust, Basil rebelled against his feeling; he loved that wretched woman better than anyone, and now his place was surely by her side. It was not for him to judge nor to condemn, but rather in her shameful humiliation to succour and protect. Could he not show his mother that there were finer things in life than admiration and amusement, jewels and fine clothes? He made up his mind to go to her and take her away to the Continent, where they could hide themselves; and perhaps this might be a means to draw closer together his mother and himself, for, notwithstanding his blind admiration, Basil had suffered a good deal because he could never reach her very heart.

Lady Vizard still inhabited her husband's house in Charles Street, and it was thither on the day after the case had been dismissed that Basil hurried. He expected to find her cowering in her room, afraid of the light of day, haggard and weeping; and his tender heart, filled only with pity, bled at the thought of her distress. He would go to her and kiss her, and say: 'Here am I, mother. Let us go away together where we can start a new life. The world is wide and there is room even for us. I love you more than ever I did, and I will try to be a good and faithful son to you.'

He rang the bell, and the door was opened by the butler he had known for years.

'Can I see her ladyship at once, Miller?' he said.

'Yes, sir. Her ladyship is still at luncheon. Will you go into the dining-room.'

Basil stepped forward, but caught sight of several hats on the hall-table.

'Is anyone here?' he asked with surprise.

But before the butler could answer there was a shout of laughter from the adjoining room. Basil started as though he had been struck.

'Is her ladyship giving a party?'

'Yes, sir.'

Basil stared at the butler with dismay, unable to understand; he wished to question him, but was ashamed. It seemed
too monstrous to be true. The very presence of that servant
seemed an outrage, for he too had given evidence at the hateful trial. How could his mother bear the sight of that unctuous,
servile visage? Miller, seeing the horror in the young man's
eyes and the pallor of his cheek, looked away with a vague
discomfort.

'Will you tell her ladyship that I am here, and should like
to speak to her? I'll go into the morning-room. I suppose no
one will come there?'

Basil waited for a quarter of an hour before he heard the
dining-room door open, and several people, talking loudly and
laughing, walk upstairs. Then his mother's voice rang out,
clear and confident as ever it had been:

'You must all make yourselves comfy. I've got to see somebody, and I forbid anyone to go till I come back.'

In a moment Lady Vizard appeared, a smile still on her lips,
and the suspicion which Basil during that interval had vainly
combated now was changed to naked certainty. Not at all
downcast was she nor abashed, but alert as ever, neither less
stately nor less proud than when last he saw her. He expected
to find his mother in sackcloth and ashes, but behold! she
wore a gown by Paquin, the flaunting audacity of which only
she could have endured. Very dark, with great flashing eyes
and magnificent hair, she had the extravagant flamboyance, the
opulence of colour of some royal gipsy. Her height was unusual, her figure splendid, and holding herself admirably, she
walked with the majesty of an Eastern queen.

'How nice of you to come, dear boy!' she cried, with a
smile showing her beautiful teeth. 'I suppose you want to congratulate me on my victory. But why on earth didn't you come
into the dining-room? It was so amusing. And you really
should begin to *décrasser* yourself a little.' She put forward
her cheek for Basil to kiss (this was surely as much as could
be expected from a fond though fashionable mother), but he
stepped back. Even his lips grew pale.

'Why didn't you tell me that this action was coming on?' he asked hoarsely.

Lady Vizard gave a little laugh, and from a box on the table took a cigarette.

'*Voyons, mon cher*, I really didn't think it was your business.'

Lighting a cigarette, she blew into the air two neat smoke-rings, and watched her son with somewhat contemptuous amusement.

'I didn't expect to find you giving a party today.'

'They insisted on coming, and I had to do something to celebrate my triumph.' She laughed lightly. '*Mon Dieu!* you don't know what a narrow shave it was. Did you read my cross-examination? It was that which saved me.'

'Saved you from what?' cried Basil sternly, two lines of anger appearing between his brows. 'Has it saved you from shameful dishonour? Yes, I read every word. At first I couldn't believe it was true.'

'*Et après?*' asked Lady Vizard calmly.

'But it was true; there were a dozen people to prove it. Oh God, how could you! I admired you more than anyone else in the world. ... I thought of your shame, and I came here because I wanted to help you. Don't you understand the horrible disgrace of it? Oh, mother, mother, you can't go on like this! Heaven knows I don't want to blame you. Come away with me, and let us go to Italy and start afresh. ...'

In the midst of his violent speech he was stopped by the amusement of Lady Vizard's cold eyes.

'But you talk as if I'd been divorced. How absurd you are! In that case it might have been better to go away for a bit, yet even then I should have faced it. But d'you think I'm going to run away now? *Pas si bête, mon petit!*'

'D'you mean to say you're going to stay here when everyone knows what you are – when they'll point at you in the street, and whisper to one another foul stories? And however foul they are, they'll be true.'

Lady Vizard shrugged her shoulders.

'*Oh, que tu m'assomes!*' she said scornfully, justly proud of her French accent. 'You know me very little if you think I'm going to hide myself in some pokey Continental town, or add another tarnished reputation to the *declassée* society of Florence. I mean to stay here. I shall go everywhere, I shall be seen at every theatre, at the opera, at the races, everywhere. I've got some good friends who'll stick to me, and you'll see in a couple of years I shall pull through. After all, I've done little more than plenty of others, and if the *bourgeois* knows a good deal about me that he didn't know before—*je m'en bats l'oeil.* I've got rid of my pig of a husband, and, for that, the whole thing was almost worth it. After all, he knew what was going on; he only rounded on me because he was afraid I spent too much.'

'Aren't you ashamed?' asked Basil, in a low voice. 'Aren't you even sorry?'

'Only fools repent, my dear. I've never done anything in my life that I wouldn't do over again – except marry the two men I did.'

'And you're just going to remain here as if nothing had happened?'

'Don't be foolish, Basil,' answered Lady Vizard ill-temperedly. 'Of course, I'm not going to stay in this particular house. Ernest Torrens has rather a nice little shanty vacant in Curzon Street, and he's offered to lend it me.'

'But you wouldn't take it from him, mother. That would be too infamous. For God's sake, don't have anything more to do with these men.'

'Really, I can't throw over an old friend just because my husband makes him a co-respondent.'

Basil went up to her, and placed his hands on her shoulders.

'Mother, you can't mean all you say. I dare say I'm stupid and awkward – I can't say what I have in my mind. Heaven knows, I don't want to preach to you, but isn't there something in honour and duty and cleanliness and chastity, and all the rest of it? Don't be so hard on yourself. What does it matter what people say? Leave all this and let us go away.'

'*T'es ridicule, mon cher,*' said Lady Vizard, her brow darkening. 'If you have nothing more amusing to suggest than that, we might go to the drawing-room. . . . Are you coming?'

She walked towards the door, but Basil intercepted her.

'You shan't go yet. After all, I'm your son, and you've got no right to disgrace yourself.'

'And what will you do, pray?'

Lady Vizard smiled now in a manner that suggested no great placidity of temper.

'I don't know, but I shall find something. If you haven't the honour to protect yourself, I must protect you.'

'You impudent boy, how dare you speak to me like that!' cried Lady Vizard, turning on him with flashing eyes. 'And what d'you mean by coming here and preaching at me? You miserable prig! I suppose it runs in your family, for your father was a prig before you.'

Basil looked at her, anger taking the place of every other feeling; pity now had vanished, and he sought not to hide his indignation.

'Oh, what a fool I was to believe in you all these years! I would have staked my life that you were chaste and pure. And yet when I read those papers, although the jury doubted, I knew that it was true.'

'Of course it was true!' she cried defiantly. 'Every word of it, but they couldn't prove it.'

'And now I'm ashamed to think I'm your son.'

'You needn't have anything to do with me, my good boy. You've got money of your own. D'you think I want a lubberly, ill-bred oaf hanging about my skirts?'

'I know what you are now, and you horrify me. I hope I shall never see you again. I would sooner my mother were a wretched woman on the streets than you!'

Lady Vizard rang the bell.

'Miller,' she said when the butler appeared, as though she had forgotten Basil's presence, 'I shall want the carriage at four.'

'Very well, my lady.'

'You know I'm dining out, don't you?'

'Yes, my lady.'

Then she pretended to remember Basil, who watched her silently, pale and scarcely able to contain himself.

'You can show Mr Kent out, Miller. And if he happens to call again you can say that I'm not at home.'

With scornful insolence she saw him go, and once again remained mistress of the situation.

Then came three years at the Cape, for Basil, unwilling to return to England, stayed after the expiration of the year for which he enlisted. At first his shame seemed unendurable, and he brooded over it night and day; but when the distance increased between him and Europe, when at length he set foot on African soil, the load of dishonour grew lighter to bear. His squadron was quickly sent up-country, and the hard work relieved his aching mind; the drudgery of a trooper's lot, the long marches, the excitement and the novelty, exhausted him so that he slept with a soundness he had never known before. Then came the sheer toil of war and its dull monotony; he suffered from hunger and thirst, from heat and cold. But these things drew him closer to the companions from whom at first he had sought to hide himself; he was touched by their rough good-humour, their mutual help, and the sympathy with which they used him in sickness; his bitterness towards mankind in general diminished when he saw human good-fellowship face to face with actual hardship; and when at last he found himself in battle, though he had looked forward to it with horrible anxiety, fearing that he might be afraid, Basil felt a great exhilaration which made life most excellent to live. For then vice and squalor and ugliness vanished away, and men stood before one another in primeval strength, the blood burning in their veins, and Death walked between contending hosts; and where Death is there can be nothing petty, sordid, nor mean.

But finally the idea came to Basil that it was not brave to remain there in concealment. For such talents as he had the Cape offered no scope, and he made up his mind to return to London, holding up his head proudly, and there show what stuff he was made of. He felt more self-reliant because he knew he could withstand cheerfully fatigue and want; and the medal on his breast proved that he lacked not courage.

Back at length in London, he entered his name at Lincoln's Inn, and while arranging for publication a little series of sketches he had written during the war, worked hard at law. Though the storm through which he passed had left him somewhat taciturn, with a leaning towards introspection, at bottom Basil was no less open-hearted and sanguine than before, and he entered upon this new phase with glowing hopes. But sometimes his chambers in the Temple seemed very lonely. He was a man who yearned for domestic ties; a woman's hands busied about him, the rustle of a dress or the sound of a loving voice were necessities of his nature. And now it seemed the last bitterness of his life would be removed, for Mrs Murray offered just that affection which he needed, and, still somewhat distrustful of himself, he looked for support to her strength.

Then, in the midst of his thought, Basil frowned, for on a sudden there had arisen in his mind a form which in his new-born joy he had momentarily forgotten. Leaving the bridge, he wandered to the greater darkness of the Mall, his hands behind him; and for a long time walked up and down beneath the trees, perplexed and downcast. It was very late, and there was scarcely a soul about; on the seats homeless wretches lay asleep, huddled in grotesque attitudes, and a policeman stealthily crept along behind them.

Some months before, Basil, instead of lunching in hall, went by chance into a tavern in Fleet Street, and there saw behind the bar a young girl whose extreme beauty at once attracted his attention. Her freshness was charming in that tawdry place, grey with London smoke notwithstanding the gaudiness of its decoration; and though not a man to gossip with barmaids over his refreshment, in this case he could not resist a commonplace remark. To this the girl answered rather saucily (a public-house is apparently an excellent school for repartee) and her bright smile gave a new witchery to the comely face. Interested and a little thrilled, for there was none on whom sheer beauty made a greater impression, Basil told Frank Hurrell, then resident physician at St Luke's, that he had found in Fleet Street of all places the loveliest woman in London. The doctor laughed at his friend's enthusiasm, and one day when they were passing, Basil, to justify himself, insisted on going again to the *Golden Crown*. Then once or twice he went alone, and the barmaid, beginning to recognize him, gave a little friendly nod of greeting. Basil had ever something of a romantic fancy, and his quick imagination decked the pretty girl with whimsical conceits: he dignified her trade by throwing back the date, and seeing in her a neat-footed maid who gave sack to cavaliers and men-at-arms; she was Hebe pouring nectar for the immortal gods; and when he told her this with other fantastic inventions, the girl, though she did not altogether comprehend, reddened as the grosser compliments of the usual frequenters of the bar – accredited admirers – had no power to make her. Basil thought he had never seen anything more captivating than that blush.

And then he began to visit the *Golden Crown* more frequently – at tea-time, when there were fewest people. The pair grew friendly; and they discussed the weather, the customers, and the news of the day. Basil found that half an hour passed very pleasantly in her company, and perhaps he was a little flattered because the barmaid set greater store on his society than on that of the other claimants to her attention. One afternoon, going somewhat later than usual, he was delighted with the bright look that lit her face like sunshine on his appearance.

'I was afraid you weren't coming, Mr Kent.'

By now she used his name, and hers he found was Jenny Bush.

'Would you have minded if I hadn't?'

'A bit.'

At that moment the second barmaid of the *Golden Crown* came to her.

'It's your evening out tonight, isn't it, Jenny?'

'Yes, it is.'

'What are you going to do?'

'I don't know,' said Jenny; 'I haven't made any plans.'

A customer came in, and Jenny's friend shook hands with him.

'Same as usual, I suppose?' she said.

59

'Would you like to come to the play with me?' asked Basil lightly. 'We'll have a bit of dinner first, and then go wherever you like.'

The suggestion flashed across his mind, and he spoke the words without thinking. Jenny's eyes sparkled with pleasure.

'Oh, I should like it. Come and fetch me here at seven, will you?'

But then came in a somewhat undersized young man, with obviously false teeth and a jaunty air. Basil vaguely knew that he was engaged to Jenny, and on most days he might be seen making sheep's eyes across the bar, and drinking innumerable whiskies-and-soda.

'Coming out to dinner, Jenny?' he said. 'I'll stand you a seat at the Tivoli if you like.'

'I'm afraid I can't tonight, Tom,' she answered, blushing slightly. 'I've made other arrangements.'

'What arrangements?'

'A friend has promised to take me to the theatre.'

'Who's that?' answered the man, with an ugly look.

'That's my business, isn't it?' answered Jenny.

'Well, if you won't tell me, I'm off.'

'I'm not stopping you, am I?'

'Just give me a Scotch-and-soda, will you? And look sharp about it.'

The man spoke impudently, wishing to remind Jenny that she was there to carry out his orders. Basil reddened, and with some sharpness was about to say that he would be discreet to use greater politeness, when Jenny's eyes stopped him. Without a word she gave the clerk what he asked for, and the three of them remained silent.

Presently the newcomer finished his liquor and lit a cigarette. He glanced suspiciously at Basil, and opened his mouth to make an observation, but catching the other's steady look, thought better of it.

'Good night then,' he said to Jenny.

When he was gone Basil asked her why she had not thrown him over; it would have been better than to vex her lover.

'I don't care,' cried Jenny: 'I'm about sick of the airs he

60

gives himself. I'm not married to him yet, and if he won't let me do as I like now he can just take himself off.'

They dined at a restaurant in Soho, and Basil, in high spirits over the little adventure, was amused with the girl's delight. It did his heart good to cause such pleasure, and perhaps his satisfaction was not lessened by the attention which Jenny's comeliness attracted. She was rather shy, but when Basil strove to entertain her laughed very prettily and flushed: the idea came to him that he would much like to be of use to her, for she seemed to have a very agreeable nature; he might give her new ideas and a view of the beauty of life which she had never known. She wore a hat, and he morning dress, so they took seats in the back-row of the dress circle at the Gaiety; but even this was unwonted luxury to Jenny, accustomed to the pit or the upper boxes. At the end of the performance she turned to him with dancing eyes.

'Oh, I have enjoyed myself,' she cried. 'I like going out with you much more than with Tom; he's always trying to save money.'

They took a cab to the *Golden Crown,* where Jenny shared a room with the other barmaid.

'Will you come out with me again?' asked Basil.

'Oh, I should love to. You're so different from the other men who come to the bar. You're a gentleman, and you treat me – as if I was a lady. That's why I first liked you, because you didn't go on as if I was a lump of dirt: you always called me Miss Bush ...'

'I'd much rather call you Jenny.'

'Well, you may,' she answered, smiling and blushing. 'All those fellows who hang about the bar think they can do anything with me. You never tried to kiss me like they do.'

'It's not because I didn't want to, Jenny,' answered Basil, laughing.

She made no reply, but looked at him with smiling mouth and tender eyes; he would have been a fool not to recognize the invitation. He slipped his arm round her waist and touched her lips, but he was astonished at the frank surrender with which she received his embrace, and the fugitive pressure turned into a kiss so passionate that Basil's limbs tingled. The cab stopped at the *Golden Crown*, and he helped her out.

'Good night.'

Next day, when he went to the public-house, Jenny blushed deeply, but she greeted him with a quiet intimacy which in his utter loneliness was very gratifying. It caused him singular content that someone at last took an interest in him. Freedom is all very well, but there are moments when a man yearns for someone to whom his comings and goings, his health or illness, are not matters of complete indifference.

'Don't go yet,' said Jenny; 'I want to tell you something.'

He waited till the bar was clear.

'I've broken off my engagement with Tom,' she said then. 'He waited on the other side of the street last night and saw us go out together. And this morning he came in and rounded on me. I told him if he didn't like it he could lump it. And then he got nasty, and I told him I wouldn't have anything more to do with him.'

Basil looked at her for a moment silently.

'But aren't you fond of him, Jenny?'

'No; I can't bear the sight of him. I used to like him well enough, but it's different now. I'm glad to be rid of him.'

Basil could not help knowing it was on his account that she had broken off the engagement. He felt a curious thrill of power, and his heart beat with elation and pride, but at the same time he feared he was doing her some great injury.

'I'm very sorry,' he murmured. 'I'm afraid I've done you harm.'

'You won't stop coming here because of this?' she asked, anxiously watching his doubtful face.

His first thought was that a sudden rupture might be best for both of them, but he could not bear that on his account pain should darken those beautiful eyes, and when he saw the gathering tears he put it aside hastily.

'No, of course not. If you like to see me I'm only too glad to come.'

'Promise that you'll come every day.'

'I'll come as often as I can.'

'No, that won't do. You must come every day.'

'Well, I will.'

He was touched by her eagerness, for he must have been a dolt not to see that Jenny cared a good deal for him, but introspective though he was, never asked himself what were his own feelings. He wished to have a good influence on her, and vowed she would never through him come to any harm. She was very unlike his notion of the ordinary barmaid, and he thought it would be simple to lead her to some idea of personal dignity; he would have liked to take her away from that rather degrading occupation, placing her where she could learn more easily: her character, notwithstanding three years at the *Golden Crown,* was very ingenuous, but in those surroundings she could not for ever remain unspoilt, and it would have seemed a justification of his friendship if he could put her in the way to lead a more beautiful life. The most obvious result of these deliberations was that Basil presently made it a practice to take Jenny on her free evenings to dinner and to the play.

As for her, she had never known anyone like the young barrister who impressed her by the courtesy of his manner and the novelty of his conversation: though often she did not understand the things he said, she was flattered nevertheless, and, womanlike, simulated a comprehension which made Basil think her less uneducated than she really was. At first she was intimidated by the grave stateliness of his treatment, for she was accustomed to less respect, and he could not have used a duchess with more polite decorum; but insensibly admiration and awe passed into love, and at last into blind adoration of which Basil not for a moment dreamed. She wondered why since that first night he had never kissed her, but at parting merely gave his hand; in three months she had advanced only so far as to use his Christian name.

At length the spring came. Along Fleet Street and the Strand flower-women offered for sale gay vernal blossoms, and their baskets gave a dash of colour to the City's hurrying grey. There were days when the very breath of the country, bland and generous, seemed to blow down the crowded thoroughfare, uplifting weary hearts despondent with long monotonous toil:

the sky was blue, and it was the same sky that overhung green meadows and trees bursting into leaf. Sometimes towards the west bevies of cloud, dazzling in the sunshine, were piled upon one another, and at sundown, all rosy and golden, would fill the street with their effulgence, so that the smoky vapours took a gorgeous opalescence, and the heart beat with sheer delight of this goodly London town.

One balmy night in May, when the air was suave and fragrant, so that the heavy step was lightened and the tired mind eased by a strange sad gaiety, Jenny dined with Basil at the little restaurant in Soho where now they were well known. Afterwards they went to a music-hall, but the noise and the glare on that sweet night were unendurable; the pleasant darkness of the streets called to them, and Basil soon proposed that they should go from that place of tedium. Jenny agreed with relief, for the singers left her listless, and an unquiet emotion, which she had never known, made her heart throb with indescribable yearning. As they passed into the night she looked at Basil for a moment with wide-open eyes, in which, strangely mingled, were terror and the primitive savagery of some wild thing.

'Let's go on the Embankment,' she whispered. 'It's quiet there.'

They looked at the silent flowing river and at the warehouses of the Surrey side, uneven against the starlit sky. From one of these gleamed like a malevolent eye one solitary light, and it gave mystery to that square mass of dingy brick, suggesting some grim story of lawless passion and crime. It was low-tide, and below the stone wall was a long strip of shining mud; but Waterloo Bridge, with its easy arches, was oddly dapper, and its lights, yellow and white, threw gay reflections on the water. Near at hand, outlined vaguely by their red lamps, were moored three barges; and there was a weird magic about them, for, notwithstanding their present abandonment, they spoke of strenuous life and passion and toil: for all their squalid brutality there was romance in the hard, strong men who dwelt there on the widening river, travelling on an eternal pilgrimage to the salt sea and the open.

They wandered slowly towards Westminster Bridge, and the lights of the Embankment in their sinuous line were strangely reflected, so that a forest was seen on the river of fiery piles on which might have been built a mystic, invisible city. But the short walk wearied them, though the night was sweet with the savour of springtime, and their limbs were heavy as lead.

'I can't walk back,' said Jenny; 'I'm too tired.'

'Let us take a cab.'

Basil hailed a passing hansom, and they got in. He gave the address in Fleet Street of the *Golden Crown*. They did not speak, but the silence told them things more significant than ever words had done. At last, in a voice not her own, as though speech were dragged from her, Jenny broke the oppressive stillness.

'Why have you never kissed me since that first night, Basil?'

She did not look at him, and he made no sign that he heard, but she felt the trembling of his limbs. Her throat grew hot and dry, and a horrible anxiety seized her.

'Basil!' she said hoarsely, insisting on an answer.

'Because I didn't dare.'

She could count now the throbbing of that torturer in her breast, and the cabman seemed to drive as for a wager. They sped along the Embankment, and it was very dark.

'But I wanted you to,' she said fiercely.

'Jenny, don't let us make fools of ourselves.'

But as though his words were from the mouth only, and a stronger power mastered him, even as he spoke he sought her lips; and because he had resisted so long their sweetness was doubly sweet. With a stifled gasp like a wild beast, she flung her arms about him, and the soft fragrance of her body drove away all thoughts but one: mindless of the passers-by, he pressed her eagerly to his heart. He was mad with her fair, yielding beauty and the passion of her surrender, mad with that never-ending kiss, than which in his whole life he had never known a greater rapture. And his heart trembled like a leaf trembling before the wind.

'Will you come back to my rooms, Jenny?' he whispered.

She did not answer, but drew herself more closely to him.

He lifted the trap in the roof of the hansom and told the cabman to drive to the Temple.

For a week, for a month even, feeling stronger and braver because this woman had given him her love, Basil enjoyed a very ecstasy of pride; he faced the world with greater assurance, and life possessed a spirit and a vigour which were quite new to him. But presently the romantic adventure gained the look of a somewhat vulgar intrigue, and when he recalled his ideal of an existence, spotless and pure, given over to noble pursuits, he was ashamed. This love of his was nothing more than a passing whim of which the knell sounded with its gratification, and he saw with dismay that Jenny had given herself to him body and soul: on her side it was a deathless passion compared with which his attachment was very cold. Each day fanned the flames in her heart, so that he became a necessity of her existence, and if by chance he was too busy to see her an anxious letter came, pitiful in its faulty spelling and clumsy expression, imploring him to visit her. Jenny was exacting, and he resigned himself to going every day to the *Golden Crown*, though that bar grew ever more distasteful. The girl was quite uneducated, and the evenings they spent together – for now, instead of going to a theatre, Jenny passed her leisure in Basil's rooms – went rather heavily; he found it sometimes hard work to make conversation. He realized that he was manacled hand and foot with fetters that were only more intolerable because they consisted of nothing more substantial than the dread of causing pain. He was a man who bore uneasily an irregular attachment of this sort, and he asked himself what could be the end; a dozen times he made up his mind to break with Jenny, but coming to the point, when he saw how dependent she was upon his love, had not the courage. For six months, degraded to a habit, the connection went on.

But it was only by reminding himself constantly that he was not free that Basil abated his nascent love for Mrs Murray, and he imagined that his feeling towards her was different from any he had known before. His desire now was overwhelming to break from the past that sullied him, and thenceforward to lead a fresher, more wholesome life: cost what it might, he must finish with Jenny. He knew that Mrs Murray meant to winter abroad, and there was no reason why he, too, should not go to Italy; there he might see her occasionally, and at the end of six months, with a free conscience, ask her to be his wife.

Thinking he saw the way more clearly before him, Basil ceased his lonely promenade and walked slowly into Piccadilly. After the stir and restless movement of the day, the silence there, unnatural and almost ghostly, seemed barely credible; and the great street, solemn and empty and broad, descended in a majestic sweep with the tranquillity and ease of some placid river. The air was pure and limpid, but resonant, so that a solitary cab on a sudden sent the whole place ringing, and the emphatic trot of the horse clattered with long reverberations. The line of electric lights, impressive by their regularity, self-asserting and staid, flung their glare upon the houses with an indifferent violence, and lower down threw into distinctness the straight park railing and the nearer trees, outlining more sombrely the leafy darkness beyond. And between, outshone, like an uneven string of discoloured gems twinkled the yellow flicker of the gas-jets. Everywhere was silence, but the houses, white except for the gaping windows, had a different silence from the rest; for in their sleep, closed and bolted, they lined the pavement helplessly, disordered and undignified, as though without the busy hum of human voices and the hurrying of persons in and out they had lost all significance.

7

On the following Sunday Basil Kent and Hurrell lunched with Miss Ley, and there met Mr and Mrs Castillyon, who came early in the afternoon. The husband of this lively lady was a weighty man, impressive by the obesity of his person and the commonplace of his conversation; his head was bald, his fleshy face clean-shaven, and his manner had the double pomposity of a landed proprietor and a member of Parliament. It seemed that Nature had taken a freakish revenge on his dullness when she mated him with such a sprightly person as his wife, who, notwithstanding his open adoration, treated him with impatient contempt. Mr Castillyon might have been suffering had he been as silent as he was tedious; but he had an interminable flow of conversation, and now, finding the company somewhat overwhelmed by his appearance, seized the opportunity to air opinions which should more properly have found utterance in that last refuge of dullards and bores, the House of Commons.

But in a little while, at the butler's heels, Reggie, with the stealthiness of a sleek cat, slouched into the room. He was pale after Saturday's amusement, but very handsome. Miss Ley, rising to welcome him, intercepted a glance at Mrs Castillyon, and, seeing in that lady's eye a malicious twinkle, was convinced that the pair had arranged this meeting. But though it amused the acute woman that an assignation should be made in her house, she would not have given Mrs Castillyon further occasion to exercise her wiles if the member of Parliament had not bored her into a bad temper. And really Emily Bassett exaggerated the care she took of her son; it irritated Miss Ley that anyone should be so virtuous as Reggie was thought to be.

'Paul,' said Mrs Castillyon, 'Mr Bassett has heard that you're going to speak in the House tomorrow, and he would so much like to hear you.... My husband – Mr Barlow-Bassett.'

'Really! How did you hear that?' asked Mr Castillyon, delighted.

It was part of Reggie's ingenuity that he never lied in haste to repent at leisure. For one moment he meditated, then fixed his eyes firmly on Frank to prevent a contradiction.

'Dr Hurrell told me.'

'Of course I shall be delighted if you'll come,' pursued the orator. 'I shall speak just before dinner. Won't you dine afterwards? I'm afraid the dinner they give you is very bad.'

'He won't mind that after he's heard you speak, Paul,' said Mrs Castillyon.

A faint smile flickered on her lips at the success of this manoeuvre. Mr Castillyon turned blandly to Miss Ley, with the little shake of his whole body which announced a display of eloquence. Frank and Basil immediately jumped up and bade Miss Ley farewell; they walked together towards the Embankment, and for a while neither spoke.

'I wanted to talk to you, Frank,' said Basil at last. 'I'm thinking of going abroad for the winter.'

'Are you? What about the Bar?'

'I don't mind about that. After all, I have enough to live on, and I mean to have a shot if I can do any real good as a writer. Besides, I want to break with Jenny, and I can think of no kinder way to do it.'

'I think you're very wise.'

'Oh, I wish I hadn't got into this mess, Frank. I don't know what to do. I'm afraid she's grown a good deal fonder of me than I ever thought she would, and I don't want to cause her pain. I can't bear it when I think of the wretchedness she'll suffer – and yet we can't go on as we are.'

Frank remained silent, with compressed lips and a stern look on his face. Basil divined the unspoken censure, and burst out passionately.

'Oh, I know I oughtn't to have given way. D'you think I've not bitterly regretted? I never thought she'd take it any more seriously than I did. And, after all, I'm a man like any other. I have passions as other men have. I suppose most men in my place would have done as I did.'

'I didn't venture to reproach you, Basil,' said Frank dryly.

'I meant to do only good to the girl. But I lost my head. After all, if we were all as cool at night as we are in the morning. . . .'

'Life would be a Sunday-school,' interrupted Frank.

At that moment they were near Westminster Bridge, and a carriage passed them. They saw that in it sat Mrs Murray, and she bowed gravely; Basil reddened and looked back.

'I wonder if she's on the way to Miss Ley.'

'Would you like to go back and see?' asked Frank coldly.

He looked sharply at Basil, who flushed again, and then threw off his momentary hesitation.

'No,' he answered firmly; 'let us go on.'

'Is it on account of Mrs Murray that you wish to throw over Jenny?'

'Oh, Frank, don't think too hardly of me. I hate the ugly sordid vulgarity of an intrigue. I wanted to lead a cleaner life than most men because of my – because of Lady Vizard; and when I've been with Jenny I'm disgusted with myself. If I'd never seen Mrs Murray, I should still do all I could to finish.'

'Are you in love with Mrs Murray?'

'Yes,' answered Basil, after a moment's pause.

'D'you think she cares for you?'

'The other night I felt sure of it, but now again I'm doubtful. Oh, I want her to care for me. I can't help it, Frank, this is quite a different love from the other; it lifts me up and supports me. I don't want to seem a prig, but when I think of Mrs Murray I can't imagine anything unworthy. And I'm proud of it because my love for her is almost spiritual. If she does care for me and will marry me, I think I may do some good in the world. I fancied that if I went away for six months Jenny would gradually think less of me – I think it's better to drift apart than just to break cruelly at once.'

'It would certainly be less painful to you,' said Frank.

'And when I'm free I shall go to Mrs Murray, tell her the whole story, and ask her to marry me.'

Basil lived in a pleasant court of the Temple to which, notwithstanding the sordid contentions of its daily life, the old red houses and the London plane-trees, with their leafy coolness, gave a charm full of repose. His rooms, on the top floor, were furnished simply, but with the taste of a man who cared for beautiful things. The ladies of Sir Peter Lely, with their sweet artificial grace, looked down in mezzotint from the panelled walls, and the Sheraton furniture gave a delicate austerity to the student's room.

Frank filled his pipe, but they had not been long seated, when there came a knock at the door.

'I wonder who the dickens that is?' said Basil. 'I don't often have visitors on Sunday afternoon.'

He went into the tiny passage and opened. Frank heard Jenny's voice.

'Can I come in, Basil? Is anyone there?'

'Only Frank,' he answered, leading the way in.

Jenny was arrayed in Sabbath garments, the colours of which to the doctor's eye seemed a little crude; the bright bow in her black hat contrasted violently with a fawn jacket, but her beauty was such as to overcome all extravagance of costume. She was rather tall, handsomely made, with the rounded hips and full breasts of a passionate woman; her features were chiselled with the clean perfection of a Greek statue, and no duchess could have had a shorter lip or a more delicate nose; her pink ears were more exquisite than the shells of the sea. But it was her wonderful colouring which chiefly attracted notice, with the rich magnificence of her hair, the brilliant eyes, and the creamy perfection of her skin. Her face had a girlish innocence which was very captivating, and Frank, observing her with critical gaze, could not deny that Mrs Murray by her side, notwithstanding all the advantages of dress and manner, would have been reduced to insignificance.

'I thought you were going home this afternoon,' said Basil.

'No, I couldn't manage it. I came here immediately after we closed at three, but you weren't in. I was so afraid that you wouldn't come before six o'clock.'

It was very clear that Jenny wished to talk with Basil, and

71

Frank, deliberately knocking out the ashes of his pipe, rose to go. His host accompanied him downstairs.

'Look here, Basil,' said Frank; 'if I were you I'd take this opportunity to tell Jenny that you're going away.'

'Yes, I mean to. I'm glad she's come. I wanted to write to her, but I think that would be funking it. Oh, I hate myself because I must cause her so much pain.'

Frank walked away. Disposed at first to envy Basil his good fortune, he had cursed his fate because pretty girls never fell desperately enamoured of him: it would certainly have been a bore, and to him more than to another an insufferable slavery, but yet the marked abstention was not flattering. Now, however, on his way to the club, wanted by no one, with no claims on him of any sort, he congratulated himself cynically because fair ladies kept their smiles for persons more fascinating than himself.

When Basil returned to his room, he found that Jenny had not, as usual, taken off her hat, but stood by the window looking at the door. He went to kiss her, but she drew back.

'Not today, Basil. I've got something to say to you.'

'Well, take off your things first, and make yourself comfortable.'

It occurred to him that Jenny had perhaps quarrelled with her employer at the *Golden Crown*, or wished to reproach him because for a couple of days he had not seen her, and, lighting his pipe, he answered with careless gaiety. He did not see that she looked at him strangely, but when she spoke there was such tragic anguish in her tone that he was startled.

'I don't know what I should have done if I'd not found you in today.'

'Good heavens, Jenny! what's the matter?'

Her voice broke with a sob.

'I'm in trouble, Basil.'

The tears cut his heart, and very tenderly he put his arms round her; but again she withdrew.

'No, please don't sit near me, or I shall never have the courage to tell you.'

She stood up, drying her eyes, and walked up and down.

'I wanted to see you this morning, Basil. I came to your door, and then I was afraid to knock. So I went away again. And then this afternoon, when I couldn't make you hear, I thought you'd gone away, and I couldn't have borne another night of it.'

'Tell me quickly what it is, Jenny.'

A horrible fear seized him, and his cheeks grew pale as hers. She watched him with anxious eyes.

'I've not been feeling very well these last few days,' she whispered, 'and yesterday I went to the doctor. He told me I was going to have a child.'

And then, hiding her face, she sobbed bitterly. Basil's heart sank within him, and when he looked at that wretched girl, bowed down with fear and shame, he was filled with remorse. If he had never regretted before, he regretted now, with all his soul.

'Don't cry, Jenny; I can't bear it.'

She looked up hopelessly, and the ugliness of that fair face, pain-distraught, tortured him. He was all confused, and many an impulse madly skeltered through his brain: he, too, feared, but at the same time, above all and overmastering, was a wonderful elation because he would be the father of a living child. His pulse throbbed with pride, and like a miracle a sudden love mysteriously burnt up his heart; he took Jenny in his arms and kissed her more passionately than he had ever done before.

'Oh, don't, for God's sake; it's nothing to you,' she cried, trying to tear herself away. 'But what about me? I wish I was dead. I'd always been straight till I knew you.'

He could bear her agony no longer, and the thought which had come to him immediately now grew irresistible. There was one way to dry those tears, one way alone to repair that wrong, and a rising flood of passion made it very easy. His whole soul demanded one definite course, uplifting him and crushing every nascent objection; but his heart beat painfully when he spoke, for he was taking an irretrievable step, and God only knew what would be the end.

'Don't cry, darling; it's not so bad as all that,' he said. 'We'd better get married at once.'

With a little gasp Jenny's sobs were stilled, and quite motionless, looking down, she clung to Basil like a thing from which all life was gone. The words sank into her mind slowly, and she puzzled over them as though they were said in a language she barely understood; and then, still silent, she began to tremble.

'Say that again, Basil,' she whispered, and after a pause: 'Did you mean it? Can you bring yourself to marry me?'

She stood up and looked at him, dishevelled and beautiful, a tragic figure in whose unutterable woe was a most noble pathos.

'I'm only a barmaid, Basil.'

'You're the mother of my child, and I love you,' he answered gravely. 'I've always longed to have children, Jenny, and you've made me very proud and very happy.'

Her eyes shone with tears, and into her anxious, terror-stricken face came a look of such ecstatic happiness that Basil felt himself ten times rewarded.

'Oh, Basil, you are good. You do mean it, don't you? And I shall be with you always?'

'Did you think so badly of me as to suppose I would throw you over now?'

'Oh, I was afraid. You've cared for me less of late, and I've been so unhappy, Basil, but I didn't dare show it. At first I hadn't the courage to tell you, because I thought you'd be angry. I knew you wouldn't let me starve, but you might just have given me money and told me to go.'

He kissed her hands, aflame as never before with her radiant beauty.

'I didn't know I loved you so much,' he cried.

She sank into his arms with a sob, but it was a sob now of uncontrollable passion, and avid of love she sought his lips.

Basil had in his passage a little gas-stove, and presently with a charming housewifely grace, Jenny set about making the tea: languorous and happy, she was proud to do things for him, and insisted, while she prepared, that he should sit still and smoke.

'I wish we needn't keep a servant, Basil, so as I might wait on you.'

'You mustn't go back to that beastly bar.'

'I can't leave them in a hole, you know. I shall have to give a week's notice.'

'Then give it at once, and as soon as you're free we'll be married.'

'Oh, I shall be so happy!' she sighed with rapture.

'Now, look here: we must be sensible and talk over things. You know I'm not very well-to-do. I've only got three hundred a year.'

'Oh, that's lots,' she cried. 'Why, dad has never had more than three-ten a week.'

Basil smiled doubtfully, for his tastes were expensive, and he had never been able satisfactorily to make ends meet. But he persuaded himself that two persons could live more economically than one; he would give serious attention to his law, and had no doubt that in time he would earn an income. While he waited for briefs he might write. They could afford a little house in the suburbs at Barnes or Putney, and, so as not to be extravagant, for their honeymoon would merely go to Cornwall for a fortnight. After that he must set to work immediately.

'Ma will be surprised when I tell her I'm going to get married,' said Jenny, laughing. 'You must come down and see them.'

Though a brother in the City sometimes came to the *Golden Crown*, Basil had never made acquaintance with any of Jenny's relations; he knew that they lived at Crouch End.

'I wouldn't have gone back to them if you hadn't said you'd marry me, Basil. Ma would have turned me out of doors. I was frightened to go down today in case she suspected something.' Suddenly, a doubt rising in her mind, she turned to him quickly. 'You do mean it, don't you? You won't go back on me now?'

'Of course not, you foolish child. Don't you think I shall be proud to have so beautiful a wife?'

Jenny was obliged to go a little before six, at which hour the *Golden Crown* opened its doors to thirsty Christians; and Basil, having accompanied her thither, walked on to consider this new state of his affairs. The capacity to stand quite alone, careless of praise or censure, is very rare among men, and he, temperamentally lacking confidence in himself, felt at that moment a most urgent need for advice and sympathy; but Frank was inaccessible, and he could not disturb Miss Ley again that day. He went to his club and wrote a note asking if he might see her the following morning.

He slept uneasily, and getting up later than usual, had scarcely finished breakfast when an answer came to say that she would be pleased to walk with him at eleven in St James's Park. He fetched her punctually. They sauntered for a while, looking at the wild-fowl, and Basil, hesitating, spoke of indifferent subjects; but Miss Ley, noting his unusual gravity, surmised that he had a difficult communication to make.

'Well, what is it?' she asked point-blank, sitting down.

'Only that I'm going to be married.'

Her thoughts at once went to Mrs Murray, and she wondered when Basil could have found opportunity for his declaration.

'Is that all?' she cried, smiling. 'It's a very proper proceeding for young things, but surely you need not look so serious over it.'

'I'm going to marry a Miss Bush.'

'Who on earth is she? I've never heard of her,' answered the good lady, turning to him with surprise; but a dim recollection flashed across her mind. 'Wasn't it a certain Jenny Bush that Frank told me you had discovered somewhere and vowed was the loveliest creature in the world?' She gave him a long and searching look. 'I suppose you're not going to marry a barmaid from a public-house in Fleet Street?'

'Yes,' he answered quietly.

'But why?'

'Presumably because I'm in love with her.'

'Nonsense! A susceptible youth falls in love with a dozen girls, but in a country where monogamy is enforced by Act of Parliament, it is impracticable to marry them all.'

'I'm afraid I can give you no other reason.'

76

'You might really have made that interesting announcement by letter,' returned Miss Ley dryly.

He looked down with a discouraged air, and for a while was silent.

'I must talk it over with someone,' he burst out at length. 'I'm so utterly alone, and I have no one to help or advise me. ... I'm marrying Jenny because I must. I've known her for some time – the whole thing was sordid and hateful – and yesterday after I left you she came to my rooms. She was half hysterical, poor thing, she hardly knew what she was saying, and she told me ...'

'What you very well might have foreseen,' interrupted Miss Ley.

'Yes.'

Miss Ley meditated, slowly drawing her initials with the point of her parasol in the gravel, and Basil stared at her anxiously.

'Are you sure you're not making a fool of yourself?' she asked finally. 'You're not in love with her, are you?'

'No.'

'Then you have no right to marry her. Oh, my dear boy, you don't know how tiresome marriage is sometimes, even with persons of the same class and inclinations. I've known so many people in my life, and I'm convinced that marriage is the most terrible thing in the world unless passion makes it absolutely inevitable. And I hate and abhor with all my soul those fools who strive to discredit and ignore that.'

'If I don't marry Jenny she'll kill herself. She's not like an ordinary barmaid. Until I knew her she was perfectly straight. It means absolute ruin to her.'

'I think you exaggerate. After all, it's not much more than a very regrettable incident due to your – innocence; and there's no need for desperate courses or histrionics. You will behave like a gentleman, and take proper care of the girl. She can go into the country till the whole thing is over, and when she comes back no one will be the wiser nor she very much the worse.'

'But it isn't a matter of people knowing; it's a matter of honour.'

'Isn't it rather late in the day to talk of morality? I don't see where precisely the honour came in when you seduced her.'

'I dare say I've been an utter cad,' he answered humbly; 'but I see a plain duty before me, and I must do it.'

'You talk as though such things had never happened before,' pursued Miss Ley.

'Oh yes, I know they happen every day. If the girl gives way, so much the worse for her; it's no business of the man's. Let her go on the streets, let her go to the devil, and be hanged to her.'

Miss Ley, pursing her lips, shrugged her shoulders. She wondered how he proposed to live, since his income was quite insufficient for the necessities of a family, and he was peculiarly unsuited to the long drudgery of the Bar. She knew the profession termed 'literary' well enough to be aware that in it little money could be earned. Basil lacked the journalistic quickness, and it took him two years to write a novel for which he would probably not get more than fifty pounds; and his passion for the analysis of mental states offered small chance of lucrative success. Besides, he was extravagant, and would hate to pinch and spare: nor had he occasion ever to learn the difficult art of getting a shilling's-worth of goods for twelve coppers.

'I suppose you've realized that people will cut your wife,' Miss Ley added.

'Then they will cut me too.'

'But you're the last man in the world to give up these things. There's nothing you enjoy more than dinner-parties and visits to country houses. Women's smiles are all-important to you.'

'You talk of me as if I were a tame cat,' he returned smiling. 'After all, I'm only trying to do my duty. I made an awful mistake, and heaven knows how bitterly I've regretted it. But now I see the way clearly before me, and whatever the cost, I must take it.'

Miss Ley looked at him sharply, and her keen grey eyes travelled over his face in a minute examination.

'Are you sure you don't admire a little too much your heroic attitude?' she asked, and in her voice was a stinging coldness at which Basil winced. 'Nowadays self-sacrifice is a luxury which few have the strength to deny themselves; people took to it when they left off sugar because it was fattening, and they sacrifice themselves wantonly, from sheer love of it, however worthless the object. In fact, the object scarcely concerns them; they don't care how much they harm it so long as they can gratify their passion.'

'When I asked Jenny to marry me, and saw the radiant joy in her poor, tear-stained face, I knew I'd done the right thing. Ah, what does it matter if I'm wretched, so long as I can make her happy!'

'I wasn't thinking of your wretchedness, Basil. I was thinking that you had done that girl harm enough already without marrying her. ... D'you think she'll be anything but utterly miserable? You're only doing this from selfishness and coward-ice, because you love your self-esteem and you're afraid to give pain.'

This point of view was new to Basil, but it seemed un-reasonable. He put it hastily aside.

'All this time you've not thought of the child, Miss Ley,' he said slowly. 'I can't let the child skulk into the world like a thief. Let him go through life with an honest name; it's hard enough without marking him with a hideous stigma. And, after all, I'm proud to be the father of a living child. Whatever I suffer, whatever we both suffer, will be worth it for that.'

'When are you to be married?' asked Miss Ley, after a pause.

'I think this day week. You won't abandon me, Miss Ley, will you?'

'Of course not,' she answered, smiling gently. 'I think you're a fool, but then most people are. They never realize that they have only one life, and mistakes are irreparable. They play with it as though it were a game of chess in which they could try this move and that, and when they get in a muddle, sweep the board clear and begin again.'

'But life is a game of chess in which one is always beaten. Death sits on the other side of the board, and for every move he has a counter-move, for all your deep-laid schemes a parry.'

They walked back to Old Queen Street, both occupied with

their thoughts, and at her door Miss Ley gave Basil her hand. He hesitated a little, but forced himself to speak.

'There's one thing more, Miss Ley: I fancied – that Mrs Murray ... I dare say I was wrong, but I shouldn't like her to think too ill of me.'

'I'm afraid you must put up with that,' replied Miss Ley sharply. 'There was nothing in the way of an engagement between you?'

'Nothing.'

'I shall see her in a day or two, and I'll tell her that you're going to be married.'

'But what will she think of me?'

'I suppose you don't want her to know the truth?'

'No. I told you only because I felt I must talk it over with someone. Of all persons, I least wish Mrs Murray to know.'

'Then you must let her think as she chooses. Good-bye.'

'Have you nothing more to say to me than that?' he asked despairingly.

'My dear, if you can suffer all things, you may venture all things.'

8

MISS LEY found the Dean alone in the library, for the Langtons returned to Tercanbury that afternoon, and Bella was spending her last morning at the Stores.

'You know, Algernon, in this world it's the good who do all the harm,' remarked Miss Ley, sitting down. 'The bad carry off their wrong-doing with a certain dash which lessens the iniquity, and common-sense robs their vice of sting; but there's no reasoning with a man conscious of his own rectitude.'

'That is a very subversive doctrine,' answered the Dean, smiling.

'Only the wicked should sin, for experience teaches them moderation, and little hurt befalls. But when the virtuous slip from the narrow path they flounder hopelessly, committing one error after another in the effort to right themselves by the methods of virtue. Under like circumstances they injure all concerned far more desperately than the entirely vicious, because they won't face the fact that a different code is applicable.'

'Pray tell me the reason of this harangue.'

'A young friend of mine has done a foolish thing, and means to cap it with another. He came to me just now ostensibly for advice, but in reality that I might applaud his magnanimity.'

Without giving names, Miss Ley told her cousin Basil's story.

'My first curacy was at Portsmouth,' the Dean said when she finished, 'and I was then very intolerant of evil, very eager to right the wrong. I remember one of my parishioners got into a similar trouble, and for the child's sake as well as for the woman's I insisted that the man should marry. I practically dragged them to the altar by the hair of their heads, and when I had properly legalized the position felt I had done a good day's work: six months afterwards the man cut his wife's throat and was duly hanged. If I hadn't been so officious two lives might have been spared.'

'Mrs Grundy is a person of excellent understanding, who does not in the least deserve the obloquy with which she is now regarded. She does not mind if a man is a little wild, and if he isn't thinks him rather a milksop; but with admirable perspicacity she realizes that for the woman a straighter rule is needed: if *she* falls Mrs Grundy, without the smallest qualm, will give the first push into the pit. Society is a grim monster, somnolent apparently, so that you think you can take every kind of liberty; but all the time he watches you, he watches slily, and when you least expect it puts out an iron hand to crush you.'

'I hope Bella won't be late,' said the Dean; 'we haven't too much time after luncheon to catch our train.'

'Society has made its own decalogue, a code just fit for middling people, who are neither very good nor very bad; but the odd thing is it punishes you just as severely if you act above its code as if you act below.'

'Sometimes it makes a god of you when you're dead.'

'But it takes precious good care to crucify you when you're alive, Algernon.'

Soon after this Bella came in, and when the Dean went upstairs, told Miss Ley that on her bookseller's advice she had purchased for Herbert Field the two portly tomes of Dowden's *Life of Shelley*.

'I hope soon he'll have enough poetry to make a little volume,' said Bella, 'and then I shall ask him if I may arrange for publication. I wonder if Mr Kent will help me to find a publisher.'

'You will find a bank balance your best friend there, my dear,' answered Miss Ley.

Basil announced the approaching marriage to his solicitor, for his small fortune was held in trust, and his mother's signature was needed for various documents. In a day or two the following letter reached him.

82

CHER ENFANT,

I find that you mean to be married, and I desire to give you my maternal blessing. Do come to tea tomorrow and receive it in due form. You have sulked with me quite long enough, and the masculine boudeur is always a trifle ridiculous. In case it has escaped your memory I venture to remind you that I am – your mother.

Yours affectionately,

MARGUERITE VIZARD

P.S.—It is one of the ironies of nature, that though a man, if his father is canaille, may console himself with the thought that this relationship is always a little uncertain, with regard to his mother he can lay no such flattering unction to his soul.

Lady Vizard was shrewd when she prophesied that a couple of years would suffice for her to regain the place in society due to her beauty, wealth, and distinction. None knew better that her position after the trial was precarious, and it required much tact to circumvent the many pitfalls. She was aware that the two best stepping-stones for social aspirants are philanthropy and the Church of Rome, but the astute creature did not think her state so desperate as to need conversion, and a certain assiduity in charitable pursuits offered all that was requisite. Lady Vizard made a dead-set for respectability in the person of a tedious old lady, whose rank and opulence gave her unlimited credit with the world, and whose benevolence made her an easy tool. Lady Edward Stringer was a little old woman with false teeth and a bright chestnut wig, always set awry; and, though immensely dull, managed to assemble in her drawing-rooms everyone in London of real importance. A relation of Lord Vizard, she had quarrelled with him desperately, and it was but natural that his wife should pour her troubles into a willing ear. Now, when she chose, Lady Vizard could assume a manner so flattering that few could resist it: she had an agile tongue and so good a memory for the lies she told that she was never caught tripping; she unfolded the story of her matrimonial unhappiness with such pathetic skill that Lady Edward, touched, promised to do everything to help her. She appeared at the old lady's parties, was seen with her in all places where fashion congregates; and presently the world concluded it could well afford to know an amusing woman who suffered from no lack of money.

When Basil arrived, obedient to her summons, he found his mother seated in that favourite attitude in which she had been painted; and the portrait, by its daring colour the sensation of its season, hung behind her to show how little in ten years the clever woman had changed. By her side were the inevitable cigarettes, smelling-salts, and a French novel which on its appearance lately had excited a prosecution. Lady Vizard held a stall at a forthcoming bazaar, and it was not altogether without satisfaction that she read at that moment the prospectus in which her name figured on a list whereof the obvious respectability was highly imposing.

Tall and statuesque, she wore her gowns with a flaunting extravagance rather than with the simplicity, often bordering on slovenliness, of most of her countrywomen. She had no desire to conceal from masculine gaze the sinuous outlines of her splendid figure, and dressed, with the bold effrontery of the sensual woman, to draw attention to her particular anatomy rather than to conceal it. Nor was she strange to the intricate art of *maquillage*: the average Englishwoman who paints her face, characteristically feeling it a first step in the descent to Avernus, paints it badly. She can never avoid the idea that cosmetics are a little wicked or a little vulgar, and a tiny devil, cloven-footed and betailed, lurks always at the bottom of her rouge-pot. Then, perversely, the plunge once taken, to reassure herself she very distinctly exaggerates. Lady Vizard used all the artifices known to the wise, but so cleverly that the result was admirable: even her hair, which to most of her sex is a block of stumbling, was dyed in complete harmony with her eyes and complexion, so that the gross male intelligence was often deceived. Her eyebrows were perfect, and the pencilled line at her eyelashes gave her flashing eyes a greater intensity; the cosmetic on her lips was applied with an artist's hand, and her mouth was no less beautiful than Cupid's bow.

Lady Vizard had not seen her son for five years, and she noted the change in him with interest but without emotion.

'Let me give you some tea,' she said. 'By the way, why didn't you come and see me on your return from the Cape?'

'You forget that you gave Miller orders not to admit me.'

'You shouldn't have taken that *au grand sérieux*; I dismiss my maid every time she does my hair badly, but she's been with me for years. I forgave you in a week.'

Their eyes met, and they realized that the position between them was unchanged. Lady Vizard shrugged her shoulders.

'I asked you to come today because I thought you might have grown more tolerant in five years. Apparently you are one of those men who never learn.'

Even a year before Basil would have answered that he hoped never to grow tolerant of dishonour, but now, ashamed, he sat in silence. His effort was to assume the air of polite indifference which his mother used so easily. He foresaw her next question, and it tortured him that he must expose part at least of his secret to that scornful woman; yet, just because it was so distasteful, he meant to answer them openly.

'And whom are you going to marry?'

'No one you have ever heard of,' he answered, smiling.

'Do you wish to make a secret of the fortunate creature's name?'

'Miss Bush.'

'That doesn't sound very distinguished, does it? Who is her father?'

'He's in the City.'

'Rich?'

'Very poor.'

Lady Vizard looked at her son keenly, then with a peculiar expression leaned forward.

'Pardon me if I ask, but is she what your tedious grandmother called a gentlewoman?'

'She's a barmaid in Fleet Street,' he answered defiantly.

Without hesitation came the next question, in a ringing voice.

'And when do you expect the *accouchement*?'

A blow could not have taken him more aback. The blood rushed to his cheeks, and he sprang to his feet. Her eyes rested on him with cool scorn, and confounded by her penetration, he found nothing to say.

'I'm right, am I? Virtue has had a fall, apparently. Ah, *mon cher*, I've not forgotten the charming things you said to me five years ago. Have you? Don't you remember the eloquence with which you spoke of chastity and honour? And you called me a name – which well-conducted sons don't usually apply to their mothers; but I take it your wife will have no fewer claims to it than I?'

'If I have lust in my blood, it's because I have the misfortune to be your son,' he cried fiercely.

'I can't help admiring you when I remember the unctuous rectitude with which you acted the upright man, and you were playing your little game all the time. But, *franchement,* your little game rather disgusts me. I don't like these hole-and-corner tricks with barmaids.'

'I dare say I did wrong, but I mean to make amends.'

'Of all fools, the saints preserve me from the fool who repents. If you can't sin like a gentleman, you'd really better be virtuous. A gentleman doesn't marry a barmaid because he's seduced her – unless he has the soul of a counter-jumper. And then you dared come to me with your impudent sermons!'

At the recollection her eyes flashed, and she stood over Basil like some wrathful, outraged goddess.

'What do you know of life and the fiery passion that burns in my veins? You don't know what devils tear at my breast. How can you judge me? But what do I care? I've had a good time in my day, and I'm not finished yet; and after all, if you weren't such a prig, you'd see that I'm a better sort than most women, for I've never deserted a friend nor hit an enemy that was down.'

This she said with an angry vehemence, fluently as though she had often uttered the words to herself, and now at last found the opportunity for which she had waited. But quickly she regained that cutting irony of manner which she well knew was most effective.

'And when I grow old I shall go into the Catholic Church and finish my days in the odour of sanctity.'

'Have you anything more to say to me?' asked Basil coldly.

'Nothing,' she replied, shrugging her shoulders. 'You were born to make a fool of yourself. You're one of those persons who are doomed to mediocrity because you haven't the spirit to go to the devil like a man. Go away and marry your barmaid. I tell you that you disgust me.'

Blind with rage, his hands clenched, Basil turned to the door, but before he reached it the butler announced Lord de Capit, and a tall fair youth entered. Basil gave him an angry glare, for he could well imagine what were the relations between his mother and the wealthy peer. Lord de Capit looked after him with astonishment.

'Who is that amiable person?' he asked.

Lady Vizard gave a little, irritated laugh.

'A foolish creature. He doesn't interest me.'

'One of my predecessors?'

'No, of course not,' answered Lady Vizard, amused. 'Give me a kiss, child.'

Profoundly despondent, Basil walked back to the Temple, and when he came to his door it was opened by Jenny. He remembered then that she had promised to come that afternoon to hear the final arrangements for their marriage, which was to take place at a registry office.

'I met my brother Jimmie in the Strand, Basil,' she said, 'and I've brought him up to see you.'

Going in, he found a weedy youth seated on the table, with dangling legs. He had sandy hair, a clean-shaven, sharp face, and pale eyes. Much commoner than his sister, he spoke with a pronounced Cockney accent, and when he smiled, showing small, discoloured teeth, had an expression of rather odious cunning. He was dressed in the height of fashion – for City sportsmen, with a rakish bowler, a check suit, and a bright violet shirt: he flourished a thin bamboo cane.

'How do?' he said, nodding to Basil. 'Pleased to make your acquaintance.'

'I'm afraid I've kept you waiting.'

'Don't apologize,' Mr Bush answered cheerfully. 'I can't stay long, because I'm a business man, but I thought I'd better just pop in and say 'ow d'ye do to my future brother-in-law. I'm a chap as likes to be cordial.'

'It's very kind of you,' said Basil politely.

'My! He was surprised when I told him I was going to marry you, Basil,' cried Jenny, with a little laugh of pleasure.

'Now then, don't mind me,' said James. 'Give 'im a slobber, old tart.'

'Go on, Jimmie; you are a caution!'

'Oh, I see you're bashful. Well, I'll be toddling.'

'Won't you have some tea before you go?' asked Basil.

'Bless you, I don't want to disturb you canary birds. And I'm not much of an 'and at tea; I leave that to females. I like something stronger myself.'

'That's Jimmie all over,' cried his sister, amused.

'I have some whisky, Mr Bush,' said Basil, raising his eyebrows.

'Oh, blow the Mister and blow the Bush. Call me Jimmie. I can't stand ceremony. We're both of us gentlemen. Now mind you, I'm not a feller to praise myself, but I will say this – I am a gentleman. That's not self-praise, is it?'

'Dear me, no. Mere statement of fact.'

'It's a thing you can't 'elp, so what's the good of being proud about it? If I meet a chap in a pub, and he wants to stand me a drink, I don't ask 'im if he's a lord.'

'But you just take it.'

'Well, you'd do the same yourself, wouldn't you?'

'I dare say. May I offer you some whisky now?'

'Well, if you are so pressing. My motto is: Never refuse a gargle. They say it's good for the teeth.'

Basil poured out.

'Hold hard, old man,' cried James. 'You needn't be too generous with the soda. Well, 'ere's luck!'

He emptied his glass at a gulp and smacked his lips.

'There are no flies about that, I lay. Now I'll be toddling.'

Basil did not press him to stay, but by way of speeding the parting guest, offered a cigar. James took and examined it.

'*Villar y Villar!*' he exclaimed. 'That's all right. How much do they run you in a 'undred?'

'I really don't know what they cost. They were given to me.'
Basil struck a match. 'Won't you take the label off?'

'Not if I know it,' said James, with much decision. 'I don't smoke a *Villar y Villar* every day, and when I do I smoke it with the label on. ... Well, so long. See you later, old tart.'

When he was gone Jenny turned to her lover.

'Kiss me. ... There! Now I can sit down quietly and talk. How d'you like my brother?'

'I scarcely know him yet,' answered Basil cautiously.

'He's not a bad sort when you do, and he can make you laugh. He's just like my mother.'

'Is he?' cried Basil, with some vivacity. 'And is your father like that too?'

'Well, you know, pa's not had the education that Jimmie's had. Jimmie was at a boarding-school at Margate. You were at a boarding-school, weren't you?'

'Yes, I was at Harrow.'

'Ah, you don't get the fine air at Harrow that you do at Margate.'

'No,' said Basil.

'Come and sit by me, ducky. ... I'm so glad we're alone. I should like to be alone with you all my life. You do love me, don't you?'

'Yes.'

'Much?'

'Yes,' he repeated, smiling.

She gave him a long, searching glance, and her eyes suddenly darkened. She looked away.

'Basil, I want to say something to you, and it's dreadfully hard.'

'What is it, darling?'

He put his arm round her waist and drew her towards him.

'No, don't do that,' she said, getting up and moving away. 'Please stay where you are. I can't say it if I look at you.'

He paused, wondering what was in her mind. She spoke brokenly, as though by an effort almost beyond her strength.

'Are you sure you love me, Basil?'

'Quite sure,' he answered, trying to smile.

89

'Because I don't want to be married out of pity or anything like that. If you're only doing it because you think you ought, I'd rather go on as I am.'

'But why d'you say this now, Jenny?'

'I've been thinking it over. The other day when you offered to marry me I was so happy I couldn't think it out. But I love you so much that I've seen things quite differently since then. I don't want to hurt you. I know I'm not the sort of woman you ought to marry, and I can't help you to get on.'

Her voice trembled, but she forced herself to continue, and Basil, motionless, listened to her gravely. He could not see her face.

'I want to know if you really care for me, Basil. If you don't, you've only got to say so, and we'll break it off. After all, I'm not the first girl that's got into trouble; I could easily manage, you know.'

For one moment he hesitated, and his heart beat painfully. Miss Ley's cold advice, his mother's scorn, recurred to him: the girl herself offered an opportunity, and would it not, after all, be best to seize it?

His freedom stood before him, and he exulted; a few easy words might destroy that horrible nightmare, and he could start life afresh, wiser and better. But Jenny turned round, and in her sad, beautiful eyes he saw a mortal anxiety; in the sickening anguish of her expectation she could scarcely breathe. He had not the strength to speak.

'Jenny, don't torture yourself,' he said brokenly. 'And you torture me, too. You know I love you, and I want to marry you.'

'Straight?'

'Yes.'

She sighed deeply, and heavy tears fell down her cheeks. For a while she remained silent.

'You've saved my life, Basil,' she said at last. 'I made up my mind that if you didn't want to marry me I'd do away with myself.'

'What nonsense you talk!'

'I mean it. I couldn't have faced it. I'd fixed it all up in my

90

head – I should have waited till it was dark, and then I'd have gone over the bridge.'

'I will do my best to be a good husband to you, Jenny,' he said.

But when Jenny left him, Basil, utterly bowed down, surrendered himself to an uncontrollable depression. It came to his mind that Miss Ley had likened existence to a game of chess, and now bitterly he recalled each move that he should have played differently: again and again the result hung as on a balance, so that if he had acted otherwise everything would have gone right; but each time the choice appeared to matter so little one way or the other, and it was not till afterwards that he saw the fateful consequence. Every move was irretrievable, but at the moment seemed strangely unimportant; it was not a fair game, for the issue was hidden constantly by a trivial mask. And then it appeared to him as though, after all, he had never had a choice in the matter; he felt himself powerless in the hand of a greater might, and Fate, for once grown ghastly visible, directed each step as though he were a puppet. Now life before him loomed black and cheerless, and even his child, the thought of which had been his greatest strength, offered no solace.

'Oh, what shall I do?' he moaned – 'what shall I do?' He remembered with a shudder Jenny's threat of suicide, and he knew that she would have carried it out, unhesitating; a sudden impulse seized him in just such a manner to finish with all that doubt and misery. But then, setting his teeth, he sprang up.

'I won't be such a funk,' he cried savagely. 'After all, I've made my bed and I must lie on it.'

9

A FEW days later Basil was married, and Frank, who had assisted him in the rather sordid proceedings of the registry office, going back to his rooms, found Reggie Bassett comfortably lounging in an armchair, with his long legs on another. By his side were Frank's cigarettes and the whisky-and-soda.

'I see you make yourself at home, my friend.'

'I was passing this way and I hadn't got anything particular to do, so I thought I'd look in: my mamma thinks your society good for me. Got your wedding over?'

'What do you know about it?' asked Frank sharply.

'More than you think, my boy,' answered Reggie, with a grin. 'The mater told me as a solemn warning. She says Kent's married a barmaid, and it's the result of keeping bad company and going to pubs. What did he do it for?'

'If I were you I'd mind my own business, Reggie.'

'If it's because she's in the family way, he's a bally ass. If I got in a mess like that, I'd see the lady shot before I married her.'

'I have some work to do, my friend,' said Frank shortly. 'You would show discretion if you took yourself off.'

'All right! I'll just have another drink,' he answered, helping himself to the whisky. 'I'm going out to tea with Mrs Castillyon.'

Frank pricked up his ears, but said nothing. Reggie looked at him, smiled with great self-satisfaction, and winked.

'Smart work, ain't it – considering I've only known her a fortnight. But that's the right way with women – rush 'em. I saw she was smitten the first time we met, so I made a dead-set for her. I knew she was all right, so I just told her what I wanted; by Jove, she is a little baggage! I've come to the conclusion I like ladies, Frank; you don't have to beat about the bush. You just come to the point at once, and there's no blasted morality about them.'

'You're a philosopher, Reggie.'

'You think I'm rotting, but I'm not. I'll read you the letter she wrote me. By the way, I'm going to give her your address – in case the mater stops anything.'

'If letters come for you here, my friend, they shall be promptly returned to the postman.'

'You are a low blackguard; it wouldn't hurt you,' said Reggie crossly. 'But if you think that'll stop her writing, it won't, as I shall just have them sent to my crammer's. I say, I must read you this; it's rather funny.'

Reggie took from his pocket a letter on which Frank recognized Mrs Castillyon's large writing.

'Don't you think it's playing it rather low down to show the private letters which a woman has written you?'

'Rot!' cried Reggie, with a laugh. 'If she didn't want anyone to see them, she oughtn't to have written.'

With manifest pride he read parts of an epistle which would have left the President of the Divorce Court few doubts as to the relations between the happy pair. The wretched woman's love tickled his vanity, and to him the pleasure lay chiefly in boasting of it: he uttered with rolling emphasis certain expressions of endearment.

'"Yours till death,"' he finished. 'Good Lord, what rot women write! and the funny thing is that it's always the same rot. But there's not much doubt about this, is there? She's as far gone as she can be.'

'Amiable youth!' said Frank. 'Does your mother know that you have struck up an acquaintance with Mrs Castillyon?'

'Rather! At first the mater thought her a bit vulgar, but she looked her up in the *Landed Gentry*, and when she found out her grandfather was a lord she thought it must be all right. The mater's a bit of a snob, you know – her governor was in the City, and she's got it into her head that the Castillyons will ask us down to Dorsetshire. By Gad, if they do I'll make things hum.'

Reggie looked at his watch.

'I shall have to be scooting, or I shall be late for tea.'

'Aren't you supposed to be working?'

'Yes, but I can let that wait. You see, I'm not going up for the exam next time. The mater gave me the fees, and I blued them, so I shall just tell her that I've got through. It'll be all right in the end.'

'Isn't that very dishonest?'

'Why?' asked Reggie, with surprise. 'She keeps me so devilish short, and I must have money somehow. It'll all be mine when she pegs out, so it can't matter, you know.'

'And what about the little lady you dined with on Saturday?'

'Oh, I've chucked her. I think Mrs Castillyon will be more economical. She's got lots of tin, and I'm blowed if I see why a man should always be expected to fork out for women.'

'You're trying to reconcile two contradictory things, my boy – love and economy.'

Reggie marched off to Bond Street, and finding that Mrs Castillyon was not yet arrived, began to walk up and down; but having waited half an hour, he grew annoyed, and it was with no smiling countenance that he met the pretty little lady when at length she drove up.

'Have I kept you waiting?' she asked airily.

'Yes, you have,' he answered.

'It's good for you.'

She tripped in, and they ordered tea.

'I can't possibly eat those cakes,' she said. 'Tell them to bring some more.'

The next plateful was as little to her taste, and she called for a third.

'I think I like the first lot best, after all,' she said, when these were produced.

'You might have taken one of them straight away, instead of disturbing the whole place,' exclaimed Reggie, very peevish himself, but peculiarly impatient of that defect in others.

'That woman has nothing else to do: why shouldn't I disturb her? And she was very impudent; I have a good mind to report her.'

'If you do, I shall go and say that she was nothing of the sort.'

94

'This is a disgusting place; I can't think why you suggested it. Anyhow, I'll have some sweets to make up.'

Looking round, she saw a box of chocolates, elaborately decorated with ribands and artificial violets.

'You can get those for me. I love sweets – don't you?'

'Yes, when somebody else pays for them.'

She threw back her head and laughed boisterously, so that people turned round and looked. Reggie grew vexed.

'I wish you wouldn't make such a row. Everyone's staring at you.'

'Well, let them! Give me a cigarette.'

'You can't smoke here.'

'Why not? There's a woman over there smoking.'

'Yes, but she's no better than she should be.'

'Nonsense! It's Lady Vizard. It's only your friends in Piccadilly who are always thinking of propriety; they're so afraid of not behaving like ladies, and you can always tell them because they're so prim.'

Mrs Castillyon, powdered and scented, was dressed in the most outrageous taste, but no one could have been more fashionable; and she displayed uncommon sagacity when she said that her flaunting manners alone distinguished her from persons of easy virtue. She looked across at Lady Vizard, no less strikingly attired, but with a sort of flamboyant discretion which marked the woman of character: she sat with the young Lord de Capit, and Mrs Castillyon told Reggie the latest scandal about the pair.

'You know she's Mr Kent's mother, don't you? By the way, is it true he married a creature off the streets?'

'Yes,' said Reggie. 'Silly ass!'

He gave a vivid account of the affair according to his lights. Unaccountably, for Frank and Miss Ley, both highly discreet, alone knew the circumstances, Basil's adventure in a very elaborate form was current among all his friends.

'I say, Reggie, will you come to the play tomorrow? Lady Paperleigh's got a box for *The Belle of Petersburg*, and she's asked me to bring my man.'

'Am I your man?' asked Reggie.

'Why not?'

'It sounds bally vulgar. I should have thought it meant your valet.'

At this Mrs Castillyon laughed as she spoke at the top of her voice, so that people, to Reggie's confusion, again turned round.

'How prim you are! Is it your mamma's bringing-up, Reggie? She's rather an old frump, you know.'

'Thanks!'

'But I intend to ask her down to Jeyston for Christmas. We're going to have a house-party, and I mean to get Miss Ley and Dr Hurrell. I don't like him much, but Miss Ley won't come without him. Pity she's not younger, isn't it? They could talk philosophy to more purpose then. They say she has a passion for young men; I wonder what she does with them. D'you think she was very gay in her youth?'

'She's a regular ripper, I know that,' answered Reggie, remembering the frequent tips which in his school-days the generous creature had slipped into his hand.

'I'm sure there was something,' expostulated Mrs Castillyon, 'or she wouldn't have lived so long in Italy.'

'My mother thinks her about the straightest woman she's ever known.'

'I wish you wouldn't keep thrusting your mother down my throat, Reggie. It's bad enough having to put up with Paul's, without getting yours as well. I suppose I shall have to ask that old cat for Christmas: she's awful, but as rich as they make 'em, and she'll get on with your mother first-rate. Let's go; I'm sick of this hole.'

When Reggie asked for the bill, he found the box of chocolates cost fifteen shillings, and preferring to spend his money exclusively on himself, was consequently none too pleased. Mrs Castillyon had kept the cab, and offered to drive her cavalier to Grosvenor Gardens, where she was going for a second tea.

'I've had a good time,' she said, when they arrived. 'You'd better give the driver five bob. Good-bye, Reggie. Mind you're not late tomorrow. Where shall we dine?'

'I don't mind as long as it's cheap,' he said, ruefully handing the cabman five shillings.

'Oh, I'll stand you a dinner,' said Mrs Castillyon.

'All right,' he answered, his face brightening. 'Let's go to the *Carlton*, then.'

Mrs Castillyon skipped into the house, and Reggie, who hated walking, to save money trudged sulkily home to Sloane Gardens: Frank showed much wisdom when he asserted that love and economy went seldom hand-in-hand.

'It's cost me over a quid,' he muttered. 'I could have dined Madge three times for that, and I'm blowed if she's so damned vulgar as that little baggage.'

But next day he met her in the *Carlton* vestibule, and they sat down to dinner. The waiter brought him a wine-card.

'What would you like to drink?' he asked.

'Somthing fizzy.'

This entirely agreed with Reggie's ideas, and since he was not to pay the bill, he took care to order the champagne he liked best, which was by no means the least expensive. Flattering himself on his educated palate, he drank the wine with added satisfaction because the price was high. Mrs Castillyon, over-powdered, with somewhat the look of a faded rose arranged under careful lights in a shop window to delude the purchaser that it had still its first freshness, was in high spirits: pleased with her own appearance and with that of the handsome youth in front of her, languid and sensual as the waking Adam of Michelangelo, she talked very quickly in an excessively loud voice. Reggie's spirits rose with the intoxicating liquor, and his doubts whether an amour with a woman of distinction was quite worth while were soon dissipated; looking at the costly splendour of her gown, the boy's flesh tingled, and his eyes rested with approval on the diamonds about her neck and in her yellow hair. It was a new sensation to dine with a well-dressed, rich woman in a crowded restaurant, and he felt himself with pride a very gay Lothario.

Handing something, he touched her fingers.

'Don't,' she said, 'you give me the shivers;' and seeing the effect she created, Mrs Castillyon displayed all her arts and graces.

'Confound this theatre! I wish we weren't bound to go to it.'

'But we are. Lady Paperleigh is going with her man, and we've got to chaperon her.'

It pleased Reggie to sit in a box with a person of title, and he knew it would gratify his mother.

'Why don't they make your hubby a Baronet?' he asked ingenuously.

'My mother-in-law won't fork out. You see, Paul ain't what you might call a genius – he'd love a handle to his name, but the price has gone up lately, and a baronetcy is one of the few things you have to pay for money down.'

Reggie's appetite was large, and he went through the long dinner with huge satisfaction. When they arrived at dessert, he lit a cigarette and gave a sigh of contented repletion.

'Yet people say the pleasures of the intellect are higher than the pleasures of the table,' he sighed.

He looked at Mrs Castillyon with heavy eyes, and since, like most men, love arose in his heart as an accompaniment to the satisfactory process of digestion, he gave her a peculiarly sensual smile.

'I say, Grace, don't you think you could come away for a week-end somewhere?'

'Oh, I couldn't risk it. It would be too dangerous.'

'Not if we go somewhere quiet. It would be a beano!'

Her heart beat quickly, and under those handsome, lazy eyes she felt a curious defaillance; his hand rested on the table, large, soft and smooth, and the sight of it sent through her an odd thrill.

'Paul's going up to the North to speak next month,' she said. 'That's our chance, isn't it?'

The risk fascinated her, and the whim for Reggie grew on a sudden to an ardent passion for which she was willing to venture all things.

'I say, I've got an idea,' she whispered, with sparkling eyes. 'Let's go to Rochester. Don't you remember, Basil Kent spoke of it the other day? I could easily say I was going down to see the view or whatever it is. I believe it's a dull hole, and nobody goes there but Americans.'

'All right,' he said. 'That'll do A1.'

'Now we must be getting off. Call for the bill.'

Mrs Castillyon felt for her pocket; then, throwing back her head, gave a little shriek of laughter.

'What's the matter?'

'I've forgotten my purse. You'll have to pay, after all. D'you mind?'

'Fortunately the mater gave me a fiver this morning,' he answered, without enthusiasm, and when he doled out the shining sovereigns, added to himself: 'By Jove, I'll punish her for this some time.'

Arriving at the theatre, they found Lady Paperleigh was not yet come and since they did not know the number of her box, were obliged to wait in the entrance. They waited for nearly half an hour, during which Mrs Castillyon grew every moment more peevish.

'It's perfectly disgusting and awfully rude of her,' she cried for the tenth time. 'I wish I hadn't come, and I wish to goodness you wouldn't stand there looking bored. Can't you say something to amuse me?'

'I should have thought you could wait for a few minutes without getting into a beastly temper.'

'I shall take care to serve that woman as she has served me. I suppose she's eating somewhere with her wretched man. Why don't you pay for the box so that we can go in?'

'Why should I? They've asked us, and we must hang about till they choose to turn up.'

'If you cared for me the least bit, you wouldn't refuse to do things I asked you.'

'If you'll ask for something reasonable I'll do it.'

Reggie had a very pretty little temper of his own, which his fond mother's upbringing had never taught him to restrain; and seeing that Mrs Castillyon raged with impatience, he assumed an exaggerated calm which was far more irritating than if he had fussed or fumed. The lady busied herself with sharp tongue to pierce his thick hide of indifference, and abused him roundly. In a little while without more ado he answered her in kind.

'If you're not satisfied with me I'll go. D'you think you're

99

the only woman in the world? I'm about sick of your vixenish temper. Good Lord, if this is what a married man has to put up with, God save me from marriage!'

They sat without speaking, and through her powder Mrs Castillyon's cheeks glowed angrily; but when at length Lady Paperleigh appeared, accompanied by a strapping youth with military airs, Mrs Castillyon greeted her with smiles and soft words, vowing that they had only that very moment arrived. Reggie, less accustomed to the ways of polite society, could not conceal his ill-humour, and shook hands in sulky silence.

After the performance Reggie put Mrs Castillyon into a cab, but he would not shake hands, and there was a malevolent scowl on his handsome face which singularly disturbed her; for what at first had seemed but a passing fancy was now unaccountably changed into a desperate passion. She had the soul of a trollop, and for years had flirted more or less seriously with one man after another; but it was chiefly admiration she sought and someone to go about with her and pay for little extravagances; and though several had taken the matter in earnest, she always kept her head, and was careful to drop them when they grew troublesome. But now, driving away alone, there was a dull and hungry pain in her heart; she was tormented by the anger of those handsome eyes, and remembered sorrowfully the hurried kiss he had given her the day before in the cab.

'Supposing he doesn't come back,' she whispered, with a painful sob.

She was a little frightened also, knowing herself in the power of a dissolute, selfish boy who cared nothing for her. Any woman would have served his purpose as well, for she saw with bitter clearness that he was merely dazzled by her wealth and her diamonds. He liked to dine at her house, and it pleased his vanity to embrace a woman in expensive clothes. But she had not the temperament to make a fight for freedom, and gave herself up to this love weakly, careless into what abyss of shame and misery it led. Going to her room, she wrote a pitiful letter to Reggie, and those with whom in time past she had cruelly played, seeing this utter abasement, might have felt abundantly revenged.

Don't be angry with me, darling; I can't bear it. I love you with all my heart and soul. I'm sorry that I was horrid this evening, but I couldn't help it, and I will try to keep my temper. Write and say you forgive me, because my head is throbbing and my heart is aching for you.

I love you – I love you – I love you.

GRACE

She folded the letter, and was about to put it in an envelope, when an idea crossed her mind. For all her flippancy, Mrs Castillyon had a good deal of observation; it had not escaped her notice that Reggie hated to spend money. She went to a drawer and took out a ten-pound note, which with a postscript she enclosed.

I'm sorry I hadn't my purse tonight, and I've only got this note here. Please take what I owe you out of it, and with the change you might buy yourself a tie-pin. I wanted to give you a little present, but I'm afraid of getting something you won't like. Please say you're not cross with me for asking you to see about it yourself.

The youth read the letter with indifference, but when he came to the last lines blushed, for his mother had instilled into him certain rules of honour, and against his will, he could not escape the notion that it was the most discreditable thing possible to accept money from a woman. For a moment he felt sick with shame, but the note was crisp and clean and inviting. His fingers itched.

His first impulse was to send it back, and he sat down at his writing-table. But when he came to put the note in an envelope, he hesitated and looked at it again.

'After all, what with the dinner and tea yesterday, she owes me a good deal of it, and I shall spend it on her if I keep it. She's so rich, it means nothing to her.'

Then he had an inspiration.

'I'll put the balance on a horse, and if it comes in I'll give her the tenner back. If it doesn't – well, it's not my fault.'

He pocketed the note.

10

THE Kents spent their honeymoon in a fisherman's cottage at Carbis Water, the very name of which, romantic and musical, enchanted Basil's ear; and from their window the cliff, grown over with odorous broom, tumbled lazily to the edge of the coloured sea. There was an amiable simplicity about the old man from whom they hired rooms, and Basil delighted to hear his long stories of the pilchard fishery, of storms that had strewn the beach with wreckage, and of fierce battles fought between the fishers of St Ives and the foreigners from Lowestoft. He told of the revivals which burned along the countryside, calling sinners to repentance, and how himself on a memorable occasion had found salvation; now he confessed his late-found faith with savage ardour, but notwithstanding made the most he could out of the strangers in his house! And the tall, gaunt figure of that ancient seaman, with furrowed cheeks and eyes bleared with long scanning of the sea, seemed a real expression of that country – wild with its deserted mines, yet tender; barren yet with the delicate colour of a pastel. To Basil, weary with the conflicting emotions of the last month, it had a restful charm unrivalled by the distincter glories of more southern lands.

One afternoon they walked up a hill to see the local curiosity, a gravestone which crowned its summit, and Basil wandered on while Jenny, indifferent and tired, sat down to rest. He sauntered through the furze, saffron and green, and the heather rich with the subdued and decorous richness of an amethyst: some child had gathered a bunch of this and thrown it aside, so that it lay on the grass dying, faded purple, like a symbol of the decay of an imperial power. For a reason that escaped him, it recalled to Basil's mind that most poetical of prose-writers, the divinely simple weaver of words, Jeremy

Taylor, and he repeated to himself that sad, passionate phrase used in the *Holy Dying*: 'Break the beds, drink your wine, crown your head with roses and besmear your curled locks with nard; for God bids you to remember death.'

Standing on the brink, he overlooked the valley of the sea – Hale in the distance, with its placid river, like some old Italian town coloured and gay even under that sombre heaven. The sky was grey and overcast, and the clouds, pregnant with rain, swept over the hill-top like the gauzy drapery of some dying pagan spirit, lingering solitary among the grotesque shapes of Christian legend. There was a line of dead trees on the crest of the hill, and Basil, visiting this place earlier in the year, had found them then incongruous with the summer, a hideous darkness against the joyous colour of the Cornish June. But now all Nature drew into harmony with them, and they stood, gnarled and leafless, with a placid silence, as though in a sense of the eternity of things they felt a singular content. The green leaves and the flowers were vanity, ephemeral as the butterflies and the light breeze of April, but they were changeless and constant. Dead ferns lay all about, brown as the earth, and they were the first of the summer plants to go, chilled to death by the mild wind of September. The silence was so great that Basil seemed to hear the wings of the rooks as they beat the air, flying overhead from field to field, and in his mind, curiously, he listened to the voice of London calling. Basil peculiarly enjoyed his solitude, for he was used to be much alone, and the constant companionship since his marriage at times proved irksome. He began to plan out his future. There was no reason why Jenny should not be induced to a wider view of things than she then possessed; she was by no means a fool, and little by little, with patience on his side, she might gain interest in the things that interested him: it would be wonderful to disclose a human soul to its own beauty. But his enthusiasm was short-lived, for, walking down the hillside, he found Jenny asleep, her head thrown back and her hat slouched over one eye, her mouth open. His heart sank, for he saw her as he had never seen her before: amid the soft grace of that scene her clothes looked tawdry and crude, and with keen eyes he detected, under her beauty, the commonness of nature for which already he loathed the brother.

But, fearing it would rain, he woke her and proposed that they should go home. She smiled at him lovingly.

'Have you been looking at me asleep? Had I got my mouth open?'

'Yes.'

'I must have looked a sight.'

'Where did you buy your hat?' he asked.

'I made it myself. Don't you like it?'

'I wish it weren't so bright.'

'Colours suit me,' she answered. 'They always did.'

The Cornish drizzle hovered over the earth, all-penetrating like human sorrow, and at length, with the closing day, the rain fell. In the mist and in the night the country sank into darkness. But in Basil's heart was a greater darkness, and already, after one short week, he feared that the task he had confidently undertaken was beyond his strength.

On their return to London Basil moved such furniture as he possessed into the little house he had taken in Barnes. He liked the old-fashioned High Street of that place because it had preserved a certain village simplicity, and the common made up for the dreary look of the long row of villas in which was his own: the builder, careful of his invention, had placed on each side fifty small houses so alike that they were distinguishable only by their numbers and the grandiloquent names on the fanlight. For two or three weeks the young couple were engaged in putting things to rights, and then Basil settled to the monotonous life he liked because it gave most opportunity for work. He went away every morning early to chambers, where he devilled for the 'silk' in whose room he sat, waiting for briefs that came not, and about five took the train back to Barnes; then followed a stroll along the tow-path with Jenny, and after dinner he wrote till bed-time. Basil felt now a certain quiet satisfaction in his marriage; his affairs were settled for good, and he could surrender himself to his literary ambition. Apparently there was a magic in the nuptial tie, since there arose within him by degrees a sober but deep affection for

104

Jenny; he was flattered by her adoration, and touched at the humility wherewith she did his bidding. With all his heart he looked forward to the birth of their child. They talked of him incessantly for both were convinced that it must be a son, and they never tired of discussing what to do with him, how he should wear his hair, when be breeched, and where to go to school. When Basil pictured the beautiful woman nursing her child – and she had never been lovelier than then – his pulse throbbed with thankfulness and pride; and he chid himself because he had ever hesitated to marry her or for a moment during the honeymoon bitterly regretted his rashness.

Jenny was radiantly happy. She was of indolent temper, and it delighted her, after the bondage of the *Golden Crown,* to do nothing from morning till night. It was very amusing to have at her beck and call a servant who called her 'ma'am', and hugely satisfactorily to watch her work while she sat idly. She was proud also of the little house and the furniture, and dusted the pictures with greater complacency because she thought them rather ugly; Basil said they were very beautiful, and she knew they cost a lot of money. In the same way Jenny admired her husband all the more because she neither understood his ideas nor sympathized with his ambitions. She worshipped him like a dog his master. It was a daily torment when he went to town, and invariably she accompanied him to the door to see the last of him; when he was due to return, she listened with held breath for his step on the pavement, and sometimes in her impatience walked to meet him.

Basil had not the amiable gift of taking people as they are, asking no more from them than they can give; but rather sought to mould after his own ideas the persons with whom he came into contact. Jenny's taste was deplorable, and the ignorance which had not been unbecoming to the pretty barmaid in the wife was a little distressing. In accordance with a plan of unconscious education whereby, like powder in jam, Jenny might acquire knowledge without realizing it, Basil gave her books to read; and though she took them obediently, his choice, perhaps, was not altogether happy, for after a diligent quarter of an hour she would mostly drop the volume, and for the rest of the morning chat familiarly with the maid-of-all-work. If, however, at any time she yearned for literary pabulum, she much preferred to buy a novelette at the station bookstall, but took care to hide it when Basil came in; and once when he found by chance a work entitled *Rosamund's Revenge*, explained that it belonged to the servant. For one penny Mrs Kent could get a long and blood-curdling romance, the handsome, aristocratic hero of which bore an unusual similarity to Basil, while the peerless creature for whom doughty deeds were so fearlessly performed was none other than herself; under the mattress in the spare bedroom she kept her favourite story, wherein a maid of high degree nobly sacrificed herself, and Jenny's heart beat fast when she thought how willingly under similar circumstances she would have risked her life for Basil. Ignorant of all this, Kent talked frequently of the books himself had given her, but in his enthusiasm was apt to be so carried away as not to notice how small her knowledge thereof remained.

'I wish you'd read me your book, Basil,' she said one evening. 'You never tell me anything about it.'

'It would only bore you, darling.'

'D'you think I'm not clever enough to understand it?'

'Of course not! If you'd like me to, I shall be only too pleased to read you bits of it.'

'I'm so glad you're a novelist. It's so uncommon, isn't it? And I *shall* be proud when I see your name in the papers. Read me some now, will you?'

No writer, however violent his protests, really dislikes being asked to read an unpublished book; it is the child of his heart, and has still the glamour which, when it is coldly set up in type and bound in cloth, will be utterly destroyed. Basil especially needed sympathy, for he was distrustful of himself, and could work better when someone expressed admiration for his efforts. It had been his ardent hope that Jenny would take interest in his writing, and it was only from diffidence that hitherto he had said little about it.

The idea of his novel, the scene of which was Italy in the early sixteenth century, came to him one day in the National Gallery soon after his return from South Africa, when his mind, fallow after the long rest from artistic things, was peculiarly sensitive to the impression of beauty. He wandered among the pictures, visiting old favourites, and the sober quiet of that place filled his soul with a greater elation than love or wine; he recalled the moment often for its singular happiness, spiritual and calm, yet very fruitful. At last he came to that portrait of an Italian nobleman by Moretto, which to an imaginative mind seems to express the whole spirit of the later Renaissance. It fitted his mood strangely. He thought that to make lovely patterns was the ultimate end of the painter's art, and noticed with keen appreciation the decorative effect of the sombre colouring and of the tall man, leaning, melancholy and languid, in that marble embrasure. Nameless through the ages, he stood in an attitude that was half weariness and half affectation; and his restrained despair was reflected by the tawny landscape of the background, blank like the desert places of the spiritual life; the turquoise sky even was cold and sad. The date was given, 1526, and he wore the slit sleeves and hose of the period (the early passion for the New Birth was passed already; for Michelangelo was dead, and Caesar Borgia rotted in far Navarre); the dark cerise of his parti-coloured dress was no less mournful than the black, but against it gleamed the delicate cambric of his shirt and ruffles. One hand, ungloved, rested idly on the pommel of his long sword, the slender, delicate hand, white and soft, of a gentleman and a student. On his head he wore a strange-shaped hat, part buff, part scarlet, with a medallion on the front of St George and the Dragon.

The face haunted Basil, paler by reason of the dark beard; and out of it looked wistfully the eyes, as though sight were weariness and the world had naught to offer but disillusion. Presently, brooding over the character which seemed there expressed, he invented a story, and to work it out for some months, steeping himself in the poets and historians of the period, spent much time in the British Museum. At last he began actually to write. Basil wished to describe Italian society at that time, its profound disenchantment after the vigorous glow with which it had welcomed the freedom of mind when the fall of Constantinople threw open to the human intellect a new horizon; and devised a man who waged life as though it were a battle, vehemently, seeking to enjoy every moment, and now, finding all things vain, looked back with despair because the world had nothing more to offer. Acquainted with the courts of princes and the tents of condottieri, he had experienced every emotion, fought bloodily, loved and intrigued, written poetry and talked platonism. The incidents of this career were stirring, but Basil referred to them only so much as was necessary to explain the state of mind, for he desired to show his scorn of commonplace by eschewing sensation and giving merely detailed analyses of a spiritual condition.

His theme gave opportunity for the elaborate style Basil affected, and he began to read, emphasizing the rhythm of his sentences and rejoicing in their music. His vocabulary, chosen from the Elizabethans, was rich and sonorous, and the beauty of certain words intoxicated him. But at last he stopped suddenly.

'Jenny?' he said.

No answer came, and he saw that she was fast asleep. Taking care not to disturb her, he put aside the book and rose from his chair. It was not worth while to ask him to read if she could not keep awake, and with some vexation he went to his desk. But his sense of humour came to the rescue.

'What a fool I am!' he cried, with a laugh. 'Why should I think it would interest her?'

Yet Mrs Murray had listened to that same chapter with most flattering attention, and afterwards was loud in its praise. Basil remembered that Molière read comedies to his cook, and if she was not amused rewrote them. By that test he should have destroyed his novel; but then impatiently he told himself that he wrote, not for the many, but for a chosen few.

No longer feeling him near her, Jenny presently awoke.

'Well, I never! I haven't been to sleep, have I?'

'Snoring!'

'I am sorry. Did I disturb you?'

'Not at all.'

'I couldn't help it. I felt so drowsy with you reading. I did enjoy it, Basil.'

'It's something to write a book which is a soporific,' he answered, smiling grimly.

'Do read me some more. I'm wide awake now, and it was beautiful.'

'I think, if you don't mind, I'll do a little work.'

A few days later Jenny's mother, who had seen neither Basil nor the house, paid them a visit. She was a stout woman with a determined manner, and wore a black satin dress so uneasily as to suggest it was her Sunday best; it gave her a queer feeling that the days had got mixed, and a Sabbath come somehow in the middle of the week. Against Basil's will, Jenny insisted on keeping for special occasions their nicest things, and when they were alone made tea in an earthenware pot.

'You don't mind if I don't get out the silver teapot, ma?' she asked, when they sat down. 'We don't use it every day.'

'No more do I come and see you every day, my dear,' answered Mrs Bush, gloomily stroking her black satin. 'But I suppose I'm nobody now you're married. Don't you sit down at table for tea?'

'Basil likes to have it in the drawing-room,' answered Jenny, pouring milk in the bottom of each cup.

'Well, I think it's messy. My tea is my best meal; you know that, Jenny.'

'Yes, ma.'

'I always say it looks mean just to have a few pieces of bread-and-butter put on a plate, with the butter just scraped on so as you can't see it.'

'Basil likes it like that.'

'In my 'ouse I 'ave things my own way. Don't begin to give way to your 'usband in the 'ouse, my dear, or he'll presume on it.'

Basil, coming in at this moment, was introduced to the visitor, and Jenny, rather nervously, watched her to see that she behaved nicely! But Mrs Bush, though somewhat awed by his reserved manner, took care to show that she was a perfect lady, and when she lifted her cup curled her little finger in the most elegant and approved fashion. Basil, after a few polite remarks, lapsed into silence, and the two women for five minutes talked difficultly of trivial subjects. Then a carriage stopped at their door, and in a minute the maid announced – Mrs Murray.

'I thought you would allow me to call on you,' she said, holding out her hand to Jenny. 'I'm an old friend of your husband.'

Jenny blushed, taken aback, but Basil, delighted to see her, shook hands warmly.

'It's awfully good of you. You've just come in time for tea.'

'I'm simply dying for some.'

She sat down, looking very handsome and self-possessed, and Mrs Bush deliberately examined her gown. But Jenny remembered that they had only the common teapot.

'I'll just go and get some fresh tea,' she said.

'Fanny will get it, Jenny.'

'Oh no, I must get it myself, and I keep the tea locked up. You know I have to,' she added to Mrs Murray; 'these girls are so dishonest.'

She went out hurriedly, and while she was gone Basil eagerly asked Mrs Murray how she had found them out.

'It was horrid of you not to write and tell me where you were. Miss Ley gave me your address.'

'Don't you think it's an amusing place? You must go into the High Street. Bits of it are so odd and quaint.'

They chattered gaily, almost turning their backs on Mrs Bush, who watched them with lowering brows. But she often said that she was not a woman to be put upon.

'It's a fine day, isn't it?' she interrupted aggressively.

'Beautiful!' said Mrs Murray, smiling.

And before Mrs Bush could make another observation Basil asked when she was starting for Italy. Fortunately, at that moment Jenny came in, but her mother noticed with indignation that she brought the silver teapot; she drew herself up very straight and sat in mute anger, a bristling figure of outraged susceptibility. Nor did it escape her that Basil, who till Mrs Murray's arrival had scarcely spoken, now talked volubly; he gave a humorous account of their troubles in moving into the house, but though it appeared to amuse Mrs Murray hugely, Mrs Bush could see nothing at all funny in it.

At last the visitor rose.

'I really must fly. Good-bye, Mrs Kent. You must get your husband to bring you to see me.'

She sailed out, with a rustle of silk, and Basil accompanied her downstairs.

'She's come in a carriage, ma,' said Jenny, looking from the window.

'I 'ave eyes in my 'ead, my dear,' answered Mrs Bush.

'Isn't he aristocratic-looking?' exclaimed the admiring wife.

'Aristocratic is as aristocratic does,' returned her mother severely.

They saw Basil at the door talk with Mrs Murray and laugh. Then she gave an order to the coachman, who followed them while they walked slowly down the street.

'Well, Jenny!' cried Mrs Bush, in tones of surprise, horror, and indignation.

'I wonder where they're going,' said Jenny, looking away.

'You take my advice, my dear, and keep your eyes on that young man. I wouldn't trust 'im too far if I was you. And you tell him that your ma can see through a brick wall as well as anyone.... 'Ad he ever said anything about his lady friend?'

'Oh yes, ma, he's spoken of her often,' said Jenny uneasily, for as a matter of fact till that day she had never even heard Mrs Murray's name.

'Well, you tell 'im you want to hear nothing about her. You must be careful, my dear. I 'ad a rare lot of trouble with your pa when I was first married. But I put my foot down, and let 'im see I wouldn't stand his nonsense.'

'I wonder why Basil doesn't come back?'

'And, if you please, he never introduced me to his lady friend. I suppose I'm not good enough.'

111

'Ma!'

'Oh, don't talk to me, my dear. I think you've treated me very bad, both of you, and it'll be a long day before I leave my pleasant home in Crouch End to cross this threshold.'

At this Basil returned, and saw at once that Mrs Bush was much disturbed.

'Hulloa, what's up?' he asked, smiling.

'It's no laughing matter, Mr Kent,' answered the ruffled matron, with dignity. 'I'm put out, and I won't deny it. I do expect to be treated like a lady, and I don't think Jenny ought to 'ave given me my tea out of a sixpenny 'alfpenny teapot – and you can't deny that's what they cost, my dear, because I know as well you do.'

'We'll behave ourselves better next time,' said Basil good-humouredly.

'It didn't take Jenny long to get the silver teapot as soon as your lady friend come in. But I suppose I'm not worth troubling about.'

'I believe tea always tastes much better in earthenware,' remarked Basil mildly.

'Oh yes, I dare say it does,' returned Mrs Bush ironically. 'And to catch sparrows you've only got to put a little salt on their tails. Good afternoon to you.'

'You're not going yet, ma?'

'I know when I'm not wanted, and you needn't trouble to show me out, because I know my way and I shan't steal the umbrellas.'

Basil was in high spirits, and this display of temper vastly amused him.

'Where did you go just now, Basil?' asked Jenny, when her mother had stalked defiantly out of the house.

'I just showed Mrs Murray the High Street. I thought it would amuse her.'

Jenny did not answer. Basil had discussed with the unexpected visitor the progress of his book, and thinking still of the pleasant things she said to him, paid no attention to his wife's silence. All the evening she scarcely spoke, but it struck

112

her that Basil had never been more cheerful; during dinner
he laughed and joked, without caring that she was irrespon-
sive; and afterwards sat down to work. Inspiration flowed in
upon him, and he wrote easily and quickly. Jenny, pretending to
read, watched him through her eyelashes.

11

ABOUT a week after Basil's marriage, Miss Ley found on her breakfast-table the following letter from Bella:

MY DEAREST MARY,

I have been very anxious lately about my friend Herbert Field, and I want you to do me a great favour. You know that he is not very strong, and some time ago he caught a horrid cold which he seems quite unable to shake off. He refuses to take proper care of himself, and he looks very ill and thin. Our doctor has been attending him, but he grows no better, and I am dreadfully alarmed. I don't know what I should do if anything happened to him. At last I have been able to persuade him to come to London to see a specialist. Do you think Dr Hurrell would look at him if I brought Mr Field up next Saturday? Of course I would pay the ordinary fees, but there is no need that Herbert should know this. He can manage to get away early on Saturday morning, and if you will get me an appointment we would drive straight to Dr Hurrell. May we come to luncheon with you afterwards?

Yours affectionately,

BELLA LANGTON

When Frank came in to tea, as was his habit whenever he had time, Miss Ley showed him the letter, and afterwards wrote back to say that Dr Hurrell would be pleased to see the invalid at twelve on the following Saturday.

'I don't suppose he has anything the matter with him,' said Frank, 'but I don't mind having a look. And tell her she can keep her confounded fees.'

'Don't be an idiot, Frank,' replied Miss Ley.

At the appointed hour Bella and Herbert were shown into his consulting-room. The youth was shy and ill at ease.

'Now, will you go into the waiting-room, Miss Langton?' said Frank. 'I'll send for you later.'

Bella, somewhat impressed by his professional manner, retired, and Frank examined his patient's face slowly, as though he sought the hidden springs of character. Herbert watched with apprehension the grave man in front of him.

'I don't think I've really got anything much the matter with me; only Miss Langton was anxious.'

'Medical men would starve if they depended only on the diseased,' answered Frank. 'You'd better take off your things.'

Herbert reddened at the discomfort of undressing himself before a stranger. The doctor noted the milky whiteness of his skin, and the emaciation of his body, which revealed the entire form of the skeleton; he took the boy's hand and looked at the long fingers with nails slightly bent over.

'Have you ever spat any blood?'

'No.'

'D'you sweat at night at all?'

'I never used to, but this last week I have a bit.'

'I believe most of your relations are dead, aren't they?'

'All of them.'

'What did they die of?'

'My father died of consumption, and my sister also.'

Frank said nothing, but his face grew somewhat graver as he heard the bad history. He began to percuss the boy's chest.

'I can find nothing abnormal there,' he said.

Then he took his stethoscope and listened.

'Say ninety-nine. Now cough. Breathe deeply.'

He went over every inch carefully, but found nothing more than might be due to an attack of bronchitis. But before putting down the stethoscope he applied it again to the apex of the lung, just above the collar-bone.

'Breathe deeply.'

Then very distinctly he heard a slight crackling sound, which the hectic flush on Herbert's cheeks, the symptoms and the history, had led him to expect. Once more he percussed, more carefully still, and the note was dull. There could be little doubt about the diagnosis.

'You can put on your clothes,' he said, sitting down at his desk to write notes of the case.

Without a word Herbert dressed himself. He waited till the doctor finished.

'Is there anything the matter with me?' he asked.

Frank looked at him gravely.

'Nothing very serious. I'll talk to Miss Langton if you'll get her to come here.'

'I'd sooner hear myself, if you don't mind,' said Herbert, flushing. 'I'm not afraid to be told anything.'

'You need not be very much alarmed, you know,' answered Frank in a moment, with a brief hesitation which did not escape Herbert. 'You have râles at the right apex. At first I didn't hear them.'

'What does that mean?' A cold shiver of dread ran through him so that his hands and feet felt horribly cold; there was a slight tremor in his voice when he asked a further question. 'Is it the same as my father and my sister?'

'I'm afraid it is,' said Frank.

And the shadow of Death stood suddenly in the room, patient and sinister; and each knew that henceforward it would never leave the young man's side; it would sit by him at table silently, and lie in his bed at night; and when he read, a long finger would underline the words to remind him that he was a prisoner condemned. When the wind, marching through the country, sang to himself like a strong-limbed ploughboy, Death, whistling in his ears, would mock the tune softly; when he looked at the rising sun which coloured the mist like a chalcedony, purple and rosy and green, Death would snigger at his delight in the sad world's beauty. An icy hand gripped his heart so that he felt sick with dread and anguish; he could not repress the sob torn from him by bitter agony. Frank was ashamed to look at that boyish face, so frank and fair, distraught with terror, and he cast down his eyes. Then, to hide himself, Herbert went to the window and looked out: opposite, the houses were grey, ugly, and monotonous, and the heavy sky lowered as though verily it would crush the earth; but he saw life like a pageant processioning before him, and the azure heaven more profound than the rich enamel of an old French jewel, the ploughed fields gaining in the sunshine the various colours of the jasper, and the elm-trees more sombre than jade. He was like a man in a deep chasm who scans at noon the stars which those who live in daylight cannot see.

Frank's voice came to him like a sound from another world.

'I wouldn't take it too much to heart if I were you. With care you may easily recover, and after all, plenty of people lived to a ripe old age with tuberculous lungs.'

'My sister was only ill for four months, and my father less than a year.'

His pale face expressed no emotion, so that Frank could only divine the fear that made his heart sink; he had seen many take the sentence of death, and knew that in comparison the final agony itself was small indeed. It was the most awful moment in life, and it must have been a cruel god who was not satisfied with that instant of hopeless misery to punish all the sins and follies of mankind: beside it all human suffering, the death of children or the ingratitude of friends, loss of honour or of wealth, sank into insignificance. It was the bitter, bitter cup that each must drink because man had raised himself above the beasts.

Frank rang the bell.

'Ask Miss Langton to be so good as to come here,' he told the servant who answered.

She looked anxiously from Frank to Herbert standing at the window, his back turned; and the two men's silence, the doctor's grave constraint, filled her with terrified foreboding.

'Herbert, what's the matter?' she cried. 'What has he told you?'

The boy turned round.

'Only that I shall never do anything in the world now. And I shall die like a dog and leave behind me the sunshine and the blue sky and the trees.'

Bella cried out, and then despair settled in her eyes, and helplessly the tears ran down her cheeks.

'How could you be so cruel?' she said to Frank. 'Oh, Herbert, perhaps it's not true. .... What's to be done, Dr Hurrell? Can't you save him somehow?'

117

She sank into a chair and sobbed. The boy placed his hand on her shoulder gently.

'Don't cry, dear. In my heart of hearts I knew, but I tried not to believe it. After all, it can't be helped. I shall just have to go through with it like everyone else.'

'It seems so hard and meaningless,' she groaned. 'It can't be true.'

Herbert looked at her without answering, as though her anguish were a curious thing which excited in him no emotion. In a little while, with a sigh, Bella rose to her feet and dried her eyes.

'Come away, Herbert,' she said. 'Let us go back to Mary.'

'D'you mind if I go by myself? I feel I can't talk to anyone just now. I should like to be alone for a bit to think it out.'

'You must do as you choose, Herbert.'

'Good-bye, Dr Hurrell, and thanks.'

With eager, pain-filled eyes Bella watched him go, and she, too, felt that something strange was in him, so that she dared not thwart his wish; when he spoke there was an inflexion in his voice which she had never heard before. But presently, with a great effort gathering herself together, she turned to Frank.

'Now, will you tell me exactly what should be done?' she said, with an attempt at the decisive manner she used in the conduct of charitable enterprises at Tercanbury.

'First of all get the fact into your head that there is no immediate cause for alarm. I'm afraid there's no doubt that tubercle is there, but the damage at present is very small. He wants care and proper treatment. ... Is he entirely dependent for means upon his occupation?'

'I'm afraid so.'

'Is it possible for him to go away? He ought to winter abroad – not only for the climate, but also because new scenes will distract his mind.'

'Oh, I would so gladly pay for him, but he'd never accept a penny from me. Is it his only chance of life?'

'I can't say that. The human body is a machine which constantly acts counter to expectation; sometimes with every organ diseased it still manages to dodder along.'

Bella did not listen, for suddenly an idea had flashed across her mind. She blushed furiously, but all the same it seemed excellent; her heart beat madly, and an ecstatic happiness lifted her up. She rose from the chair.

'I dare say I can manage something, after all. I must go and talk to Miss Ley. Good-bye.'

She gave him her hand and left him wondering what had caused in her this sudden change, for the depression had vanished before something which quickened her gait and rendered her step elastic.

'Well, what did Frank tell you?' asked Miss Ley, when she had kissed Bella.

'He says that Herbert has consumption and must spend the winter abroad.'

'I'm very sorry; but is that possible?'

'Only if I take him.'

'My dear, how can you?' cried Miss Ley, astonished.

Bella hesitated and blushed.

'I'm going to ask him to marry me. It's no good now to counterfeit modesty and all the rest of it. It's the only way I can save his life, and after all, I love him better than anyone else in the world. When I told you a month ago that it was impossible I should care for a boy almost young enough to be my son, I lied. I fought against it then as something shameful and ridiculous, but I've loved him from the very first day I saw him.'

Bella's vehement seriousness alone prevented Miss Ley from indulging in her usual irony. She carefully repressed the smile which struggled to gain possession of her lips.

'Your father will never consent, my dear,' she said gravely.

'I hope he will when I explain the circumstances. I'm afraid he'll be dreadfully distressed, but if he refuses I shall remember that I'm a grown woman, capable of judging for myself.'

'I don't know what he'll do with you. He's entirely dependent on you for all his comfort and all his happiness.'

'I've served him for forty years. I gave him all my youth, not because it was my duty, but because I loved him. Now

119

someone needs me more than he does. My father is rich; he has a comfortable home, books and friends, and health. Herbert has nothing but me. If I take care of him, I may give him a few more years of life, and if he dies I can soothe his last days.'

Miss Langton spoke rapidly, with such determination that the elder woman saw it was useless to argue; her whole mind was set on this idea, and neither the persuasion of friends nor the entreaties of a father would hinder her.

'And what does the young man say to it?' asked Miss Ley.

'The thought has never entered his head. He looks upon me as a middle-aged woman to whom all things of love are absurd. Sometimes he's laughed at me because I'm so practical and matter-of-fact.'

'Where is he?'

Before Bella could answer there was a ring at the door, and they heard Herbert ask the butler if Miss Langton had come in.

'There he is!' cried Bella. 'Let me go to him now, Mary. He's going up to the drawing-room. Oh, I feel so dreadfully nervous.'

'Don't be ridiculous, Bella,' answered Miss Ley, smiling. 'I've never seen a woman about to propose marriage to the object of her affections who was quite so self-possessed as you.'

But at the door Miss Langton stopped, and with a very piteous expression looked at her friend.

'Oh, I wish I weren't so old, Mary. Tell me honestly, am I awfully plain?'

'You're a great deal too good for a silly young hobbledehoy, my dear,' said Miss Ley, hiding by roughness of manner something very like a sob. 'If he had any sense, he'd have insisted on marrying you three months ago.'

When Bella closed the door, Miss Ley's eye caught the bronze statue of Narcissus, standing on a pedestal in that eternal attitude of adorable affectation, one long forefinger outstretched, and his listening head bent slightly to one side. She addressed him irritably.

120

'I wish you wouldn't look so shocked and puzzled and self-conscious of your beauty. You ought to know that when love and self-sacrifice are combined in the heart of a middle-aged woman, nothing on earth will prevent her from acting like a perfect lunatic. In your day the old maid was unknown, and you can't possibly understand her emotions, for, extraordinary as it may appear, even old maids are human. And if you are scandalized at this disproportion of ages, know that you are an idiot, ignorant of the elements both of psychology and of physiology. And I myself have adored generations of young men, though the relations between us have invariably remained strictly platonic.'

Narcissus, listening intently to the dying cries of Echo, remained indifferent to Miss Ley's harangue, and she turned away impatiently.

Entering the drawing-room, Bella found Herbert standing at the window, and he came towards her with a smile. She saw that already he was more collected, and though his face was pale and grave, it bore no longer that disfigurement of fear.

'You didn't think it unkind of me to leave you to come home by yourself, did you?' he asked gently. 'I was a little bothered just then, and I felt if I weren't alone I should make a fool of myself.'

She took his hand and held it.

'You know that I can never think anything you do unkind. But tell me now if you have decided anything.' She hesitated, but it seemed futile to utter expressions of regret; for at that moment how could they comfort him? 'I should like you to know that you can depend on me always.'

'It's very good of you. I don't know that there's anything much to decide. I dare say I shall soon get used to the idea of not looking into the future, but it'll be rather hard at first, because it was all I had at that dreary bank. I shall stay there as long as I can, and when I grow too ill I must try and get into the hospital. I dare say the Dean will help me to be admitted.'

'Oh, don't talk like that! It's too horrible,' cried Bella wretchedly. 'Isn't there anything I can do? I feel so utterly helpless.'

He looked at her for a while.

'Well, yes, there is,' he answered presently. 'There's one thing I wished to ask you, Bella. You've been an awfully good friend to me, and now I want you more than ever.'

'I'll do anything you wish,' she said, with a beating heart.

'I'm afraid it's very selfish. But I don't want you to go away this winter – in case anything happened. You know my sister died three months after the first symptoms were noticed.'

'I'd do so much more for you than that.'

She placed her hands on his shoulders, and gazed into his blue, sad eyes; searchingly she scrutinized his face, paler than ever and more exquisitely transparent, and his soft mouth, tremulous still with the horror of death. She remembered his mouth and his eyes when they were merry with boyish laughter and his cheeks flushed with excitement at his own gay rhetoric. Then she looked down.

'I wonder if you could bring yourself to marry me.'

Although her eyes were turned away, she knew that he blushed deeply, and hopelessly, full of shame, she dropped her hands. It seemed an intolerable time before he answered.

'I'm not so selfish as all that,' he whispered, his voice trembling.

'Yes, I was afraid the thought would disgust you,' she said, with a sob.

'Bella, how can you say that! Don't you know that I should have been proud? Don't you know that you're the only woman I've ever liked? But I won't let you sacrifice yourself for me. I've seen people die of consumption, and I know the ghastliness of it. D'you think I would let you nurse me and do all the odious things that are needful? And you might get ill, too. Oh no, Bella, don't think me ungrateful, but I couldn't marry you.'

'D'you think it would be a sacrifice to me?' she asked in tragic tones. 'My poor boy, you never saw that I loved you with all my soul, and when you were so happy and careless my heart felt as though it would break because I was old and plain. You've forgotten that one day you kissed my hands: it was only a joke to you, but when you'd gone I cried bitterly. You'd never have done it except that you thought I was forty and it couldn't matter. And when you took my arm sometimes I felt sick with love. And now, I suppose, you utterly despise me.'

She broke down, sobbing; but in a little while impatiently she brushed away her tears and faced him with a sort of despairing pride.

'After all, what am I but a middle-aged woman? I've never been even pretty, and my mind is narrow because I've lived all my life among paltry things, and I'm stupid and dull. Why should I think you would care to marry me because I love you like a fool?'

'Oh, Bella, Bella, don't say that. You break my heart.'

'And you thought it was self-sacrifice on my part! I was only asking you because I wanted to be with you every moment – if you fell ill, I couldn't bear that anyone else should touch you. I've been lonely in my life, so dreadfully lonely, and I was making one last bid for happiness.'

She sank into a chair and hid her face, but Herbert, kneeling beside her, took her hands.

'Look at me, Bella. ... I thought you only suggested it because you know I ought to leave the bank, and have someone to look after me. I never suspected that you really cared for me. And I'm ashamed because I was blind. But don't you know that there's nothing I should like better than to be with you always? Then I should care nothing for my illness, because it would have brought me a greater happiness than I ever dared to hope for. Bella, if you don't mind that I'm poor and ill and unworthy of you, will you marry me?'

On a sudden she stopped in the middle of her silent crying and a radiant smile chased away the sorrow. For one moment, while she realized the meaning of his words, she looked at him half in doubt; then, bending down, she kissed his hands.

'Oh, my dearest, you've made me so happy.'

When at last they went to Miss Ley, Bella's tear-filled eyes shone with unspeakable bliss; and the elder woman, looking at Herbert, no longer wondered at her cousin's infatuation for him, for his face, so candid and sweet, was like the face of a young beautiful saint in an old picture.

12

It was Frank's habit after his work at the hospital to have tea with Miss Ley, but when, that afternoon, he arrived at Old Queen Street she was surprised at the pallor of his face, from which shone with unnatural brilliancy the dark eyes. They seemed larger than ever she had seen them, and his harassed look told her that he was suffering: the square jaw was set firmly, as though with strong deliberation he held himself in hand.

'You're so late,' she said. 'I thought you wouldn't come.'

'I'm very tired,' he answered, in a strained voice.

She poured out tea, and while he ate and drank, to give him opportunity to collect himself, read the evening paper. With admirable insight, she alone, of his friends, had divined Frank's emotional temper; and though never hinting at the knowledge, for she was aware it humiliated him to have so little self-control, could in consequence handle him with very subtle skill. Presently fetching his tobacco, for they sat in the library, he lit his pipe; he blew the smoke from his mouth in heavy clouds.

'Is it very comforting?' asked Miss Ley, smiling.

'Very!'

Waiting till he was ready to speak, she returned to her news-sheet, and though she felt his eyes rest curiously upon her, took no notice.

'I wish to goodness you'd put that paper down,' he cried at last irritably.

With a faint smile she did as he suggested.

'Have you had a very hard day, Frank?'

'Oh, it was awful!' he answered. 'I don't know why, but it all seemed to have a greater meaning for me than ever before. I couldn't get out of my head the utter misery of that poor boy when I told him his chest was affected.'

125

'I wish the whole thing weren't so ordinary,' murmured Miss Ley. 'The consumptive poet and the devoted old maid! It's so fearfully hackneyed. But the gods have no originality; they always make their aesthetic effects by confounding the tragic and the commonplace. ... I suppose you're quite certain he has phthisis?'

'I found bacilli in the sputum. Where are they both now?'

'Bella took him back to Tercanbury, and I've promised to follow on Monday. She's going to marry the boy!'

'What!' cried Frank.

'She wants to take him abroad. Don't you think if he winters in the South Nature will have some chance with him?'

'In nine cases out of ten Nature doesn't want to cure a man; she wants to put him in his coffin.'

Rising from his chair, Frank walked restlessly up and down the room. On a sudden he stopped short in front of Miss Ley.

'D'you remember your friend Mr Farley telling us the other day that pain ennobles a man? I should like to conduct him through the wards of a hospital.'

'I have no doubt that when he has a tooth drawn Mr Farley takes care that gas should be properly administered.'

'I suppose divines can only justify pain by ascribing to it elevation of character,' cried Frank savagely. 'If they weren't so ignorant they'd know it requires no justification. You might as well assert that a danger-signal elevates a train; for, after all, pain is nothing more than an indication by the nerves that the organism is in circumstances hurtful to it.'

'Don't lecture me, Frank, there's a dear!' murmured Miss Ley mildly.

'But if that man had seen as much pain as I have he'd know that it doesn't refine; it brutalizes. It makes people self-absorbed and selfish – you can't imagine the frightful egoism of physical suffering – querulous, impatient, unjust, greedy. I could name a score of petty vices that it engenders, but not a single virtue. ... Oh, Miss Ley, when I look at all the misery of the world I am so thankful I don't believe in God.'

As though seeking to break through the iron bars of the flesh, like a wild beast unquietly he paced the room.

'For years I've toiled night and day to distinguish truth from falsehood; I want to be clear about my actions, I want to walk with sure feet; but I find myself in a labyrinth of quicksands. I can see no meaning in the world, and sometimes I despair; it seems as senseless as a madman's dream. After all, what does it tend to, the effort and the struggle, hope, love, success, failure, birth, death? Man emerged from savagery merely because he was fiercer than the tiger and more cunning than the ape; and nothing seems to me less probable than that humanity advances to any ideal condition. We believe in progress, but progress is nothing but change!'

'I confess,' interrupted Miss Ley, 'that I sometimes ask myself how it benefits the Japanese that they have assumed the tall-hat and the trousers of Western civilization. I wonder if the Malays in their forests or the Kanakas on their islands have cause vastly to envy the London slummer.'

'What does it all end in?' pursued Frank, too much absorbed in his own thoughts to listen. 'Where is the use of it? For all my labour I haven't the shadow of an answer. And even yet I don't know what is good and what is evil, what is high and what is low; I don't even know if the words have any sense in them. Sometimes men seem to me cripples ever seeking to hide their deformity, huddled in a stuffy room, lit by one smoky taper; and they crowd together to keep warm, and they tremble at every unexpected sound. And d'you think in the course of evolution it was the best and noblest who survived to propagate their species? It was merely the shrewd, the hard, and the strong.'

'It would bore me dreadfully to be so strenuous, dear Frank,' answered Miss Ley, with a slight shrug of the shoulders. 'It was a wise man who said that, with regard to the universe, few questions could be asked and none could be answered. In the end we all resign ourselves to the fact, and we find it possible to eat our dinner with no less satisfaction because at the back of our minds stands continually a discreet mark of interrogation. For my part, I think there is as little justification for

127

ascribing an end to the existence of man as there was for the supposition of the Middle Ages (pardon me if I seem erudite), that the heavenly bodies moved in circles because that was the most perfect figure; but I assure you that my night's rest is not in the least impaired. I, too, went through a stormy period in my youth, and if you'll promise not to think me tedious I'll tell you about it.'

'Please do,' said Frank.

He sat down, fixing upon her his piercing eyes, and Miss Ley, as though she had given the matter frequent thought, spoke fluently, with ordered ideas and balanced phrase.

'You know, I was reared on the strictest Evangelical principles to believe certain dogmas on pain of eternal damnation, but at twenty, why I scarcely can tell, all I had learnt fell away from me. Faith presumably is a matter of temperament; good-will has nothing to do with it, and when I look back on my ignorance I am astounded that such ill-considered reasons sufficed to destroy the prejudices of so many years. I was certain then that no God existed; but now I make a point of being certain of nothing: it saves trouble. Besides, each time you make up your mind you rob yourself of a subject for cogitation. But theoretically I cannot help thinking that for a quite reasonable view of life it is necessary to be convinced that no immortality of the soul exists.'

'How can a man lead his life uniformly on the earth if he is disturbed by the thought of another life to come?' broke in Frank eagerly. 'God is a force throwing man's centre of gravity out of his own body.'

'We agreed, Frank, that I was to expound *my* views,' answered Miss Ley, with some asperity, for interruption she never suffered easily.

'Forgive me,' said Frank, smiling.

'But I agree that your remark, though ill-timed, was not without point,' she proceeded deliberately. 'When man is assured that the insignificant planet on which he lives, and the time, are everything so far as he is individually concerned, he can look about him and order himself according to the surroundings. He is a chess-player with his definite number of

128

pieces, capable of definite moves; and none asks why the castle must run straight, but the bishop obliquely. These things are to be accepted, and with these rules, careless of what may befall when the game is finished, the wise man plays – not to win, for that is impossible, but to make a good fight of it. And if he is wise indeed he will never forget that, after all, it is but a game, and therefore not to be taken too seriously.'

Miss Ley paused, thinking it high time to give Frank opportunity for some remark, but since he remained silent she went on slowly.

'I think the most valuable thing I have learnt in my life is that there is so much to say on both sides of every question that there is little to choose between them. It has made me tolerant, so that I can listen with equal interest to you and to my cousin Algernon. After all, how can I tell whether Truth has one shape only, or many? In how many errors does she linger with a smiling face and insufficient raiment; in what contrary and irreconcilable places does she dwell, more wilful than April winds, more whimsical than the Will-o-the-wisp! My art and science is to live. It is an argument of weak men to say that all things are vanity because the pleasure of them is ephemeral: it may console the beggar to look upon the tomb of kings, but then he must be a fool as well. The pleasures of life are illusion, but when pessimists complain that human delights are negligible because they are unreal, they talk absurdly; for reality none knows, and few care about: our only interest is with illusion. How foolish is it to say that the mirage in the desert is not beautiful merely because it is an atmospheric effect!'

'Is life, then, nothing but a voyage which a man takes, bound nowhither and tossed perpetually upon a treacherous sea?'

'Not quite. Storms don't rage continually, nor is the wind for ever boisterous: sometimes it blows fair and strong, so that the ship leaps forward with animal delight; the mariner exults in his skilful power and in the joy of the limitless horizon. Sometimes the sea is placid like a sleeping youth, and the scented air, balmy and fresh, fills the heart with lazy pleasure. The ocean has its countless mysteries, its thoughts and manifold emotions. Why on earth should you not look upon the passage as a pleasure-trip, whereon the rough weather must necessarily be taken with the smooth – looking regretlessly towards the end, but joyful even amid hurricane or gale in the recollection of happy, easy days? Why not abandon life, saying: I have had evil fortune and good, and the pains were compensated by the pleasures; and though my journey, with all its perils, has led me nowhither, though I return tired and old to the port whence with my many hopes I started, I am content to have lived.'

'And so, for all your experience, your study, and your thought, you've found absolutely no meaning,' cried Frank, profoundly discouraged.

'I invented a meaning of sorts; like a critic explaining a symbolical picture, or a school-boy construing a passage he doesn't at all understand, I at least made the words hang sensibly together. I aimed at happiness, and I think, on the whole, I've found it. I lived according to my instincts, and sought every emotion that my senses offered; I turned away deliberately from what was ugly and tedious, fixing my eyes with all my soul on Beauty – seen, I hope, with a discreet appreciation of the Ridiculous. I never troubled myself much with current notions of good and evil, for I knew they were merely relative, but strove always to order my life so that to my eyes at least it should form a graceful pattern on the dark inane.'

Miss Ley stopped, and a whimsical smile flickered across her face.

'But I should tell you that, like Mr Shandy, who was so long about his treatise on the education of his son that by the time it was finished Tristram's growth made it useless, I did not formulate my philosophy till it was too late to set much of it in practice.'

'Dinner is served, madam,' said the butler, coming into the room.

'By Jove!' cried Frank, springing up, 'I had no idea it was so late.'

'But you're going to stay? I think you'll find a place laid for you.'

'I've ordered my dinner at home.'

'I'm sure it won't be so good as mine.'

'I never saw anyone quite so conceited as you about the excellence of your cook, Miss Ley.'

'Just as it is far easier for a man to be a philosopher than a gentleman, my dear, it is less difficult to cultivate a Christian disposition than good cooking.'

They went downstairs, and Miss Ley ordered a bottle of Miss Dwarris' champagne to be opened. She had a cynical belief in the efficacy of a square meal to relieve most spiritual torments; but besides, heroically – for she was an indolent woman – took pains to amuse her guest. She talked of many things, gaily and tenderly, while Frank, the dinner finished, smoked innumerable pipes. At last Big Ben struck twelve, and cheerful now, resigned to philosophic doubt, he rose to his feet. Frank took both Miss Ley's hands.

'You're a jewel of a woman. I was quite wretched when I came, and you've put new life into me.'

'Not I!' she cried. 'The chocolate soufflé and the champagne. I have always observed that the human soul is peculiarly susceptible to the culinary art. Personally, I never feel so spiritual as when I've slightly overeaten myself. I wish you wouldn't squeeze my hands.'

'You're the only woman I know who's as interesting to talk to as a man.'

'Faith, and I believe if I were twenty years younger the child would propose to me!'

'You have only to say the word, and I'll lead you to the altar.'

'I'm a proud woman this day to get an offer of marriage in my fifty-seventh year. But where, my dear, if I married you, would you go to have tea in the afternoon?'

Frank laughed, but in his voice when he answered there was something very like a sob.

'You're a dear, kind thing. And I'm sure I shall never be half so devoted to any other woman as I am to you.'

The emotion must have been catching, for Miss Ley's tones had not their usual cold steadiness.

'Don't be a drivelling idiot, my dear!' she answered, and when the door was closed behind him added to herself, half in irritation: 'Bless the boy, I wish I were his mother.'

13

Two days later Miss Ley duly travelled down to Tercanbury, and was met at the station by Bella, who told her that, according to their arrangement, no mention had yet been made of the proposed marriage. She had announced merely that Herbert Field, whom she desired to make acquainted with her father, would come to tea that day. The Dean welcomed Miss Ley with joy.

'It's very gracious and charming of you to shed your light on our provincial darkness, my dear,' he exclaimed, taking her hand.

'Don't hold my hand, Algernon. I had a proposal of marriage on Saturday night, and I'm palpitating still.'

'Oh, Mary, do tell us all about it,' cried Miss Langton, with delight.

'I shan't! I told Algernon simply because I notice the average man has no consideration at all for a single woman unless she's marriageable.'

'But why didn't you bring your friend, Dr Hurrell?' asked the Dean. 'Only today I bought a Latin herbary, written in the seventeenth century, which I'm sure would interest him.'

'As if he'd understand a word of it, my dear Algernon! Besides, I thought it quite enough for you to snatch one brand at a time from the burning.'

'Ah, Polly, I shouldn't like to stand in your shoes on the Last Day,' he answered, with twinkling eyes.

'I very much doubt if you could get into them,' replied Miss Ley quickly, protruding a small and elegant foot.

'The sin of pride, my dear!' said the Dean, shaking his finger at her. 'Pride of all sorts, for not Lucifer himself was more satisfied with the excellence of his understanding.'

'I don't care, Algernon – if I frizzle, I frizzle,' laughed Miss Ley. 'I know I'm no fool, and after all, my gloves *are* sixes.'

Tea was brought in, and presently Herbert Field made his appearance. The Dean, who liked all young things, shook hands with him warmly.

'I've heard about you from Bella. I don't know why she has never before allowed me to set eyes on you.'

He talked to the boy about his old school, and finding him interested in the antiquities of Tercanbury, gave way to his own enthusiasm. He fetched from his study certain lately-acquired plates of old churches in that city, and Bella watched the pair, the youth's fair head contrasting with her father's white hair and benign face, bending over them under the lamp. She was delighted with the friendship that seemed about to spring up between them, and wished with all her heart that they might thus spend many charming evenings interchanging views on books and pictures; while she sat by tending them as though both were her children.

'Now that you've broken the ice, you must come again often,' said the Dean, holding the boy's hand, when Herbert bade him good-bye. 'I must show you my library, and, if you're fond of old books, I dare say there are some I have in duplicate which you might care to have.'

'It's very kind of you,' answered Herbert, flushing, for the Dean's old-fashioned courtesy was a little overwhelming, and the stately kindness hard to bear when soon he must distress him so enormously by taking away his daughter.

When Herbert was gone, the Dean said he would return to his study to finish an article he was preparing for a learned magazine on one of the later Roman orators.

'Would you stay a few minutes longer, father?' said Bella; 'I have something I wish to talk to you about.'

'Certainly, my dear,' he replied, sitting down. He turned with a quiet smile to Miss Ley. 'When Bella used to announce an important communication, my heart sank to my boots, for I always expected she would inform me of her approaching marriage; but I bear it now with equanimity, because it is invariably only to wheedle me into getting a boy into the choir who has every qualification except a voice, or to provide a home for some deserving widow.'

'D'you think I'm too old to marry now?' asked Bella, smiling.

'My dear, for twenty years you've refused the most eligible aspirants. Shall we tell Polly about the last one?'

'She wouldn't tell us.'

'Only two months ago one of our Canons solemnly asked whether he might pay his addresses to Bella. But she wouldn't hear of it, because he had seven children by his first wife.'

'He was a singularly dull man into the bargain,' answered Bella.

'Nonsense, my dear; he has a first edition of the *Pilgrim's Progress*.'

'Did you like Mr Field?' asked Bella quietly.

'Very much,' answered the Dean. 'He seems a quiet, modest young man.'

'I'm glad of that, father, because I'm engaged to be married to him.'

The Dean gasped; the shock was so great that for a moment he could not speak, and then he began to tremble. Miss Langton watched him anxiously.

'It's impossible, Bella,' he muttered at last. 'You must be joking.'

'Why?'

'He's twenty years younger than you.'

'Yes, that's true. I should never have thought of marriage only he has consumption. I want to be his nurse more than his wife.'

'But he isn't a gentleman,' said the Dean, looking at her gravely.

'Father, how can you say that!' cried Bella indignantly, reddening. 'I've never met anyone with such a gentle soul. He's all goodness and purity.'

'Women know nothing about such things. They can never tell if a man's a gentleman or not. What was his father?'

'His father was a tradesman. But kind hearts are more than coronets.'

The Dean tightened his lips. He had recovered now from his surprise, and stood before Bella, stern and cold.

'I dare say. But a kind heart doesn't make a gentleman. Polly can tell you that as well as I.'

'Quite the biggest scoundrel I ever knew was Lord William Heather,' said Miss Ley reflectively. 'He was a cheat and a blackmailer. He had committed every crime, great and mean, and kept out of prison only by miracle and the influence of his family; yet no one for a moment could deny that to his very finger-tips he was a gentleman. I never saw a better in my life. Gentility has nothing whatever to do with the Ten Commandments.'

'Mary, don't go against me, too,' cried Bella. 'I want your help.' She went up to the Dean and took his hands. 'Father dear, this isn't a rash whim of mine. I've considered it gravely, and I promise you that my motives are neither low nor unworthy. I would give the world not to cause you pain, and if I do, it's only because I think my duty here is clear. I beg you to give me your consent, and I beg you to remember that for many years I've devoted myself to your comfort.'

The Dean released his hands.

'I didn't know that you looked upon it as an irksome task,' he answered frigidly. 'And why do you suppose this man wants to marry you?' He seized Bella's arm, and with energy surprising in one of so fragile appearance, led her to the glass. 'Look at yourself. Is it natural for a boy to wish to marry a woman old enough to be his mother?' With hard eyes he scrutinized his daughter's face and the wrinkles about her mouth. 'Look at your hands; they're almost the hands of an old woman. I was mistaken in your friend; he can be nothing better than an unscrupulous fortune-hunter.'

Bella turned away with a groan; she could not understand that her father, gentleness itself, should suddenly be so horribly cruel.

'I know I'm old and plain,' she cried, 'and I don't think for a moment that Herbert loves me. He would never have thought of marrying me unless I had asked him. But I can only save his life by taking him abroad.'

For a while the Dean looked down in deep thought.

'If he's ill and must go abroad, Bella, I will willingly give him all the money he needs.'

'But I love him, father,' she answered, with a blush.

'Do you mean that seriously?'

'Yes.'

Then heavy tears came to his eyes, and ran slowly down his cheeks; the hardness was gone out of his voice when he answered, and it was half choked with sobs.

'Would you leave me alone, Bella? Can't you wait till I'm dead? I shan't last very much longer.'

'Oh, father, don't say that. Heaven knows I don't want to pain you. It tears my heart to think of leaving you. Let me marry him, and come with us to Italy. We may be very happy all three of us.'

But at this the Dean drew back from Bella's appealing hands, and brushing away his tears, drew himself up sternly.

'No, I will never do that, Bella. I've tried to remember all my life that first of all I'm a Christian minister, but pride of race is in my blood. I'm proud of my stock, and in my small way I've sought to add honour to it. By marrying this man you dishonour yourself and you dishonour me. How can you suffer to change the glorious name you bear for that of a miserable little counter-jumper! I have no right to ask you to refrain from marriage because I'm old and helpless, and you've made me utterly dependent on you, but I have a right to ask you not to disgrace the name of my family.'

Miss Ley had never before seen such severity in the gentle Dean; an unwonted fire had driven away the delightful sweetness which was his most charming trait, and two red spots burned on his cheeks. His very voice was harsh, and he held himself upright, austere and cold, like some Roman senator conscious of his royal responsibility. But Bella was unmoved.

'I'm very sorry, father, that you should look at it in such a narrow way. I can never think it dishonourable to take the name of the man I love. I'm afraid that if you won't consent I must still do as I think right.'

He gave her a long and searching look.

'It's a very grave step absolutely to disobey your father, Bella. I think it's the first time in your life.'

'I realize that.'

137

'Then let me tell you that if you leave the Deanery to marry this wretched tradesman, neither you nor he shall ever enter it again.'

'You must do as you think fit, father. I shall follow my husband.'

Slowly the Dean walked out of the room.

'He'll never change his mind,' said Bella in despair, turning to Miss Ley. 'He refused ever to see Bertha Ley because she married a farmer. His manner is so gentle, so sweet, that you might think his heart overflowed with humility, but he's right when he says pride of race is in his blood. I think I alone know how enormous it is in him.'

'What will you do now?' asked Miss Ley.

'What can I do? It means that I must choose between Herbert and my father; and Herbert needs me most.'

They did not see the Dean again till dinner, when he came down, dressed as was his fastidious habit, with silk stockings and buckled shoes, in the full array of his degree. He sat at the table silently, scarcely eating, and paid no attention to the conversation, forced and trivial, between Bella and Miss Ley. Now and then a heavy tear rolled down his cheek. He was a man of methodical habits, and till ten o'clock always remained in the drawing-room; on this occasion, therefore, as on others, he sat down and took up the *Guardian*, but Bella saw that he did not read, since for an hour his gaze was fixed vacantly on the same place, and now and then he drew out a handkerchief to dry his eyes. When the clock struck he rose, and his face was worn and grey with utter wretchedness.

'Good night, Polly,' he said. 'I hope Bella has seen that you have everything you require.'

He walked towards the door, but Miss Langton stopped him.

'You're not going without kissing me, father? You know it cuts my heart to make you so unhappy.'

'I don't think we need discuss the matter again, Bella,' he answered coldly. 'As you reminded me, you are of an age to decide your own affairs. I have nothing more to say, but I shall remain steadfast to my resolution.'

138

He turned on his heels and closed the door behind him; they heard him lock himself in his study.

'He's never gone to bed without kissing me before,' said Bella painfully. 'Even when he stayed out late, he used to come into my room to bid me good night. Oh, poor man, how frightfully unhappy I've made him!'

She looked at Miss Ley with anguish in her eyes.

'Oh, Mary, how hard it is that in this life you can't do good to one person without hurting another! Duty so often points in two contrary directions, and the pleasure of doing the one duty is so much less than the pain of neglecting the other.'

'Would you like me to speak to your father?'

'You can do no good. You don't know what immovable determination lies behind his meek and gentle manner.'

The Dean sat at his study table, his face buried in his hands, and when at last he went to bed, could not sleep, but brooded continually over the change that must occur in all his habits. He knew not what he should do without Bella, but could have reconciled himself to the loss if the youth and station of Herbert Field had not to his mind made the union unnatural and outrageous. He was paler than ever next day, bowed and haggard, and went about the house restlessly, silent, avoiding Bella's compassionate eyes: with an old man's weakness, he could not restrain the tears of which he was ashamed, and hid himself that he might not excite his daughter's pity. Miss Ley attempted to reason with him, but no good came; he was by turns obstinate and imploring.

'She can't leave me now, Polly,' he said. 'Can't she see how old I am, and how much I want her? Let her wait a little, I don't want to die alone with strange hands to close my eyes.'

'But you're not going to die, my dear Algernon. Our family to its uttermost branches has two marked characteristics, pigheadedness and longevity; and you'll live for another twenty years. After all, Bella has done a great deal for you. Don't you realize that she wants to live her own life for a little? You haven't noticed the change in her during the last few years; she's no longer a girl, but a woman of decided views;

and when a spinster develops views there's the devil to pay, my dear. I always think the one duty of human beings is not to hinder their neighbours in fulfilling themselves. Why don't you change your mind, and go with them to Italy?'

'I would sooner remain solitary to the end of my days,' he cried, with sudden vehemence. 'The women of our family have always married gentlemen. You pretend to despise birth, and consider yourself in consequence broad-minded; but I was brought up with the belief that my ancestors had handed down to me an honoured name, and I must sooner die than disgrace it. In all the temptations of my life I've remembered that, and if I've been too proud of my race I ask God to forgive me.'

He was immovable; and Miss Ley, to whom the point of view seemed quite ridiculous, turned away with a shrug of the shoulders. A special licence had been obtained, and on the following Friday, the day fixed for the marriage, Bella with a heavy heart put on a travelling-dress. They were to take the train immediately after the ceremony, catch the afternoon boat to Calais, and thence travel directly to Milan. The Dean, informed by Miss Ley of the arrangements, had said no word. Before starting for church Bella went to her father's study to bid him good-bye; she wished to make one more effort to soften him and to gain his forgiveness.

She knocked at the door, but no answer came, and turning the handle, she found it locked.

'May I come in, father?' she cried.

'I'm very busy,' he answered, in a trembling voice.

'Please open the door. I'm just going away. Let me say good-bye to you.'

There was a pause, while Bella waited with beating heart.

'Father,' she called again.

'I tell you I'm very busy. Please don't disturb me.'

She gave a sob and turned away.

'I think nothing makes one so hard as virtue,' she muttered.

Miss Ley was waiting in the hall, and very quietly the two women walked to the church where the marriage was to take place. Herbert stood at the chancel, and when Bella saw his bright smile of welcome she took courage; she could not doubt that she was acting wisely. Miss Ley gave her away. It was a very matter-of-fact ceremony, but afterwards in the vestry Herbert tenderly kissed his bride; then she gave a hysterical laugh to choke down her tears.

'Thank heaven it's over!' she said.

The luggage had preceded them to the station, whither they now walked demurely; soon the train arrived, and the happy pair set off on their long journey. But when the Dean knew that his daughter was gone from his house for good and all, he came out of his study; with aching heart he went to her room and noted the loneliness which seemed already to fill it; he went to the drawing-room, and that was bare and empty, too. For a while he sat down, and since none could see, surrendered helplessly to his grief; he asked himself to what he could now look forward, and with joined hands prayed that death might soon release him from his utter misery. Presently, taking his hat, he walked through the cloister, thinking in the cathedral he loved so well to gain at least a measure of peace; but in the transept his eye caught the large plate of polished brass on which were graven the names of all the Deans his predecessors: first there were strange Saxon names, half mythical in appearance, and then the sonorous names of Norman priests, names of divines remembered still in the stately annals of the English Church, great preachers, scholars, statesmen; and lastly his own. And the fire came to his cheeks, anger inflamed him, when he thought that his name, not a whit behind the proudest of them all in dignity and honour, must henceforth be utterly shameful.

At luncheon the Dean, exerting himself to shake off his despondency, spoke with Miss Ley of indifferent topics. In a little while she glanced at the clock.

'Bella must be just leaving Dover now,' she said.

'I would rather you didn't talk to me of her, Polly,' he answered, with a shaking voice which he strove to render firm. 'I must try to forget that I ever had a daughter.'

'I believe that the most deep-rooted of human passions is

that which makes men cut off their nose to spite their face,' she answered dryly.

Afterwards Miss Ley expressed a wish to drive over to Leanham and Court Leys, and invited the Dean to accompany her, but on his refusal ordered the carriage to be ready at three. For several years she had not seen the house wherein her ancestors, since the time of George II, had been born; nor was it without a discreet emotion that she recognized the well-known fields, the flat marshes, and the shining sea, which at that spot, to her partial eyes, had a peculiar charm not to be found elsewhere. She drove to Leanham Church, and getting the key, walked in to look at the stones and brasses which preserved the memory of her forebears: a new tablet recorded the birth, death, and qualities of Edward Craddock, and underneath a space was left for the name of his widow. She could not repress a sigh when she remembered that herself and Bertha, wife of the said Edward Craddock, would bring that long list to an end: after them the chapter of the Family of Ley would be closed for ever, and the pages of Burke know them no more.

'Algernon can say what he likes,' she muttered, 'but they were a dull lot. Families, like nations, only grow interesting in their decadence.'

Driving on, she came to Court Leys, which stood as ever white and square, as though placed upon the ground like a house of cards. Closed since the death of Craddock, husband to her niece, it wore a desolate and forsaken look; the trim and well-mown lawns were choked with weeds, and the flower-beds bare of flowers; the closed gates, the shuttered windows, gave it a sinister appearance, and with a shudder Miss Ley turned away. She bade the coachman to go back to Tercanbury, and deep in meditation, paid no more attention to the surrounding scenes. She started at hearing her name called in tones of astonishment, and noticed that Miss Glover, sister to the Vicar of Leanham, was staring after her. She stopped the carriage, and Miss Glover quickly walked up.

'Who ever thought of seeing you, Miss Ley? It's quite like old times.'

'Now, don't gush, my dear. I'm staying with my cousin at the Deanery, and I thought I would come over and see if Court Leys still stood in its place.'

'Oh, Miss Ley, you must be very much upset. The poor Dean, they say he's quite broken-hearted! You know young Field's father was a linen-draper at Blackstable.'

'It looks as if the *mésalliance* were endemic in my family. You must never be surprised to hear that I have married my butler, a most respectable man.'

'Oh, but poor Edward was different, and he turned out so well. Where is Bertha now? She never writes.'

'I believe she's in Italy. I mean her to marry Frank Hurrell, the son of old Dr Hurrell of Ferne.'

'Oh, but, Miss Ley, will she?'

'She's never set eyes on him yet,' answered Miss Ley, smiling dryly. 'But they'd suit one another admirably.'

'Doesn't it make you feel sad to see the old house shut up?'

'My dear, I take care never to give way to regret, which is nearly as sinful as repentance.'

'I don't understand you,' answered Miss Glover. 'I don't believe it means anything to you that, as far as ever you can see, it's Ley land.'

'There you wrong me. I do feel a certain satisfaction in revisiting the place; it makes me so glad that I live somewhere else. But I dare say it's a fine thing to be born in the country on your own land, even if you're only a woman. I like to feel that my roots are here. When I look round, I can hardly resist the temptation to take off my clothes and roll in a ploughed field.'

'I hope you won't, Miss Ley,' answered Fanny Glover, somewhat shocked; 'it would look so odd.'

'Don't be ridiculous, my dear,' smiled the other. 'You're so innocent that each time I see you I expect to find wings sprouting on your shoulders.'

'I see you're just the same as ever.'

'Pardon me, I grow distinctly younger every year. Upon my word, sometimes I don't feel more than eighteen.'

Then Miss Glover made the only repartee of her life.

'I confess I think you look quite twenty-five, Miss Ley,' she replied with a grim smile.

'You impudent creature!' laughed the other, and, telling the coachman to drive on, with a wave of the hand bade good-bye to Miss Glover, the scenes of her youth, and the fields which seemed part of her very blood and her bones.

Since the Dean somewhat curtly declined her offer to stay longer with him, Miss Ley set out next day for London. But a curious unrest had seized her, and she began much to regret her determination to spend the winter in England; Mrs Murray was already gone to Rome, and the sight of Bella leaving for the Continent had excited still more in Miss Ley's veins the travel-fever. She pictured to herself all the little delightful bothers of the Custom House, the mustiness of hotel 'buses, the sweet tediousness of long journeys by train, the grateful discomforts of foreign hostelries; she thought with dazzled eyes of the dingy greyness of Boulogne, and her nostrils inhaled the well-known odours of the port and station. Her nerves tingled with eagerness to forsake her house, her servants, and to plunge into the charming freedom of the idle tourist. But the train she was in stopped at Rochester, and her abstracted gaze fixed suddenly on that scene which, she remembered, Basil Kent had once highly extolled: the sky with its massive clouds was sombre, and its restfulness was mirrored on the flat surface of the Medway; tall chimneys belched winding smoke, a sinuous pattern against the greyness, and the low factory buildings were white with dust; to the observant there was indeed a decorative quality, recalling in its economy of line, in its subdued and careful colour, the elegance of a Japanese print.

Miss Ley sprang up.

'Give me my dressing-bag,' she said to her astonished maid. 'You can go on to London. I shall stay here.'

'Alone, madam?'

'D'you think anyone will run away with me! Be quick, or I shall be taken on.'

She seized her bag, jumped out of the carriage, and when the train steamed away gave a great sigh of relief; it quietened her nerves to be alone in a strange town, where none knew her, and walking downstairs she felt a most curious exhilaration. She surveyed the hotel 'buses, chose the most elaborate, and drove off.

With characteristic wilfulness, Miss Ley set no great store on the more celebrated objects that tourists visited; she had an idea that a work of art could arouse but a limited amount of enthusiasm, and this, with such as were world-renowned, seemed exhausted before ever she came to them. On the Continent, when she visited a fresh town, it was her practice to wander at random, watching the people, and nothing delighted her more than to discover some neglected garden or a decorated doorway, which the good Baedeker, carefully left at home, did not mention. That afternoon, then, in the lamplight, the inhabitants of Rochester might have seen a little old woman, plainly dressed, sauntering idly down the High Street, observing with keen eyes, amused and tolerant, and upborne, evidently, by a feeling of great self-satisfaction. At that moment the house in Old Queen Street seemed a prison, of which the faithful butler was head-gaoler; and the admirable dinner, all prepared, was more abhorrent than skilly and hard bread.

Presently, growing tired, Miss Ley returned to the hotel, and after resting went down to the dining-room. The waiter placed her at a little table, and while waiting for dinner to be brought she played absently with the Renaissance jewel which never left her. It had not yet occurred to her to examine the people who sat in the large room, and now, slowly raising her eyes, she saw fixed upon her, with a terrified expression, those of – Mrs Castillyon; her face was livid with anxiety. At first Miss Ley did not understand, but then she perceived that Reggie Bassett was there also. No sign of recognition passed between the two women; Mrs Castillyon looked down, and with scarcely a movement of the lips, spoke to Reggie. He started, and instinctively was about to turn around, but a quick word from his neighbour prevented him. Though seated some way from Miss Ley, they spoke in hurried whispers, as though afraid the very air should hear them. Miss Ley curiously glanced up once more, and once more Mrs Castillyon's eyes were hastily lowered. The ghastly pallor of her face was such that Miss Ley thought she would faint. Reggie poured out a tumbler of champagne which Mrs Castillyon quickly drank.

'I don't think they'll have a very pleasant dinner,' murmured the elderly spinster, repressing a smile. 'I wonder why on earth they chose Rochester.'

Then, mentally, she abused Frank for not telling her what she felt certain he very well knew. Indeed, Miss Ley was scarcely less confused than Mrs Castillyon, for she had no idea there existed such a relationship between the pair as to occasion a visit to the country from Saturday to Monday. But she put two and two together. She pursed her lips when she remembered that Paul Castillyon was at that time in the North of England speaking at a political meeting, and again smiled quietly to herself. She was devoured with eagerness to know how her neighbours would conduct themselves, for it always amused her to see in what manner people acted in untoward circumstances. She appeared not to look at them, but was able, notwithstanding, to note the hurried colloquy, followed by an uneasy silence, with which they finished their meal. It could not be denied that Miss Ley ate her dinner not only with equanimity, but with added zest.

'I didn't know they cooked so well in English hotels,' she murmured. She called the waiter. 'Can you tell me who that lady is at the fifth table from here?'

'Mrs Barlow, madam. They only arrived this afternoon.'

'And is the gentleman her husband or her son?'

'Her husband, madam, I think.'

'Pray bring me a newspaper.'

Mrs Castillyon and Reggie were bound to pass her on their way to the door, and Miss Ley, somewhat ill-naturedly, determined to remain where she was. Her sight was good enough for her to notice a look of utter despair on the pretty woman's face when a *Westminster Gazette* accompanied the coffee. Miss Ley arranged it in front of her, and was soon engrossed in the perusal of a leading article.

There was no help, and Mrs Castillyon was obliged to make the best of it. Reggie got up and strolled out, his eyes glued to the floor, with a scowl on his handsome features which indicated that Mrs Castillyon would suffer for the mischance. But she was bolder; she walked a few steps behind him, uprightly, with a swaying movement of the hips that was habitual to her, and arriving in front of Miss Ley, stopped with a very natural cry of surprise.

'Miss Ley, of all people! How delightful to find you down here!'

She held out her hand with every appearance of joy. Miss Ley smiled coldly.

'I hope I see you well, Mrs Castillyon.'

'Have you been dining here? How extraordinary that I didn't see you! But it's been a day of odd things for me. When I came into the hotel, the first person I ran across was Mr Bassett. So I asked him to dine with me. It appears he's staying in the neighbourhood. I wonder you didn't see him.'

'I did.'

'Why on earth didn't you come and speak to us? We might all have dined together.'

'What a prodigious fool you must think me, my dear!' drawled Miss Ley, with a mingled expression of scorn and amusement.

At this Mrs Castillyon started, her face grew on a sudden horribly grey, and her eyes were filled with abject terror. She had not the strength to continue the pretence on which she had at first counted; she saw, moreover, that it was useless.

'You won't give me away, Miss Ley,' she whispered, in a tone that fear made scarcely articulate.

'I have no doubt that curiosity is my besetting sin,' answered Miss Ley, 'but not indiscretion. Only fools discuss the concrete; the intelligent are more concerned with the abstract.'

'D'you know that Paul's mother would give half her fortune to know that I was down here with a man? Oh, how glad she'd be of the chance of hounding me down! For God's sake promise that you'll never say a word. You don't want to ruin me, do you?'

'I promise faithfully.'

Mrs Castillyon gave a sigh of relief that was half a sob of

pain. The room was empty except for the waiter clearing away, but she thought he watched suspiciously.

'But now I'm in your power, too,' she groaned. 'I wish to God I'd never come here. Why doesn't that man go away. I feel I could scream at the top of my voice.'

'I wouldn't if I were you,' answered Miss Ley quietly.

Valuing nothing so much as self-restraint, she observed Mrs Castillyon with a certain scorn, for this pitiful exhibition of shame and terror somewhat disgusted her. None was more indifferent to convention than herself, and the marriage tie especially excited her ridicule, but she despised entirely those who disregarded the by-laws of society, yet lacked courage to suffer the results of their boldness: to seek the good opinion of the world, and yet secretly to act counter to its idea of decorum, was a very contemptible hypocrisy. Mrs Castillyon, divining the sense of Miss Ley's scrutiny, watched anxiously.

'You must utterly despise me,' she moaned.

'Don't you think you'd better come back to London with me tonight?' answered Miss Ley, fixing on the terrified woman her cold, stern grey eyes.

Mrs Castillyon's buoyant sprightliness had completely disappeared, and she sat before the elder woman haggard and white, like a guilty prisoner before his judge. But at this proposition a faint blush came to her cheeks, and a look of piteous anguish turned down the corners of her mouth.

'I can't,' she whispered. 'Don't ask me to do that.'

'Why?'

'I daren't leave him; he'll go after some of those women in Chatham.'

'Has it come to that already?'

'Oh, Miss Ley, I've been so awfully punished. I didn't mean to go so far. I only wanted to amuse myself – I was so bored; you know what Paul is. Sometimes he was so tedious and dull that I flung myself on my bed and just screamed.'

'All husbands sometimes are tedious and dull,' remarked Miss Ley reflectively, 'just as all wives are often peevish. But he's very fond of you.'

'I think it would break his heart if he knew. I'm so utterly wretched. I couldn't help myself; I love Reggie with all my soul. And he doesn't care two straws for me! At first he was flattered because I was what he calls a gentlewoman, but now he only sticks to me because I pay him.'

'What!' cried Miss Ley.

'His mother doesn't give him enough money, and I manage to help him. He pays all the bills with notes I give, and I pretend to think there's never any change. Oh, I hate and despise him, and yet if he left me I think I should die.'

Hiding her face in her hands, she wept irresistibly. Miss Ley meditated. In a moment Mrs Castillyon looked up, clenching her fists.

'And now when I go to him he'll abuse me like a fishwife because I suggested Rochester. He'll say it was my fault that we came here. Oh, I wish we'd never come; I knew it was madness. I wish I'd never set eyes on him.'

'But why did you hit upon Rochester?' asked Miss Ley.

'Don't you remember Basil Kent talked about it? I thought no one ever came here, and Paul said wild-horses wouldn't drag him. That settled it.'

'Basil must apply his aesthetic theories to less accessible places,' murmured Miss Ley. 'For that is why I came also. You know, our place is not far from here, and I've been staying at Tercanbury.'

'I forgot that.'

For a little while they remained silent. The hotel dining-room, with most of the lights extinguished, the tables clear but for white table-cloths, was gloomy and depressing. Mrs Castillyon shuddered as painfully she took in the scene, and dimly felt that this passion, which had seemed so wonderful, in Miss Ley's eyes must appear most sordid and mean.

'Can't you help me at all?' she moaned.

'Why don't you break with Reggie altogether?' asked Miss Ley. 'I know him pretty well, and I don't think he will ever bring you much happiness.'

'I wish I had the strength.'

Miss Ley gently placed her hand on the thin, jewelled fingers of the unhappy woman.

'Let me take you up to London tonight, my dear.'

Mrs Castillyon looked at her with tear-filled eyes.

'Not tonight,' she begged. 'Give me till Monday, and then I'll break with him altogether.'

'It must be now or never. Don't you think it had better be now?'

None would have thought that Miss Ley's cold voice was capable of such persuasive tenderness.

'Very well,' said Mrs Castillyon, utterly exhausted. 'I'll go and tell Reggie.'

'If he raises any objection, say that I make it a condition of holding my tongue.'

'Much he'll care!' replied Mrs Castillyon, with a sob of anger.

She went away, but immediately returned.

'He's gone,' she said.

'Gone?'

'Without a word. All the things are out of his room. He's always been a coward, and he's just run away.'

'And left you to pay the bill. How like dear Reggie!'

'You're right, Miss Ley: no good can come of the whole thing. This is the end. I'll drop him. Take me up to London, and I promise you I'll never see him again. I will try from now to do my duty to Paul.'

Their traps were soon collected, and they caught the last train to town. Mrs Castillyon sat in the corner of the carriage, her face woebegone and white against the blue cushions; she looked out into the night and never spoke. Her companion meditated.

'I wonder what there is in respectability,' she thought, 'that I should take such pains to lead back that woman to its dull, complacent paths. She's a poor creature, and I don't suppose she's worth the trouble; and I haven't seen Rochester after all. But I must take great care, I'm becoming quite a censor of morals, and soon I shall grow positively tedious.'

She glanced at the pretty woman, looking then so old and worn, the powder on her cheeks emphasizing their wan hollowness. She was crying silently.

'I wonder if that beast Frank knew all the time, and basely kept the secret.'

When at last they drew near London, Mrs Castillyon roused herself. She turned to her friend with a sort of despairing scorn.

'You're fond of aphorisms, Miss Ley,' she said. 'Here's one that I've found out for myself: One can despise no one so intensely as the person one loves with all one's heart.'

'Frank can say what he likes,' answered the other, 'but there's nothing like mortal pain for making people entertaining.'

A few days later Miss Ley, who prided herself that she made plans only for the pleasure of breaking them, started for Italy.

PART TWO

1

MISS LEY returned to England at the end of February. Unlike the most of her compatriots, she did not go abroad to see the friends with whom she spent much time at home; and though Bella and Herbert Field were at Naples, Mrs Murray in Rome, she took care systematically to avoid them. Rather was it her practice to cultivate chance acquaintance, for she thought the English in foreign lands betrayed their idiosyncrasies with a pleasant and edifying frankness. In Venice, for example, or at Capri, the delectable isle, romance might be seized as it were in the act, and all manner of oddities were displayed with a most diverting effrontery. In those places you meet middle-aged pairs, uncertainly related, whose vehement adventures startle the decorum of a previous generation. You discover how queer may be the most conventional, how ordinary the most eccentric. Miss Ley, with her discreet knack for extracting confidence, after her own staid fashion enjoyed herself immensely. She listened to the strange confessions of men who for their souls' sake had abandoned the greatness of the world, and now spoke of their past zeal with indulgent irony; of women who for love had been willing to break down the very pillars of heaven, and now shrugged their shoulders in amused recollection of passion long since dead.

'Well, what have you fresh to tell me?' asked Frank, having met Miss Ley at Victoria, when he sat down to dinner in Old Queen Street.

'Nothing much. But I've noticed that when pleasure has exhausted a man he's convinced that he has exhausted pleasure; then he tells you gravely that nothing can satisfy the human heart.'

But Frank had more important news than this, for Jenny, a week before, was delivered of a still-born child, and had been so ill that it was thought she could not recover. Now, however, the worst was over, and if nothing untoward befell she might be expected slowly to regain health.

'How does Basil take it?' asked Miss Ley.

'He says very little. He's grown silent of late, but I'm afraid he's quite heart-broken. You know how enormously he looked forward to the baby.'

'D'you think he's fond of his wife?'

'He's very kind to her. No one could have been gentler than he after the catastrophe. I think she was the more cut up of the two. You see, she looked upon it as the reason of their marriage – and he's doing his best to comfort her.'

'I must go down and see them. And now tell me about Mrs Castillyon.'

'I haven't set eyes on her for ages.'

Miss Ley observed Frank with deliberation. She wondered if he knew of the affair with Reggie Bassett, but, though eager to discuss it, would not risk to divulge a secret. In point of fact, he was familiar with all the circumstances, but it amused him to counterfeit ignorance that he might see how Miss Ley guided the conversation to the point she wanted. She spoke of the Dean of Tercanbury, of Bella and her husband; then, as though by chance, mentioned Reggie. But the twinkling of Frank's eyes told her that he was laughing at her stratagem.

'You brute!' she cried. 'Why didn't you tell me all about it, instead of letting me discover the thing by accident?'

'My sex suggests to me certain elementary notions of honour, Miss Ley.'

'You needn't add priggishness to your other detestable vices. How did you know they were carrying on in this way?'

'The amiable youth told me. There are very few men who can refrain from boasting of their conquests, and certainly Reggie isn't one of them.'

'You don't know Hugh Kearon, do you? He's had affairs all over Europe, and the most notorious was with a foreign Princess who shall be nameless. I think she would have bored him to death if he hadn't been able to flourish ostentatiously a handkerchief with a royal crown in the corner and a large initial.'

Miss Ley then gave her account of the visit to Rochester, and certainly made of it a very neat and entertaining story.

'And did you think for a moment that this would be the end of the business?' asked Frank ironically.

'Don't be spiteful because I hoped for the best.'

'Dear Miss Ley, the bigger blackguard a man is, the more devoted are his lady-loves. It's only when a man is decent and treats women as if they were human beings that he has a rough time of it.'

'You know nothing about these things, Frank,' retorted Miss Ley. 'Pray give me the facts, and the philosophical conclusions I can draw for myself.'

'Well, Reggie has a natural aptitude for dealing with the sex. I heard all about your excursion to Rochester, and went so far as to assure him that you wouldn't tell his mamma. He perceived that he hadn't cut a very heroic figure, so he mounted the high horse, and full of virtuous indignation, for a month took no notice whatever of Mrs Castillyon. Then she wrote most humbly begging him to forgive her; and this, I understand, he graciously did. He came to see me, flung the letter on the table, and said: "There, my boy, if anyone asks you, say that what I don't know about women ain't worth knowing." Two days later he appeared with a gold cigarette-case!'

'What did you say to him?'

'"One of these days you'll come the very devil of a cropper."'

'You showed wisdom and emphasis. I hope with all my heart he will.'

'I don't imagine things are going very smoothly,' proceeded Frank. 'Reggie tells me she leads him a deuce of a life, and he's growing restive. It appears to be no joke to have a woman desperately in love with you. And then, he's never been on such familiar terms with a person of quality, and he's shocked by her vulgarity. Her behaviour seems often to outrage his sense of decorum.'

'Isn't that like an Englishman! He cultivates propriety even in the immoral.'

Then Miss Ley asked Frank about himself, but they had

155

corresponded with diligence, and he had little to tell. The work at St Luke's went on monotonously – lectures to students three times a week, and out-patients on Wednesday and Saturday. People were beginning to come to his consulting-room in Harley Street, and he looked forward, without great enthusiasm, to the future of a fashionable physician.

'And are you in love?'

'You know I shall never permit my affections to wander so long as you remain single,' he answered, laughing.

'Beware I don't take you at your word, and drag you by the hair of your head to the altar. Have I no rival?'

'Well, if you press me, I will confess.'

'Monster, what is her name?'

'Bilharzia hoematobi.'

'Good heavens!'

'It's a parasite I'm studying. I think authorities are all wrong about it. They've not got its life-history right, and the stuff they believe about the way people catch it is sheer footle.'

'It doesn't sound frightfully thrilling to me, and I'm under the impression you're only trumping it up to conceal some scandalous amour with a ballet-girl.'

Miss Ley's visit to Barnes seemed welcome neither to Jenny nor to Basil, who looked harassed and unhappy, and only with a visible effort assumed a cheerful manner when he addressed his wife. Jenny was still in bed, very weak and ill, but Miss Ley, who had never before seen her, was surprised at her great beauty; her face, whiter than the pillows against which it rested, had a very touching pathos, and notwithstanding all that had gone before, that winsome, innocent sweetness which has occasioned the comparison of English maidens to the English rose. The observant woman noticed also the painful, questioning anxiety with which Jenny continually glanced at her husband, as though pitifully dreading some unmerited reproach.

'I hope you like my wife,' said Basil, when he accompanied Miss Ley downstairs.

'Poor thing! She seems to me like a lovely bird imprisoned

156

by fate within the four walls of practical life, who should by rights sing careless songs under the open skies. I'm afraid you'll be very unkind to her.'

'Why?' he asked, not without resentment.

'My dear, you'll make her live up to your blue china teapot. The world might be so much happier if people wouldn't insist on acting up to their principles.'

Mrs Bush had been hurriedly sent for when Jenny's condition seemed dangerous, but in her distress and excitement had sought comfort in Basil's whisky bottle to such an extent that he was obliged to beg her to return to her own home. The scene was not edifying. Surmising an alcoholic tendency, Kent, two or three days after her arrival, locked the sideboard and removed the key. But in a little while the servant came to him.

'If you please, sir, Mrs Bush says, can she 'ave the whisky; she's not feelin' very well.'

'I'll go to her.'

Mrs Bush sat in the dining-room with folded hands, doing her utmost to express on a healthy countenance maternal anxiety, indisposition, and ruffled dignity. She was not vastly pleased to see her son-in-law instead of the expected maid.

'Oh, is that you, Basil?' she said. 'I can't find the sideboard key anywhere, and I'm that upset I must 'ave a little drop of something.'

'I wouldn't if I were you, Mrs Bush. You're much better without it.'

'Oh, indeed!' she answered, bristling. 'P'raps you know more about me inside feelings than I do myself. I'll just trouble you to give me the key, young man, and look sharp about it. I'm not a woman to be put upon by anyone, and I tell you straight.'

'I'm very sorry, but I think you've had quite enough to drink. Jenny may want you, and you would be wise to keep sober.'

'D'you mean to insinuate that I've 'ad more than I can carry?'

'I wouldn't go quite so far as that,' he answered, smiling.

'Thank you for nothing,' cried Mrs Bush indignantly. 'And I should be obliged if you wouldn't laugh at me, and I must say it's very 'eartless with me daughter lying ill in her bedroom.

I'm very much upset, and I did think you'd treat me like a lady; but you never 'ave, Mr Kent – no, not even the first time I come here. Oh, I 'aven't forgot, so don't you think I have. A sixpenny 'alfpenny teapot was good enough for me; but when your lady friend come in out pops the silver, and I don't believe for a moment it's real silver. Blood's all very well, Mr Kent, but what I say is, give me manners. You're a nice young feller, you are, to grudge me a little drop of spirits when me poor daughter's on her death-bed. I wouldn't stay another minute in this 'ouse if it wasn't for 'er.'

'I was going to suggest it would be better if you returned to your happy home in Crouch End,' answered Basil, when the good woman stopped to take breath.

'Were you indeed! Well, we'll just see what Jenny 'as to say to that. I suppose my daughter is mistress in 'er own 'ouse.'

Mrs Bush started to her feet and made for the door, but Basil stood with his back against it.

'I can't allow you to go to her now. I don't think you're in a fit state.'

'D'you think I'm going to let you prevent me? Get out of my way, young man.'

Basil, more disgusted than out of temper, looked at the angry creature with a cold scorn which was not easy to stomach.

'I'm sorry to hurt your feelings, Mrs Bush, but I think you'd better leave this house at once. Fanny will put your things together. I'm going to Jenny's room, and I forbid you to come to it. I expect you to be gone in half an hour.'

He turned on his heel, leaving Mrs Bush furious, but intimidated. She was so used to have her own way that opposition took her aback, and Basil's manner did not suggest that he would easily suffer contradiction. But she made up her mind, whatever the consequences, to force her way into Jenny's room, and there set out her grievance. She had not done repeating to herself what she would say, when the servant entered to state that, according to her master's order, she had packed the things. Jenny's mother started up indignantly, but pride forbade her to let the maid see she was turned out.

'Quite right, Fanny! This isn't the 'ouse that a lady would stay in; and I pity you, my dear, for 'aving a master like my son in-law. You can tell 'im, with my compliments, that he's no gentleman.'

Jenny, who was asleep, woke at the slamming of the front-door.

'What's that?' she asked.

'Your mother has gone away, dearest. D'you mind?'

She looked at him quickly, divining from knowledge of her parent's character that some quarrel had occurred, and anxious to see that Basil was not annoyed. She gave him her hand.

'No; I'm glad. I want to be alone with you. I don't want anyone to come between us.'

He bent down and kissed her, and she put her arms round his neck.

'You're not angry with me because the baby died?'

'My darling, how could I be?'

'Say that you don't regret having married me.'

Jenny, realizing by now that Basil had married her only on account of the child, was filled with abject terror; his interests were so different from hers (and she had but gradually come to understand how great was the separation between them) that the longed-for son alone seemed able to preserve to her Basil's affection. It was the mother he loved, and now he might bitterly repent his haste, for it seemed she had forced marriage upon him by false pretences. The chief tie that bound them was severed, and though with meek gratitude accepting the attentions suggested by his kindness, she asked herself with aching heart what would happen on her recovery.

Time passed, and Jenny, though ever pale and listless, grew strong enough to leave her room. It was proposed that in a little while she should go with her sister for a month to Brighton. Basil's work prevented him from leaving London for long, but he promised to run down for the week-end. One afternoon he came home in high spirits, having just received from his publishers a letter to say that his book had found favour, and would be issued in the coming spring. It seemed the first step to the renown he sought. He found James Bush, his brother-in-law, seated with Jenny, and in his elation greeted him with unusual cordiality; but James lacked his usual facetious flow of conversation, and wore, indeed, a hang-dog air which at another time would have excited Basil's attention. He took his leave at once, and then Basil noticed that Jenny was much disturbed. Though he knew nothing for certain, he had an idea that the family of Bush came to his wife when they were in financial straits, but from the beginning had decided that such inevitable claims must be satisfied. He preferred, however, to ignore the help which Jenny gave, and when she asked for some small sum beyond her allowance, handed it without question.

'Why was Jimmie here at this hour?' he asked carelessly, thinking him bound on some such errand. 'I thought he didn't leave his office till six.'

'Oh, Basil, something awful has happened. I don't know how to tell you. He's sacked.'

'I hope he doesn't want us to keep him,' answered Basil coldly. 'I'm very hard up this year, and all the money I have I want for you.'

Jenny braced herself for a painful effort. She looked away, and her voice trembled.

'I don't know what's to be done. He's got in trouble. Unless he can find a hundred and fifteen pounds in a week, his firm are going to prosecute.'

'What on earth d'you mean, Jenny?'

'Oh, Basil, don't be angry. I was so ashamed to tell you, I've been hiding it for a month; but now I can't any more. Something went wrong with his accounts.'

'D'you mean to say he's been stealing?' asked Basil sternly; and a feeling of utter horror and disgust came over him.

'For God's sake, don't look at me like that,' she cried, for his eyes, his firm-set mouth, made her feel a culprit confessing on her own account some despicable crime. 'He didn't mean to be dishonest. I don't exactly understand, but he can tell you how it all was. Oh, Basil, you won't let him be sent to prison! Couldn't he have the money instead of my going away?'

Basil sat down at his desk to think out the matter, and resting his face thoughtfully on his hands, sought to avoid Jenny's fixed, appealing gaze. He did not want her to see the consternation, the abject shame, with which her news oppressed him. But all the same she saw.

'What are you thinking about, Basil?'

'Nothing particular. I was wondering how to raise the money.'

'You don't think because he's my brother I must be tarred with the same brush?'

He looked at her without answering. It was certainly unfortunate that his wife's mother should drink more than was seemly, and her brother have but primitive ideas about property.

'It's not my fault,' she cried, with bitter pain, interrupting his silence. 'Don't think too hardly of me.'

'No, it's not your fault,' he answered, with involuntary coldness. 'You must go away to Brighton all the same, but I'm afraid it means no holiday in the summer.'

He wrote a cheque, and then a letter to his bank begging them to advance a hundred pounds on securities they held.

'There he is,' cried Jenny, hearing a ring. 'I told him to come back in half an hour.'

Basil got up.

'You'd better give the cheque to your brother at once. Say that I don't wish to see him.'

'Isn't he to come here any more, Basil?'

'That is as you like, Jenny. If you wish, we'll pretend he was unfortunate rather than – dishonest; but I'd rather he didn't refer to the matter. I want neither his thanks nor his excuses.'

Without answering Jenny took the cheque. She would have given a great deal to fling her arms gratefully round Basil's neck, begging him to forgive, but there was a hardness in his manner which frightened her. All the evening he sat in moody silence, and Jenny dared not speak. His kiss when he bade her good night had never been so frigid, and unable to sleep, she cried bitterly. She could not understand the profound abhorrence with which he looked upon the incident. To her mind it was little more than a mischance occasioned by Jimmie's excessive sharpness, and she was disposed to agree with her brother that only luck had been against him. She somewhat resented Basil's refusal to hear any defence, and his complete certainty that the very worst must be true.

A few days later, coming unexpectedly, Kent found Jenny in earnest conversation with her brother, who had quite regained his jaunty air, and betrayed no false shame at Basil's knowledge of his escapade.

'Well met, 'Oratio!' he cried, holding out his hand. 'I just come in on the chance of seeing you. I wanted to thank you for that loan.'

'I'd rather you didn't speak of it.'

'Why, there's nothing to be ashamed of. I 'ad a bit of bad luck, that's all. I'll pay you back, you know. You needn't fear about that.'

He gave a voluble account of the affair, proving how misfortune may befall the deserving, and what a criminal complexion the most innocent acts may wear. Basil, against his will admiring the fellow's jocose effrontery, listened with chilling silence.

'You need not excuse yourself,' he said at length. 'My reasons for helping you were purely selfish. Except for Jenny, it would have been a matter of complete indifference to me if you had been sent to prison or not.'

'Oh, that was all kid. They wouldn't have prosecuted. Don't I tell you they had no case. You believe me, don't you?'

'No, I don't.'

'What d'you mean by that?' asked James angrily.

'We won't discuss it.'

The other did not answer, but shot at Basil a glance of singular malevolence.

'You can whistle for your money, young feller,' he muttered under his breath. 'You won't get much out of me.'

He had but small intention of paying back the rather large sum, but now abandoned even that. During the six months of Jenny's married life he had never been able to surmount the freezing politeness with which Basil used him. He hated him for his supercilious air, but needing his help, took care, though sometimes he could scarcely keep his temper, to preserve a familiar cordiality. He knew his brother-in-law would welcome an opportunity to forbid him the house, and this, especially now that he was out of work, he determined to avoid. He stomached the affront as best he could, but solaced his pride with the determination sooner or later to revenge himself.

'Well, so long,' he cried, with undiminished serenity; 'I'll be toddling.'

Jenny watched this scene with some alarm, but with more irritation, since Basil's frigid contempt for her brother seemed a reflection on herself.

'You might at least be polite to him,' she said, when Jimmie was gone.

'I'm afraid I've pretty well used up all my politeness.'

'After all, he is my brother.'

'That is a fact I deplore with all my heart,' he answered.

'You needn't be so hard on him now he's down. He's no worse than plenty more.'

Basil turned to her with flaming eyes.

'Good God, don't you realize the man's a thief! Doesn't it mean anything to you that he's dishonest? Don't you see how awful it is that a man –'

He broke off with a gesture of disgust. It was the first quarrel they had ever had, and a shrewish look came to Jenny's face, her pallor gave way to an angry flush. But quickly Basil recovered himself. Recollecting his wife's illness and her bitter disappointment at the poor babe's death, he keenly regretted the outburst.

'I beg your pardon, Jenny. I didn't mean to say that. I should have remembered you were fond of him.'

But since she did not answer, looking away somewhat sulkily, he sat down on the arm of her chair and stroked her wonderful rich tresses.

'Don't be cross, darling. We won't quarrel, will we?'

Unable to resist his tenderness, tears came to her eyes, and passionately she kissed his caressing hands.

'No, no,' she cried. 'I love you too much. Don't ever speak angrily to me; it hurts so awfully.'

The momentary cloud passed, and they talked of the approaching visit to Brighton. Jenny was to take lodgings, and she made him promise faithfully that he would come every Saturday. Frank had offered a room in Harley Street, and while she was away Basil meant to stay with him.

'You won't forget me, Basil?'

'Of course not! But you must hurry up and get well and come back.'

When at length she set off, and Basil found himself Frank's guest, he could not suppress a faint sigh of relief. It was very delightful to live again in a bachelor's rooms, and he loved the smell of smoke, the untidy litter of books, the lack of responsibility. There was no need to do anything he did not like, and for the first time since his marriage he felt entirely comfortable. Recalling his pleasant rooms in the Temple, and there was about them an old-world air which amiably fitted his humour, he thought of the long conversations of those days, the hours of reverie, the undisturbed ease with which he could read books; and he shuddered at the poky villa which was now his home, the worries of housekeeping, and the want of privacy. He had meant his life to be so beautiful, and it was merely sordid.

'There are advantages in single blessedness,' laughed the doctor, when he saw Basil after breakfast light his pipe, and putting his feet on the chimney-piece, lean back with a sigh of content.

But he regretted his words when he saw on the other's mobile face a look of singular wistfulness. It was his first indication that things were not going very well with the young couple.

'By the way,' Frank suggested presently, 'would you care to come to a party tonight? Lady Edward Stringer is giving some sort of function, and there'll be a lot of people you know.'

'I've been nowhere since my marriage,' Basil answered irresolutely.

'I shall be seeing the old thing today. Shall I ask if I can bring you?'

'It would be awfully good of you. By Jove, I should enjoy it.' He gave a laugh. 'I've not had evening clothes on for six months.'

2

LADY EDWARD STRINGER said she would be delighted to see Basil that evening, and Frank, whose toilet was finished in a quarter of an hour, with scornful amusement watched the care wherewith the young man dressed. At last, with a final look at the glass, he turned round.

'You look very nice indeed,' said the doctor ironically.

'Shut up!' answered Basil, reddening; but it was evident all the same that he was not displeased with his appearance.

They dined at Frank's very respectable club, surrounded by men of science with their diverting air of middle-aged schoolboys, and soon after ten drove off to Kensington. Basil hated the economy which since his marriage he had been forced to practise, and the signs of wealth in Lady Edward's house were very grateful to him. A powdered footman took his hat, another seized his coat; and after the cramped stuffiness of the villa at Barnes it pleased him hugely to walk through spacious and lofty rooms, furnished splendidly in the worst Victorian manner. Lady Edward, her fair wig more than usually askew, dressed in shabby magnificence, with splendid diamonds round her withered neck, gave him the indifferent welcome of a fashionable hostess, and turned to the next arrival. Moving on, Basil found himself face to face with Mrs Murray.

'Oh, I *am* glad to see you!' he cried, enthusiastic and surprised. 'I didn't know you were back. Come and sit down, and tell me all you've seen.'

'Nonsense! I'm not going to say a word. You must give me all the news. I see your book is announced.'

Basil was astonished to find how handsome she was. He had thought of her very frequently, against his will, but the picture in his mind had not that radiant health nor that spirited vitality. Rather had his imagination exaggerated the likeness to a Madonna of Sandro Botticelli, dwelling on the sad passion of

165

her lips and the pallid oval of her languid face. Tonight her vivacity was enchanting; the grey eyes were full of laughter, and her cheeks delightfully flushed. He looked at her beautiful hands, recognizing the rings, and at the picturesque splendour of her gown. The favourite scent which vaguely clung to her recalled the past with its pleasant intercourse, and he remembered her drawing-room in Charles Street where they had sat so often talking of charming things. His heart ached, and he knew that for all his efforts he loved her no less than that night before his marriage when he became convinced that she also cared.

'I don't believe you're listening to a word I say,' she cried.

'Yes, I am,' he answered, 'but the sound of your voice intoxicates me. It has all the music of Italy. I haven't heard it for such ages.'

'When did I see you last?' she inquired, remembering perfectly well, but curious to know his answer.

'You were driving near Westminster Bridge one Sunday afternoon, but I've not spoken to you since the Thursday before that. I remember the cloak you wore then. Have you still got it?'

'What a memory!'

She laughed flippantly, but there was triumph in her eyes; for he seemed to have forgotten completely the visit to Barnes, and his recollection was only of their mutual love.

'I often think of the long talks we used to have,' he said. 'Except for you, I should never have written my book.'

'Ah, yes, before you married, wasn't it?'

She uttered the words carelessly, with a smile, but she meant to wound; and Basil's face grew on a sudden deathly pale, an inexpressible pain darkened his eyes, and his lips trembled. Mrs Murray observed him with a cruel curiosity. Sometimes in her anger she had prayed for an occasion of revenge for all the torture she had suffered, and this was the beginning. She hated him now, she told herself – she hated him furiously. At that moment she caught sight of Mr Farley, the fashionable parson, and smiled. As she expected, he came forward.

'Did you get a letter from me?' she asked, holding out her hand.

'Thanks so much. I've already written to accept.'

Her question was not without malice, for she wished Basil to understand that she had sent Mr Farley some invitation. Unwillingly, the younger man rose from her side, and the Vicar of All Souls' took the vacant place. As Basil sauntered away, sore at heart, she addressed the newcomer with a flattering, though somewhat unusual, cordiality.

'*Tiens!* There's chaste Lucretia. How on earth did you get here?'

Basil started, and his face grew suddenly cold and hard when at his elbow he heard his mother's mocking voice.

'Dr Hurrell brought me,' he answered.

'He showed discretion in bringing you to the dullest house in London, also the most respectable. How is Camberwell, and do you have high tea?'

'My wife is at Brighton,' replied Basil, feeling, as ever, humiliated by Lady Vizard's banter.

'I didn't expect she was here. You're really very good-looking. What a pity it is you're so absurd!'

She nodded to her son and passed on. Presently she came to Miss Ley, who stood by herself watching with amusement the various throng.

'How d'you do?' said Lady Vizard.

'I had no idea that you remembered me,' answered the other.

'I saw in the paper that you had inherited the fortune of that odious Miss Dwarris. Haven't you found that lots of people have remembered you since then?' She did not wait for an answer. 'Aren't you a friend of my young hopeful? I've just seen him, and I can't imagine why he dislikes me so much. I suppose he thinks I'm wicked, but I'm not in the least, really. I'm not conscious of ever having committed a sin in my life. I've done foolish things and things I regret, but that's all.'

'It's very comfortable to have the approval of one's own conscience,' murmured Miss Ley.

Lord de Capit at that moment advanced to Lady Vizard, and

167

Miss Ley took the opportunity to go to Mrs Barlow-Bassett, superbly imposing as usual, who was talking with the Castillyons.

'It's a great comfort to me to know he's such a good boy,' she heard her saying. 'He has no secrets from me, and I can assure you he hasn't a thought which he needs to hide from anyone.'

'Who is this admirable person?' asked Miss Ley.

'I was thanking Mrs Castillyon for being so good to Reggie. He's just of an age when the influence of a woman of the world – a good woman – is so important.'

'Reginald is a compendium of all the virtues,' remarked Miss Ley quietly; 'and Mrs Castillyon is a pattern of charity.'

'You overwhelm me with confusion,' cried the little woman, with the lightest laugh, but only the powder hid a crimson blush of shame.

She managed in a little while to get Miss Ley to herself, and they sat down. Mrs Castillyon's manner was so airy and flippant that none could have guessed she dealt with tragic issues.

'You must utterly despise me, Miss Ley,' she said.

'Why?'

'I promised you I'd never see Reggie again, and what must you have thought when you heard Mrs Bassett!'

'At least it saved you the trouble of telling me fibs.'

'I wouldn't have lied about it. I must have someone to whom I can talk openly. Oh, I'm so unhappy!'

These words also she said with so expressionless a countenance that an onlooker out of earshot would have been persuaded she spoke of most trivial things.

'I did my best,' she went on. 'I bore it for a month. Then I couldn't do without him any longer. I feel like a woman in one of those old stories, under some love-spell so that no power of hers could help her. I suppose you'll say I'm a fool, but I think Isolde or Phèdre must have had just that same sensation. I haven't any will and I haven't any courage, and the worst is that the whole thing's so absolutely degrading. There's no reason why you shouldn't despise me, because I utterly despise myself. And Heaven knows what'll be the end of it; I feel that

168

something awful will happen. Some day or other Paul is certain to find out, and then it means ruin, and I shall have thrown away everything for such a miserable, poor-spirited cur.'

'Don't talk so loud,' said Miss Ley, for the other had slightly raised her voice. 'D'you think he'd marry you?'

'No; he's often told me he wouldn't. And I wouldn't marry him now; I know him too well. Oh, I wish I'd never seen him. He doesn't care two straws for me; he knows I'm in his power, and he treats me as if I were a woman off the streets. I've been so bitterly punished.'

Her eyes wandered across the room, and she saw Reggie talking to Mrs Murray.

'Look at him,' she said to Miss Ley. 'Even now I would give my soul for him to take me in his arms and kiss me. I wouldn't mind the danger, I wouldn't mind the shame, if he only loved me.'

Self-possessed and handsome, immaculately attired, Reggie chatted with the ease of a man of forty; his dark, lustrous eyes fixed on Mrs Murray, his red lips smiling sensually, indicated plainly enough that her beauty attracted him. Mrs Castillyon watched the pair with jealous rage and with agony.

'She's got every chance,' she muttered; 'she's a widow, and she's rich, and she's younger than I am. But I wouldn't wish my worst enemy the wretchedness of falling in love with that man.'

'But, good heavens! why don't you pull yourself together? Have you given up all thought of breaking with him?'

'Yes,' she answered desperately; 'I'm not going to struggle any more. Let come what may. It's not I that is concerned now, but fate. I won't leave him till he throws me aside like a toy he's tired of.'

'And what about your husband?'

'Paul? Paul's worth ten of the other. I didn't know his value till I was so unhappy.'

'Aren't you a little ashamed to treat him so badly?'

'I can't sleep at night for thinking of it. Every present he gives me is like a stab in my heart; every kindness is the bitterest anguish. But I can't help it.'

Miss Ley meditated for a moment.

'I've just been talking to Lady Vizard,' she said then. 'I suppose there's no one in London whom a pious person would more readily consign to eternal flames, and yet she looks upon herself as a very good woman indeed. Also I feel sure that our mutual friend, Reggie, has no qualms about any of his proceedings. It suggests to me that the only wicked people in the world are those who have consciences.'

'And d'you think I have a conscience?' asked Mrs Castillyon bitterly.

'Apparently. I never saw any trace of it till I met you at Rochester. But I suppose it was there in a rudimentary condition, and events have brought it to the front. Take care it doesn't get the better of you. I see a great danger staring you in the face.'

'What do you mean?'

Mrs Castillyon's face, notwithstanding the rouge, was haggard and white. Miss Ley looked at her with piercing keenness.

'Have you never thought of confessing the whole thing to your husband?'

'Oh, Miss Ley, Miss Ley, how did you guess that?'

In her uncontrollable agitation she forgot her self-control, and wrung her hands with anguish.

'Take care. Remember everyone can see you.'

'I forgot.' With an effort she regained her wonted ease of manner. 'It's been with me night and day. Sometimes, when Paul is good to me, I can hardly resist the temptation. Some awful fascination lures me on, and I know that one day I shan't be able to hold my tongue, and I shall tell him everything.'

During the last six months Mrs Castillyon had aged, and bitterly conscious of her failing beauty, resorted now to a more extravagant artifice; the colour of her hair was more obviously unnatural, she pencilled her eyebrows, and used too much paint on her cheeks. The unquiet of her manner had increased, so that it was somewhat painful to be with her. She talked more than ever, more loudly, and her laughter was shriller and more frequent; but the high spirits, which before were due to an entire unconcern for the world in general, now were deliberately assumed to conceal, if possible even from

170

herself, a most utter wretchedness. Life had been wont to go most smoothly. She had wealth to gratify every whim, admiration to give a sense of power, a position of some consequence; and she had never wanted anything so desperately that it was more than tiresome to do without it: but now, with no previous experience to guide her, she was beset on every side with harassing difficulties. This ardent passion had swept her off her feet, and the wakening was very bitter when she learnt that it was her turn to suffer. She had no illusions with regard to Reggie. He was immeasurably selfish, callous to her pain, and she had long since discovered that tears had no effect upon him. He meant to get his own way, and when she rebelled gave her the truth in brutal terms.

'If you don't like me, you can go to the devil. You're not the only woman in the world.'

But on the whole he was fairly good-humoured – it was his best quality – and she had a certain hold over him in his immense love of pleasure. She could always avoid his peevishness by taking him to the theatre; he was anxious to move in polite circles, and an invitation to some great house made him affectionate for a week. But he never allowed her to dictate, and an occasional display of jealousy was met with an indifferent cynicism which nearly drove her to distraction; besides, she was afraid of him, knowing that to save his own skin he would not hesitate to betray her. Yet, notwithstanding, she loved Reggie still so passionately that it affected her character. Mrs Castillyon, who had never sought to restrain herself, now took care to avoid causes of offence to the dissolute boy. She made herself complaisant so that he might not again throw in her face her age and waning charms; in bitter misery she learnt a gentleness and a self-control which before she had never known. In the general affairs of life she exhibited a new charity, and especially with her husband was less petulant. His sure devotion was singularly comforting, and she knew that in his eyes she was no less adorable than when first he loved her.

3

MISS LEY took care to learn at which hotel Bella meant to stay in Milan, and when the pair arrived, at the beginning of their honeymoon, they found awaiting them in their friend's neat and scholarly writing a little ironical letter, enclosing as wedding-present a cheque for five hundred pounds. This enabled them to travel more sumptuously than at first seemed possible, and meaning to spend the worst of the winter at Naples, without fearing the expense they could linger on their way in one charming town after another. Herbert was full of enthusiasm, and for a while seemed entirely to regain health. He forgot the disease which ate away silently his living tissue, and formed extravagant hopes for the future. His energy was such that Bella had much difficulty in restraining his eagerness to see the sights of which for so many years he had vainly dreamed. His passion for the sunshine, the blue skies and the flowers, was wonderful to see, yet Bella's heart ached often, though with greatest care she trained her countenance to cheerfulness, because this singular capacity for life to her anxious mind seemed to forebode a short continuance. He was gathering into one feverish moment all that others spread over a generation.

In the constant companionship his character unfolded itself, and she learnt how charming was his disposition, how sweet and unselfish his temper. Admiring him each day more ardently, she enjoyed his little airs of masculine superiority, for he would not consent to be treated as an invalid, and somewhat resented her motherly care. On the contrary, he was full of solicitude for her comfort, and took upon himself all necessary arrangements, the ordering of details and so forth, of which she would most willingly have relieved him. He had ingenuous ideas about a husband's authority, to which Bella, not without a sly amusement, delighted to submit. She knew herself stronger not only in health, but in character, yet it diverted her to fall in with his fancy that she was the weaker vessel. When she feared that Herbert would tire himself, she simulated fatigue, and then his anxiety, his self-reproach, were quite touching. He never forgot how great was his debt to Bella, and sometimes his gratitude brought tears to her eyes, so that she sought to persuade him nothing at all was due. Ignorant of the world, his behaviour formed chiefly on books, Herbert used his wife with the gallant courtesy of some Shakespearian lover, writing sonnets which to her mind rang with the very nobility of marital passion; and under the breath of his romantic devotion the dull years fell away from her heart, so that she felt younger and fairer and more gay. Her sobriety was coloured by a not unpleasing flippancy, and she leavened his strenuous enthusiasm with kindly banter. But as though the sun called out his own youth, dissipating the dark Northern humours, sometimes he was boyish as a lad of sixteen, and then, talking nonsense to one another, they shouted with laughter at their own facetiousness. The world, they say, is a mirror whereon, if you look smiling, joyous smiles are reflected; and thus it seemed to them as if the whole earth approved their felicity. The flowers bloomed to fit their happiness, and the loveliness of Nature was only a frame to their great content.

'D'you know, we began a conversation two months ago,' he said once, 'and we've never come to an end yet. I find you more interesting every day.'

'I am a very good listener, I know,' she answered, laughing. 'Nothing gives one a surer reputation for being a conversationalist.'

'It's no good saying spiteful things to me when you look like that,' he cried, for her eyes rested on him with the most caressing tenderness.

'I think you're growing very vain.'

'How can I help it when you're my wedded wife? And you're so absolutely beautiful.'

'What!' she exclaimed. 'If you talk such rubbish to me, I'll double your dose of cod-liver-oil.'

'But it's true,' he said eagerly, so that Bella, though she knew

173

her comeliness existed only in his imagination, flushed with delight. 'I love your eyes, and when I look into them I feel I have no will of my own. The other day in Florence you called my attention to someone who was good-looking, and she wasn't a patch on you!'

'Good heavens, I believe the boy's serious!' she cried, but her eyes filled with tears and her voice broke into a sob.

'What *is* the matter?' he asked, astonished.

'It's so good to be loved,' she answered. 'No one has ever said such things to me before, and I'm so ridiculously happy.'

But as though the gods envied their brief joy, when they arrived at Rome, Herbert, exhausted by the journey, fell desperately ill. The weather was cold, rainy, dismal; and each day when he awoke, and the shutters were thrown back, Herbert looked eagerly at the sky, but seeing that it remained grey and cloudy, with a groan of despair turned his face to the wall. Bella, too, watched with aching heart for the sunshine, thinking it might bring him at least some measure of health, for she had given up all hope of permanent recovery. The doctor explained the condition of the lungs. Since Frank's examination the left side, which before was whole, had become affected, and the disease seemed to progress with a most frightful rapidity.

But at length the weather changed, and the warm wind of February, that month of languor, blew softly over the old stones of Rome; the sky once again was blue with a colour more intense by reason of the fleecy clouds that swayed across its dome, whitely, with the grace of dancers. The Piazza di Spagna, upon which looked Herbert's window, was brilliant with many flowers; the models in their dress of the Campagna, lounged about Bernini's easy steps; and the savour of the country and the spring was wafted into the sick man's room.

He grew better quickly; his spirits, of late very despondent, now became extravagantly cheerful, and hating Rome, the scene of his illness, he was convinced that it only needed change of place to complete his recovery. He insisted so vehemently that Bella should take him down to Naples that the doctor agreed it would be better to go, and therefore, as soon as he could be moved, they went further South.

They arrived in Naples no longer a pair of light-hearted children, but a middle-aged woman, haggard with anxiety, and a dying youth. Herbert's condition betrayed itself in an entire loss of his old buoyancy, so that the new scenes among which he found himself aroused no new emotions. The churches of Naples, white and gold like a ballroom of the eighteenth century, fit places of worship to a generation whose faith was a flippant superstition, chilled his heart; the statues in the museum were but lifeless stones; and the view itself, the glorious crown of Italian scenery, left him indifferent. Herbert, whose enthusiasm had once been so facile, now, profoundly bored, remained listless at all he saw, and discovered in Naples only its squalor and its vicious brutality. But on the other hand a restless spirit seized him, so that he could not remain quietly where he was, and he desired passionately to travel still further afield. With an eager longing for the country which above all others – above Italy, even – had fired his imagination, he wished before he died to see Greece. Bella, fearing the exertion, sought to dissuade him, but for once found him resolute.

'It's all very well for you,' he cried. 'You have plenty of time before you. But I have only now. Let me go to Athens, and then I shan't feel that I have left unseen the whole of the beautiful world.'

'But think of the risk.'

'Let us enjoy the day. What does it matter if I die here, in Greece, or elsewhere? Let me see Athens, Bella. You don't know what it means to me. Don't you remember that photograph of the Acropolis I had in my room at Tercanbury? Every morning on waking I looked at it, and at night before blowing out my candle it was the last thing I saw. I know every stone of it already. I want to breathe the Attic air that the Greeks breathed; I want to look at Salamis and Marathon. Sometimes I longed for those places so enormously that it was physical pain. Don't prevent me from carrying out my last wish. After that you can do what you like with me.'

There was such yearning in his voice and such despair that Bella, much as she dreaded the journey, could not resist. The doctor at Naples warned her that at any time the catastrophe might occur, and she could no longer conceal from herself the frightful ravage of the disease. Herbert, according to the course of his illness, was at times profoundly depressed, and at others, when the day was fine or he had slept well, convinced that soon he would entirely recover. He thought then that if he could only get rid of the cough which racked his chest, he might grow perfectly well; and it was Bella's greatest torture to listen to his confident plans for the future. He wished to spend the summer at Vallombrosa among the green trees, and buying a guide-book to Spain, made out a tour for the following winter. With smiling countenance, with humorous banter, Bella was forced to discuss schemes which she knew Death would utterly frustrate.

'Two years in the South ought to put me quite right again,' he said once; 'and then we'll take a little house in Kent where we can see the meadows and the yellow corn, and we'll work together at all sorts of interesting things. I want to write really good poetry, not for myself any more, but for you. I want you never to think that you threw yourself away on me. Wouldn't it be glorious to have fame! Oh, Bella, I hope some day you'll be proud of me.'

'I shall have to keep a very sharp eye on you,' she answered, with a laugh that to herself sounded like a sob of pain: 'poets are notoriously fickle, and you're sure to philander with pretty milkmaids.'

'Oh, Bella, Bella,' he cried, with sudden feeling, 'I wish I were more worthy of you. Beside you I feel so utterly paltry and insignificant.'

'I dare say,' she replied ironically. 'But that didn't prevent you from writing a sonnet in Pisa about the ankles of a peasant woman.'

He laughed and blushed.

'You didn't really mind, did you? Besides, it was you who called my attention to the way she walked. If you like, I'll destroy it.'

Boylike, he took her mocking seriously, and was indeed half afraid he had annoyed her. She laughed again, more sincerely, but still her laughter rang softly with the tears that filled it.

'My precious child,' she cried, 'when will you grow up!'

'You wait till I'm well, and then you shall put on these airs at your peril, madam.'

Next morning, the spell of health continuing, he proposed that they should start at once for Brindisi, where they could wait one day, and then take the boat directly to Greece. Bella, who counted on making delay after delay till it was too late, was filled with consternation; but Herbert gave her no opportunity to thwart his will, for he said nothing to her till he had looked out the train, called for the bill, and given the hotel-keeper notice of his intention. Once started, his excitement was almost painful to see: his blue eyes shone and his cheeks were flushed: a new energy seemed to fill him, and he not only looked much better, but felt it.

'I tell you I shall get quite well as soon as I set my foot on the soil of Greece,' he cried. 'The immortal gods will work a miracle, and I will build a temple in their honour.'

He looked with beating heart at the country through which they sped, fresh and sunny in the spring, with vast green tracts spread widely on either side. on which browsed herds of cattle, shaggy-haired and timid. Now and again they saw a herdsman, a rifle slung across his back, wild and handsome and debonair; and finally – the trembling of the sea.

'At last!' the boy cried. 'At last!'

Next morning he was feverish and ill, and on the day after, notwithstanding his entreaties, Bella absolutely refused to start. He stared at her sullenly, with bitter disappointment.

'Very well.' he said at length. 'But next time you must promise to go whatever happens, even if I'm dying: you must have me carried on the boat.'

'I promise faithfully,' answered Bella.

A certain force of will gave him an imaginary strength, so that in a couple of days he was on his feet again; but the elation, which during a fortnight had upborne him, now was quite gone, and he was so silent that Bella feared he had not forgiven the delay on which she insisted. They were obliged to spend a week in Brindisi, that dull, sordid, populous town, and together wandered much about its tortuous and narrow streets. It pleased Herbert chiefly to go down to the port, for he loved the crowded ships, loading and unloading, and dreamt of their long voyages over the wild waste of the sea; and he loved the lounging sailormen, the red-sashed, swarthy porters, the urchins who played merrily on the quay. But the life which thrilled through them, one and all, caused him sometimes an angry despair; they seemed to possess such infinite power to enjoy things, and with all his heart he envied the poorest stoker because his muscles were like iron and his breathing free. The week passed, and on the afternoon before their boat sailed Herbert went out alone; but Bella, knowing his habits, was presently able to find him: he sat on a little hill, olive-clad, and overlooked the sea. He did not notice her approach, for his gaze, intent as though he sought to see the longed-for shores of Greece, was fixed upon the blue Ægean distance, and on his wan and wasted face was a pain indescribable.

'I'm glad you've come, Bella: I wanted you.'

She sat beside him, and taking her hand, his eyes wandered again to the far horizon. A fishing-boat, with a white, strange-shaped sail, sped like a fair sea-bird over the water's shining floor. The sky was a hard, hot blue like the lapis-lazuli, and not a cloud broke its serene monotony.

'Bella,' he said at last, 'I don't want to go to Greece. I haven't the courage.'

'What do you mean?' she asked, enormously surprised. All his thoughts had tended to this one object, and it seemed a sign of ill omen that when at length it lay within reach he should draw back.

'You thought I was angry because we didn't start last week. I tried to be, but in my heart I was glad of the respite. I was afraid. I've been trying to screw up my courage, but I can't.'

He did not look at her, but gazed straight out to sea.

'I daren't run the risk, Bella. I'm afraid to put my fancies to the test of reality. I want to keep my illusions. Italy has shown me that nothing is so lovely and enchanting as the image of it in my mind. Each time that something hasn't quite come up to my expectations I've said to myself that Greece would repay me

178

for everything. But now I know that Greece will have just the same disappointments, and I can't bear them. Let me die with the picture still in my heart of the long-beloved country as I have fancied it. What is it to me when fauns no longer scamper through the fields, and dryads aren't in the running brooks? It's not Greece I go to see, but the land of my ideal.'

'But, my dearest, there's no need to go. You know I'd much rather not,' cried Bella.

He looked at her at length, and his glance was long and searching. It seemed that he wished to speak, yet for some reason hesitated strangely. Then he made an effort.

'I want to go home, Bella,' he whispered. 'I feel I can't breathe here; the blue sky overwhelms me, and I long for the grey clouds of England. I didn't know I loved my country till I left it. . . . D'you think I'm an awful prig?'

'No, dear,' she answered, with choking voice.

'The clamour of the South tires my ears, and the colours are overbright, the air is too thin and too brilliant, the eternal sunshine blinds me. Oh, give me my own country again. I can't die down here; I want to be buried among my own people. I've never said a word to you, Bella, but lately I've lain awake at night thinking of the fat Kentish soil. I want to take it up in my hands, the cool, rich mould, and feel its coldness and its strength. When I look up at that blue fire, I think of my beautiful Kentish sky, so grey, so soft, so low; and I yearn for those rounded clouds, all pregnant with rain.'

His excitement was unbearable as the thoughts crowded upon him, and he pressed his hands to his eyes so that nothing should disturb.

'My mouth is parched for the spring showers. D'you know, we've not seen a drop of rain for a month. Now at Leanham and at Ferne the elm-trees and the oaks are all in leaf, and I love their fresh young green. There's nothing here like the green of the Kentish fields. Oh, I can feel the salt breeze of the North Sea blowing against my cheek, and in my nostrils are all the spring smells of the country. I must see the hedgerows once more, and I want to listen to the birds singing. I long for the cathedral with its old grey stones, and the dark, shady streets of Tercanbury. I want to hear English spoken around me; I want to see English faces. Bella, Bella, for God's sake take me home, or I shall die!'

There was such agony in his passionate appeal that Bella was more than ever alarmed. She thought he had some mysterious premonition of the end, and it was only with difficulty that she brought herself to utter words of consolation and of reassurance. They settled to start at once. Herbert, in his anxiety, wished to travel directly to London; but his wife, determined to take no risk that could possibly be avoided, insisted on going by very easy stages. Through the winter she had written every week to the Dean, telling him of their doings and the places they saw, but he had never once replied, and for news of him she had been forced to rely on friends in Tercanbury. Now she wrote to him immediately.

MY DEAREST FATHER,

My husband is dying, and I am bringing him home at his own wish. I do not know how long he can continue to live, but at the most I'm afraid it can only be a question of very few months. I beg you most earnestly to put aside your anger. Let us come to you. I have nowhere to take Herbert, and I cannot bear that he should die in a stranger's house. I beseech you to write to me at Paris.

Your affectionate daughter,

BELLA

Her first two letters the Dean had enough resolution not to open, but he could not grow used to his solitude, and each day missed more acutely his daughter's constant care. The house was very empty without her, and sometimes in the morning, forgetting what had happened, he expected when he went down to breakfast to find her as ever, alert and trim, at the head of his table. The third letter he could not resist, and afterwards, though his pride forbade him to answer, looked forward intensely to the weekly communication. Once, when by some chance it was two days delayed, he was so anxious that he went to a friend in the chapter whose wife, he knew, corresponded with Bella, and asked whether anything had been heard.

On opening this final note, the Dean was surprised to find it so short, for Bella, to comfort and interest him, was used to write a sort of diary of the week. He read it two or three times. He gathered first that Bella was on her way home, and if he liked might once more sit at his solitary table, go about the house gently as of old, and in the evening play to him the simple melodies he loved so well; but then he became aware of the restrained despair in those few hurried lines, and reading deeper than the words, understood for the first time her overwhelming love for that poor sick boy. From his daughter's letters the Dean had come to know Herbert somewhat intimately, for with subtle tenderness Bella related little traits which she knew would touch him, and for long he had struggled with an uneasy feeling of his own injustice. He remembered now the lad's youth and simplicity, that he was poor and ill, and his heart went out to him strangely. Contrition seized him. A portrait of his wife, dead for five-and-thirty years, hung in the Dean's study, showing her in the first year of marriage with the simpering air, the brown ringlets, of a middle Victorian young lady; and though a work of no merit, to the sorrowing husband it seemed a real masterpiece. He had often gathered solace and advice from those brown eyes, and now, pride and love contending in his breast, looked at it earnestly. The face seemed to wear an expression of reproach, and in mute self-abasement the Dean bent his head. The hungry had come to him, and he had given no meat; the stranger he had cast out, and the sick turned from his door.

'I have sinned against heaven and in Thy sight,' he mutttered painfully, 'and am no more worthy to be called Thy son.'

His eyes caught a photograph of Bella, which, for a while banished from the room, now again occupied its accustomed place, and as though to take her in his arms, he stretched his hands towards it. He smiled happily, for his mind was made up. Notwithstanding the words uttered in his wrath, he would go to Paris and bring home his daughter with her dying husband; and if in the last months of the boy's life he could make up for past harshness, perhaps it would be taken as some atonement for his cruel pride.

Announcing his intention to no one, the Dean set out at

once. He had no means to communicate with Bella, but knew the hotel to which she would go, and determined there to await her arrival. Finding at what hour she must reach it, he lingered in the hall, but twice was grievously disappointed. On the third day, however, when he began to feel the tension unbearable, a cab drove up, and trembling with excitement, he saw Bella step out. Desirous that she should not see him immediately, the Dean withdrew a little to one side. He noted the care with which she helped Herbert to get out of the cab: she took his arm to lead him in. He was apparently very weak, wrapped up to his eyes though the evening was warm, and while she asked for rooms he sat down in sheer exhaustion.

The Dean was very remorseful when he saw the change in him, for when last they met Herbert Field was full of spirits and gay; and these months of anxiety had left their mark on Bella also, whose hair was beginning to turn quite grey. Her expression was tired and wan. When they were gone upstairs, the Dean asked for the number of their room, but to give them time to get off their things, forced himself to wait half an hour by the clock. Then, going up, he knocked at the door. Bella, thinking it was a maid, called out in French.

'Bella,' he said in a low voice, and he remembered how once she had begged to be admitted to his study and he had refused.

With a cry she flung open the door, and in a moment they were clasped in one another's arms; he pressed her to his heart, but in his emotion found no word to say. She drew him in eagerly.

'Herbert, here's my father.'

The youth was lying on the bed in the next room, and Bella led the Dean in. Herbert was too tired to rise.

'I've come to take you both home,' said the old man, tears of joy in his voice.

'Oh, father, I'm so glad. You're not angry with me any longer. It'll make me so happy if you forgive me.'

'It's not you that need forgiveness, but I, Bella. I want to ask your husband to pardon my unkindness. I've been harsh and proud and cruel.'

He went to Herbert and took his hand.

'Will you forgive me, my dear? Will you allow me to be your father as well as Bella's?'

'I shall be very grateful.'

'And will you come back to Tercanbury with me? I should like you to know that so long as I live my home will be yours. And I will try and make you forget that I was ever –'

The Dean broke off with a gesture of appeal, unable to finish.

'I know you're very good,' smiled Herbert, 'and you see I have brought Bella back to you.'

The Dean hesitated a moment shyly, then bent down and very tenderly kissed the pale, suffering lad.

4

SOME days after the party at Lady Edward Stringer's Basil went to Brighton, and was met at the station by Jenny and her sister. Sending the traps by porter, they set out for the lodgings, but were quickly joined by a very smart young man, introduced to Basil as Mr Higgins, who paired off with Annie Bush. When they had gone ahead, Basil asked who he was.

'He's Annie's latest,' answered Jenny, laughing.

'Have you known him long?'

'We got to know him the second day we were down. I noticed him look at us, and I said to Annie: "There you are, my dear; there's company for you when Basil comes, because I can't stick walking three in a row." '

'Who introduced him to you?'

'What a silly you are!' laughed Jenny. 'He just came up and said good evening, and Annie said good evening, and then he began to talk. He seems to have lots of money. He took us to a concert last night, to the best places. It was nice of him, wasn't it?'

'But, my dear child, you can't go about with people you don't know.'

'You must let Annie enjoy herself, and he's a very respectable young fellow, isn't he? You see, living at home, she hasn't the opportunity to get to know men that I had. And he's quite a gentleman.'

'Is he? I should have thought him a most awful bounder.'

'You're so particular,' said Jenny. 'I don't see anything wrong in him.'

Arriving at the lodging-house, Annie, engaged in lively conversation with her new acquaintance, stopped till the others came up. She resembled Jenny as much as it was possible for a somewhat plain woman to resemble a beautiful. She had the same graceful figure, but her hair, arranged with needless elaboration, was colourless, and her complexion had not the mellow delicacy which distinguished her elder.

'Jenny,' she cried, 'he won't come in to tea because he says you want to be alone with your hubby. Tell him it's all right.'

'Of course it's all right,' said Jenny. 'You come in and take a cup of tea with us, and then we'll all go on the front.'

He was evidently a facetious person, for while Basil washed he heard the two women in the adjoining room shout with uproarious merriment. Presently Jenny called out that tea was ready, and somewhat against his will, he was forced to go in. His wife, much better in health, talking and laughing loudly, was in high spirits; and the three had evidently enjoyed thoroughly the last two weeks, for they were full of remembered jokes. Basil, annoyed by the stranger's intrusion, sought not to join in the conversation, but sat silently, and after a while took up a newspaper. Annie gave him an angry glance, and Mr Higgins looked once or twice uncertainly, but then went on with his rapid string of anecdote. Perhaps he also had cause for irritation, since his best stories were heard by Basil with all the appearance of profound boredom.

'Well, who says a stroll on the parade?' he cried at last.

'Come on, Jenny,' answered Annie Bush, and turned to Basil. 'Are you coming?'

He looked up from his paper indifferently.

'No; I have some letters to write.'

Jenny preferred to remain with her husband, and, once alone, they talked for a time of domestic affairs; but there seemed a certain constraint between them, and presently Basil began to read. When Annie, after some while, came back, she glanced at him aggressively.

'Better?' she asked.

'What?'

'I thought you didn't seem well at tea.'

'Thanks, I'm in the best of health.'

'You might make yourself obliging, then, instead of sitting there like a funeral-mute when I have a gentleman to visit me.'

'I'm sorry my behaviour doesn't meet with your approval,' he answered quietly.

'Mr Higgins says he won't come here till your husband's taken himself off, my dear. He says he knows where he's not wanted, and I don't blame him, either.'

'Oh, Annie, what nonsense!' cried Mrs Kent. 'Basil was only tired.'

'Yes, a journey to Brighton's very tiring, isn't it? I tell you straight, Basil, I expect my friends to be treated like gentlemen.'

'You're an amiable creature, Annie,' he answered, shrugging his shoulders.

After supper Annie waited somewhat impatiently till the servant came in to say that Mr Higgins was at the door; then hurriedly put on her hat. Basil hesitated for one moment, unwilling to give offence, but decided that some word of warning was necessary.

'I say, Annie, d'you think you ought to go out alone at night with a man you've picked up casually on the pier?'

'What I do is no business of yours, is it?' she answered angrily. 'I'd thank you to give me your advice when I ask for it.'

'Shall I come with you, Annie?' said her sister.

'Now, don't you interfere. I can look after myself, as you know very well.'

She went out, vindictively slamming the door, and Basil, without another word, a frown on his brow, returned to his book. But in a little while he heard that Jenny was crying very quietly.

'Jenny, Jenny, what's the matter?' he exclaimed.

'Oh, nothing,' she answered, drying her eyes and doing her best to smile. 'Only I've been having such a good time down here; I only wanted you to make it perfect. I did look forward so to your coming, and now you've upset everything.'

'I'm very sorry,' he sighed, with complete discouragement.

He did not know what to say nor how to comfort her, for he realized, too, that his appearance had disturbed her enjoyment, and for all his goodwill he appeared able to bring her only unhappiness. She was most herself in the company of such as Mr Higgins; her greatest pleasure was to walk on the parade, staring at the people, or to listen to nigger-minstrels' sentimental ditties; she wanted gaiety and noise and garish colour. On the other hand, things which affected him painfully left her unmoved, and she was perfectly content in the sordid, vulgar lodging which overwhelmed him with disgust. It seemed that he was in a labyrinth of cross-purposes wherefrom was no issue.

Next morning occurred a trifling incident which showed Basil how his wife regarded him. Annie, dressed for church, came downstairs in a costume which was positively outrageous, so that one wondered at the perverse ingenuity with which the colours were blended; and she wore much cheap finery.

'Well, my dear, you're never going out like that!' she cried, seeing that Jenny was no differently attired from the day before. (An antipathy to Sunday clothes was to his wife one of Basil's most incomprehensible fads.) 'Aren't you going to put on your new hat?'

Mrs Kent looked somewhat uneasily at her husband.

'I saw such a smart hat in a shop, Basil, and Annie simply made me buy it. And I must say it was dirt cheap – only six and eleven.'

'This is evidently an occasion to put it on,' he smiled.

In a few minutes she came back, radiant and flushed, but Basil could not persuade himself that her headgear was cheap at the price.

'D'you like it?' she asked anxiously.

'Very much,' he replied, wishing to please.

'There, Jenny, I knew he wouldn't mind. If you heard all the fuss she made about your being angry and not liking it, and I don't know what all!'

'Basil says I look best in black,' said Jenny in self-defence.

'Men never know what's dressy, my dear,' Annie answered. 'If you went by what Basil said, you would be a dowd.'

It was rather distressing to find that his wife still somewhat feared him. In her eyes, apparently, he was a bearish creature whose whimsical fancies must be humoured, and he thought bitterly of the confidence which he hoped would exist between them, of the complete union in which not a thought nor an emotion should be unshared. And knowing that his own love was long since dead, Basil sought to persuade himself that hers also was on the wane. The week-end bored him immensely, and it was not without relief that he found himself on Monday morning at the station, whither his wife accompanied him.

'I'm awfully busy; I don't know whether I can manage to come down next Saturday,' he said tentatively.

But Jenny's eyes filled on a sudden with tears.

'Oh, Basil, Basil, I can't live without you! I'd rather come up to town. If you don't like Annie, she can go away. Promise me you'll come. I look forward to it all the week.'

'You'll have a very good time without me. I've only made you wretched by my visit.'

'No, you haven't. I want you so badly. I'd rather be utterly unhappy with you than happy without. Promise me you'll come.'

'All right. I will.'

The chains that bound him were as fast as ever. And as the train sped towards London his heart beat madly because each minute he drew nearer to Hilda Murray. It was very plain now that he loved her passionately, more than ever he had done, and with violent rage he told himself that she was lost to him for always. Intoxicated by the ring of her voice, by the sweep of her dress, by the tender look in her eyes, he repeated every word she had said at Lady Edward's. On Wednesday he was to dine with Miss Ley, and already he felt sick with hope at the thought of meeting Hilda. In the afternoon, leaving chambers, he went home by way of Charles Street, and like a lover of eighteen, looked up at her windows. There were lights in the drawing-room, so that he knew she was at home, but he dared not go in. Mrs Murray had not asked him to visit her, and he could not tell whether she had no wish to see him, or whether she thought a call so obvious as to need no special invitation. The windows seemed to beckon, the very door offered a mute welcome; but while he lingered someone came out, Mr Farley, and Basil wondered angrily why he should go to that house so often. At length with a desperate effort he walked away.

Though Basil went on Wednesday to Miss Ley almost trembling with excitement, he managed to ask gaily who was expected to dinner, but his heart sank when she made no mention of Mrs Murray. Then he wondered how to pass the dreariness of that evening to which he had so enormously looked forward. Since the meeting at Lady Edward Stringer's, the passion, hitherto dormant, had blazed into such a vehement flame that he could scarcely bear himself. It seemed impossible to live through the week without seeing Hilda; he could think of nothing else, and foresaw with sheer horror his excursion on Saturday to Brighton. Of course it was madness, and he knew well enough it was no use to see Mrs Murray again – it would have been better if they had never met; but the sound sense which he preached to himself seemed folly, and his eagerness to see her overcame all prudence. He thought there could be no harm in speaking to her just once more, only once, after which he vowed entirely to forget her.

Next day he walked again through Charles Street, and again saw the light in her windows. He hesitated, walking up and down. He could not tell if she wished any longer to know him, and feared horribly to discern on her face that he intruded, but at length in sullen anger decided to adventure. He could not love Hilda more if he saw her, and perhaps by some miracle the sight might console him, helping him to bear his captivity. He rang.

'Is Mrs Murray at home?'

'Yes, sir.'

She was reading when he entered the room, and with dismay Basil fancied that a very slight look of vexation crossed her eyes. It disconcerted him so that he could think of nothing to say. Then he imagined that his behaviour must astonish her, and asked himself whether she knew the cause of his sudden marriage. He listened to the polite or flippant things she said, and did his best to answer fittingly; but his words sounded so unnatural that he scarcely recognized his voice. Yet they laughed and jested as though neither had a care in the world; they spoke of Miss Ley and of Frank, of the plays then to be seen in London, of one trivial topic after another, till Basil was forced to go.

'I came in fear and trembling,' he said gaily, 'because you certainly never asked me to call.'

'I thought it wasn't needful,' she answered, smiling; but she looked straight into his eyes with an odd air of defiance.

Basil flushed, glancing at her quickly, for there seemed a double meaning in her words, and he knew not how to take them. He lost momentarily his urbane, courteous manner.

'I wanted so much to come and see you,' he said, in a low voice, which he strove to keep firm. 'May I come again?'

'Of course!' she replied; but her tone was full of cold surprise, as though she wondered at his question and resented it.

Suddenly she found his eyes fixed upon her with such an expression of deadly anguish that she was troubled. His face was very white, and his lips twitched as though he sought to command himself. All through the night she thought of that look of utter agony; it stared at her from the darkness, and she knew that if she needed revenge the fates had given it. But she was not pleased. For the hundredth time, unable to get it out of her head that he loved her still, she asked herself why he had married so strangely; but she would not inquire into her own feelings. She tightened her lips.

Knowing well that he would come again, it was Mrs Murray's impulse to tell the butler not to admit him; but something, she knew not what, prevented her. She wished to observe once more the terrible wretchedness of his face; she wished to make sure that he was not happy in what seemed his cruel treachery. One afternoon of the following week, coming in from a drive, she found his card. She took it in her hand and turned it over.

'Shall I ask him to luncheon?' With a frown of annoyance she put it down. 'No; if he wants to see me, let him come again.'

Basil was bitterly disappointed that day when the servant said that Mrs Murray was not at home, and at first determined that there he must leave it. He waited for a note, but none came. He waited for a week, able to do nothing but think of her, restless and preoccupied. With stricken conscience he went to Brighton, and so far as possible avoided to be alone with

Jenny. He took her to a play one night, to a concert the next, and insisted that Mr Higgins, still faithful, should be constantly with them; but the whole thing disgusted him, and he felt utterly ashamed.

Then he made it a practice every evening to take Charles Street on his way to Frank, and ever the windows appeared to invite him. When he looked back, the whole street beckoned, and at length he could resist no longer. He knew that Mrs Murray was in. If the butler sent him away it must be taken as definite, for it would mean that Hilda had given orders he was not to be admitted.

This time better fortune was his, but when he saw her the many things on the tip of his tongue seemed impossible of utterance, and it was an effort to speak commonplace. Mrs Murray was disconcerted by the look of pain which darkened his face, and the constraint between them made conversation very difficult. Basil dared not prolong his visit, yet it was dreadfully hard to go leaving unspoken all that lay so heavily on his heart. Talk flagged, and presently silence fell upon them.

'When is your book to be published?' she asked, oppressed, she knew not why.

'In a fortnight. . . . I wanted to thank you for your help.'

'Me!' she cried, with surprise. 'What have I done?'

'More than you know. I felt sometimes as if I were writing for you only. I judged of everything by what I thought would be your opinion of it.'

Mrs Murray, somewhat embarrassed, did not answer. He looked away, as though forcing himself to speak, but nervous.

'You know, it seems to me as though everyone were surrounded by an invisible ring which cuts him off from the rest of the world. Each of us stands entirely alone, and each step one must judge for one's self, and none can help.'

'D'you think so?' she answered. 'If people only knew, they would be so ready to do anything they could.'

'Perhaps, but they never know. The things about which it's possible to ask advice are so unimportant. There are other things, in which life and death are at stake, about which a man can never say a word; yet if he could it would alter so much.'

191

He turned and faced her gravely. 'A man may have acted in a certain way, causing great pain to someone who was very dear to him, yet if all the facts were known that person might – excuse and pardon.'

Mrs Murray's heart began to beat, and she had some difficulty in preserving the steadiness of her voice.

'Does it much matter? In the end everyone resigns himself. I think an onlooker who could see into human hearts would be dismayed to find how much wretchedness there is which men bear smiling. We should all be very gentle to our fellows if we realized how dreadfully unhappy they were.'

Again there was silence, but strangely enough, the barrier between them appeared suddenly to have fallen, and now, though neither spoke, there was no discomfort. Basil got up.

'Good-bye, Mrs Murray. I'm glad you let me come today.'

'Why on earth shouldn't I?'

'I was afraid your servant would say you weren't at home.'

He looked at her steadily, as though meaning to say far more than was expressed in the words.

'I shall always be very glad to see you,' she answered, in a low voice.

'Thank you.'

A look of deep gratitude softened away the pain on his face.

At that moment Mrs Barlow-Bassett was announced. She shook hands with Basil somewhat coldly, thinking that a man who had married a barmaid could be no proper companion for her virtuous son, and she determined not to renew the old acquaintance. He went out.

'D'you know whom Mr Kent married, and why?' asked Mrs Murray.

The question had been often on her lips, but pride till this moment had ever prevented her from making an effort to clear up a difficulty which had long puzzled her.

'My dear Hilda, don't you know? It's a most shocking story. I must say I was surprised to find him here, but of course, if you didn't know, that explains it. He got into trouble with some dreadfully low creature.'

'She's very beautiful. I've seen her.'

192

'You?' cried Mrs Bassett, with astonishment. 'It seems there was going to be a baby, and he was forced to marry.'

Mrs Murray blushed to the roots of her hair, and for one moment bitter anger blazed in her heart. Again she told herself that she hated and loathed him, but remembering on a sudden the woe in his eyes, knew it was no longer true.

'D'you think he's very unhappy?'

'He must be. When a man marries beneath him he's always unhappy, and I must say I think he deserves it. I told my boy the whole story as a warning. It just shows what comes of not having good principles.'

Mrs Murray's eyes dwelt on the speaker absently, as though she thought of other things.

'Poor fellow! I'm afraid you're right. He is very unhappy.'

5

In his distress Basil could scarcely bear the thought of resuming his old life at Barnes, so unprofitable to the spirit, mean and illiberal; and though ill able to afford it, pretexting Jenny's health, he insisted that she should remain at Brighton longer than was at first intended. But at length she was evidently quite well, and no persuasions of Basil could induce her to prolong her visit. They returned to the little house in River Gardens, and outwardly things went very much as in the past. Yet certain differences there were. They seemed more strange to one another after the temporary separation, and on each side trifles arose occasionally to embitter their relations. Basil observed his wife now in a more critical spirit, and certain little vulgarities which before had escaped him now set his teeth on edge. He thought that the company of her sister for two months had affected her somewhat badly. She used expressions which he found objectionable, and he could not help it if her manners at table offended his fastidious taste. He loathed the slovenly way with which she conducted her household affairs, and the carelessness of her dress. Though what she bought was ever in outrageous taste, indoors she took no pains to be even tidy, and spent most of the day in a dirty dressing-gown, with bedraggled hair. But since alteration seemed impossible, Basil determined rather to ignore things, leading his own life apart, and allowing Jenny to lead hers. When she did anything of which he disapproved, he merely shrugged his shoulders and pursed his lips. He grew much more silent, and did not now attempt to discuss with her matters wherein he was aware she took no interest.

But he had reckoned without his wife's passionate affection, no less than when first they married. Realizing the change in him, of which the causes were to her quite incomprehensible, Jenny was profoundly disturbed. Sometimes she wept helplessly, wondering what she had done to lose his love, and at others, conscious of his injustice, broke irritably into sharp speeches. She resented his reserve, and the indifference with which he put aside her questions on topics which before he would have eagerly discussed. Brooding over all this, she concluded that only a woman could have wrought this difference, and remembered on a sudden her mother's advice to keep a sharp eye on him. Basil one morning told her that he was dining out that day. He had accepted the invitation before he knew she would be back.

'Who with?' asked Jenny, quickly suspicious.

'Mrs Murray.'

'Your lady friend who came down here to see you last year?'

'She came to see *you*,' replied Basil, smiling.

'Yes, I believe that. I don't think a married man ought to go dining in the West End by himself.'

'I'm sorry. I've accepted the invitation, and I must go.'

Jenny did not answer, but when Basil came home in the afternoon watched him. She saw how restless he was. His eyes shone with excitement, and he looked at his watch a dozen times to see if it were time to dress. The moment he was gone, determined to find out on what terms he was with Mrs Murray, and hindered by no scruple, she went to the pockets of the coat he had just taken off, but his pocket-book was not there. A little surprised, for he was careless about such things, she thought there might be a letter in the desk, and with beating heart went to it. But it was locked, and this unaccustomed precaution doubled her suspicions. Remembering that there was a duplicate key, she fetched it, and on opening the drawer at once came upon a note signed *Hilda Murray*. It began with *Dear Mr Kent*, and ended *Yours Sincerely* – a merely formal invitation to dinner. Jenny glanced through the other letters, but they related to business matters. She replaced them in the old order and locked the drawer. She felt sick with shame now that she had actually done this thing.

'Oh, how he'd despise me!' she cried.

And in terror lest she had left any trace of her interference, she opened the drawer again, and once more smoothed out and tidied everything. Basil had asked her not to wait up for him, but she could not go to bed. She looked at the clock, ticking so slowly, and with something like rage told herself that Basil all this time enjoyed himself, and never thought of her. When he came home, flushed and animated, she fancied that a look of annoyance crossed his face when he saw her still sitting in the armchair.

'Are you very sleepy?' he asked.

'Yes.'

'Why don't you go to bed? I'm just going to have one more pipe.'

'I'll wait till you're ready.'

She watched him walk up and down the room, excited with his thoughts, and he never spoke to her. He seemed to have forgotten that she was present. Then rage and jealousy overcame all other feelings.

'All right, my young fellow,' she whispered to herself, 'I'll find out if there's anything in this.'

She had taken note of Mrs Murray's writing, and thenceforward examined closely the addresses of all letters that came for him, to see if one was written by her. Basil had been used to leave his correspondence lying about, but now took care to lock up everything, and this convinced her that he had something to conceal. But she flattered herself, with a little bitter laugh, that she was fairly sharp, and he did not know that every day after he went out she ransacked his desk. Though she never found anything, Jenny was none the less assured that there were good grounds for her jealousy. One morning she noticed that he was dressed in new clothes, and it flashed across her mind that in the afternoon he meant to see Mrs Murray. It seemed to her that if he actually went it would be a confirmation of her fears, while if not she could put aside all these tormenting fancies. Knowing at what time he left chambers, Jenny, veiled and dressed soberly, that she might not attract his attention, took up her stand in good time on the other side of the square, and waited. Presently he came out, and she followed. She followed him sauntering down the Strand, she followed him to Piccadilly Circus, and here was obliged to come a little closer, for fear of losing him in the throng. On a sudden he wheeled round and quickly strode up to her. She gave a stifled cry, and then, seeing his face white with rage, was overwhelmed with shame.

'How dare you follow me, Jenny?'

'I wasn't following you. I didn't see you.'

He called a cab, and told her to get in, jumped up, and bade the driver go to Waterloo. They were just in time to catch a train to Barnes. He did not speak to her, and she watched him in frightened silence. He said no word during the walk back to the house. They went to the drawing-room, and he closed the door carefully.

'Now will you have the goodness to tell me what you mean by this?' he asked.

She gave no answer, but looked down in sullen anger.

'Well?'

'I won't be bullied,' she answered.

'Look here, Jenny, we had better understand one another. Why have you been going to my drawer and reading my letters?'

'You've got no right to accuse me of that. It's not true.'

'You leave my desk in such disorder when you've been to it.'

'Well, I've got a right to know. Where were you going to-day?'

'That is absolutely no business of yours. I'm simply ashamed that you should do such horrible things. Don't you know that nothing is so disgraceful as to follow anyone in the street, and I'd sooner you stole than read private letters.'

'I'm not going to stand by and let you run after other women, so you needn't think I am.'

He gave a laugh, partly of scorn, partly of disgust.

'Don't be absurd. We're married, and we must make the best of it. You may be quite sure that I'll give you no cause for reproach.'

'You're always after your fine friends that I'm not good enough for.'

'Good heavens!' he cried bitterly, 'you can't grudge me a little relaxation. It surely does you no harm if sometimes I go and see the people I knew intimately before my marriage?'

197

Jenny did not answer, but pretended to order anew flowers in a vase; then she smoothed down cushions on the sofa and set a picture straight.

'If you've done preaching at me, I'll go and take off my hat,' she said at length viciously.

'You may do exactly as you choose,' he answered, with cold indifference.

Shortly after this Basil's novel was published. Knowing that it could not interest her, and conscious of her small sympathy, he gave a copy to Jenny somewhat shyly, but said no more than the truth when he wrote to Mrs Murray that great part of his pleasure in the book's appearance lay in the fact that he was able to send it to her. He waited for her letter of thanks with as much anxiety as for the first reviews. She wrote twice, first to acknowledge the receipt and say that she had already read a chapter; then, having finished, to bestow enthusiastic praise. Her appreciation lifted him to a very heaven of delight. When Jenny, after an obvious struggle, reached the last page, he waited for some criticism, but since none came, was forced to ask what she thought.

'I liked it very much,' she said.

But there was in her tone an unconcern which not a little incensed him, and though he knew this indifference pointed to no particular fault in his book, he was none the less profoundly humiliated. Yet a bitterer disappointment awaited him in the reviews which now began to come in. For the most part they were short, somewhat scornful, somewhat patronizing, and it appeared that this book, which he had imagined would raise him at once to a literary position of some eminence, was no more than prentice work, showing more promise than performance. Its merits, indeed, were not few, but scarcely such as to excite any sudden admiration; his construction was faulty, and in parts his attention to the environment suggested rather the essay or the treatise. The result, notwithstanding many qualities, was neither very good romance nor very good history. Two literary papers at length offered salve to his wounded vanity in long and appreciative notices, doing full justice to his passion for beauty, his measured and careful style, the clear-cut perfection of his portraits. The first of these was sent him with a note of congratulation by Mrs Murray, and he read it with leaping heart. It gave him new confidence, and a firmer resolution to do better in future. But though careful to hand over to Jenny all unfavourable criticisms, these, which from a literary standpoint were more important than all the others put together, with a kind of inverted pride he forbore to show.

The consequence of this was that Jenny gained a rather false impression of the book's failure, and the idea came that Basil, after all, was perhaps not such a wonderful person as once she fancied. She sought not to analyse her feelings, but had she done so would have found in them a strange medley. She adored Basil passionately, jealously, but at the same time felt against him a sort of confused irritation which made her welcome the published sneers that wounded him so keenly; they seemed to draw him down to her, for if he was less clever than at first she thought it lessened the distance between them. Yet the gulf which separated them grew daily greater, and quarrels were of more frequent occurrence. Basil, hating his life at Barnes, wrapped himself in a reserve which he strove to make impenetrable; he was very silent, going about his work methodically, and doing his best to avoid the acrimonious discussions which Jenny forced upon him. He tried to relieve his unhappiness with unceasing toil, and to counter his wife's ill-temper with philosophic indifference. It drove her to furious anger that, however she taunted, he seldom replied, and then only with cold sarcasm. But sometimes remorse seized her. Then she went to her husband in tears, begging him to forgive and asserting again her great love; and this for some days would be followed by a measure of peace.

But one morning a more serious quarrel arose, for Basil, somewhat pressed for money, had discovered that James Bush, still out of work, was steadily borrowing from Jenny. He had begged her not to lend any more, and finding her unwilling to give a promise, was obliged somewhat peremptorily to insist that not another penny should go into the grasping hands of the Bush family. On both sides there was a good deal of irritation, and finally Basil flung out of the house. Presently James Bush, cause of all the trouble, sauntered in.

'Where's his lordship this afternoon?' he asked, helping himself to Basil's cigarettes.

'He's gone out for a walk.'

'That's what he tells you, my dear,' he answered with a malevolent laugh.

'Have you seen him anywhere?' asked Jenny quickly, full of suspicion.

'No, I can't say I 'ave, an' if I 'ad I wouldn't boast about it.'

'What did you mean, then?' she insisted.

'Well, whenever I come here he's out for a walk.'

He glanced at her, and then without more ado asked for the loan of a couple of sovereigns; but Jenny, mindful of the morning's dispute, and regretfully conscious that herself had brought it about, firmly refused. Since he insisted, accusing her of meanness, she was forced to explain how heavy of late had been their expenses; the doctor had sent in a bill for fifty pounds, the visit to Brighton cost a great deal, and they would have much difficulty to make both ends meet.

'It was a wonderful fine thing you did when you married him, Jenny, and you thought you'd done precious well for yourself too.'

'I won't have you say anything against him,' she cried impetuously.

'All right; keep your shirt in. I'm blowed if I know what you've got to stick up for him about. He don't care much about you.'

She looked up with a quick drawing-in of breath.

'How d'you know?'

'Think I can't see!' He chuckled slily at his own acuteness. 'I suppose you 'aven't been crying today?'

'We had a little tiff this morning,' she answered. 'Oh, don't say he doesn't care for me. I couldn't live.'

'Go along with you,' he laughed. 'Basil Kent ain't the only pebble on the beach.'

Jenny went to the window and looked out. She saw her husband walk slowly along, his head bent down, betraying in his whole appearance the most profound depression, and thinking of their wretchedness, she could not restrain her tears. Everything went against them, and though loving him so tenderly, some mysterious power seemed ever to force her to anger him. With entire despair she turned to her brother and spoke words which had long been in her heart, but which till then she had not uttered to a living soul.

'Oh, Jimmie, Jimmie, sometimes I don't know which way to turn, I'm that unhappy. If the baby had only lived, I might have kept my husband – I might have made him love me.'

She sank on a chair and hid her face, but in a moment, hearing the door close, looked up.

'He's just come in, Jimmie. Mind you don't say anything to put him out.'

'I'd just like to give 'im a piece of my mind.'

'Oh, Jimmie, don't. It was my fault that we quarrelled this morning. I wanted to make him angry, and I nagged at him.' She knew the best way to influence her brother. 'Don't let him see that I've said anything to you, and I'll try and send you a pound tomorrow.'

'Well, he'd better not start patronizing me, because I won't put up with it. I'm a gentleman, and every bit as good as he is, if not better.' At this Basil came in, noticed James, but did not speak. ' 'Afternoon, Basil.'

'You here again?' he remarked indifferently.

'Looks like it, don't it?'

'I'm afraid it does.'

'Are you? I suppose I can come and see my own sister.'

'I suppose it's inevitable. Only I should be excessively grateful if you'd time your coming with my going, and *vice versa.*'

'That means you want me to get out, I reckon.'

'You show unusual perspicacity, dear James,' said Basil with a frigid smile.

'Look here, Basil, let me give you a bit of advice. Don't put on quite so much side, or you'll hurt yourself.'

'I observe that you have not acquired the useful art of being uncivil without being impertinent.'

There was nothing James could brook less easily than the

201

irony and the deliberate sarcasm with which Basil invariably answered him, and now in his exasperation, forgetting all prudence, he jumped up.

'Look 'ere, I've 'ad about enough of this. I'm not going to stand you sneerin' and snarlin' at me when I come here. You seem to think I'm nobody. I should just like to know why you go on as if I was I don't know what.'

'Because I choose,' answered Basil, looking him up and down with chilling scorn.

Jenny's heart beating furiously as she foresaw the approaching quarrel and in an undertone, hurriedly, she begged James to hold his tongue. But he would not be restrained.

'You can bet anything you like I don't come 'ere to see you.'

'It has been borne in upon me that the length of my purse attracts you more than the charm of my conversation. I wonder why you imagined, because I married your sister, I was bound to support the whole gang of you for the rest of your lives? Would you have the intense amiability to inform your family that I'm sick and tired of giving money?'

'I wonder you don't forbid us your house while you're about it,' snarled James.

Basil shrugged his shoulders.

'You may come here when I'm not at home – if you behave yourself.'

'I'm not good enough for you, I suppose?'

'No, you're not,' answered Basil, with deliberation.

'I dare say you'd like to get me out of the way. But I mean to keep my eye on you.'

'What d'you mean by that?' asked Basil, so sharply that James saw he had touched him on the raw.

He pursued his advantage.

'You think I don't know what sort of a feller you are. I can just about see through two of you. Jenny has something to put up with, I lay.'

But Basil recovered himself quickly, and turned to Jenny with a smile of contempt, which, since it was undeserved, most deeply wounded her.

'Has she been telling you my numerous faults? You must

202

have had plenty to talk about, my dear.' He saw her motion of protest, and gave a laugh. 'Oh, my dear girl, if it amuses you, by all means discuss me with your relations. I should be so dull if I had no failings.'

'Tell him I've not said anything against him, Jimmie,' she cried.

'It's not for want of something to say, I'll be bound.'

Basil was growing bored, and saw no reason for concealing the fact. He sat down at his desk to write a letter, and took a sheet of note-paper. Jimmie watched him viciously, smarting under the bitter things the other had said, and wondering what the next move would be. Basil glanced at him indifferently.

'I'm getting rather tired, brother James. I'd go if I were you.'

'I shan't go till I choose,' answered Bush very aggressively.

Basil looked up with a smile.

'Of course, we're both of us Christians, dear James, and there's a good deal of civilization kicking about the world nowadays. But the last word is still with the strongest.'

'What d'you mean by that?'

'Merely that discretion is the better part of valour. They say that proverbs are the wealth of nations.'

'That's just the sort of thing you'd do – to 'it a feller smaller than yourself.'

'Oh, I wouldn't hit you for worlds,' laughed Basil bitterly. 'I should merely throw you downstairs.'

'I should just like to see you try it on,' cried the other, edging a little towards the door.

'Don't be silly, James. You know you wouldn't like it at all.'

'I'm not afraid of you.'

'Of course not. But still – you're not very muscular, are you?'

Rage driving away prudence, James shook his fist in Basil's face.

'Oh, I'll pay you out before I've done. I'll pay you out.'

'James, I told you to get out five minutes ago,' said Basil, in a more peremptory fashion.

Jimmie looked at him for one moment, furious and impotent; then, without another word, flung out of the room, slamming the door behind him. Basil smiled quietly and shrugged his shoulders. He felt almost as disgusted with himself as with James, but supposed that as such scenes grew more frequent he would acquire a certain callousness. In his self-contempt he told himself that without doubt the time would come when he would be proud of his triumph in repartee over an auctioneer's clerk. He glanced at Jenny, who sat with sewing in her hands, but without working gazed straight out of the window.

'The only compensation in brother James is that he causes one a little mild amusement,' he murmured.

'I don't know what's wrong with him,' she answered. 'Why d'you treat him as if he was a dog?'

'My dear child, I don't. I'm very fond of dogs.'

'Isn't he as good as I am? And you condescended to marry me.'

'I really can't see that because I married you I must necessarily take the whole of your amiable family to my bosom.'

'Why don't you like them? They're honest and respectable.'

Basil gave a little sigh of fatigue. They had discussed the matter often during the last month, and though he did his best to curb his tongue, his patience was nearly exhausted.

'My dear Jenny,' he said, 'we don't choose our friends because they're honest and respectable, any more than we choose them because they change their linen daily. But I'm willing to acknowledge that they have every grace and every virtue, only they rather bore me.'

'They wouldn't if they were swells.'

He looked at her curiously, wondering why she imputed to him such despicable motives, and reflected that he could have been very good friends with his wife's relations if they had been simple country folk, unassuming and honest; but the family of Bush joined the most vulgar pretentiousness to a code of honour which could only in charity be called eccentric. Jenny brooded over his words, and after a silence of some minutes burst out impatiently.

'After all, we're not in such a bad position as all that. My mother's father was a gentleman.'

204

'I wish your mother's son were,' answered Basil, without looking up from the letter he wrote.

'D'you know what Jimmie says *you* are?'

'I don't vastly care, but if it pleases you very much you may tell me.'

She shot at him an angry glance, but did not answer. Then Basil got up, and going to her, placed his hands on her shoulders. Making his tone very gentle, he explained that it was really not his fault if he did not care for her people. Could she not resign herself to the fact, and make the best of it? Surely it would be better than to make themselves miserable. But Jenny, refusing the offer of reconciliation, turned away.

'You don't think they're good enough for you to associate with because they're not in swell positions.'

'I don't in the least object to their being grocers and haberdashers,' he answered, with a flush of annoyance. 'I only wish they'd sell us things at cost price.'

'Jimmie isn't a grocer or a haberdasher. He's an auctioneer's clerk.'

'I humbly apologize. I thought he was grocer, because last time he did us the honour of calling he asked how much a pound we paid for our tea, and offered to sell us some at the same price. But then he also offered to insure our house against fire, and to sell me a gold-mine in Australia.'

'Well, it's better to make a bit as best one can than to moon around like you do.'

'Really, even to please you I'm afraid I can't go about with little samples of tea in my pocket, and sell my friends a pound or two when I call upon them. Besides, I don't believe they'd ever pay me.'

'Oh no,' cried Jenny scornfully, 'you're a gentleman, and a barrister, and an author, and you couldn't do anything to dirty those white hands that you're so proud about. How do other fellows manage to get briefs?'

'The simplest way, I believe, is to marry the wily solicitor's daughter.'

'Instead of a barmaid?'

'I didn't say that, Jenny,' he answered very gravely.

'Oh no, you didn't say it. But you hinted it. You never say anything, but you're always hinting and insinuating till you drive me out of my senses.'

He held out his hands.

'I'm very sorry if I hurt your feelings. I promise you I don't mean to. I always try to be kind to you.'

He looked at her wistfully, expecting some word of regret or affection; but sullenly, with tight-closed lips, she cast down her eyes, and went on with her sewing.

With darkened brows he returned to his letters, and for an hour they remained silent. Then Jenny, unable any longer to bear that utter stillness, which seemed more marked because he sat so near, hostile and unapproachable, went out to sit in her own room. Her anger was past, and she was frightened at herself. She wanted to think the matter out, and with despair remembered that there was none to whom she could go for advice. It would be impossible to make her own folk understand these difficulties, and instead of help they would give only flouts and cruel jibes. It crossed her mind to go to Frank, the only friend of Basil whom she knew with any intimacy, for he came not infrequently to Barnes, and his manner, always so kind and gentle, made her think that she could trust him; but what should he care for her misery, and what assistance could he offer? She knew well enough the expressions of helpless sympathy he would use. It seemed that she stood quite alone in the world, weak and without courage, separated at once from those among whom her life had been spent, and from those into whose class her marriage had brought her. With throbbing brain, like a puppet driven round endlessly in a circle of pain, she could not see an end to her troubles. But the very confusion, the terror and uncertainty of it, forced her to make some desperate attempt, and she sought within herself for strength to gain the happiness she so woefully desired. She pondered over the events of the last year, picturing distinctly each passing scene, and saw the gradual bitterness that darkened the bliss of the beginning; then she told herself that some great effort was needed, or it would be too late. She was losing her husband's love, and in bitter self-reproach took all the blame therefor upon her own shoulders. The only chance now was to change herself completely. She must try to be less exacting, less insanely jealous; she must at least attempt to be more worthy of him. In an agony of repentance she reviewed all her faults. At last, with flushed cheeks and eyes still shining with tears, she went to Basil, and laid her hand on his shoulder.

'Basil, I've come to beg your pardon for what I said just now. I was carried away, and forgot myself.'

There was a gentleness in her voice which he had almost forgotten. He stood up and took her hands, smiling brightly.

'My dear girl, what does it matter? I'd forgotten all about it.'

'I've been thinking it all over. We haven't been getting on very well of late, and I'm afraid I've been to blame. I did things I regret. I have been reading your letters' – she blushed deeply with intense shame – 'but I swear I won't do it any more. I will try to be a good wife to you. I know I'm not your equal, but I want to try to get up to you. And you must be patient with me – you must remember I've got a lot to learn.'

'Oh, Jenny, don't talk like that; you make me feel such a cad.'

She smiled through her tears. He spoke in just the same eager tone which in time past had so charmed her. But then a wistful look came to her face.

'You do love me still a little, Basil, don't you?'

'My darling, you know I do.'

He took her in his arms and kissed her. She burst into tears, but they were tears of joy, for she thought, poor thing! that there ended their troubles. The future would be brighter and quite different.

6

PART of Frank's work as assistant-physician was to make post-mortem examinations of patients who died in the hospital, and in the performance of this duty, some time after Easter, he contracted a septic inflammation of the throat. Characteristically making nothing of it till quite seriously ill, he was at length taken to St Luke's in a high fever, delirious, and there for more than a week remained in a somewhat dangerous condition. For a fortnight more he found himself so languid that, though with vexation rebelling against his weakness, he was obliged to keep his bed; but finally convalescent, he arranged to go for a little to Ferne, near Tercanbury, where his father had a large general practice; then he meant to stay at Jeyston in Dorsetshire, where the Castillyons were giving a small house-party for Whitsun. Nor was there much inconvenience in his taking then a needed holiday, for the absence during August and September of the physician whose place in the wards he must fill would keep him in town for the hottest months.

The night before his departure Frank dined with Miss Ley, alone as both preferred, and during the meal, as was their wont, they discussed the weather and the crops. Each was sufficiently fond of his own ideas to brook no interruption from the service of food, and chose rather to keep till afterwards any topic that needed free discussion. But when the coffee was brought into the library, Miss Ley being comfortably stretched on a sofa, and Frank, with his legs on an armchair, lit his cigar, they looked at one another with a sigh of relief and a smile of self-satisfaction.

'You are going down to Jeyston, aren't you?' he asked.

'I don't think I can face it. As the time grows nearer, I begin to feel more wretched at the prospect, and I'm convinced I shall have worried myself into a dangerous illness by the appointed day. I don't see why at my age I should deliberately expose myself to the tedium of a house-party. Paul Castillyon has notions of old-fashioned hospitality, and every morning after breakfast asks what you would like to do; (as if any sensible woman knew at that preposterous hour what she wanted to do in the afternoon!) but it's a mere form, because he has already mapped out your day, and you'll find every minute has its fixed entertainment. Then, it bores me to extinction to be affable to people I despise, and polite – Oh, how I hate having to be polite! A visit of two days makes me feel as if I should like to swear like a Billingsgate fishwife, just to relieve the monotony of good manners.'

Frank smiled, and drinking his Benedictine, settled himself still more comfortably in his chair.

'By the way, talking of good manners, did I tell you that just before I grew seedy I went to three dances?'

'I thought you hated them?'

'So I do, but I went with a special object. The chief thing that struck me was the execrable breeding of the people. Supper was to be ready at midnight, and at half-past eleven they began to gather round the closed doors of the supper-room; by twelve there was as large a crowd as at the pit-entrance of a theatre, and when the doors were thrown open they struggled and pushed and fought like wild beasts. I'm sure the humble pittite is never half so violent, and they just flung themselves on the tables like ravening wolves. Now, I should have thought polite persons showed no excessive anxiety to be fed. By Jove! they made a greater clamour than the animals at the Zoo.'

'You're so *bourgeois*, dear Frank,' smiled Miss Ley. 'Why do you suppose people go to a dance, if not to have a good square meal for nothing? But that was surely not your object.'

'No; I went because I'd made up my mind to marry.'

'Good heavens!'

'Having arrived at the theoretical conclusion that marriage is desirable, I determined to go to three dances to see whether I could find anyone with whom it was possible, without absolute distaste, to contemplate passing the rest of my days. I danced and sat out with seventy-five different persons, Miss Ley,

209

ranging in age from seventeen to forty-two, and I can honestly say I've never been so hideously bored in my life. It's no good; I'm doomed to a career of single blessedness. I didn't think I should fall desperately in love on the spot, but it seemed possible that one of those five-and-seventy blooming maidens would excite in me some faint thrill: not one disturbed my equilibrium for a single moment. Besides, they were mostly phthisical or anaemic or ill-developed; I hardly saw one who appeared capable of bearing healthy children.'

For a moment they were silent, while Miss Ley, not without amusement, pondered over Frank's fantastic scheme for finding a wife.

'And what are you going to do now?' she asked.

'Shall I tell you?' He put aside the light manner which prevented one from seeing how much of what he said was seriously meant, and how much deliberate nonsense, and leaned forwards, his square strong chin on his hand, looking at Miss Ley with steady gaze. 'I think I'm going to chuck everything.'

'What on earth d'you mean?'

'I've been thinking of it more or less for some months, and during this last fortnight in bed I've put two and two together. I'm going home partly to sound my people. You know my father has toiled year after year, saving every penny he could, so that I might have the best possible medical education, and take at once to consulting work without any anxiety about my bread-and-butter. He knew it entailed earning very little for a long time, but he was determined to give me a chance; it's a poorish practice round Ferne, and he's never had a holiday for thirty years. I want to find out if he could bear it if I told him I intend to abandon my profession.'

'But, my dear boy, d'you realize that you wish to give up a very brilliant career?' exclaimed Miss Ley in some consternation.

'I've considered it pretty carefully. I suppose no one of my years in the medical has quite such a brilliant chance as I. Luck has been on my side throughout. I fell into the post of resident at St Luke's by the death of the man above me, and at the end of my time got the assistant-physicianship at a very early age. I have friends and connections in the world of fashion, so that I shall soon have a rich and important practice. In due course, I dare say, if I stick to it, I may earn ten or fifteen thousand a year, be appointed a royal physician, and eventually be baroneted; and then I shall die, and be buried, and leave rather a large fortune. That is the career that awaits me: I can see myself in the future portly and self-complacent, rather bald, with the large watch-chain, the well-cut frock-coat, and the suave manner of the modish specialist; I shall be proud of my horses, and fond of giving anecdotes about the royal personages I treat for over-eating.'

He paused, looking straight in front of him at this imaginary Sir Francis Hurrell who strutted pompously, sleek and prosperous, under a load of honours. Miss Ley, deeply interested in all stirrings of the soul, observed keenly his look of scorn.

'But it seems to me at the end of it I may look back, intensely bored with my success, and say to myself that, after all, I haven't really lived a single day. I'm thirty now, and my youth is beginning to slip away – callow students in their first year think I'm quite middle-aged – and I haven't lived yet; I've only had time to work, and by Jove! I have worked – like the very devil. When my fellow-students spent their nights in revelry, at music-halls, kicking up a row and getting drunk, or making love to pretty wantons, when they played poker into the small hours of the morning, reckless and light of heart, I sat working, working, working. Now, for the most part, they've settled down as sober, tedious general practitioners, eminently worthy members of society, and respectably married; and a fool would say I have my reward because I'm successful and somewhat distinguished, while they for past dissipation must pay to their life's end with the stupidest mediocrity. But sometimes their nerves must tingle when they look back on those good days of high spirits and freedom; I have nothing to look back on but the steady acquirement of knowledge. Oh, how much wiser I should have been to go to the deuce with them! But I was just a virtuous prig. I've worked too much, I've been altogether too exemplary, and now my youth is going, and I've known none of its follies; my blood burns for the hot, mad riot of the devil-may-cares. And this medical life isn't as I thought once, broad and catholic; it's warped and very narrow. We only see one side of things; to us the world is a vast hospital of sick people, and we come to look upon mankind from the exclusive standpoint of disease; but the wise man occupies himself, not with death, but with life – not with illness, but with radiant health. Disease is only an accident; and how can we lead natural lives when we deal entirely with the abnormal? I feel I never want to see sick persons again; I can't help it, they horrify and disgust me. I thought I'd busy myself with science, but that, too, seems dead to me and irksome; it wants men of different temper from mine to be scientists. There are plenty to whom the world and its glories are nothing, but I have passions – hot, burning passions; my senses are all alert, and I want to live. I wish life were some rich fruit, that I could take it in my hands and tear it apart, and eat it piece by piece. How can you expect me to sit down at my microscope hour after hour when the blood is racing through my veins and my muscles are throbbing for sheer manual labour!'

In his excitement he jumped up, and walked up and down, blowing out the smoke furiously in white clouds. The old fable of the ant and the grasshopper came to Miss Ley's mind, and she reflected that so at the approach of autumn might have reasoned the ant when she contemplated her store of food laboriously collected; perhaps she, too, bitterly envied the grasshopper who had spent the glorious days in idle singing, and in her heart, notwithstanding an empty larder and the cold winter to come, felt that the careless songster had made a better use than she of the summer-time.

'Do you think you'll have the same ideas after a fortnight in the country has brought you back again your full health?' asked Miss Ley meditatively.

She was astonished at the effect of this question, for he turned on her with an anger which she had never seen in him before.

'D'you think I'm an absolute fool, Miss Ley?' he cried. 'D'you think these are mere idle womanish fancies? I've been thinking of this for months, and my illness has left my brain clearer than ever it was. We're all tied to the wheel, and when one of us tries to escape the rest do all they can by jibes and sneers to hold him back.'

'I didn't mean to hurt your feelings, my son,' smiled Miss Ley indulgently. 'You know I have a certain discreet affection for you.'

'I beg your pardon; I didn't mean to be so violent,' he answered, quickly penitent. 'But I feel as though chains were eating into my flesh, and I want to get free.'

'I should have thought London offered a fairly spirited and various life.'

'London doesn't offer life at all – it offers culture. Oh, they bore me to extinction, the people I go and see, all talking of the same things and so self-satisfied in their narrow outlook! Just think what culture is. It means that you go to first-nights at the theatre and to private views at the Academy; you rave over Eleonora Duse and read the *Saturday Review*; you make a point of wading through the latest novel talked of in Paris, discuss glibly the books that come out here, and occasionally meet at tea the people who write them. You travel along the beaten track in Italy and France, much despising the Cook's Tourist, but really no better than a vulgar tripper yourself; you're very fond of airing your bad French, and you have a smattering of worse Italian. Occasionally, to impress the vulgar, you consent to be bored to death by a symphony concert, you go into fashionable raptures over Wagner, collect paste buckles, and take in the *Morning Post*.'

'Spare me,' cried Miss Ley, throwing up her hands; 'I recognize a particularly unflattering portrait of myself.'

Frank in his vehemence paid no attention to her remark.

'And the dull stupidity of it just chokes me, so that I pant for the fresh air. I want to sail in ships, and battle with hurricane and storm; I want to go far away among men who actually do things – to new countries, Canada and Australia, where they fight hand to hand with primitive nature; I desire the seething scum of great cities, where there's no confounded policeman to keep you virtuous. My whole soul aches for the

East, for Egypt and India and Japan; I want to know the corrupt, eager life of the Malays and the violent adventures of South Sea Islands. I may not get an answer to the riddle of life out in the open world, but I shall get nearer to it than here; I can get nothing more out of books and civilization. I want to see life and death, and the passions, the virtues and vices, of men face to face, uncovered; I want really to live my life while there's time; I want to have something to look back on in my old age.'

'That's all very fine and romantic,' replied Miss Ley; 'but where are you going to get the money?'

'I don't want money; I'll earn my living as I go. I'll ship before the mast to America, and there I'll work as a navvy; and I'll tramp from end to end picking up odd jobs. And when I know that, I'll get another ship to take me East. I'm sick to death of your upper classes; I want to work with those who really know life at the bottom, with its hunger and toil, its primitive love and hate.'

'That's nonsense, my dear. Poverty is a more exacting master than all the conventions of society put together. I dare say one voyage before the mast would be interesting, and would certainly teach you the advantage of ample means and the comfort of useless luxuries. But remember that as soon as anything becomes a routine it ceases to be true.'

'That sounds epigrammatic,' interrupted Frank; 'but does it by any chance mean something?'

Miss Ley, uncertain that it did, went on quickly.

'I assure you that no one can be free who isn't delivered from the care of getting money. For myself, I have always thought the philosophers talk sheer silliness when they praise the freedom of a man content with little; a man with no ear for music will willingly go without his stall at the opera, but an obtuseness of sense is no proof of wisdom. No one can really be free, no one can even begin to get the full value out of life, on a smaller income than five hundred a year.'

Frank looked straight in front of him, without answering; his quick mind still thrilled with the prospect his imagination offered. Miss Ley continued reflectively.

214

'On the other hand, it seems to me proof of great dullness that a person of ample fortune should devote himself to any lucrative occupation, and I have no patience with the man of means who from sheer habit or in poverty of spirit pursues a monotonous and sordid industry. I know a millionaire who makes his only son work ten hours a day in a bank, and thinks he gives him a useful training! Now, I would have the rich leave the earning of money to such as must make their daily bread, and devote their own energies exclusively to the spending thereof. I should like a class, leisured and opulent, with time for the arts and graces, in which urbanity and wit and comeliness of manner might be cultivated; I would have it attempt curious experiments in life, and like the Court of Louis XV, offer a frivolous, amiable contrast to the dark strenuousness in which of necessity the world in general must exist. A deal of nonsense is now talked about the dignity of labour, but I wonder that preachers and suchlike have ever had the temerity to tell a factory hand there is anything exalting in his dreary toil. I suppose it is praised usually because it takes men out of themselves, and the stupid are bored when they have nothing to do. Work with the vast majority is merely a refuge from ennui, but surely it is absurd to call it noble on that account; on the contrary, there is probably far more nobility in indolence, which requires many talents, much cultivation, and a mind of singular and delicate constitution.'

'And now for the application of your harangue,' suggested Frank, smiling.

'It's merely that in this short life of ours it's never worth while to be bored. I set no such value on regular occupations as to blame you if you abandon your profession; and for my part neither honours nor wealth would tempt me to a career wherein I was imprisoned by any kind of habit, tie, or routine. There's no reason why you should continue to be a doctor if it irks you, but for Heaven's sake don't on that account despise the fleshpots of Egypt. Now, I have a proposition to make. As you know, my income is much greater than my needs, and if you will graciously accept it, I shall be charmed to settle upon you five hundred a year – the smallest sum, as I have often

215

told you, on which may be played the entertaining game of life.'

He shook his head, smiling.

'It's awfully good of you, but I couldn't take it. If I can bring my father round, I shall go to Liverpool, and get on a ship as ordinary seaman. I don't want anybody's money.'

Miss Ley sighed.

'Men are so incurably romantic.'

Frank bade her good night, and next day went to Ferne. But Miss Ley considered what he had said, and the morning after solemnly visited her solicitor at Lancaster Gate – an elderly, rubicund gentleman with mutton-chop whiskers.

'I wish to make my will,' she said, 'but I really don't know what to do with this blessed fortune of mine; no one much wants it, and now my brother is dead there's no one I can even annoy by leaving him nothing. By the way, can I during my lifetime settle an annuity on a person against his will?'

'I'm afraid you can't force anyone to take money,' answered the solicitor, with a chuckle.

'How tiresome your laws are!'

'I should have said they applied perfectly, because a man who refuses an income is certainly fit only for a lunatic asylum.'

Beside her house in Old Queen Street, Miss Ley had somewhat less than four thousand a year, and the necessity of leaving it in a more or less rational fashion had of late much tormented her.

'I think,' she said, after a moment's thought, 'I'll just divide it into three – one part to my niece, Bertha Craddock, who won't in the least know what to do with it; one part to my nephew, Gerald Vaudrey, who's a scamp and will squander it in riotous living; and one part to my friend, Francis Hurrell.'

'Very well; I'll have it drawn out, and send it down to you.'

'Fiddlesticks! Take a sheet of paper and write it now. I'll wait till you're ready.'

The solicitor, sighing over this outrage to the decorum of legal delays, but aware that his client was of a peremptory nature, did her bidding, and calling in a clerk, with him wit-

216

nessed her signature. She departed, feeling singularly pleased with herself, for whatever happened Frank would never suffer from financial difficulties, and she thought, not without sly amusement, of his extreme surprise when he found himself at her demise a man in comfortable circumstances.

7

DURING his fortnight at home Frank observed his father and mother with great attention, and realized, really for the first time, how enormous were the sacrifices they had made for his sake. Every day, fine or rainy, old Dr Hurrell drove out to visit his scattered patients, and in the afternoon trudged round on foot. From five till seven he saw patients in the surgery, and often enough was called up in the middle of the night to go to a farmhouse five miles away in the very heart of the country. To all these people he dispensed the fruits of his long experience, medical knowledge perhaps a little rough-and-ready, but serviceable enough; and of a surety his old-fashioned drugs, his somewhat drastic surgery, were more popular with yokel and farmer than would have been any new-fangled methods of treatment. Besides, he gave to all and sundry good, cheery advice, and a piece of his mind when they did what they shouldn't, so that it was no wonder not a practitioner for twenty miles around was so beloved and trusted. But it was a monotonous life, without rest, without a single break from year's end to year's end, ill-paid if paid at all; and for thirty years the good man and his wife had looked upon every sovereign earned as held in trust for their only son. They had demanded economy neither at Oxford nor afterwards in London, but rather pressed money upon him. They had received with proud enthusiasm his desire to take up consulting practice, though knowing he must for a long time still be a charge upon them, and insisted that he should rent in Harley Street the very best rooms obtainable. The constant drudgery had been happiness unalloyed, because it gave every chance to the beloved boy whose brilliant talents seemed a thing so surprising that they could only thank God humbly for an unmerited mercy.

'Don't you get tired of the practice sometimes, father?' asked Frank.

'It's a matter of habit, and it's all I'm fit for – country practice. And then I have my reward, because some day you may
be at the head of the profession; and when afterwards they
write your life, a chapter will be devoted to the old G.P. at
Ferne, who first gave you a love for medicine.'

'But we shan't work very much longer,' said Mrs Hurrell,
'for soon we shall be able to afford to retire and live close to
you. Sometimes we do want to see you often, Frank. It's very
hard to be separated from you for so long at a time.'

There was trembling in that strong even voice, so that Frank
felt powerless. How could he, for reasons they would never
understand, destroy that edifice of hope on which they had
spent so many years of striving? He could never cause them
such bitter, bitter pain. So long as they lived he must bear the
yoke which they had put upon him, and go on with the steady,
not inglorious routine of his existence in London.

'You've been very good to me,' he said, 'and I'll try so to live
as to prove to you that I'm grateful for all you've done. I'll be
very ambitious, so that you may not think you've wasted your
time.'

But Frank's humour was inclined to the satiric when he
arrived at Jeyston, the Castillyon's place in Dorsetshire.
Miss Ley had finally decided that her health prevented her
from indulging in any dissipation, but Mrs Barlow-Bassett
with Reggie came by the same train as himself, and Paul's
mother, who with her companion made up the small party, a
few hours later.

A wizened little woman with white hair and a preposterous
cap, the elder Mrs Castillyon babbled incessantly of nothing in
particular, but for the most part of her own family, the Bain-
bridges of Somersetshire, whereof now she was the only living
representative. Immensely proud of her stock, she took small
pains to hide her contempt for all whose names figured less im-
portantly than her own in the *Landed Gentry*. Ignorant, narrow, ill-educated and ill-bred, she pursued her course through
this vale of sorrow with a most comfortable assurance of her
superiority to the world in general; and not only in her hus-

band's time, but even now that Paul reigned in his stead, by virtue of the purse-strings, whereof she kept tight hold, tyrannized systematically over Jeyston and all the villages surrounding. Her abominable temper, unchecked since in early youth she awoke to the fact that she was an heiress of old family, was freely vented on Miss Johnston, her companion, a demure maiden of forty, who ate with admirable complacency the bread of servitude; but also to some extent on her daughter-in-law, whom the old lady detested heartily, never hesitating to remind her that it was her good money which she so lightly squandered. Paul alone, whom she spoke of always as The Squire, had influence with her, for it was Mrs Castillyon's belief, innate as the capacity of ducks to swim, that the holder of this title was God's representative on earth, a person of superhuman attributes whose word was law, and whose commands must be obeyed; and Frank, who had seen Mr Castillyon somewhat flouted in London as a notorious bore, was amazed to find that here he was ultimate arbiter of all questions. His judgement was unquestioned in matters of opinion as in matters of fact; his ideas upon art or science were as necessarily final as his political theories were the only ones an honest man could hold. When he had spoken all was said, and it would have been as rational to contradict him as to argue with an earthquake. But even Paul was relieved when his mother's periodic visits came to an end, for her forcible and unique repartee made intercourse somewhat difficult.

'Thank God *I*'m not a Castillyon,' she said habitually. 'I'm a Bainbridge, and I think you'll have some difficulty in finding a better family in this part of England. You Castillyons hadn't a penny to bless yourselves with till *I* married into you.'

At dinner on his first evening Frank attempted to join intelligently in the conversation, but soon found that nothing he could say in the least interested the company; he had imagined innocently that it was ill-mannered to speak of one's ancestors, but now learned that there were households wherein it was the staple of conversation: this rested chiefly between the elder Mrs Castillyon, the Squire, and his brother Bainbridge, agent for the property, an obese man with a straggling beard, rather untidy and dressed in shabby old clothes, who talked very slowly, with a broad Dorsetshire accent, and to Frank seemed not a whit better that the farmers with whom he mostly consorted. They spoke besides of local affairs, of the neighbouring gentry, and of the Rector's vulgar independence. Afterwards Grace Castillyon went up to Frank.

'Aren't they awful?' she asked. 'I have to put up with this day after day for weeks at a time. Paul's mother rubs her money and her family into me; Bainbridge, that lout who should dine with the housekeeper instead of with us, discusses the weather and the crops; and Paul plays at being God Almighty.'

But Mrs Barlow-Bassett was somewhat impressed by the pomposity of her environment, and took an early opportunity again to peruse the account given by the worthy Burke of the family whose guest she was; she found the page much thumbed and boldly marked with blue pencil. Every article in the house had its history, which old Mrs Castillyon the elder narrated with gusto, for though from her exalted standpoint despising the family into which she had married, she had no doubt they were a great deal better than anyone else. Here were the books collected by Sir John Castillyon, grandfather of the present Squire; there the Eastern curiosities of the Admiral his great-uncle; in fine array were portraits of frail ladies in the time of Charles II, and of fox-hunting, red-faced gentlemen in the reign of King George. Mrs Bassett had never so felt her own insignificance.

After two days Frank retired to his room to compose a wrathful letter to Miss Ley.

O WISE WOMAN!

I know now why the thought of a visit to Jeyston drove you to such a state of desperation; I am so bored that I feel perfectly hysterical, and except that I dare not risk to make myself ridiculous even in the privacy of my bedchamber, would fling myself on the floor and howl. It would have been charitable to warn me, but I take it that you had a base desire I should eat the bread of hospitable persons, and then betray to you all their secrets: to gain your ends you have stifled the voice of conscience, and deafened

221

your ears to the promptings of good feeling. It would serve you right if I discoursed for six pages on things in general, but I so overflow with indignation that, even though I feel a mean swine because I abuse my hosts, I must let myself go a little. Imagine a Georgian house, spacious and well-proportioned and dignified, filled with the most delicate furniture of Chippendale and Sheraton, portraits on the walls by Sir Peter Lely and Romney, and splendid tapestries; a park with wide meadows and magnificent trees before which you feel it possible to kneel down and worship; all around the country is undulating, lovely and fertile; and it belongs, lock, stock, and barrel, to people who have not a noble idea, no thought above the commonplace, no emotion that is not petty and sordid. Pray observe also that they heartily despise me because I am what they call a materialist. It makes my blood boil to think that this wonderful place is enjoyed by a pompous ass, a silly woman, an ill-tempered harridan, and a loutish boor, all of whom, if things went by deserts, would inhabit the back-room of a grocer's shop in Peckham Rye. Bainbridge, who will eventually come into the estate unless Mrs Castillyon can bring herself so to endanger her figure as to produce an heir, is a curious phenomenon: he went to Eton and spent a year at Oxford, from which he was sent down because he could pass no examination, but in manners and conversation is no better than a labourer at thirteen shillings a week. He has lived all his life here, and goes to London once in two years to see the Agricultural Show. But let me not think of him. The day is passed by Mrs Barlow-Bassett listening with open mouth to Mrs Castillyon's family anecdotes, by Reggie in eating and drinking and sucking up to the Squire, by myself in desperation. I fancied that I might get entertainment from Miss Johnston, the companion, and was at some pains to make myself amiable; but she has the soul of a sycophant. When I asked whether she was never bored, she looked at me severely, and answered: 'Oh no, Dr Hurrell, I'm never bored by gentlefolks.' Whenever there is a pause in the conversation or Mrs Castillyon is out of temper, she points to some picture or ornament of which she has already heard the history a thousand times, and asks how it came into the family. 'Fancy your not knowing that!' cries the old lady, and breaks into an endless rigmarole about some beery Squire, happily deceased, or about a simpering dame whose portrait shows that her liver from tight-lacing must have been quite out of shape. The things a single woman is driven to for thirty pounds a year and board and lodging! I would far sooner be a cook. Oh, how I long for the smoking-room in Old Queen Street and your conversation! I am coming to the conclusion that I only like two kinds of society – yours on the one hand, and that of the third-class actor on the other: where the men are all blackguards, the women frankly immoral, and no fuss is made when you drop an aitch, I feel thoroughly comfortable. I don't think I have any overwhelming desire to omit aspirates, but it is a relief to be in company where no notice would be taken if I did.

Yours ever,
FRANK HURRELL

Miss Ley would have used her sharp eyes at Jeyston to more purpose than Frank, and seen enacted a little comedy which on one side verged somewhat to the tragic. Tired and unhappy, Grace Castillyon with all her soul looked forward to Reggie's visit as a respite from the anxiety of her life; for of late more than ever tormented by her conscience, only the actual presence of her lover was able to make her forget how abominably she treated Paul. She had learnt to see the tenderness behind her husband's pompous manner, and his complete loving confidence gave a very despicable air to her behaviour; she felt guilty before him and vile. But with Reggie by her side Grace knew she would forget everything save her insatiable passion; she resolved only to see his good points, and forget how ill he had used her; it seemed that she could only keep the bare shreds of her self-respect by holding on to his love, and if she lost that nothing would remain but the dark night of despair and shame. And her heart rejoiced because at Jeyston no conflicting desires would take Reggie from her side; they could walk together delightfully, and in the quiet country enjoy somewhat of that great bliss which glorified the memories of their early friendship.

But to her dismay, Mrs Castillyon found that Reggie systematically avoided to be alone with her. The morning after his arrival she asked him to come for a stroll in the park, and he accepted with alacrity; but after going upstairs to put on her hat she found that Paul and Mrs Bassett waited for her in the hall.

'Reggie says you've offered to show us the park,' said Mrs Bassett. 'It'll be so nice for us all to go together.'

'Charming,' answered Mrs Castillyon.

She shot an angry glance at Reggie, which he sought not to elude, but took calmly, with a faint smile of amusement; and when they walked he dawdled so as to be well within earshot of the others. After luncheon again he remained with Frank, and it was not till the evening that Mrs Castillyon had opportunity even to say half a dozen words.

'Why did you ask your mother to come out with us this morning?' she asked hurriedly, in a low voice. 'You knew I wanted to talk to you alone.'

'My dear girl, we must be careful. Your mother-in-law is watching us like a cat, and I'm sure she suspects something. I don't want to get you into a mess.'

'I *must* see you alone; I must talk to you,' cried Mrs Castillyon desperately.

'Don't be a fool!'

'Well, I shall wait for you here after the others have gone to bed.'

'You'll jolly well have to wait, because *I*'m not going to take any risks.'

She gave him a look of hatred, but could not answer, for at that moment Miss Johnston joined them, and Reggie, with alertness unusual to him, engaged her in the conversation. Grace, for the moment discountenanced, and careless if she betrayed her distress, stared at him fixedly, wondering what was in that mind which revelled in crooked ways. She felt horribly powerless in his hands, and knew, though it sickened her to know it, that now he would play with her cruelly, catlike, till he was sufficiently amused, and not till then deal the final blow. For two days more he pursued the same tactics, more carefuly still, so that he never saw Mrs Castillyon, even for a moment, except when others were present; and he appeared to take a malicious pleasure in hurting her. He made extravagant compliments which excited Paul's ponderous hilarity, and using her like an intimate friend with whom he was on confidential terms, chaffed and bantered and laughed at her. Old Mrs Castillyon, who liked to be amused, took a great fancy to him, which was no way diminished when she discovered, with the clear vision of dislike, that her daughter-in-law winced at these good-natured jokes. Grace bore them with a smiling face, with little shrieks of laughter; but it seemed there was a great raw wound in her heart, which Reggie, callously joyful because he inflicted pain, probed with a red-hot knife. When she was alone and could surrender to her wretchedness, she wept bitterly, wondering, half mad with agony, why her passionate love should be repaid by this inexplicable hatred. She had done everything possible to make Reggie love her, and beside giving him her whole soul, had been very good to him.

'He's found me a real brick all through,' she sobbed. 'I'd have done anything to help him.'

Of late even she had sought to influence him for his own weal, persuading him to drink less and to be less extravagant. In her adoration she was capable of any sacrifice for his sake; and the result was only that he loathed her. She could not understand. At length she could bear the torment no longer, and since Reggie gave no opportunity, determined at all costs to make one. But it was the last day of the visit, and he doubled his precautions. With an inkling that Grace would force an interview, he took care not to be alone for one moment, and sighed with relief when, after a smiling good night, he retired with the other men to the smoking-room. But Mrs Castillyon was decided not to let him go without an explanation of his behaviour; and although the danger of her contemplated step was enormous, her frame of mind was so desperate that she did not hesitate. When Reggie, chuckling slily because he had circumvented her, went to his bedroom, he found Grace quietly seated, waiting for him.

'Good Lord! what are you doing here?' he cried, for once startled from his self-possession. 'Frank might very well have come in with me.'

She did not answer his question, but stood up and faced him, more haggard and pale for the magnificence of her gown and the brilliancy of her diamonds. She sought to compose herself and to talk deliberately.

'Why have you been avoiding me all these days?' she asked. 'I want an explanation. What are you up to?'

'Oh, for God's sake, don't bring that up again! I'm sick to death of it. You didn't suppose I was coming down here to stay with your husband, and then play the fool with you? After all, I flatter myself I'm a gentleman.'

Mrs Castillyon gave a low angry laugh.

'It's rather late in the day to develop honourable sentiments, isn't it? Haven't you got some better story to tell me than that?'

'What d'you take me for? Why should you always think I'm lying to you?'

'Because experience has shown me that you generally are.'

He shrugged his shoulders and lit a cigarette, then looked at Grace with deliberation, as though meditating what he should now do.

'Haven't you got anything to say to me at all?' she asked, her voice suddenly breaking.

'Nothing, except that you'd better go back to your own room. It's devilish unsafe for you to be here, and I can tell you *I* don't want to get into a mess.'

'But what does it all mean?' she cried desperately. 'Don't you care for me any more?'

'Well, if you insist, it means that I think the whole thing had better stop.'

'Reggie!'

'I want to turn over a new leaf. I'm going to give up racketing about, and settle down. I'm sick of the whole thing.'

He did not look at her now, but kept his eyes away nervously. A sob caught Grace's throat, for what she feared was true.

'I suppose you're gone on somebody else.'

'That's no business of yours, is it?'

'Oh, you cad! I wonder how I could ever have been such a fool as to care for you.'

He gave a short, dry laugh, but did not answer. She went up to him quickly and took hold of his arms.

'You're hiding something from me, Reggie. For God's sake, tell me the whole truth now!'

He turned his eyes to her slowly, that sulky look of anger on his face which she knew so well.

'Well, if you want to know, I'm going to be married.'

'What?' For a moment she could not believe him. 'Your mother never said a word about it.'

He laughed.

'You don't suppose she knows, do you?'

'And what if I tell her?' whispered Grace hurriedly, distracted, only knowing that this horror must be prevented. 'You can't marry; you haven't the right to now. It's too infamous. I won't let you. I'll do anything to stop it. Oh, Reggie, Reggie, don't leave me! I can't bear it.'

'Don't be a fool! It had got to come to an end some day or other. I want to marry and settle down.'

Mrs Castillyon looked at him, and despair and anger and vehement hatred chased one another across her mobile face.

'We'll see about that,' she whispered vindictively.

Reggie went up to her and caught her violently by the shoulders, so that she could hardly bear the pain.

'Look here, none of your little games! If I find out that you've been putting a spoke in my wheel, I'll give you away. You'd better hold your tongue, my dear; and if you don't, every letter you've written to me shall be sent to your mother-in-law.'

Grace turned deathly pale.

'You promised me you'd burn them.'

'I dare say, but you're not the only woman I've had to do with. I always like to have a weapon or two in my hands, and I thought it might be useful if I kept your letters. They'd make pretty reading, wouldn't they?'

He saw the effect of his words on Grace, and let go; she tottered to a chair, shaken with terror. Reggie rubbed it in.

'I'm not a bad-tempered chap, but when people put my back up I know how to get even with them.'

For a moment she gazed straight in front of her, then looked up with a curious expression in her eyes. She spoke in a hoarse voice, jerkily.

'I don't think you'd come out of it very well if there were a public scandal.'

'Don't you have any fear about me, my girl,' he answered.

'What d'you suppose I care if I'm made a co? The mater would be a bit sick, but it don't really matter a button to a man.'

'Not if it gets known that he's taken a good deal of money off the woman unlucky enough to fall in his clutches? You forget that I've paid you – paid you, my friend, paid you. In the last six months you've had two hundred pounds out of me; d'you think anyone would ever speak to you again if they knew?'

She saw the deep blush of shame which coloured his dark cheeks, and with a ring of bitter triumph in her voice, continued.

'The first time I sent you money I never thought for a moment you'd accept; and because you did I knew what a low cur you were. I've got letters, too, in which you ask for money, and letters in which you thank me because I sent it. I kept them, not because I wanted a weapon against you, but because I loved you and treasured everything you'd touched.'

She stood up, and with cold, sneering lips flung out the words; she hoped they would rankle; she wanted to wound his self-esteem, to sear him so that he should writhe before her.

'Make a scandal, by all means, and let all the world see that you're nothing but a blackguard and a cad. Oh, I should like to see you expelled from your club, I should like to see people cut you in the street! Don't you know that there are laws to imprison men who get money in no filthier a way than you?'

Reggie strode up to her, but now she was no longer frightened. She laughed at him. He thrust his face close to hers.

'Look here, get out of this, or I'll give you such a thrashing as you'll never forget. Thank God, I'm done with you now. Get out – get out!'

Without a word, swiftly, she passed him, and went to the door. Not caring who might be about, she crossed the long passage that led from Reggie's room to hers, her brain beating as though devils within it hammered madly; she could not realize what had occurred, but felt that the world was strangely coming to its end; it seemed to her the finish of life and of everything. Her wan cheeks were flushed still with anger and

228

hatred. She had just reached her door, when Paul walked towards her up the great staircase; for one moment she was panic-stricken, but the danger extraordinarily cleared her mind.

'Grace, I've been looking for you,' he said; 'I wondered where you were.'

'I've been talking to Mrs Bassett,' she answered quickly. 'Where on earth did you suppose I was?'

'I couldn't think. I've just been downstairs to see if you were there.'

'I wish you wouldn't follow me about and spy on my movements,' she cried irritably.

'I'm very sorry, my darling; I didn't mean to do that.' He stood at the door of her room.

'For Heaven's sake, come in or go out,' she said; 'but don't stand there with the door wide open.'

'I'll just come for two minutes,' he answered mildly.

'What do you want?'

She took off her jewels, which burnt her neck like a circle of fire.

'I've got something I wish to talk to you about. I'm much distressed by a thing that has happened on the estate.'

'Oh, my dear Paul,' she cried impatiently, 'for goodness' sake don't worry me tonight; you know I don't care twopence about the estate. Why don't you consult Bainbridge, who's paid to look after it?'

'My love, I wanted your advice.'

'Oh, if you knew how my head was aching! I feel as if I could scream in sheer agony.'

He stepped forward, full of affectionate concern.

'My poor child, why didn't you tell me before? I'm so sorry, and I've been bothering you. Is it very bad?'

She looked up at him, and her mouth twitched. He was so devoted, so kind, and whatever she did he could overlook and forgive.

'What a pig I am!' she cried. 'How can you like me when I'm so absolutely horrid to you?'

'My darling,' he smiled, 'I don't blame you for having a headache.'

A sudden impulse seized her; she flung her arms round his neck and burst into a flood of tears.

'Oh, Paul, Paul, you are good to me. I wish I were a better wife. I've not done my duty to you.'

He folded his arms about her, and kissed tenderly her painted, wan, and wrinkled face.

'My darling, I couldn't want a better wife.'

'Oh, Paul, why can't we be alone? We seem so separated. Let's go away together, where we can be by ourselves. Can't we go abroad? I'm sick of seeing people – I'm sick of society.'

'We'll do whatever you like, my dearest.'

A great happiness filled him, and he wondered how he had deserved it. He wished to stay by his wife, helping her to undress, but she begged him to go.

'My poor child, you look so tired,' he said, kissing her forehead gently.

'I shall be better in the morning, and then we'll start a new life. I'll try and be better to you – I'll try and deserve your love.'

'Good night, darling.'

He closed the door very softly, leaving her to her thoughts.

8

MRS CASTILLYON passed a sleepless, unquiet night, and looking at herself in the glass next morning, was shocked at her haggard countenance; but she was determined that Reggie during this final interview should discern no sign of her distress, and coming down to breakfast, was to all appearance in the highest spirits. She noticed the hang-dog air with which he avoided her glance, and with angry resolution began to rally him in the somewhat obvious fashion often mistaken by persons of her sort for wit. To conceal her poignant misery she kept up a flow of vapid conversation, intermingled with little shrieks of laughter and pointed by much gesticulation; but she exaggerated her spiritless vivacity so that the effect was somewhat hysterical, and Frank, whom this did not escape, wondering what thus affected her, mentally prescribed a sedative. The carriage drove round before breakfast was over, and Mrs Bassett, fearful of missing her train, began to bid the company farewell. Mrs Castillyon held out her hand frankly to Reggie.

'Good-bye. You must come and see us again when you have time. I hope you've enjoyed yourself.'

'A1,' he answered.

He could not understand the smiling carelessness of her look, wherein he saw no reproach nor anger, and asked himself uncomfortably what Grace could have in mind. He pondered slowly over the harm she could possibly do him. But he was glad of the decisive rupture, and heartily thankful the final meeting was over. He hated her the more because of the reminder that a good deal of money had passed from her hands to his.

'She knew I couldn't afford to go about with her on my allowance, and I've spent it all on her,' he muttered to himself in extenuation.

They were in the train now, and he looked at his mother, who sat in the opposite corner of the carriage, reading the *Morning Post*. He would not have liked her to know the details of the affair. Again he repeated excuses to himself, at the end of which he settled to a sullen resentment against Grace because she had tempted him. Finally his thoughts went elsewhere and his heart began to beat more quickly.

But after the Bassetts and Frank were gone, Mrs Castillyon was seized by a great dismay, and shuddered as though a cold wind blew, because she must spend two days more under the stern eyes of Paul's mother, who seemed to watch with a vindictive triumph, as though she knew the abominable secret, and to reveal it only waited for an opportunity. Grace stood looking out of the window at the wide stretch of meadow-land and the splendid trees of the park. The sky was grey, covering the earth with a certain sad monotony which answered her mood, depressed after the forced excitement of the early morning. Paul came up behind her, and placed his arm round her waist.

'Are you very tired, darling?' he asked.

She shook her head, trying to smile, touched, as of late she had been often, by the gentleness of his voice.

'I'm afraid you exhaust yourself. You were the life and spirit of the whole party. Without you we should have been almost dull.'

From force of habit an ironic and obvious repartee came to her lips, but she did not say it. She leaned her head against his shoulder.

'I'm beginning to feel so dreadfully old, Paul.'

'Nonsense! You've scarcely reached your prime. You're looking prettier than ever.'

'D'you think so really? I suppose it's because you care for me a little still. This morning I thought I looked a hundred and two.'

He did not answer, being more accustomed to debate than to conversation, but pressed his arm a little more closely round her waist.

'Have you never regretted that you married me, Paul?

232

I know I'm not the sort of wife you wanted, and I've never brought you any children.'

He was profoundly moved, for his wife had never spoken to him in such a way before. For once the pompousness fell away from his delivery, and he answered in trembling tones, almost whispering.

'My darling, each day I thank God for you. I feel I'm not worthy of the blessing I've received, and I'm grateful to my Maker, very grateful, because He has given me you to be my wife.'

Grace's lips twitched, and she clenched her hands to prevent herself from bursting into tears. He looked at her with a fond smile.

'Grace, I bought a little present for your birthday next week. May I give it you now instead of waiting?'

'Yes, do,' she smiled. 'I knew you had something, and I'm so impatient.'

Quite jauntily, he went off, and in a minute, somewhat out of breath from his haste, returned with a diamond ornament. Mrs Castillyon knew something of jewellery, and her eyes glistened at the magnificence of this.

'Paul, how could you!' she cried. 'How perfectly gorgeous! But I didn't want anything half so valuable. I have so much that you've given me. I only wanted a tiny present to show that you still cared for me.'

He beamed with satisfaction and rubbed his hands gleefully.

'As if anything was too good for my loving faithful wife!'

'We mustn't show it to your mother, Paul. She's scold awfully,' answered Grace archly.

He burst into a shout of laughter.

'No, no, hide it from her.'

Mrs Castillyon raised her lips to his, and with ardent passion, unexpected in that stout, complacent man, he kissed her. At that moment the dogcart came to the door, and Paul, in some surprise, asked his wife if she needed it.

'Oh, I forgot,' she cried. 'I'm going up to town for the

day. I ought to have told you. Miss Ley is much worse than she pretends, and I think I should go and see if I can do anything.'

The night's dreary meditation had left her with a sensible resolve to consult Miss Ley, and when the maid came to draw the blinds she had ordered the trap to take her to the station for the train after that by which her guests were going. Now glibly she invented an excuse for her journey, and refused to hear Paul's remonstrance, who feared she would make herself ill; nor would she allow him to accompany her.

'I feel I mustn't prevent you when you're bent on an errand of mercy,' he said at length. 'But come back as early as you can.'

Miss Ley was finishing luncheon when Mrs Castillyon was announced.

'I thought you were entertaining at Jeyston,' she exclaimed, much surprised to see her.

'I felt I must see you or I should go mad. Oh, why didn't you come down? I wanted you so badly.'

Miss Ley, evidently in robust health, could not repeat her plea of indisposition, and therefore, instead of explaining, offered her guest food.

'I couldn't eat anything,' cried Grace, with a shiver of distaste. 'I'm simply distracted.'

'I surmised that you were in some trouble,' murmured Miss Ley, 'for I think you've rather overdone the – slap. Isn't that the technical expression?'

Mrs Castillyon put both hands to her cheeks.

'It burns me. Let me go and wash it off. I had to put it on this morning, I looked such an absolute wreck. May I go and bathe my face? It'll cool me.'

'By all means,' answered Miss Ley, smiling, and while Mrs Castillyon was absent asked herself what could be the cause of this sudden excursion.

Presently Grace returned and looked in the glass. Her skin, bare of rouge and powder, was yellow and lined, and the cosmetic on her eyebrows and lashes, which water did not re-

234

move, threw into more violent contrast the ghastly pallor. Instinctively she took a puff from her pocket, and quickly powdered her face; then she turned to Miss Ley.

'Did *you* never make up?' she asked.

'Never. I was always afraid of making myself absurd.'

'Oh, one gets over that – but I know it's silly; I'm going to give it up.'

'You say that as tragically as though you announced your intention of going into a nunnery.'

Mrs Castillyon glanced at the door suspiciously.

'Will no one come in?' she asked.

'No one; but for all that I recommend you to keep calm,' retorted the other, who suspected that Grace wished to make a scene, and somewhat resented the infliction.

'It's all finished between Reggie and me. He's thrown me over like a worn-out tie; he's got somebody else.'

'You're well rid of him, my dear.'

Miss Ley's sharp eyes were intent on Mrs Castillyon's face, seeking therein to read the inner secret of her heart.

'You don't care for him any more, do you?'

'No, thank God, I don't. Oh, Miss Ley, I know you won't believe me, but I am going to try to turn over a new leaf. During these last months I've seen Paul so differently. Of course, he's absurd and pompous and dull – I know that better than anyone – but he *is* so kind; even now he loves me with all his heart. And he's honest. You don't know what it means to be with a man who's straight to the very bottom of his soul. It's such a relief and such a comfort!'

'My dear, it surely requires no excuses to find good qualities in one's husband. You show a state of mind which is not only laughable, but highly original and ingenious.'

'It makes it so much harder for me,' answered Mrs Castillyon, woebegone and tragic; 'I feel such an awful cad. I can't bear that he should trust me implicitly when I've behaved in such a disgusting way; I can't bear his kindness. You guessed before that I was tortured by the desire to make a clean breast of it, and now I can't resist any longer. This morning, when he was so sweet and gentle, I could hardly restrain myself. I

235

can't go on; I must tell him and get it over. I would rather be divorced than continue with this perpetual lie between us.'

Miss Ley observed her for some while calmly.

'How selfish you are!' she murmured at length in an even, frigid voice. 'I had an idea you were beginning to care for your husband.'

'But I do care for him,' answered Mrs Castillyon, with astonishment.

'Surely not, or you wouldn't wish to cause him such great unhappiness. You know very well that he dotes upon you; you are the only light and brightness in his life; if he loses his faith in you, he loses everything.'

'But it's only honest to confess my sin.'

'Don't you remember the proverb that open confession is good for the soul? There's a lot of truth in it – it *is* very good indeed for the soul of the person who confesses; but are you sure it's good for the listener? When you wish to tell Paul what you have done, you think only of your own peace of mind, and you disregard entirely your husband's. It may be only an illusion that you are a beautiful woman of virtuous temper, but all things are illusion, and why on earth should you insist on destroying that of all others which Paul holds dearest? Haven't you done him harm enough already? When I see a madman wearing a paper crown under the impression that it is fine gold, I haven't the brutality to undeceive him; let no one shake our belief in the fancies which are the very breath of our nostrils. There are three good maxims in the conduct of life: Never sin; but if you sin, never repent; and above all, if you repent, never, never confess. Can't you sacrifice yourself a little for the sake of the man you've treated so badly?'

'But I don't understand,' cried Grace. 'It's not self-sacrifice to hold my tongue – it's just cowardly. I want to take my punishment; I want to start fair again, so that I can look Paul in the face.'

'My dear, you have an incurable passion for rodomontade. You're really not thinking of Paul in the least; you have merely an ardent desire to make a scene; you wish to be a

236

martyr and abase yourself in due form. Above all, you want to rid yourself of the burden of a somewhat guilty conscience, and to do that you are perfectly indifferent how much you make others suffer. May I suggest that if you're really sorry for what you've done, you can show it best by acting differently in the future; and if you hanker after punishment, you can get as much as ever you want by taking care that no word or deed of yours lets your husband into this rather odious secret.'

Mrs Castillyon looked down, following with her eyes the pattern of the carpet; she thought over all that Miss Ley said.

'I came to you for advice,' she moaned helplessly, 'and you've only made me more undecided than ever.'

'Pardon me,' answered the other, with considerable asperity: 'you came with your mind perfectly made up, for me to approve your disinterestedness; but as I think you uncommonly stupid and selfish, I reserve my applause.'

The result of this conversation was that Mrs Castillyon promised to hold her tongue; but on leaving Old Queen Street to catch the train back to Jeyston, she would have been puzzled to tell whether there was in her mood more of relief or of disappointment.

Mrs Castillyon arrived at Jeyston just in time to dress for dinner, and somewhat tired by her journey, did not notice the gravity which affected the family party; she was accustomed to their dullness, and ate her food silently, wishing the meal were over. When Paul and Bainbridge came into the drawing-room afterwards, with an effort she gave her husband a smile of welcome, and made room for him on the sofa whereon she sat.

'Tell me what it is you wanted to speak about last night,' she said; 'you asked for my advice, and I was too cross to give it you.'

He smiled, but his face quickly regained its serious look.

'It's too late now; I had to decide at once. But I'd better tell you about it.'

'Fetch me my cloak, then, and we'll stroll up and down

237

the terrace; the light tires my eyes, and I hate talking to you always in the presence of other people.'

Paul was only too pleased to do as she suggested, and found it very delightful to wander in the pleasant starlit night; the clouds which had darkened the morning were vanished with the setting sun, and there was a delicate softness in the air. Grace took her husband's arm, and her need for support made him feel very strong and masculine.

'A dreadful thing has happened,' he said, 'and I've been very much upset. You remember Fanny Bridger, who went up to London last year in service? Well, she's come back. It appears that she got into trouble. ...' He hesitated a moment in the discomfort of telling his wife the brutal fact. 'The man deserted her, and she's returned with a baby.'

He felt a tremor pass through his wife, and wished that he had kept his second resolution, to say nothing to her.

'I know you hate to speak of such things, but I must do something. She can't go on living here.' Fanny Bridger's father was an under-gamekeeper on the estate, and his two sons were likewise employed. 'I saw Bridger today, and told him his daughter must be sent away; I can't in my position connive at immorality.'

'But where is she to go?' asked Mrs Castillyon in a voice that was scarcely more than a whisper.

'That is no business of mine. The Bridgers have been good servants for many years, and I don't wish to be hard on them. I've told the old man that I'll give him a week to find somewhere for his daughter to go.'

'And if he can't?'

'If he can't, it'll be because he's a stupid and obstinate dolt. He began to make excuses this afternoon; he talked a deal of nonsense about keeping her in his care, and that it would break his heart to send her away, and he couldn't afford to. I thought it was no good mincing matters, so I told him if Fanny wasn't gone for good by Tuesday next I should dismiss him and his two sons.'

Abruptly Mrs Castillyon snatched her arm from his, and a coldness seized her; she was indignant and horrified.

238

'We'd better go in to your mother, Paul,' she said, knowing to whom this determination of her husband was due. 'We must talk this out at once.'

Surprised at the change in her tone, Castillyon followed his wife, who walked quickly to the drawing-room and flung aside her cloak. She went up to Mrs Castillyon the elder.

'Did you advise Paul that Fanny Bridger should be sent away?' she asked, her eyes flaming with anger.

'Of course I did. She can't stay here, and I'm happy to see that Paul has behaved with spirit. People in our position have to take great care; we must allow no contamination to enter the parish.'

'What d'you think will happen to the wretched girl if we turn her out? The only chance for her is to remain in her family.'

Paul's mother, by no means a patient woman, vastly resented the scornful indignation apparent on Grace's face; she drew herself up, and spoke with tight lips, acidly.

'Perhaps you're not very capable of judging matters of this sort, my dear. You've lived so much in London that I dare say your notions of right and wrong are not quite clear. But, you see, I'm only a country bumpkin. I'm happy to say I think differently from you. I've always been under the impression that there is something to be said for morality. To my mind, Paul has been absurdly lenient in giving them a week. My father would have turned them out bag and baggage in twenty-four hours.'

Grace shuddered at the cruel self-righteousness of that narrow, bigoted face, and then slowly examined Paul, whose eyes were upon her, dreadfully pained because she was angry, but none the less assured of his own rectitude. She pursed her lips, and saying not a word more, went to her room. She felt that nothing could be done then, and made up her mind next morning to visit for herself the unlucky girl. Paul, disturbed because she did not speak to him, was about to follow further to expostulate; but his mother, sharply rapping the table with her fan, prevented him.

'Now, don't run after her, Paul,' she cried peremptorily.

239

'You behave like a perfect fool, and she just turns you round her little finger. If your wife has no sense of morality, other people have, and you must do your duty, however much Grace dislikes it.'

'I dare say we might manage to find Fanny Bridger some place.'

'I dare say you'll do nothing of the sort, Paul,' she answered. 'The girl's a little wanton. I've known her since she was a child, and she always was. I wonder she had the impudence to come back here, but if you have any sense of decency *you* won't help her. How d'you suppose you're going to keep people moral if you pamper those who fall? Remember that I have some claims upon you, Paul, and I don't expect my wishes to be entirely disregarded.'

In her domineering way she looked round the room, and it was obvious in every repellent feature – in her narrow lips, in her thin nose and little sharp eyes – that she remembered how absolute was her power over the finances of that house. Paul indeed was the Squire, but the money was hers, if she chose, to leave every penny to Bainbridge. Next day she came in to luncheon in a towering passion.

'I think you should know, Paul, that Grace has been to Bridger's cottage. I don't know how you expect the tenants to have any regard for modesty and decorum if your wife openly favours the most scandalous indecency.'

Grace turned on her mother-in-law with flashing eyes.

'I felt sorry for the girl, and I went to see her. Poor thing! she's in great distress.'

She saw again that little cottage at one of the park gates – a pretty rural place overgrown with ivy, the tiny garden vivid with carefully-tended flowers. Here Bridger was working, a man of middle age, hard-featured and sullen, his face tanned by exposure. He turned his back on her approach, and when she bade good morning answered unwillingly.

'I've come to see Fanny,' said Mrs Castillyon. 'May I go in?'

He faced her with a dark scowl, and for a moment did not answer.

240

'Can't you leave the girl alone?' he muttered at last huskily.

Mrs Catillyon looked at him doubtfully, but only for a moment. She passed by quickly, and without another word entered the house. Fanny was seated at the table, sewing, and close to her was a cradle. Seeing Grace, she rose nervously, and a painful blush darkened her white cheeks. Once a pretty girl with fresh colours, active and joyful, deep lines of anxiety now gave a haggard look to her eyes. Her cheeks were sunken, and the former trimness of her person had given way to slovenly disorder. She stood before Grace like a culprit, conscience-stricken, and for a moment the visitor, abashed, knew not what to say. Her eyes went to the baby, and Fanny, seeing it, anxiously stepped forward to get between them.

'Was you looking for father, mum?' she asked.

'No; I came to see you. I thought I might be of some use. I want to help you if you'll let me.'

The girl looked down stubbornly, white again to her very lips.

'No, mum, there's nothing I want.'

Facing her, Grace understood that there was something common to them both, for each had loved with her whole soul and each had been very unhappy. Her heart went out strangely to the wretched girl, and it was torture that she could not pierce that barrier of cold hostility. She knew not how to show that she came with no thought of triumphing over her distress, but rather as one poor weak creature to another. She could have cried out that before her Fanny need fear no shame, for herself had fallen lower even than she. The girl stood motionless, waiting for her to go, and Mrs Castillyon's lips quivered in helpless pity.

'Mayn't I look at your baby?' she asked.

Without a word the girl stepped aside, and Mrs Castillyon went to the cradle. The little child opened two large blue eyes and lazily yawned.

'Let me take it in my arms,' she said.

Again the fleeting colour came to Fanny's cheeks as with a softer look she took the baby and gave it to Grace. With

241

curious motherly instinct Grace rocked it, crooning gently, and then she kissed it. Against her will a cry was forced from her.

'Oh, I wish it were mine!'

She looked at Fanny with pitiful longing in her eyes all bright with tears; and her own emotion thawed at length the girl's cold despair, for she buried her face in her hands and burst into passionate weeping. Grace placed the child again in the cradle, and gently leaned over Fanny.

'Don't cry. I dare say we can do something. Do talk to me, and let me see how I can help.'

'No one can help,' she moaned. 'We've got to go in a week; the Squire says so.'

'But I'll try and make him change his mind, and if I can't I'll see that you and the baby are well provided for.'

Fanny shook her head hopelessly.

'Father says if I go he goes, too. Oh, the Squire can't turn us out! What are we to do? We shall starve, all of us. Father's not so young as he was, and he won't get another job so easy, and Jim and Harry have got to go, too.'

'Won't you trust me? I'll do whatever I can. I'm sure he'll let you stay.'

'The Squire's a hard man,' muttered Fanny. 'When he sets his mind to anything he does it.'

And now at luncheon, looking at Paul and his mother, Bainbridge and Miss Johnston, she felt a bitter enmity against them all because of their narrow cruelty. What did they know of the horrible difficulties of life, when their self-complacency made the way so easy to their feet?

'Fanny Bridger is no worse than anyone else, and she's very unhappy. I'm glad I went to see her, and I've promised to do all I can to help her.'

'Then I wash my hands of you,' cried the elder Mrs Castillyon violently. 'But I can tell you this, that I'm shocked and scandalized that you should be quite dead to all sense of decency, Grace. I think that you should have some regard for your husband's name, and not degrade yourself by pampering an immoral woman.'

'I think it was unwise of you to go to Bridger's cottage,' said Paul gently.

'You're all of you so dreadfully hard. Have you none of you pity or mercy? Have *you* never done anything in your lives that you regret?'

Mrs Castillyon turned to Grace severely.

'Pray remember that Miss Johnston is a single woman, and unaccustomed to hearing matters of this sort discussed. Paul has been very lenient. If he were more so, it would seem as if he connived at impropriety. It's the duty of people in our position to look after those whom Providence has placed in our care. It's our duty to punish as well as to reward. If Paul has any sense remaining of his responsibilities, he will turn out neck and crop the whole Bridger family.'

'If he does that,' cried Grace, 'I shall go too.'

'Grace!' cried Mr Castillyon, 'what do you mean?'

She looked at him with shining eyes, but did not answer. They were too many against her, and she knew it useless to attempt anything more till next day, when Paul's mother departed. Yet it was almost impossible to hold her tongue, and she was desperately tempted to cry out before them all the story of her own shameful misery.

'Oh, these virtuous people!' she muttered to herself. 'They're never content unless they see us actually roasting in hell! As if hell were needed when every sin brings along with it its own bitter punishment. And they never make excuses for us. They don't know how many temptations we resist for the one we fall to.'

9

BUT Grace found her husband more obstinate than ever before, and though she used every imaginable device he remained unmoved; by turns she was caressing and persuasive, scornful, bitter, and angry, but at length, because of his unperturbed complacency, was seized with indignant wrath. He was a man who prided himself on the accomplishment of every resolve he formed, and his determination once made, that the Bridgers at the end of their week's warning should go, no appeals to his reason or to his emotion would induce him to another mind. Though it hurt him infinitely to thwart his wife, though it was very painful to feel her cold antagonism, his duty seemed to point clearly in one direction, and the suffering it caused made him only more resolute to do it. Paul Castillyon had a very high opinion both of the claims his tenants had upon him and of his great responsibilities towards them; and he never imagined for a moment that their private lives could be no concern of his: on the contrary, convinced that a merciful Providence had given him a trust of much consequence, he was fully prepared to answer for all who were thus committed to his charge; and he took his office so seriously that even in London he was careful to inform himself of the smallest occurrences on his estate. To all these people he was a just and not ungenerous master, charitable in their need, sympathetic in their sickness, but arrogated to himself in return full authority over their way of life. In this instance his moral sense was sincerely outraged; the presence of Fanny Bridger appeared a contamination, and with the singular prudery of some men, he could not think of her case without a nausea of disgust. It horrified him somewhat that Grace not only could defend, but even visit her; it seemed to him that a pure woman should feel only disdain for one who had so fallen.

The week passed, and Grace had been able to effect nothing;

bitterly disappointed, angry with her husband and with herself, she made up her mind that no pecuniary difficulties should add to Fanny's distress; if she had to go, at least it was possible so to provide that some measure of happiness should not be unattainable. But here she was confronted by Bridger's obstinate determination not to be separated from his daughter; he had got it into his slow brain that the trouble came only because she had gone away, and no argument would convince him that in future little need be feared; somehow, also, he was filled with sullen resentment against the Squire, and, himself no less self-willed, refused to yield one inch. He repeated over and over that if the girl went, he and his sons must go too.

Late in the afternoon of the day before that on which Fanny was to leave for ever the village of her birth, Mrs Castillyon sat moodily in the drawing-room, turning over the pages of a periodical, while Paul, now and then glancing at her anxiously, read with difficulty a late-published Blue-Book. A servant came in to say that Bridger would like to speak with the Squire. Paul rose to go to him, but Mrs Castillyon begged that he might come there.

'Send him in,' said the Squire.

Bridger entered the room somewhat timidly, and stood at the door cap in hand; it was raining, and the wet of his clothes gave out an unpleasant odour. There was a certain grim savagery about the man, as though his life spent among wild things in the woods had given him a sort of fawnlike spirit of the earth.

'Well, Bridger, what do you want?'

'Please, Squire, I came to know if I was really to go to-morrow?'

'Are you accustomed to hear me say things I don't mean? I told you that if you did not send away your daughter within a week I should dismiss you and your sons from my service.'

The gamekeeper looked down, revolving these words in his mind: even then he could not bring himself to believe that they were spoken in grim earnest; he felt that if only he could make Mr Castillyon understand how impossible was what he asked, he would surely allow him to stay.

'There's nowhere Fanny can go. If I send her away, she'll go to the bad altogether.'

'You doubtless know that Mrs Castillyon has promised to provide for her. I have no doubt there are homes for fallen women where she can be looked after.'

'Paul,' cried Grace indignantly, 'how can you say that!'

Bridger stepped forward and faced the Squire; he looked into his eyes with surly indignation.

'I've served you faithfully, man and boy, for forty years, and I was born in that there cottage I live in now. I tell you the girl can't go; she's a good girl in her heart, only she's 'ad a misfortune. If you turn us out, where are we to go? I'm getting on in years, and I shan't find it easy to get another job. It'll mean the workus.'

He could not express himself, nor show in words his sense of the intolerable injustice of this thing; he could only see that the long years of loyal service counted for nothing, and that the future offered cold and want and humiliation. Paul stood over him cold and stern.

'I'm very sorry,' he said. 'I can do nothing for you. You've had your chance, and you've refused to take it.'

'I've got to go tomorrow?'

'Yes.'

The gamekeeper turned his cap round nervously, and to his face came an expression of utter distress; he opened his mouth to speak, but no words came, only an inarticulate groan. He turned on his heel and walked out. Then Grace went up to Paul desperately.

'Oh, Paul, you can't do it,' she cried. 'You'll break the man's heart. Haven't you any pity? Haven't you any forgiveness?'

'It's no good, Grace. I'm sorry that I can't fall in with your wishes. I must do my duty. It wouldn't be fair to the other people on the estate if I let this go by without notice.'

'How can you be so hard!'

He wouldn't see, he couldn't see, that it was out of the question to drive Bridger away callously from the land he loved with all his soul; in one flash of inspiration she realized all that his little cottage signified to him, the woods and

246

coverts, the meadows, the trees, the hedges: with all these things his life was bound up; like a growing thing, his roots were in the earth which had seen his birth and childhood, his marriage, and the growth of his children. She took hold of her husband's arms and looked up into his face.

'Paul, don't you know what you're doing? We've come nearer to one another of late. I've felt a new love grow up in my heart for you, and you're killing it. You won't let me love you. Can't you forget that you're this and that and the other, and remember that you're only a man, weak and frail like the rest of us? You hope to be forgiven yourself, and you're utterly pitiless.'

'My darling, it's for your sake also that I must be firm with this man. It's because you are so good and pure that I dare not be lenient.'

'What on earth d'you mean?'

She disengaged herself roughly from his arms and stepped back. Her face, without powder or rouge, was ashen grey, and in her eyes was a look of panic fear.

'I can't allow that creature to live in the same place as you. Because you're a virtuous and a good woman, it's my duty to protect you from all contact with evil. It horrifies me to think that you may meet her on your walks – her and her child.'

Mrs Castillyon's cheeks flamed with red, and there was such a catching at her throat that she put her hand to it.

'But I tell you, Paul, that compared with me that woman is innocent and virtuous.'

'Nonsense, my dear,' he laughed.

'Paul, I'm not what you think. That woman sinned because she was ignorant and unhappy, but I knew what I was doing. I had everything I wanted, and I had your love; there were no excuses for me. I was nothing better than a wanton.'

'Don't be absurd, Grace! How can you talk such rubbish?'

'Paul, I'm talking perfectly seriously. I've not been a good wife to you. I'm very sorry. It's best that you should know.'

He stared at her incredulously.

'Are you mad, Grace? What do you mean?'

247

'I've been – unfaithful.'

He said nothing, he did not move, but a trembling came over his fleshy limbs and his face turned deathly white. Still he could scarcely believe. She went on with dry throat, forcing out the words that came unwillingly.

'I'm unworthy of the love and confidence that you gave me. I've deceived you shamefully. I've committed – adultery!'

The word hit him like a blow, and with a cry of rage he stepped forward to his wife, cowering before him, and seized her shoulders. He seized her roughly, cruelly, with strong hands, so that she set her teeth to repress the cry of pain.

'What d'you mean? Have you been in love with someone else? Tell me who it is.'

She did not answer, looking at him in terror, and he shook her angrily; he was blind with rage now, in a condition which she had never seen before.

'Who is it?' he repeated. 'You'd better tell me,'

She shrank away from him, but he held her fast with ruthless hands, and he tightened them so that she could have screamed with pain.

'Reggie Bassett,' she cried at last.

He released her roughly, so that she fell against a table.

'You dirty little beast!' he cried.

Mrs Castillyon's breath came quickly. She felt about to faint, and steadied herself against the table; she was trembling still with the pain she had suffered; her shoulders ached from the violence of his hands. He faced her, looking as though even now he scarcely understood what she had said; he passed his hands over his face wearily.

'And yet I loved you with all my heart; I did everything I could to make you happy.' Suddenly he remembered something. 'The other night when you kissed me and said we must come closer together, what did you mean?'

'I'd just broken with Reggie for ever,' she gasped.

He laughed savagely.

'You didn't come back to me till he'd thrown you over.'

She stepped forward, but he put out his hands to prevent her.

248

'For God's sake, don't come near me, or I shall hit you.'

She stopped dead, and for a moment they confronted one another strangely. Then again he passed his hands across his face, as though he wished to push away some horrible thing before him.

'Oh God, oh God! what shall I do?' he moaned.

He turned away quickly, and sinking in a chair, hid his face and burst into tears. He sobbed uncontrollably, with all the agony and the despair of a man who has cast shame from him.

'Paul, Paul, for Heaven's sake don't cry; I can't bear it.' She went up to him, and tried to take away his hands. 'Don't think of me now; you can do what you like with me afterwards. Think of these wretched people. You can't send them away now.'

He pushed her away more gently, and stood up.

'No, I can't send them away now. I must tell Bridger that he and the girl can stay.'

'Go to them at once,' she implored. 'The man's heart is breaking, and you can give him happiness. Don't let them wait a minute longer.'

'Yes, I'll go to him at once.'

Paul Castillyon seemed now to have no will of his own, but acted as though under some foreign impulse. He went to the door, walking heavily as if grown suddenly old, and Grace saw him go out into the rain, and disappear into the mist of the approaching night. She stood at the window wondering what he would do, and imagined with a shiver of dismay the shame of proceedings for divorce; she looked at the great trees of Jeyston as though for the last time, and tried to picture to herself the life that awaited her. Reggie would make no offer of marriage, nor, if he did, would she accept, since no trace remained of her vehement passion, and she thought of him merely with loathing. She hoped the case, going undefended, would excite small attention; and afterwards she was rich enough in her own right to live on the Continent as she chose. At all events, peace of sorts would be hers, and she could drag out somehow the rest of her years; she was thank-

249

ful now that she had no child from whom separation would be unendurable. Wearily Grace pressed her eyes.

'What a fool I've been!' she cried.

Quickly the events of her life marshalled themselves before her, and she looked back with shame and horror on her old self, flippant and egoistic, worthless.

'Oh, I hope I'm not like that now.'

The minutes passed like hours, so that she was surprised because Paul did not return; she glanced at the clock, and found that half an hour had gone. The Bridgers' cottage was not more than five minutes' walk from the house, and it was incomprehensible that Paul delayed so long. She was seized with fear of impending disaster, and the mad thought came that the gamekeeper, without waiting for his master's words, in his rage and grief had committed some horrible deed. She was on the point of sending a servant to see what had become of her husband. Suddenly she saw him running along the drive towards the house; dusk had set in, and she could not see plainly. At first she thought herself mistaken, but it was Paul. He ran with little quick steps, like a man unused to running, and his hat was gone; the rain pelted down on him. Quickly she flung open the glass doors that led into the garden, and he came in.

'Paul, what's the matter?' she cried.

He stretched out his hands to support himself against a chair; he was soaked to the skin, muddy and dishevelled; his large white face was set to an expression of sheer horror, and his eyes started out of his head. For a moment he pressed his hand to his heart, unable to speak.

'It's too late,' he gasped; and his voice was raucous and strange. It was a dreadful sight, this pompous man, ordinarily so self-composed, all disarrayed and terror-struck. 'For God's sake, get me some brandy!'

Quickly she went into the dining-room, and brought him a glass and the decanter. Though by habit so temperate that he drank little but claret and water, now with shaking hand he poured out half a tumbler of neat spirit, and hastily swallowed it. He took a handkerchief, and wiped his face, streaming with rain and sweat, and sank heavily into the nearest chair. Still his eyes stared at her as though filled with some ghastly sight; he made an effort to speak, but no words came; he gesticulated with aimless hands, like a madman; he groaned inarticulately.

'For Heaven's sake, tell me what it is,' she cried.

'It's too late! She threw herself in front of the London express.'

She stepped forward impulsively, and then some strange power seemed to pluck her back. She threw up her hands, and gave a loud cry of horror.

'Be quiet, be quiet!' he cried angrily. Then words came to him, and he uttered his story rapidly, voluble and hysteric; he was all out of breath, and did not think of what he spoke. 'I went down to the cottage, and Bridger wasn't there. He was at the public-house, and I went on. A man met me, running, and said there'd been an accident on the railway; I knew what it was. I ran with him, and we came to them just when they were taking her along. Oh God, oh God! I saw her.'

'Oh, Paul, don't tell me! I can't bear it.'

'I shall never get it out of my eyes.'

'And the child?'

'The child's all right; she didn't take it.'

'Oh, what have we done, Paul – you and I?'

'It's my fault,' he cried – 'only mine!'

'Have you seen Bridger?'

'No; they went to tell him, and I couldn't bear it any more. Oh, I wish I could get it out of my eyes.'

He looked at his hands and shuddered; then he got up.

'I must go and see Bridger.'

'No, don't do that. Don't see him now when he's mad with drink and rage. Wait till tomorrow.'

'How are we going to spend the night, Grace? I feel I shall never sleep again.'

Next day, when Mr Castillyon came downstairs, his wife saw that he had slept as badly as herself; for though dressed now very carefully in the rough tweeds of the country gentleman, his face was drawn and white, his eyes heavy with watching. He advanced to kiss her as usual, but on a sudden stopped, and a flush rapidly darkened his cheek; he drew back, and without a word sat down to breakfast. Neither could eat, and after a decent interval, meant to impress the servants that nothing very unusual had happened, Paul rose heavily to his feet.

'Where are you going?' she asked. 'You'd better not go to Bridger's; he's been drinking hard all night, and he might hurt you. You know he's violent-tempered.'

'D'you think I should care if he killed me?' he answered hoarsely, his face distorted by a look of dreadful pain.

'Oh, Paul, what have I done!' she cried, breaking down.

'Don't talk of that now.'

He moved towards the door, and she sprang up.

'If you are going to see Bridger, I must come, too. I'm so afraid.'

'Would you mind if anything happened to me?' he asked bitterly.

She looked at him with utter pain.

'Yes, Paul.'

He shrugged his massive shoulders, and together in silence they walked along the drive. The fine weather of the last three weeks was gone, and the day was chilly, and an east wind blew. A low white mist lay over the park, and the dripping trees were very cheerless. No sign of life was seen at Bridger's cottage, but the little garden, usually so trim and neat, was trampled and torn, as though many men had gone carelessly over the beds. Paul knocked at the door and waited, but no answer came; he lifted the latch, and followed by Grace, walked in. Bridger, seated at the table, was looking straight in front of him, stupefied still with grief and liquor. He gazed vacantly at the intruders, as though he recognized them not.

'Bridger, I've come to tell you how dreadfully sorry I am for the awful thing that has happened.'

The sound of the voice seemed to bring the man to his senses, for he gave a low cry and lurched forward.

'What d'you want? What 'ave you come here for? Couldn't

you leave me alone?' He stared at Paul, rage gradually taking possession of him. 'D'you still want me to go – me and the boys? Give us time, and we'll clear.'

'I hope you'll stay. I want to do everything I can to make up for your horrible loss. I can't tell you how deeply I blame myself. I would give anything that this dreadful thing hadn't occurred.'

'She killed 'erself so as I shouldn't be turned off. You're a hard master – you always was.'

'I'm very sorry. In future I will try to be gentler to you all. I thought I only did my duty.'

Mr Castillyon, that man so conscious of his dignity, had never before spoken to his inferiors in apologetic tones. Apt to take others to account, he had never dreamed that some day himself might need to make excuses.

'She was a good girl, after all,' said Bridger. 'In her heart she was as good as your wife, Squire.'

'Where's the child?' asked Grace, almost in a whisper.

He turned upon her savagely.

'D'you want that, too? Aren't you satisfied yet? Has the child got to go, too, before we stay?'

'No, no!' she cried hastily. 'You must keep the child, and we'll do all we can to help you.'

Paul looked at the man.

'Won't you shake hands with me, Bridger? I should like you to tell me you forgive me.'

Bridger drew back his hands and shook his head. Paul saw that no good could come of staying, and turned to the door. The gamekeeper's eye, following him, caught sight of his gun, which leaned against a chair; he stretched out his hand and took it. Grace gave a start, but managed to repress her cry of alarm.

'Squire!' he called.

'Well?'

Paul turned round, and when he saw that the man held that weapon in his hand he straightened himself; he looked at him steadily.

'Well, what do you want?'

Bridger stepped forward, and roughly gave the gun into his master's hand.

'Take it and keep it, Squire. I swore last night I'd blow your bloody brains out, and swing for it. I'm not fit to have this gun yet. Keep it, or if I get in drink I'll kill you.'

An indescribable look of pride came into Paul's face, and the humiliation and shame were banished. Grace's heart beat fast when she saw what he was about to do, and a sob broke from her. He gave back the gun.

'You'll need it for your work,' he said coldly. 'I don't think I'm afraid. I will take my chance of your wanting to shoot me.'

The man looked with wonder at his master, and then violently flung the gun into the corner of the room.

'By God!' he said.

Paul waited for one moment to see if Bridger had anything more to say, then gravely opened the door for his wife.

'Come, Grace.'

He walked with long steps back to the house, and for the first time in her life Grace admired her husband; she felt that, after all, he was not unworthy of his authority. She touched his arm.

'I'm glad you did that, Paul. I felt very proud.'

He removed his arm quickly, so that she shrank away.

'Did you think I was likely to be afraid of my gamekeeper?' he answered disdainfully.

'What are you going to do about me?' she asked.

'I don't know yet. I must think it over. All that you told me last night was true?'

'Quite true.'

'Why did you tell me?'

'It was the only way to save those people. If I'd had the courage to do it a couple of hours earlier, that poor girl wouldn't have killed herself.'

He said no more, and silently they reached the house.

For some days Paul made no reference to his wife's confession, but went about the work of his estate, his Parliamen-

254

tary labours, with stolid method, and only Grace's new sympathy discerned the awful torment from which he suffered. He took care to speak naturally before the servants and his brother, but avoided to be alone with her. His back seemed strangely bent, and he walked with a listless torpor, as though his large limbs were grown suddenly too heavy to bear; his fleshy face was drawn and sallow, his eyelids puffy from want of sleep, and his eyes dim. At length Grace could stand her misery no longer; she went to the library, where she knew he was alone, and softly opened the door. He sat at the table with Blue-Books and paper spread in front of him, striving industriously to fit himself for the duties which he took so seriously; but he did not read: he rested his face on his hands, staring straight in front of him. He started when his wife entered, and looked at her with harassed eyes.

'I'm sorry to disturb you, Paul, but we can't go on much longer in this way. I want to know what you're going to do.'

'I don't know,' he said. 'I wish to do my duty.'

'I suppose you're going to divorce me.'

He gave a groan, and pushing back his chair, stood up.

'Oh, Grace, Grace, why did you do it? You know how I worshipped you; I would have given my life to save you a moment's uneasiness. I trusted you with all my soul.'

'Yes, I know all that. I've repeated it to myself a thousand times.'

He looked at her so helplessly that she could not restrain her pity.

'Would you like me to go away? Your mother can easily come down to you, and you can talk it over with her.'

'You know what she'd advise me to do,' he cried.

'Yes.'

'D'you *want* me to divorce you?'

She gave him a look of utter agony, but would not allow the gathering tears to fall from her eyes; with fierce self-reproach, she wished to excite in him no atom of commiseration. He glanced away, with a certain shame of his next question.

'D'you still care for – Reggie Bassett?'

'No,' she cried, exultantly; 'I loathe and detest and despise him. I know he's not worth a quarter of you.'

He threw up his hand helplessly.

'Oh God! I wish I knew what to do. At first I could have killed you, and now – I feel we can't go on as we are, ought to do something; I can't forget the whole thing. I ought to hate you, but I can't; notwithstanding everything, I love you still. If you go, I think I shall die.'

She looked at him thoughtfully, divining in some measure the emotions which tore him in sundry directions. It seemed due to his honour that he should divorce the errant wife, and yet he had not the heart to do it; anger and shame were banished by utter sorrow; and then, he could not bear the scandal and the public disgrace. Paul Castillyon was a man of old-fashioned ideas, and it seemed to him proper for a gentleman to keep his name out of the newspapers. Nor did he like the modern notion that the wronged husband cuts a somewhat heroic figure; he remembered vividly his disgust when a member of his club, divorcing his wife, had sought in the smoking-room to excite sympathy by narration of the lady's infidelities. He was proud of his name, and could not bear that it should be covered with ridicule; the very thought shamed him, so that he could scarcely face his wife.

'I leave myself entirely in your hands,' she said at length. 'I will do whatever you wish.'

'Can't you give me a little more time to think it over? I don't want to do anything hastily.'

'I think we'd better decide at once. It'll be much better for you to settle it; you're making yourself ill. I can't bear to see you so awfully unhappy.'

'Don't think about me; think about yourself. What will you do if –' He stopped, unable to continue.

'If you divorce me?'

'No, I can't do that,' he cried quickly. 'I dare say I'm a doting, weak fool, and you'll despise me even more than you do; but I can't lose you altogether. Oh, Grace, you don't want me to divorce you?'

She shook her head.

'It would be very generous if you could spare me that. Will you be satisfied if I go and live abroad? I promise that you'll have no cause to blame me again. We need tell people nothing; they'll think it's a sort of amicable separation.'

'I dare say that would be the best thing,' he said quietly.

'Then, good-bye.'

She stretched out her hand to him, and the tears in her eyes made everything dim about her. He took it silently.

'I want to tell you once more, Paul, how bitterly I regret all the unhappiness I've caused you. I was never a good wife to you. I hope with all my heart that you'll be happier now.'

'How can I be happy, Grace? You were all my happiness. I can't help it; all these days I've fought against it, I've done all I could, but still even now – now that I know you've never cared for me at all, and the rest – I love you with all my heart.'

The tears ran down her wasted, colourless cheeks, and for a while she could not speak. She withdrew her hand, and stood in front of him with head bent down.

'I don't ask you to believe me, Paul. I've lied to you and betrayed you, and you have the right to take my words as worthless. But I should like to tell you this before I go: I do love you now honestly. During these last months of wretchedness I've understood how kind and good you were, and I've been awfully touched by your great love for me; you made me utterly ashamed of myself. Oh, I've been worthless and selfish; I've sacrificed you blindly to all my whims, I've never tried to make you happy; but if I'm less of a cad than I was, it's because of you. And the other day, when you gave that man his gun, I was so proud of you, and I felt such a poor mean creature I could have fallen on my knees before you and kissed your hands.'

She took her handkerchief and dried her eyes; then, forcing a smile, for one moment she flashed at him a gay look such as she had been accustomed to give.

'Don't think too badly of me, will you?'

'Oh, Grace, Grace,' he cried, 'I can't bear it! Don't go. I want you so badly. Let us try again.'

The colour rushed to her face, and she went to him quickly.

'Paul, d'you think you ever can forgive me? I tell you I love you as I never loved you before.'

'Let us try.'

He opened his arms, and with a cry of joy she flung herself into them; she lifted her lips to him, and when he kissed her she pressed more closely to him.

'My darling husband,' she whispered.

'Oh, Grace, let us thank God for His mercy to us.'

10

THE summer passed, and Miss Ley went her way as usual, going industriously, with the vivacity of a young girl, to the various entertainments offered by the season. She had a knack for extracting amusement from functions which others found entirely tedious, and with sprightly, good-natured malice related her adventures conscientiously to the faithful Frank.

He, of course, remained in London, but once a fortnight went to see Herbert Field at Tercanbury. His visits, though himself knew they were useless, were of singular consolation to the Deanery household; his kindly humour and his sympathy had so endeared him that all looked forward with the keenest pleasure to his arrival; and he had a way of arousing confidence so that even Bella felt nothing more could be done for her husband than Frank did. On reaching home from Paris, they had settled down very quietly, and though at first the Dean felt some uneasiness in Herbert's presence, this was soon replaced by a very touching affection; he learnt to admire the unflinching spirit with which the youth looked forward to inevitable death, the courage with which he bore pain. When the weather grew warmer, Herbert lay all day in the garden, rejoicing in the green leaves and the flowers and the singing of the birds; and forsaking his erudite studies, the Dean sat with him, talking of ancient authors or of the roses he loved so well. They played chess interminably, and Bella loved to watch them, the sun, broken into patches of green and yellow by the leaves, colouring them softly; it amused her to see the little smile of triumph with which her father looked up when he made a move to puzzle his opponent, and the boyish laugh of Herbert when he found a way out of the difficulty. They both seemed her children, and she could not tell which was dearer to her.

But cruelly the disease progressed, and at length Herbert

was confined to bed; a terrible haemorrhage exhausted him, so that Frank could not conceal from Bella his fear that at length the end was coming.

'For months he's been hanging on a thread, and the thread is breaking. I'm afraid you must prepare yourself for the worst.'

'D'you mean it can only be a question of weeks?' she asked with agony.

He hesitated for a while, but decided it was better to tell her the truth.

'I think it's only a question of days.'

She looked at him steadily, but her face by now was so trained to self-command that no expression of horror or of pain disturbed its steadfast gravity.

'Can nothing be done at all?' she asked.

'Nothing. I can be of no more use to you; but if it will comfort you at all, you'd better wire for me if he has another haemorrhage.'

'It will be the last?'

'Yes.'

When she went back to Herbert he smiled so brightly that it seemed impossible Frank's gloomy judgement could be true.

'Well, what does he say?'

'He says you keep your strength wonderfully,' she answered, smiling. 'I hope soon you'll be able to get up again.'

'I feel as well as possible. In another fortnight we can go to the seaside.'

Each knew that the other hid his real thought, but neither had the heart to put aside the false hopes with which they had so long tried to reassure themselves. Yet to Bella the strain was growing unendurable, and she besought Miss Ley to come and stay with them. Her father was grown so fond of Herbert that she dared not tell him the truth, and desired Miss Ley to distract his attention. She could not unaided continue much longer her own cheerfulness, and only the presence of someone else might make it possible to preserve a certain sober hilarity. Miss Ley consented, and forthwith arrived; but perceiving that it was her part to add some gaiety to that last act of life, she felt

260

it a little gruesome; it was as though she were invited to some grim festival to watch the poor boy die. However, with unusual energy she exerted herself to amuse the Dean, and having an idea that her powers of conversation were not altogether contemptible, took pains to be at her best; it did Herbert infinite good to hear her talk with the old man, bantering him gently, playing about his words with the agility of a light-winged butterfly, propounding hazardous theories which she defended with all possible ingenuity. The Dean took pleasure in the contest, and opposed her with all the resources of his learning and his common sense; with questions apparently guileless, he strove to lure her to self-contradiction, but when he managed this it profited him little, for she would extricate herself with a verbal quip, a prance, a flourish, and a caper; or else, since the only importance lay in the aesthetic value of a phrase, assert her utter indifference to the matter of the argument. To prove a commonplace, she would utter paradox after paradox – to make the fantastic obvious, would argue with the staid logic of Euclid.

'Man has four passions,' she said – 'love, power, food, and rhetoric; but rhetoric is the only one that is proof against satiety, ennui, and dyspepsia.'

A fortnight passed, and one morning Herbert Field, alone with Bella, had another attack of haemorrhage, so that for a while she thought him dying. He fainted from exhaustion, and in terror she sent for the local doctor. Presently he was brought round to consciousness, but it was obvious that the end had come; from this final attack he could never rally. Yet it seemed impossible that human skill should have no further power; surely there must be some last desperate remedy for which the moment was now at hand, and Bella asked Miss Ley whether Frank might be sent for.

'Anyhow, we shall never trouble him again,' she said.

'You don't know Frank,' answered Miss Ley. 'Of course he'll come at once.'

A telegram was despatched, and within four hours Frank arrived, only to see that Herbert's condition was hopeless. He hovered between life and death, kept alive by constant stimulants, and they could do nothing but sit and wait. When Bella repeated to her father, from whom so far as possible she had hidden her husband's desperate state, that the boy could scarcely outlast the night, he looked down for a moment, then turned to Frank.

'Is he strong enough for me to administer the Holy Sacrament?'

'Does he want it?'

'I think so. I have talked to him before, and he told me that he wished to take it before he died.'

'Very well.'

Bella went to prepare her husband, and the Dean assumed the garments of his office. Frank also went into the bedroom to be at hand if needed, and stood by the window apart from those three who performed the sacred mystery; it seemed to him as though the Dean were invested strangely with a greater, more benignant dignity. A certain majesty had descended upon the minister of God, and while he read the prayers a light shone on his face like that on the face of a pictured saint.

Verily, verily I say unto you, He that heareth My word, and believeth on Him that sent Me, hath everlasting life, and shall not come into condemnation; but is passed from death unto life.

Bella knelt at the bedside, and Herbert Field, emaciated and extraordinarily weak, his sombre eyes shining unnaturally from his white and wasted face, listened attentively. There was no fear now, but only resignation and hope; it could be seen that with all his heart he believed those promises of life everlasting and of pardon for sins past; and Frank, storm-tossed on the sea of doubt, envied that undisturbed assurance.

The Body of our Lord Jesus Christ, which was given for thee, preserve thy body and soul unto everlasting life: Take and eat this in remembrance that Christ died for thee, and feed on Him in thy heart by faith with thanksgiving.

The dying man took the bread and wine which should mystically prepare the Christian soul for her journey to the life beyond, and they seemed to give a peace ineffable; the tortured body was marvellously eased, and a new serenity descended upon the mind.

The Dean read the last solemn lines of the service, and rising from his knees, kissed the boy's forehead. Herbert was too weak to speak, but the faintest shadow of a smile crossed his lips. Presently he dozed quietly. It was late in the afternoon now, and Frank suggested that he should take the Dean into the fresh air.

'There is no immediate danger, is there?' asked the old man.

'I don't think so. He will probably live till the morning.'

They went out from the Deanery garden into the precincts. There was a large patch of green upon which the boys of Regis School played cricket at nets, but they were away for the holidays, and only the cawing rooks, flying heavily about the elm-trees, disturbed the stillness. On one side was the cathedral, adorably grey in the rosy light of evening, and the stately magnificence of the central tower rose towards heaven like a strong man's ideal turned to stone. All round were the houses of the Canons. The day had been hot and cloudless, but now a very light breeze fanned the cheeks of those two slowly sauntering. It was a spot which breathed a peace so exquisite that Frank wished dreamily his life had been cast in such pleasant ways. At intervals the cathedral bells rang out the quarters. Neither spoke, but they walked till the setting sun warned them that it grew late. When they returned to the house Miss Ley said that Herbert was awake, asking for the Dean; she proposed they should eat something, and then go to his room. He seemed slightly better, so that she asked Frank if any hope remained.

'None. It can only be a question of a few hours more or less.'

When they went into his bedroom, Herbert greeted them with a smile, for his mind at the end seemed to regain a greater lucidity. Bella turned to them.

'Father, Herbert would like you to read to him.'

'I was going to suggest it,' answered the Dean.

The night was fallen, and all the stars shone out with a vehement splendour; through the casements, wide open, entered the fresh odours of the garden, suave and unwearied. Frank sat in a window, his face in shadow, so that none could see, and watched the lad lying so still that one might have thought him dead already. Then Bella so arranged the lamp that the Dean might be able to read; and when he sat down the light fell on his face wonderfully, and it seemed transparent as alabaster.

'What shall I read, Herbert?'

'I don't mind,' the boy whispered.

The Dean took the Bible which lay at his hand, and thoughtfully turned the pages; but a strange idea came to him, and he put it down. The perfume of the night, of the leaves and of the roses, the savour of the dew, filled that room with a subtle delicacy, as though some light spirit of a poet's fancy had taken possession of it; and by instinct he felt that the boy, who through life had loved so passionately the world's sensuous beauty, must desire other words than those of Hebrew prophets. His great love and sympathy lifted him from the common level of his calling to a plane of higher charity, and the knowledge came what reading would give Herbert the most delectable comfort; bending forward, he whispered to Bella, who gave a look of utter astonishment, but none the less rose to do his bidding. She brought him a small book bound in blue cloth, and slowly he began to read.

Courting Amaryllis with song I go, while my she-goats feed on the hill, and Tityrus herds them. Ah, Tityrus, my dearly beloved, feed thou the goats, and to the well-side lead them, Tityrus. . . .

Miss Ley looked up with amazement, and even at that moment could not suppress an inward ironical laughter, for she recognized an iydll of Theocritus. Very gravely, dwelling on the pictures called up to his mind stored with classical learning, the good Dean read through the charming dialogue recounting preciously, with the elaborate simplicity of a decadent age, the amours of Sicilian shepherds. Herbert listened with quiet satisfaction, a happy smile set lightly on his pallid lips; and he too, his imagination curiously quickened by approaching death, saw the shady groves and babbling streams of Sicily, heard the piping of love-lorn goatherds, the coy responses of fair maids refusing the kisses so sweet to give only that surrender at length might be the more complete. Even in the translation a breath of pure poetry was there, and the spirit was preserved of a life consciously free from the artifice of civilization, wherein sunshine and shade, spring and summer, the perfume of flowers, offered satisfying delights.

The Dean finished, and closed the book; and silence fell upon them all, and they sat through the night. The words whereto they had listened seemed to have left with them a singular tranquillity, so that all the stress and passion of the world were banished; and even to Bella, though her husband lay a-dying, there came a strange sense of gratitude for the fullness and the beauty of life. The hours passed marked by the deep-tongued chiming of the cathedral bells; every quarter they pealed their warning, ominous, yet not terrifying, and to all it seemed that the parting soul waited only for the day to take her flight.

The silence was extraordinary, more lovely than sweet music; it seemed a living thing that filled the chamber of death with peace unspeakable; and the night was dark, for the stars now were vanished before the full moon, but the goddess spared the room her frigid brilliancy, and left the garden tenebrous. No breath of wind touched the trees, and not a rustle of leaves disturbed the stilly calm; the muteness of the sleeping town seemed all about them, so profound that one felt some spirit had descended thereon, throwing over all things, to emphasize the wakefulness of those who watched, a shroud of death. Then a sound stole through the air, so gradual and delicate a sound that none could tell how it began; one might have thought it born miraculously of the very silence; it was a silvery, tenuous note that travelled through the stillness like light through air, and all at once, with a suddenness that startled, broke into passionate, vehement song. It was the nightingale. The placid night rang like a sounding-board, and each breath of air took up the tremulous magic; the bird sang in a haw-thorn-tree below the window, and its rapture rang through the garden, rang into the large room to the ears of the dying youth. He started from his sleep, and it seemed as though he were called back from death. None stirred, all fascinated and im-

265

prisoned by that miracle of song. Passion and anguish and exultation, rising and falling in perpetual harmony, sometimes the beauty was hardly sufferable (as though was reached at length the heart's limit of endurance) so that one could have cried out with the sorrow of it. The music was poured upon the listening air, – trembling and throbbing with pain; joyous, triumphant, and conscious of might; it hesitated like a lover who knows that his love is hopeless; it was like the voice of a dying child lamenting the loveliness it would never know; it was the mocking laughter of a courtesan for whose sake a man has died; it wept and prayed, and gloried in the joy of living; it was all sweetness and tenderness, offering pardon for sins past, and charity and peace and the rest that ever endures; it exulted in the sweet scents of the earth, the multicoloured flowers, the gentle airs, the dew, and the white beam of the moon. Inhuman, ecstatic, defiant, the nightingale warbled, drunk with the beauty that issued from his throat. To Herbert, curiously alert, all his senses gathered to one last effort of appreciation, it recalled the land which he had never seen: Hellas – Hellas with its olive-gardens and its purling streams, its grey rocks all rosy in the setting sun, and its sacred groves, its blithe airs and its sonorous speech. Passed through his mind Philomel chanting for ever her distress, and Pan the happy shepherd, and the fauns and the flying nymphs; all the lovely things whereof he had read and dreamed appeared before him in one last passionate vision of a glory that was long since set. At that moment he was happy to die, for the world had given him much, and he had been spared the disillusion of old age. But to Frank the nightingale sang of other things – of the birth which follows ever on the heel of death, of life ever new and desirable, of the wonder of the teeming earth and the endless cycle of events. Men came and went, and the world turned on; the individual was naught, but the race continued its blind journey toward the greater nothingness; the trees shed their leaves and the flowers drooped and withered, but the spring brought new buds; hopes were dead before the desired came about; love perished, the love that seemed immortal; one thing succeeded another restlessly, and the universe was ever fresh and wonderful. He, too, was thankful for his life. And then, suddenly, in the very midst of his song, when he seemed to gather his heart for a final burst of infinite melody, the nightingale ceased, and through all the garden passed a shudder, as though the trees and the flowers and the taciturn birds of the day were distraught because they awoke suddenly to common life. For an instant the night quivered still with the memory of those heavenly notes, and then, more profoundly, the silence returned. Herbert gave a low sob, and Bella went to him quickly; she bent down to hear what he said.

'I'm so glad,' he whispered – 'I'm so glad.'

Again the cathedral bells rang out, and the watchers counted the deliberate striking of the hour. They sat in silence. And then the darkness was insensibly diminished; as yet there was no light, but they felt the dawn was at hand. A chilliness came into the room, the greater cold of the departing night, and the velvet obscurity took on a subtle hue of amethyst. A faint sound came from the bed, and the Dean went over and listened; the end was very nearly come. He knelt down, and in a low voice began to repeat the prayers for the dying.

O Almighty God, with whom do live the spirits of great men made perfect, after they are delivered from their earthly prisons: We humbly commend the soul of this Thy servant, our dear brother, into Thy hands, most humbly beseeching Thee that it may be precious in Thy sight. Wash it, we pray Thee, in the blood of that Immaculate Lamb, that was slain to take away the sins of the world; that whatsoever defilements it may have contracted in the midst of this miserable world, through the lusts of the flesh or the wiles of Satan, being purged and done away, it may be presented pure and without spot before Thee.

Miss Ley stood up and touched Frank's arm.

'Come,' she whispered; 'you and I can do no more good. Let us leave them.'

He rose silently, and following her, they stole very gently from the room.

'I want to walk in the garden,' she said, her voice trembling. But once in the open air, her nerves, taut till then by a great effort of will, gave way on a sudden, and the strong, collected

267

woman burst into a flood of tears. Sinking on a bench, she hid her face and wept uncontrollably. 'Oh, it's too awful,' she cried. 'It seems so horribly stupid that people should ever die.'

Frank looked at her gravely, and in a reflective fashion filled his pipe.

'I'm afraid you're rather upset; you'd better let me write you out a little prescription in the morning.'

'Don't be a drivelling idiot,' she cried. 'What do you think I want with your foolish bromides!'

He did not answer, but deliberately lit his pipe; and though Miss Ley knew it not, his words had the calming effect he foresaw. She brushed away the tears and took his arm. They walked up and down the lawn slowly; but Miss Ley, unused to give way to her emotions, was shaken still, and he felt her trembling.

'It's just at such times as these that you and I are so utterly helpless. When people's hearts are breaking for a word of consolation, when they're sick with fear because of the unknown, we can only shrug our shoulders and tell them that we know nothing. It's too awful to think that we shall never see again those we have loved so deeply; it's too awful to think that nothing awaits us but cold extinction. I try to put death from my thoughts – I wish never to think of it; but it's hateful, hateful. Each year I grow older I'm more passionately attached to life. After all, even if the beliefs of men are childish and untrue, isn't it better to keep them? Surely superstition is a small price to pay for that wonderful support at the last hour, when all else fades to insignificance. How can people have the heart to rob the simple-minded of that great comfort?'

'But don't you think most of us would give our very souls to believe? Of course we need it, and sometimes so intensely that we can hardly help praying to a God we know is not there. It's very hard to stand alone and look forward – without hope.'

They wandered still, and the birds began to sing blithely; Nature awoke from her sleep, slowly, with languid movements. The night was gone, and yet the day was not come. The trees and the flowers stood out with a certain ghostly dimness, and the air in those first moments of dawn was fresh and keen: all things were swathed in a strange violet light that seemed to give new contours and new hues. There was a curious self-consciousness about the morning, and the leaves rustled like animate beings; the sky was very pale, cloudless, grey, and amethystine; and then suddenly a ray of yellow light shot right across it, and the sun rose.

'D'you know,' said Frank, 'it seems to me that just as there is an instinct for life there must be an instinct for death also; some very old persons, here and there, long for the release, just as the majority long for existence. Perhaps in the future this will be more common; and just as certain insects, having done their life's work, die willingly, without regret, from sheer cessation of the wish to live, so it may happen that men, too, will develop some such feeling. And then death will have no terrors, for we shall come to it as joyfully as after a hard day we go to our sleep.'

'And meanwhile?' asked Miss Ley, with a painful smile.

'Meanwhile we must have courage. In our sane moments we devise a certain scheme of life, and we must keep to it in the hour of trouble. I will try to live my life so that when the end comes I can look back without regret, and forward without fear.'

But now the sun flooded the garden with its magnificence, and there was a beauty in the morning that told more eloquently than human words the good lesson that life is to the living and the world is full of joy. Still the birds sang their merry songs – throstle and merle, and finch and twittering sparrow – and the flowers, defiant, squandered their perfume. There were roses everywhere, and side by side were the buds and the full-blown blossoms and the dead, drooping splendours of yesterday; the great old trees of the Deanery garden were fresh and verdant as though they had not bloomed and faded for a hundred years; the very air was jocund and gay, and it was a delight merely to stand still and breathe.

But while they walked Miss Ley gave a cry, and leaving Frank's arm, stepped forward; for Bella was seated on a bench under a tree, with the sun shining full on her face; she stared in front of her with wide-open eyes, unblinded by the brilliance, and the lines of care were suddenly gone from her face. Her expression was radiant, so that for a momest she was a beautiful woman.

'Bella, what is it?' cried Miss Ley. 'Bella!'

She lowered her eyes and passed her hand over them, for now they were dazzled with shining gold. An ecstatic smile broke upon her lips.

'He died when the sun came into the room; a bridge of gold was set for him, and he passed painlessly into the open.'

'Oh, my poor child!'

Bella shook her head and smiled again.

'I'm not sorry; I'm glad that his suffering is over. He died so gently that at first I didn't know it. I could hardly believe he was not asleep. I told father. And then I saw a lovely butterfly – a golden butterfly such as I've never seen before – hover slowly about the room. I couldn't help looking at it, for it seemed to know its way, and then it came into the sunbeam and floated out along it – floated into the blue sky; and then I lost it.'

A week later Miss Ley was in London, where she meant to stay through August, partly because it bored her to decide where to spend that holiday season, partly because Mrs Barlow-Bassett had been forced to go to a private hospital for an operation; but still more because Frank's presence gave her the certainty that she would have someone to talk to whenever she liked. That month vastly amused her, for London gained then somewhat the air of a foreign capital, and since few of her acquaintance remained, she felt free to do whatever she chose without risk of being thought wilfully eccentric. Miss Ley dined with Frank in shabby little restaurants in Soho, where neither the linen nor the frequenters were of a spotless character; but it entertained her much to watch bearded Frenchmen languishing away from their native land, and to overhear the voluble confidences of ladies whose position in society was scarcely acknowledged. They went together to music-halls over the river or drove on the tops of buses, and discussed interminably the weather and eternity, the meaning of life, the foibles of their friends, Shakespeare, and the *Bilharzia hoematobi.*

Miss Ley had left Bella and the Dean at Tercanbury. The widow never for a moment lost her grave serenity. She attended the burying of her husband with dry eyes, absently as though it were a formal ceremony that had no particular meaning to her; and the Dean, who could not understand her point of view, was dismayed, for he was broken down with grief, and it was his daughter who sought to console him. She repeated that Herbert was there among them now; and the furniture of the house, the roses of the garden, the blue of the sky, gained a curious significance, since he seemed to be in all things, partaking of their comfortable beauty, and adding to theirs a more subtle loveliness.

Soon Miss Ley received from her friend a letter, enclosing one from Herbert, scribbled in pencil but a few days before his death. She said:

This is apparently for you, and though it is the last thing he ever wrote, I feel that you should have it. It seems to refer to a conversation that you had with him, and I am glad to have found it. My father keeps well, and I also. Sometimes I can scarcely realize that Herbert is dead, he seems so near to me. I thought I could not live without him, but I am singularly content, and I know that soon we shall be united, and then for ever.

The letter was as follows:

DEAR MISS LEY,

You wanted to ask me a question the other day, and were afraid, in case you pained me; but I guessed it, and would have answered very willingly. Did you not wish to know whether, notwithstanding poverty and illness and frustrated hopes and the prospect of death, I was glad to have lived? Yes, notwithstanding everything. Except that I must leave Bella, I am not sorry to die, for I know at last well enough that I should never have been a great poet; and Bella will join me soon. I have loved the world passionately, and I thank God for all the beautiful things I have seen. I thank God for the green meadows round Tercanbury, and the elm-trees, and the grey monotonous sea. I thank Him for the loveliness of the cathedral on rainy afternoons in winter, and for the jewelled glass of its

271

painted windows, and for the great clouds that sway across the sky. I thank God for the scented flowers and the carolling birds, for the sunshine and the spring breezes, and the people who have loved me. Oh yes, I am glad to have lived; and if I had to go through it all again, with the sorrows and disappointments and the sickness, I would take it willingly, for to me at least the delight of life has been greater than the pain. I am very ready to pay the price, and I would wish to die with a prayer of thanksgiving on my lips.'

The letter broke off thus abruptly, as though he had meant to say much more, but wanted opportunity. Miss Ley read the letter to Frank when next he came.

'Do you notice,' she asked, 'that every one of the things he speaks of appeals to the senses? Yet the only point upon which philosophers and divines agree is that this is the lower part of us, and must be resolutely curbed. They put the intellect on an altogether higher plane.'

'They lie in their throats. And you can prove that really they believe nothing of the kind by comparing the concern with which they treat their stomachs, and the negligence with which they use their minds. To make their food digestible, nourishing, and wholesome, enormous trouble is taken, but they will stuff into their heads any garbage they come across. When you contrast the heedlessness with which people choose their books from Mudie's, and the care with which they order their dinner, you can be sure, whatever their protestations, that they lay vastly more store on their bellies than on their intellects.'

'I rather wish I'd said that,' murmured Miss Ley reflectively.

'I have no doubt you will,' he returned.

11

MRS BARLOW-BASSETT, who cultivated the fashion with the assiduity of a woman not too well assured of her position in society, was preparing to spend August in Homburg, when a sudden illness prostrated her, and it was found that an immediate operation was needful. She went into a private hospital with the presentiment that she would never recover, and her chief sorrow was that she must leave Reggie, so ill-prepared for the mundane struggle, to go his way alone just when a mother's loving care was most needed for his guidance. Her heart ached to keep him continually by her side, but she had trained herself to sacrifice every amiable tenderness, and when he told her of an arrangement to read in the country with his tutor, would not hear of its being disturbed. Her possible demise made it all the more necessary that he should be standing on his own feet as a professional man, and resolutely she crushed, not only her natural inclinations, but also all evidence of anxiety for her own condition; she made light of the approaching ordeal, so that his attention should be in no way diverted from his work. Reggie promised to write every day, and went so far (a trait which touched her deeply) as to insist on remaining in London till after her operation; he would not be able to see her, but at least could inquire how she had borne it. Mrs Barlow-Bassett drove to Wimpole Street with her son, and bade him a very tender farewell; at the end, just before he left, her courage partly failed, and she could not prevent a cry of distress.

'And if something happens, Reggie, and I don't recover, you will be a good boy, won't you? You will be honest and straightforward and loyal?'

'What do *you* think?' answered Reggie.

She folded him in her arms, and with a firmness not unbecoming her appearance, fashioned somewhat in the grand style, let him go with dry eyes and with smiling lips. But Mrs Bassett had exaggerated a little the perils of her condition; she bore the operation admirably, and after the first two days proceeded without interruption to complete recovery. Reggie wrote with considerable regularity from Brighton, where it appeared the tutor had established himself for the summer, and gave his mother accounts of the work he did; he went into considerable detail, and, indeed, seemed so industrious that Mrs Bassett was minded to remonstrate with his tutor. After all, it was holiday time, and scarcely fair that Reggie's goodwill should be thus taken advantage of. Towards the end of the month she was well enough to move back to her own house, and the morning after her return came downstairs in a very contented frame of mind, rejoicing in her new health and in the splendid summer weather. Carelessly she opened her *Morning Post*, and as usual ran her eye down the announcements of birth, death, and marriage. Suddenly it caught her own name, and she read the following intelligence:

BARLOW-BASSETT – HIGGINS. – On the 30th ult., at St George's, Hanover Square, W., Reginald, only son of the late Frederick Barlow-Bassett, to Annie (Lauria Galbraith), second daughter of Jonathan Higgins, of Wimbledon.

For a moment Mrs Bassett did not understand, and she read the paragraph twice, hopelessly mystified, before she realized that it announced to the world in general the marriage of her son. The date of the occurrence was the day after her operation, and on that very morning Reggie had called at Wimpole Street to inquire after her. The butler was still in the room, and helplessly Mrs Bassett handed him the paper.

'D'you know what this means?' she asked.

'No, madam.'

Her first thought was that it must be a practical joke; and then, what was the meaning of that second name in parentheses – Lauria Galbraith? She rang for the servant, and told him at once to send a wire, which she directed to Reggie at Brighton, asking for an explanation of the extraordinary announcement; after breakfast she telegraphed to her solicitor and to the

274

tutor's London address. The tutor's reply came first, to the effect that he had not seen Reggie since July; and in answer to her second question, he added that himself had been in London all the summer. At length Mrs Bassett began to understand that something awful had happened. She went into Reggie's room, and coming upon a locked drawer, had it broken open; she found in it a writing-case, and with horror and indignation turned out a motley collection of bills, pawn-tickets, and letters. She examined them all carefully, and first discovered that accounts for which she had given money were unpaid, and that others, enormous to her economical view, existed of which she knew nothing; then from the pawn-tickets she learned that Reggie had pledged his father's watch, all his own trinkets, a dressing-case she had given him, and numberless other things. For an instant she hesitated at the letters, but only for an instant; it seemed her right now to know the worst, and little by little it dawned upon her that hitherto she had lived in a strange fool's paradise. First there came epistles from duns, polite, supplicatory, menacing; then a couple of writs, smacking to her inexperienced eye of prison bars and unimagined penalties; letters from women in various writings, most of them ill-spelt, and the cheap stationery betrayed the senders' rank. With frowning brow she read them, horrified and aghast; some were full of love, others of anger, but all pointed distinctly to Reggie's polygamous tendency. At length came a bundle whereof the paper was quite different – thick, expensive, scented; and though not at once recognizing the hand when she opened the first, Mrs Bassett cried out; on the left side, at the top, in little letters of gold, surrounded by a scroll, was the name *Grace,* and though there was no address she knew that they were from Mrs Castillyon. She read them all, and her dismay turned to abject shame and anger. It appeared that this woman had given Reggie cheques and bank-notes. One letter said, '*I hope you can change the cheque*'; another, '*So sorry you're hard up; here's a fiver to go on with*'; a third, '*What a pig-dog your mother is to be so mean! What on earth does she spend her money on?*' At first they were burning with passion, but soon began to complain of unkindness or cruelty,

275

and one letter after another was filled with bitter reproaches.

Mrs Bassett took the whole contents of the writing-case, and locked them in her own cabinet, then hurried to Reggie's tutor. Here she discovered that what she already suspected was true. She went home again, and called the upper servants. It humiliated her enormously that she must catechize them on the conduct of her son, but now she had no scruples. At first they would say nothing, but by dint of promise and threat she extracted from them the full story of how Reggie had lived during the last two years. At length, as a final blow, came an epistle from Reggie himself.

371, Vauxhall Bridge Road

MY DEAR MATER,

You will have seen in this morning's *Post* that I was married at the end of last month to Miss Higgins, professionally known as Lauria Galbraith, and we are now staying at the above address. I am sure you will like Lauria, who is the best woman in the world, and has saved me from going to the dogs. You might let us have a line to say when we can come and see you. Lauria is most anxious to make your acquaintance. I should tell you that I have decided to chuck the Bar, and I am going on the stage. Lauria and I have got an engagement for the autumn tour of *The Knave of Hearts*, and we have come up to town for rehearsals. I am sure this will meet with your approval, because law is a rotten profession, awfully overcrowded, and as Lauria says, on the stage there is always room for talent. I know I shall get on, and Lauria and I hope in a few years to run our own company. I am working very hard, for although I'm only walking on in this drama (I wouldn't have accepted the offer, only Lauria has a ripping part, and, of course, as I hadn't been on the stage before, I had to take what I could get) I am learning *Hamlet*. Lauria and I think of giving some recitations of that and *Romeo and Juliet* in town next spring.

Your affectionate son,

REGGIE

P.S. – You needn't worry about the money, because on the stage I can earn far more than I ever should have done at the Bar. An actor-manager simply makes thousands.

Mrs Bassett burst into tears, for she had never imagined that

Reggie could be so callous, so inanely flippant; but rage succeeded all other emotions in her breast, and she wrote angrily, telling her son never again to show his face at her house, or the servants would throw him into the street – telling him that no farthing of her money should ever be his; then silence seemed more dignified, and she determined merely to leave unanswered that impudent letter. But it was necessary to express her indignation to someone, and she sent an urgent note to Miss Ley, begging her at once to come.

When the good lady, obedient to the summons, arrived, she found Mrs Bassett in a very hysterical condition, walking up and down the room excitedly; and in the disorder of her majestic manner she reminded her somewhat of a middle-aged bacchante.

'Thank God you've come!' she cried. 'Reggie's married an actress, and I've disinherited him. I won't ever see him again, and for all I care he may starve.'

Miss Ley made no movement of surprise, merely noting the fact that herself was a woman of prevision. All she had expected was come about.

'I've been utterly deceived in him. He's not passed a single examination, and the servants have told me that he often came home at night tipsy. He's lied to me systematically; he's deceived me in every possible way; and all the time I flattered myself he was a good, honest boy, he's been leading the life of a rip and a libertine.'

Her words were interrupted by a fit of crying, while Miss Ley watched her reflectively. Presently Mrs Bassett recovered herself.

'I confess the marriage surprises me,' murmured Miss Ley. 'Your daughter-in-law must be a woman of character and tact, Emily; but all the rest has been known to your friends for the last year.'

'D'you mean to say you knew he was a drunken sot, and little better than a thief and a liar?'

'Yes.'

'Why didn't you tell me?'

'I thought you'd find out quite soon enough; and really,

Emily, you're such a fool you would probably have only made things worse.'

Mrs Bassett was too much crushed to resent this plain speech.

'But you don't know everything. I've found a lot of letters from women. It's they who've led him astray. And d'you know whose are the worst?'

'Mrs Castillyon's?'

'Did you know that, too? Did everyone know my shame, and that my boy was being ruined, and did no one warn me? But I'm going to pay her out. I shall send every one to her husband. It's she who's done the mischief.'

She took from a drawer the bundle of letters, and excitedly gave them to Miss Ley.

'Is this all?' she asked.

'Yes.'

Miss Ley had with her a black satin bag, in which she kept her handkerchief and her purse, and swiftly opening it, she put the letters in.

'What are you doing?'

'My dear, don't be a fool! You're not going to send these letters to anyone, and as soon as I get home I mean to burn them. Reggie was a dissolute rip before ever he met Grace Castillyon, and the only woman who ruined him is – yourself! You were very angry when I told you once that the greatest misfortune which could befall a man was to have a really affectionate mother, but I assure you, except for your bad influence, Reggie would have been no worse a boy than any other.'

Mrs Bassett turned livid.

'I think you must be mad, Mary. I've done all I could by example and precept to make him a gentleman. I've devoted my life to his education, and I've sacrificed myself to him absolutely from the day he was born. I can honestly say that I've been a good mother.'

'Pardon me,' answered Miss Ley coolly, 'you've been a very bad mother, a very selfish mother, and you've systematically sacrificed him to your own whims and fancies.'

'How can you talk to me like that when I want sympathy and help? Haven't you any pity for me?'

'None! All that has happened you've brought entirely on yourself. You made him a liar by compelling him to tell you his most private affairs, you drove him to deception by expecting from him an impossible purity, you warned him of temptation so as to make it doubly attractive. You never let him have a free will or a natural instinct, but insisted on his acting and feeling like a middle-aged and rather ill-educated woman. You thwarted all his inclinations, and forced upon him yours. Good heavens! you couldn't have been more selfish, cruel, and exacting if you'd detested the boy!'

Mrs Bassett stared at her, overwhelmed.

'But I only asked common honesty and truthfulness. I only wanted to keep him from spot and stain, and I only expected the morality which religion and everything else enforces upon us.'

'You starved his instincts – the natural desire of a boy for gaiety and amusement, the natural craving of youth for love. You applied to him the standards of a woman of fifty. A wise mother lets her son go his own way, and shuts her eyes to youthful peccadillos; but you made all these peccadillos into deadly sins. After all, moralists talk a deal of nonsense about the frailty of mankind. When you come to close quarters with vice, it's not really so desperately wicked as all that. A man may be a very good fellow though he does sit up late and occasionally drink more than is discreet, gamble a little and philander with ladies of doubtful fame. All these things are part of human nature, when youth and hot blood are joined together, and for some of them foreign nations, wiser than ourselves, have made provision.'

'I wish I'd never had a son!' cried Mrs Bassett. 'How much luckier you are than I!'

Miss Ley got up, and a curious expression came over her face.

'Oh, my dear, don't say that! I tell you, that even though I know Reggie to be idle and selfish and dissolute, I would give all I have in the world if he were only mine. There's not a soul on this wide earth that cares for me – except Frank, because I amuse him – and I'm so dreadfully lonely. I'm growing old. Often I feel so old I wonder how I can continue to live, and I want someone so badly to whom it's not a matter of absolute indifference if I'm well or ill, dead or alive. Oh, my dear, thank God for your son!'

'I can't now I know he's wicked and vicious.'

'But what is vice, and what is wickedness? Are you sure we know? I suppose I have been a virtuous woman. I've done nobody any harm; I've helped a good many; I've done the usual moral things that women do; and when anything was possible that I particularly wanted, I've withstood because it was ingrained in me that nice things were naughty. But sometimes I think I've wasted my life, and I dare say I should be a better woman if I hadn't been so virtuous. When I look back now it's not the temptations I fell to that I regret, but the temptations I resisted. I'm an old woman, and I've never known love, and I'm childless and forsaken. Oh, Emily, if I had my time over again I promise you I wouldn't be so virtuous. I would take all the good that life offered, without thinking too much of propriety. And above all things I would have a child.'

'Mary, what are you saying?'

Miss Ley shrugged her shoulders, and was silent; her voice was broken, and she could not trust herself to speak. But Mrs Bassett's thoughts went back to the injury which Reggie had done her, and she gave Miss Ley his letter to read.

'There's not a word of regret in it. He seems to have no shame and no conscience. He was married on the very day of my operation, when I might have died any moment. He must be absolutely heartless.'

'D'you know what I would do if I were you?' asked Miss Ley, pleased to get away from her own emotions. 'I would go to him, and ask forgiveness for all the harm you've done him.'

'I? Mary, you must be mad! What need have I for forgiveness?'

'Think it over. I have an idea that presently it will occur to you that you never gave the boy a chance. I'm not sure whether you don't owe him a good deal of reparation; anyhow, you can't undo the marriage, and it's just possible it may be the saving of him.'

'You're not going to ask me to receive an actress as my daughter-in-law!'

'Fiddledidee! She'll make your son a much better wife than a duchess.'

When Mrs Barlow-Bassett showed her friend Reggie's letter, Miss Ley carefully noted the address, and next day, in the afternoon, proceeded to call upon the new-married couple. They lived in a somewhat shabby lodging-house in the Vauxhall Bridge Road – that long, sordid street – and Miss Ley was shown into an attic which served as sitting-room. It was barely fitted with tawdry furniture, much the worse for wear, but to give a homelike air photographs were pinned on the wall, each with a sprawling flourish for a signature, of persons connected with the stage, but unknown to fame. When Miss Ley entered, Reggie, dressed in a suit of somewhat pronounced pattern, with a Homburg tweed hat on his head, was reading the *Era*, while his wife stood in front of the glass doing her hair. Notwithstanding the late hour, she still wore a dressing-gown of red satin, covered with inexpensive lace, which was certainly neither very new nor very clean. Miss Ley's appearance caused some embarrassment, and it was not without awkwardnesss that Reggie made the necessary introduction.

'Excuse me being in such a state,' said Mrs Reggie, gathering up her hairpins, 'but I was just going to dress.'

She was a little woman, plainly older than her husband, and to Miss Ley's astonishment, by no means pretty; her eyes were handsome, used with full knowledge of their power, and her black hair very fine; but chiefly noticeable was a singular determination of manner, a shrewishness about the mouth, which suggested that if she did not get her own way someone would suffer. She looked rather suspiciously at Miss Ley, but treated her with sufficient cordiality to indicate a readiness to be friendly if the visitor did not prove hostile.

'I only heard you were married yesterday,' Miss Ley

hastened to say as affably as possible, 'and I was anxious to make your wife's acquaintance, Reggie.'

'You've not come from the mater?' he asked.

'No.'

'I suppose she's in a hell of a wax.'

'Reggie, don't swear; I don't like it,' said his wife.

Miss Ley shrugged her shoulders and smiled vaguely. Since she was not offered a chair, she looked round for the most comfortable, and sat down. Mrs Reggie glanced uncertainly from her husband to Miss Ley, and then at her own disarranged dress, hesitating whether to leave the pair alone or to sacrifice her appearance.

'I am untidy,' she said.

'Good heavens! it's so refreshing to find someone who doesn't dress till late in the day. When I take off my dressing-gown I put on invariably a sense of responsibility. Do sit down and tell me all about your plans.'

Miss Ley had the art of putting people at their ease, and the bride succumbed at once to the elder woman's quiet but authoritative way. She glanced at her husband.

'Reggie, take off your hat,' she said peremptorily.

'Oh, I'm sorry. I forgot.'

When he removed his headgear Miss Ley noticed that his hair was very long, worn with a dramatic flamboyance. His speech was deliberate, with a certain declamatory enunciation which vastly amused his old friend; his nails were none too clean, and his boots needed polish.

'What does the mater think of my going on the stage?' he asked, passing his hand with a fine gesture through his raven locks. 'It's the best thing I could do, isn't it, Lauria? I feel that I've found my vocation. Nature intended me for an actor. It's the only thing I'm fit for – an artistic career. Tell my mother that I will sacrifice everything to my art. I hope you'll come and see me play.'

'It will give me great pleasure.'

'Not in this piece. I only – walk on, don't you know. But in the spring Lauria and I are going to give a series of recitations.'

282

He rose to his feet, and standing in front of the fireplace, stretched out one dramatic hand.

> 'To be, or not to be: that is the question:
> Whether 'tis nobler in the mind to suffer
> The slings and arrows of outrageous fortune,
> Or to take arms against a sea of troubles,
> And by opposing end them?'

He bellowed the words at the top of his voice, uttering each syllable with profound and dramatic emphasis.

'By Jove!' he said, 'what a part! They don't write parts like that now. An actor has no chance in a modern play, where there's not a speech more than two lines long.'

Miss Ley looked at him with astonishment, for it had never occurred to her that such a development could possibly be his; then, glancing quickly at Lauria, she fancied that a slight ironical smile trembled on her lips.

'I tell you,' said Reggie, beating his chest, 'I feel that I shall be a great actor. If I can only get my chance, I shall just stagger creation. I must go and see Basil Kent, and ask him to write a play for us, Lauria.'

'And are you going to stagger creation too?' asked Miss Ley, blandly turning to Mrs Reggie.

The young woman restrained her merriment no longer, but burst into such a hearty peal of laughter that Miss Ley began to like her.

'Will you stay to tea, Miss Ley?'

'Certainly; that is why I came.'

'That's fine. I'll make you some tea in less than no time. Reggie, take the can, and go out and get half a pint of milk.'

'Yes, my dear,' he replied obediently, putting on his tweed hat with a rakish swagger, and taking from a table littered with papers, articles of apparel, and domestic utensils a small milk-can.

'How much money have you got in your pocket?'

He pulled out some coppers and one silver coin.

'One and sevenpence halfpenny.'

'Then, you'll have one and sixpence halfpenny when you

come home. You can buy a packet of straighters for three-pence, and mind you're back in ten minutes.'

'Yes, dear.'

He walked out meekly, and closed the door behind him. Mrs Reggie went to the door and looked out.

'His mother brought him up very badly,' she explained, 'and he's not above listening at keyholes.'

Miss Ley, shaking with inward laughter, had listened to the scene with amazement. Lauria continued her apologetic explanations.

'You know, I have to keep a sharp eye on his money because he's rather inclined to tipple. I've got him out of it, but I'm always afraid he'll drop into a pub if I don't look out. His mother must be about the biggest fool you've met, isn't she?'

Mrs Reggie glanced at a box of cigarettes, and the other, noticing the yellow on her forefinger, concluded she was an eager smoker; it was easy to put her in comfort.

'Would you give me a cigarette?'

'Oh, d'you smoke?' cried Lauria, with a bright look of pleasure. 'I was simply dying for a fag, but I didn't want to shock you.'

They lit up, and Miss Ley drew towards her another chair.

'D'you mind if I put my feet up? I always think that only quadrupeds should keep their longer extremities constantly dangling.'

With a faint smile, she essayed to make smoke-rings.

'You're all right,' said Lauria, with a little nod. 'I'm glad you came. I wanted to have a talk with someone who knew Reggie's mother. I suppose she's in a fury. I wanted him to tell her beforehand, but he didn't dare. Besides, he never does a thing straightforwardly if he can do it crooked. And as for lying – well, he's worse than a woman. You can tell his mother it'll take me all my time to make a gentleman of her son.'

Miss Ley smiled dryly.

'I have seldom seen a newly-married woman so keenly alive to the defects of her husband's character.'

'Reggie's not a bad boy really,' answered his wife, shrugging her shoulders, 'but he wants licking into shape.'

'I wonder why you married him?' asked the other, reflectively, knocking off the ash of her cigarette.

Lauria looked at her sharply, hesitating, then made up her mind to speak openly.

'You seem a good sort and a woman of the world; and, after all, I'm married, and you'll just have to make the best of me. Reggie's good-looking, isn't he?' She glanced at a photograph which stood on the chimneypiece. 'And I like him. You know, I've been on the stage eight years; I went on when I was sixteen. How much does that make me?'

'Twenty-seven, I should say,' answered Miss Ley with deliberation.

Lauria smiled good-naturedly.

'Nasty people say I'm twenty-eight; but, anyhow, I'm sick to death of the stage, and I want to get off it.'

'I thought you were going to play Juliet to Reggie's Romeo.'

'Yes, I can see myself! For one thing, I'm quite sure Reggie can't act for nuts, and when they start they all want to play Hamlet. Why, I never knew a super who carried a banner in a panto who didn't think that if he got his opportunity he'd be another Irving. Oh, I've heard it so often! Every girl I know has come to me and said: "Lauria, I feel I've got it in me, and I only want a chance." I'm sick of the whole thing. I don't want to go traipsing about the provinces, working like a nigger all the week, and travelling on Sundays, living in dingy apartments, and all the rest of it. I just let Reggie gas away, and it keeps him out of mischief to learn plays. I thought it would take his mother three months to come round, and by that time he'll be sick of it. I like Reggie, and when I've had him in hand for a few months I shall make a decent boy of him; but I don't pretend for a moment I'd have married him if I hadn't known that his mother had money.'

'You're a wise woman. In the first place, I can't think how you got him to marry at all. I never thought he'd do it.'

'My dear Miss Ley, I thought you were a woman of the world. Don't you know that if a girl of my age makes up her mind to marry a man, he must be awfully cute to save himself?'

'I confess I had often suspected it,' smiled Miss Ley.

'Of course, you have to choose your man. I saw Reggie was gone on me, and I led him a dance. You know, we've got a reputation for being wrong uns on the stage, but that's all rot. We're no worse than anyone else, only we've got more temptation, and when anything happens the papers take it up just because we're professional. But I've known how to take care of myself, and I just let Master Reggie understand that I wasn't going to be made a fool of. I played up to him for a fortnight, and then told him I wouldn't see him any more, and by that time he was fairly stage-struck, and so he asked me to marry him.'

'It sounds very simple. And how did you manage to tame him?'

'I just let him see that if he wanted to have a decent time he'd got to be nice to me, and he very soon tumbled to it. You wouldn't think it, but I've got a nasty temper when I'm roused. He looks up to me like anything, and he knows I don't mean to stand any nonsense. Oh, he'll be all right in six months.'

'And what do you want me to tell his mother?'

'Just tell her not to interfere. We're all right with regard to money, and when she calms down she can make us an allowance. Six hundred a year will do, and we'll take a house at Bournemouth. I don't want to live in London till I'm sure of Reggie.'

'Very well,' answered Miss Ley. 'I'll say that, and I'll say besides that she ought to thank her stars Reggie has found a decent woman. I have no doubt in a little while you'll make him into quite a respectable member of society.'

'Here he comes with the milk!'

Reggie entered, and together they began to make tea. When Miss Ley departed Lauria sent him downstairs to show her out.

'Ain't she a ripper?' he exclaimed. 'And I tell you what, Miss Ley, she's a real good sort. Tell the mater that she's not beneath me at all.'

'Beneath you! My dear boy, she's worth six of you. And I dare say under her charge you'll turn into a very passable imitation of a gentleman, after all.'

Reggie looked at her with tragic countenance, flung back his head, and pressed both hands to his manly bosom.

' "*Oh, what a rogue and peasant slave am I!*" ' he cried.

'For goodness' sake, hold your tongue!' she interrupted quickly.

She gave him her hand, and while pressing it he leaned forward confidentially and exclaimed:

> 'I'll have grounds
> More relative than this.   The play's the thing
> Wherein I'll catch the conscience of the king.'

12

MEANWHILE things with Basil and Jenny had gone from bad to worse. There had been no power in their reconciliation to pacify the Fates, and presently another violent quarrel proved that under no circumstances could they live without discord. Basil, training his tongue to silence whatever the provocation, maintained over himself the most careful restraint; but it was very irksome, and in his breast there arose gradually a blind and angry hatred for Jenny because she made him suffer such unspeakable torture. They had so fallen out of sympathy that he never realized how ardent her love for him still was, and that she tormented him only on this account. So passed the summer, for Basil, crippled with debts, felt bound to remain in chambers through the vacation on the chance of picking up a stray brief which no one else was on hand to take.

A profound depression settled upon him, and he brooded hopelessly over the future. What had it to offer but a continuance of this unceasing pain? He looked into the years dragging out their weary length, and it seemed to him impossible to live under such conditions. Only his passion for Hilda Murray supported him, for therein he seemed to find strength to face the world, and at the same time resignation. He had learnt to ask for little from the gods, and was content to love without hope of reward. He was immensely grateful for her friendship, and felt that she understood and sympathized with his distress. Mrs Murray spent the summer abroad, but wrote often, and her letters made him happy for days. In his solitary walks he analysed his feelings endlessly, telling himself that they were very pure; and just because he thought of her so much it seemed to him that he grew better and simpler. In October she returned, and two days later Basil called upon her, but was grievously disappointed to find Mr Farley already on the scene. Basil detested the Vicar of All Souls, detecting in him a rival who lay under no such disadvantage as himself. Mr Farley was still a handsome man, with the air and presence of a person of importance. His conversation smacked of the diner-out who could discuss urbanely all the topics used at the tables of the cultured. He was diverting and easy, knowing well the discreet thing to say; and about his manner towards Mrs Murray was a subtle but significant flattery. Basil was hugely annoyed by the familiarity with which he used the woman whom himself could only treat quite formally. They appeared to have little understandings which made him furiously jealous. Hilda had busied herself in certain charitable concerns of the Vicar of All Souls, and with much laughter they discussed the various amusing things to which these had given rise.

Basil went home sullen and resentful, thinking through the whole evening of Hilda, whom he had left with Mr Farley, and when he went to bed gained no repose. He heard the hours strike one after the other, and turned from side to side restlessly, striving to get a little sleep; his love now was uncontrollable, and he was mad with grief and pain. He tried not to think of Hilda, but each subject he forced upon his brain gave way to her image, and in hopeless woe he asked himself how he could bear with life. He tried to reason, saying that this height of passion could only be temporary, and in a very few months he would look upon the present madness with scorn; he tried to soothe his aching heart by turning his emotion to literary uses, and set himself to describe his agony in words, as though he were going to write it in a novel. But nothing served. When the clock struck five he was thankful that only three hours remained before he could reasonably get up. He thought to read, but had not the heart to do anything which should disturb the bitter-sweet of his contemplation. Next morning at breakfast Jenny noticed that his eyes were heavy with want of rest, his mouth drawn and haggard, and with jealous intuition guessed the cause. She sought to make him angry, and the opportunity coming, made some spiteful remark; but he was listless; he looked up wearily, too exhausted to reply. They ate breakfast in silence, and then with heavy heart he set out for his daily work.

So things continued through the autumn, and with November the winter set in cold, dark, and wet. Coming home in the evenings, Basil's heart sank when he entered the street in which was his house; he felt sick with the sordid regularity of all those little dwellings exactly like one another. Miss Ley, perhaps ironically, had once remarked that life in a suburb must be quite idyllic; and Basil laughed savagely when he thought that only the milk-cart and the barrel-organ disturbed the romantic seclusion. He loathed his neighbours, with whom he knew Jenny discussed him, and shuddered with horror at their narrow lives, from which was excluded firmly all that made existence comely and urbane.

It was inevitable that quarrels should occur between the pair, notwithstanding Basil's determination to avoid friction, and of late these on both sides were grown more bitter. On a certain occasion, taking up his letters, he noticed that one had already been opened, and then somewhat clumsily fastened down; he glanced at Jenny, who was watching him, but she quickly dropped her eyes. Her suspicions had been aroused evidently because of the pink paper; *Private* was written above the address, and on the back was a golden initial. It was merely an offer from a money-lender to accommodate him with any sum between five pounds and five thousand, and he could not help a little laugh of scorn because Jenny, on steaming it open, had found nothing but an impudent circular : when she heard this she coloured furiously. She waited for him to speak, but he, only wondering why she had not the sense altogether to suppress that communication, said nothing. In a minute or two he gathered up his correspondence, and taking some paper, walked towards the door.

'Where are you going?' she asked abruptly. 'Can't you write in here?'

'Certainly, if it pleases you, but I have some rather bothering letters, and I want to be perfectly quiet.'

She flung aside the work on which she was engaged, and faced him angrily, stung to the quick by the indifference of his tone and manner.

'I suppose you have no objection to my talking to you when I want to say something? You seem to think I'm only fit to see

290

after the house and mend your clothes, and after that I can go and sit in the kitchen with the servant.'

'D'you think it's worth while making a scene? We seem to have said all this before so many times.'

'I want to have it out.'

'We've been having it out twice a week for the last six months,' he answered, bored to extinction, 'and we've never got anywhere yet.'

'Am I your wife or not, Basil?'

'You have your marriage lines carefully locked up to prove it.' He looked at her reflectively, putting back the letters in his desk. 'They say the first year of marriage is the worst; ours has been bad enough, in all conscience, hasn't it?'

'I suppose you think it's my fault?'

She spoke aggressively, with a sort of brutal sneer, but somehow it seemed no longer to affect him; he was able in a manner to look on this scene with a curious detachment, as though he were a spectator at a theatre watching players acting their parts.

'After all, I tried my best to make you happy.'

'Well, you haven't succeeded very well. Did you think I was likely to be happy when you left me alone all day and half the night for the swell friends for whom I'm not good enough?'

He shrugged his shoulders.

'You know very well that I scarcely ever see any of my old friends.'

'Except Mrs Murray, eh?' she interrupted.

'I've seen Mrs Murray a dozen times in the last year.'

'Oh, you needn't tell me that; I know it. She's a lady, isn't she?'

Basil stared coolly at his wife; though asking himself why that name had occurred to her, it never dawned on him that she could suspect how violent was his passion. But he meant to ignore the charge.

'My work takes me away from you,' he said. 'Think how bored you'd be if I were always here.'

'A precious lot of good your work does,' she cried scornfully. 'You can't earn enough money to keep us out of debt.'

291

'We are in debt, but we share that very respectable condition with half the nobility and gentry in the kingdom.'

'All the neighbours know that we've got bills with the tradesmen.'

Basil flushed and tightened his lips.

'I'm sorry that you shouldn't have made so good a bargain as you expected when you married me,' he replied acidly.

'I wonder what you do succeed in. Your book was very successful, wasn't it? You thought you were going to set the Thames on fire, and it fell flat, flat, flat!'

'That is a fate which has befallen better books than mine,' he answered, with a laugh.

'It deserved it.'

'I didn't expect you to appreciate it. Unfortunately, it's not given to all of us to write about wicked earls and beautiful duchesses.'

'The papers praised it, didn't they?'

'The unanimity of their blame was the only thing that consoled me. I often wonder if the reviewer who abuses you realizes what pleasure he causes to the wife of your bosom.'

It was Basil's apparent indifference to her taunts, his disdain and bitter sarcasm, that made Jenny lose all restraint. Often she could not see the point of his replies, but vaguely felt that he laughed at her; and then her passionate wrath knew no limits.

'Oh, I've learnt to know you so well since the baby died,' she said, clenching her hands. 'You've got no cause to set yourself up on a pedestal. I know what you are now; I was such a fool as to think you a hero. You're merely a failure. In everything you try you're a miserable failure.'

He faced her steadily, but a look of complete despair came into his eyes, for she had voiced with sufficient emphasis the thought which for so many months had wormed its way into his soul, destroying all his energy; he saw the future like a man condemned to death, for whom the beauty of life is only bitterness.

'Perhaps you're right, Jenny,' he replied. 'I dare say I'm only a rotten failure.'

He walked up and down the room, reflecting bitterly, and then stared out of the window at the even row of houses, somehow more sordid than ever in the dim light of gas-jets. He shuddered when he looked round this parlour, so common, so uninteresting; and like a sudden rush of water overwhelming, came the recollection of all the misery he had suffered within those four walls. Jenny had again taken up her sewing, and was hemming dusters; he sat down beside her.

'Look here, Jenny, I want to have a rather serious talk with you. I should like you to listen quietly for a few minutes, and I want to put away all passion and temper, so that we may discuss the matter quite reasonably. We don't seem able to get on very well, and I see no chance of things going any better. You're unhappy, and I'm afraid I'm not very happy, either; I don't want to seem selfish, but I can't do any work or anything while this sort of thing continues. And I feel that all these quarrels are so awfully degrading. Don't you think it would be better for both of us if we lived apart for a bit? Perhaps later on we might try again.'

While he spoke Jenny had watched with startled eyes, but, though vaguely alarmed, did not till quite the end understand to what his words tended. Then she could scarcely answer.

'D'you mean to say you want to separate? And what'll you do?'

'I should go abroad for awhile.'

'With Mrs Murray?' she cried excitedly. 'Is that it? You want to go away with her. You're sick of me. You've had all you want out of me, and now I can go. The fine lady comes along, and you send me away like a housemaid. D'you think I can't see that you're in love with her? You'd sacrifice me without a thought to save her a moment's unpleasantness. And because you love her you hate me.'

'How can you talk such nonsense! You've no right to say things like that.'

'Haven't I? I suppose I must shut my eyes and say nothing. You're in love with her. D'you think I've not seen it in these months? That's why you want to leave me.'

'It's impossible for us to live together,' he answered desperately. 'We shall never agree, and we shall never be happy. For God's sake, let us separate and have done with it.'

Basil was standing up now, and Jenny went up to him, close, so that they stood face to face.

'Look here, Basil: will you swear that you're not in love with that woman?'

'Certainly,' he answered scornfully.

'It's a lie. . . . And she's just as much in love with you as you are with her.'

'What d'you mean by that?' he cried, the blood running to his head and his heart beating painfully. He seized her wrists. 'What d'you mean, Jenny?'

'D'you think I haven't got eyes in my head? I saw it that day she came here. D'you suppose she came to see me? She despises me because I'm not a lady. She came here to please you; she was polite to me to please you; she asked me to go and see her to please you.'

'It's absurd. Of course she came. She was an old friend of mine.'

'I know that sort of friend. D'you think I didn't see the way she looked at you, and how she followed you with her eyes? She simply hung on every word you said. When you smiled she smiled; when you laughed she laughed. Oh, I should think she was in love with you; I know what love is, and I felt it. And when she looked at me, I knew she hated me because I'd robbed her of you.'

'Oh, what a dog's life it is we lead!' he cried, unable to contain himself. 'We've both been utterly wretched, and it can't go on. I do my best to hold myself in, but sometimes I feel it's impossible. I shall be led to saying things that we shall both regret. For Heaven's sake, let us part.'

'No. I won't consent.'

'We can't go on having these awful quarrels. It was a horrible mistake that we ever married. You must see that as well as I. We're utterly unsuited to one another, and the baby's death removed the only necessity that held us together.'

'You talk as if we only remained together because it was convenient.'

'Let me go, Jenny; I can't stand it any more,' he cried passionately. 'I feel as if I shall go mad.' He stretched out his hands, appealing. 'I did my best for you a year ago. I gave you all I had to give; it was little enough, in all conscience. Now I ask you to give me back my freedom.'

She was perfectly distracted; it had never occurred to her for a moment that things would go so far.

'You only think of yourself!' she exclaimed. 'What's to become of me?'

'You'll be much happier,' he answered eagerly, thinking she would yield. 'It's the best thing for both of us.'

'But I love you, Basil.'

'You!' He stared at her with dismay and consternation. 'Why, you've tortured me for six months beyond all endurance. You've made all my days a burden to me. You've made my life a perfect hell.'

She stared at him, sheer panic in her eyes; each word was like a death-blow, and she gasped and shuddered. Like a hunted thing, she looked this way and that for means of escape, but nothing offered; and then, groping strangely, seeking to hide herself, she staggered to the door.

'Give me time to think it over,' she said hoarsely.

Next morning at breakfast Basil, with elaborate politeness, spoke of trivial things, but Jenny noticed that he kept his eyes averted, and it cut her to the quick because he used her as he might a chance acquaintance. It seemed then that even stony silence would have been more easy to endure. Rising from the table, he asked whether she had considered his proposal.

'No; I didn't think you really meant it.'

He shrugged his shoulders, and did not answer. He made ready to go out, and she watched him with trembling heart, hoping with most sickening anguish that he would say one kind word to her before he left.

'You're going very early this morning,' she remarked.

'I've got to devil a case at eleven, and I want to see someone before I go into court.'

'Who?'

He coloured and looked away.

'My solicitor.'

This time it was she who kept silence; but when he went out into the street she watched him from the window, carefully, so that he should not see her if he looked up. But he never turned back. He walked slowly with bowed shoulders, as though he were very tired; then she gave way to her bitter sorrow and wept uncontrollably. She did not know what to do, and more than ever before needed advice. On a sudden she made up her mind to see Frank Hurrell; for during the summer he had come fairly often to Barnes, and she had been always grateful for his sober kindness; him at least she could trust, and unlike the others, he would not scorn her because she was of mean birth. Part of her difficulties arose from the fact that of late she had grown quite out of sympathy with her own people, seeing things from a different standpoint, so that it was impossible to appeal to their sympathy; she was a stranger to all the world, disaccustomed now to her own class, and still outside that into which she had married. Desperately she fancied that the very universe stood against her, and it appeared vaguely that she struggled like a drowning man against the overwhelming waters of humanity.

Jenny hurriedly dressed, and took the train to Waterloo. She did not know at what time Frank went out, and was terrified at the thought of missing him. But her training prevented her from taking a cab, and she got into a bus. It seemed to crawl along, and the minutes were hours; each stoppage drove her to such a pitch of nervous exasperation that she could scarcely sit still, and only persuaded herself with difficulty that, however slowly it went, the omnibus must go faster than she could walk. Arrived at length, Jenny to her great relief found that Frank was in, but he was so obviously surprised to see her that for a moment, disconcerted, she knew not how to explain her visit.

'May I speak to you for a few minutes? I won't keep you long.'

'By all means. Where is Basil?'

He made her sit down, and tried to take from her the umbrella which she held firmly; but she refused to be parted from it, and sat on the edge of the chair, ill at ease, with the awkward formality of a person unused to drawing-rooms. To Frank, seeking to make her comfortable, she seemed like a house-keeper applying for a situation.

'Can I trust you?' she broke out abruptly, with an effort. 'I'm in awful trouble. You're a good sort, and you've never looked down on me because I was a barmaid. Tell me I can trust you. There's no one I can speak to, and I feel if I don't speak I shall go off my head.'

'But, good heavens! what's the matter?'

'Everything's the matter. He wants to separate. He's gone to his solicitor today. He's going to turn me out in the street like a servant; and I shall kill myself – I tell you I'll kill myself.' She wrung her hands, and the tears rolled down her cheeks. 'Before you we've always kept up appearances, because he was ashamed to let you see how he regrets having married me.'

Frank knew well enough that for some months things had not gone very smoothly with the pair, but it had never occurred to him that they were come to such a pass. He did not know what to say nor how to reassure her.

'It's nonsense. It can only be a little passing quarrel. After all, you must expect to have those.'

'No, it isn't. I shouldn't mind if I thought he loved me, but he doesn't. He calls it a dog's life, and he's right.' She hesitated, but only for an instant. 'Will you tell me the truth if I ask you something – on your honour?'

'Of course.'

'Is there anything between Basil and Mrs Murray?'

'No, certainly not!' he cried emphatically. 'How can such an idea have come to you!'

'You wouldn't tell me if there was,' she answered distract-edly; and now the words, which before had come so hardly, poured out in a disordered torrent. 'You're all against me be-cause I'm not a lady. . . . Oh, I'm so unhappy! I tell you he's in love with Mrs Murray. The other day he was going to dine there, and you should have seen him! He was so restless he couldn't sit still; he looked at his watch every minute. His eyes simply glittered with excitement, and I could almost hear his heart beating. He was there twice last week, and twice the week before.'

'How d'you know?'

'Because I followed him. If I'm not ladylike enough for him, I needn't play the lady there. You're shocked now, I suppose?'

'I wouldn't presume to judge you,' he answered quietly.

'He never loved me,' she went on, feverish and overwrought. 'He married me because he thought it was his duty. And then, when the baby died – he thought I'd entrapped him.'

'He didn't say so.'

'No,' she shouted hysterically, 'he never says anything; but I saw it in his eyes.' She clasped her hands passionately, rocking to and fro. 'Oh, you don't know what our life is. For days he never says a word except to answer my questions. And the silence simply drives me mad. I shouldn't mind if he black-guarded me; I'd rather he hit me than simply look and look. I could see he was keeping himself in, and I knew it was getting towards the end.'

'I'm very sorry,' said Frank helplessly.

Even to himself the words sounded formal and insincere, and Jenny broke out vehemently.

'Oh, don't you pity me, too. I've had a great deal too much pity; I don't want it. Basil married me from pity. Oh, God, I wish he hadn't! I can't stand the unhappiness.'

'You know, Jenny, he's a man of honour, and he'd never do anything that wasn't straight.'

'Oh, I know he's a man of honour,' she cried bitterly. 'I wish he had a little less of it; one doesn't want a lot of fine sentiments in married life – they don't work.' She stood up and beat her breast. 'Oh, why couldn't I fall in love with a man of my own class? I should have been so much happier. I used to be so proud that Basil wasn't a clerk or something in the City. He's right – we shall never be happy. It isn't a matter of yesterday, or today, or tomorrow. I can't alter myself. He knew I wasn't a lady when he married me. My father had to bring up five children on two-ten a week. You can't expect a

298

man to send his daughters to a boarding-school at Brighton on that, and have them finished in Paris. ... He doesn't say a word when I do something or say something a lady wouldn't, but he purses up his lips and looks. Then I get so mad I do things just to aggravate him. Sometimes I try to be vulgar. One learns a good deal in a bar in the City, and I know so well the things that'll make Basil curl up. I want to get a bit of revenge out of him sometimes, and I know exactly where he's raw and where I can hurt him. You should see the way he looks when I don't eat properly, or call a man a Johnny.'

'It opens up endless possibilities of domestic unhappiness,' answered Frank dryly.

'Oh, I know it isn't fair to him, but I lose my head. I can't always be refined. Sometimes I can't help breaking out; I feel I must let myself go.'

Her cheeks were flaming, and she breathed rapidly. Never before had she disclosed her heart so completely to anyone, and Frank, watching her keenly, could not understand this curious mingling of love and hate.

'Why don't you separate, then?' he asked.

'Because I love him.' Her voice, hard and metallic before, grew suddenly so tender that the change was extraordinary; the bitterness went out of her face. 'Oh, you don't know how I love him! I'd do anything to make him happy; I'd give my life if he wanted it. Oh, I can't say it, but when I think of him my heart burns so that sometimes I can hardly breathe. I can never show him that he's all the world to me; I try to make him love me, and I only make him hate me. What can I do to show him? Ah, if he only knew, I'm sure he'd not regret that he married me. I feel – I feel as if my heart was full of music, and yet something prevents me from ever bringing it out.'

For a while they sat in silence.

'What is it you wish me to do?' asked Frank at last.

'I want you to tell him I love him. I can't; I always make a mess of it. Tell him he's all in the world to me, and I *will* try to be a good wife to him. Ask him not to leave me, and say that I mean everything for the best.' She paused and dried her eyes. 'And couldn't you go to Mrs Murray and tell her?

Ask her to have mercy on me. Perhaps she doesn't know what she's doing. Ask her not to take him away from me.'

She seized his hands in appeal, and he had no power to resist.

'I'll do my best. Don't be too downhearted. I'm sure it'll all come right and you'll be very happy again.'

She tried to smile through her tears and to thank him, but her voice refused to help her, and she could only press his hands. With a sudden impulse she bent down and kissed them; then quickly, leaving him strangely moved, went out.

13

JENNY had not given Frank a very easy task, and when she was gone he cursed her irritably – her father, mother, husband, and all her stock. He knew Mrs Murray fairly well, had treated her in illness, and also gone somewhat frequently to the house in Charles Street; but, for all that it was awkward to attack her on a subject of so personal a nature, and he was aware that he laid himself open to an unpleasant rebuke. He shrugged his shoulders, making up his mind to call on her that afternoon and say his say.

'She can snub me till she's blue in the face,' he muttered.

Ignorant of what was in store, Hilda Murray, coming in from luncheon, went into her drawing-room, and since the day was wet and dismal, ordered the curtains to be drawn, the lights to be turned on. She relished enormously the warm and comfortable cosiness of that room, furnished pleasantly, with a good deal of taste, if without marked originality; there were dozens of such apartments in Mayfair, with the same roomy, chintz-covered chairs, Chippendale tables and marquetry cabinets, with the same pictures on the walls. Wealth was there without ostentation, art without eccentricity; and Mr Farley, the Vicar of All Souls, who came early, recognized with sleek content that a woman who dwelt in such a room must possess a due sense of the proprieties and a gratifying belief in the importance of the London clergy. Meeting her for the first time a year before in Old Queen Street, the amiable parson had quickly grown intimate with Hilda. The robust common sense of Protestantism has made it lawful for the clerical bosom to be affected in due measure by the charms of fair women, and the Vicar of All Souls had ever looked upon a good marriage as the culmination of his parochial activities. Hilda was handsome, rich, and sufficiently well born to be the equal of a minister of Christ who stayed with

Duchesses for three days at a time; nor could he think she was quite indifferent to his attentions. Mr Farley determined to abandon the imperfect state of single blessedness, falling like a ripe apple at the feet of this comely and opulent widow; and as Othello, making love to Desdemona, poured into her astonished ears brave tales of pillage and assault, of hair-breadth 'scapes and enterprises perilous, the Rev Collinson Farley spoke of charities and sales of work, encounters with churchwardens, and the regeneration of charwomen. Hilda took great interest in All Souls, and willingly presented the church with an entire set of hassocks, so that, as the Vicar said, the pious should have no excuse for not kneeling at their prayers; somewhat later she consented to take a stall at a bazaar for getting a new organ; and then, the Rubicon of philanthropy once crossed, her efforts were untiring. These things brought them constantly together and afforded endless matter for conversation; but Mr Farley flattered himself he was a brilliant talker, and it would have been contrary to all his principles to allow their intercourse to be confined to affairs of business. The claims of culture were not forgotten. He lent Hilda books, and went with her to picture-galleries and to exhibitions; sometimes they read Tennyson together, at others visited the theatre and discussed the moral aspects of the English drama; on fine mornings they frequently studied the Italian masters in Trafalgar Square or the Elgin marbles at the British Museum. Mr Farley had a vast fund of information, and could give historic details or piquant anecdotes about every work of art; and Hilda, with a woman's passion for being lectured, found him in consequence an entertaining and instructive friend. But it had never occurred to her that any warmer feeling agitated the heart which lay beneath his immaculate silk waistcoat, and it was not without alarm that now she found the conversation verging to topics that before they had never touched upon. Mr Farley had at length made up his mind, and since he was not a man to hesitate from feelings of diffidence, went straight to the point.

'Mrs Murray,' he said, 'I have a matter of some importance which I desire to impart to you.'

'More charities, Mr Farley?' she cried. 'You'll ruin me.'

'You are a veritable angel of mercy, and your purse is ever open to the needs of the parish; but on this occasion it is of a more personal matter that I desire to speak.' He stood up and went to the fireplace, against which he stood so that no heat should enter the room at all. 'I feel it my duty to preface the question I am about to ask by some account of my position and of my circumstances. I think it better to run the risk of being slightly tedious than to fail to make myself perfectly clear.'

Certainly Hilda could not help seeing to what his words tended, and after the first moment of consternation was seized with an almost irresistible desire to laugh. Perhaps because her love for Basil was so great, she had never dreamed that another man could desire her; and Mr Farley in this connection had not for a moment occupied her thoughts. When she looked at him now, well dressed, his grey hair carefully done, his hands manicured, with his easy assurance and his inclination to obesity, the Vicar of All Souls seemed a profoundly ridiculous object. Gravely, with deliberation, he set out the advantages of his state, and not without decorum explained that he was no penniless fortune-hunter. It was a fair exchange that he offered, and many women would have been grateful. Hilda knew she should stop him, but had not the readiness; nor was she without a malicious desire to know in what precise terms he would make the proposal. He paused abruptly, smiled, and stepped forward.

'Mrs Murray, I have the honour to ask you to be my wife.'

Now she was confronted by the necessity to answer, and with all her heart wished she had possessed strength of mind to prevent the man from going so far.

'I'm sure I feel enormously flattered,' she replied awkwardly. 'It never struck me that you – cared for me in that way.'

He put out a deprecating hand.

'I don't want an immediate answer, Mrs Murray. It's a matter that requires grave consideration, and we're neither of us children to plunge into marriage recklessly. It's a great responsibility that we are proposing to take on ourselves, but I should like you to reflect on the real good that you could do as

303

my wife. Do you remember that beautiful passage in Tennyson: "And hand in hand we will go towards higher things"?'

The door opened, and the Vicar of All Souls was able to conceal his annoyance only because he was a very polite man; but Hilda, enormously relieved, turned to Frank Hurrell, the incoming visitor, with the greatest cordiality. Frank had been to Basil's chambers, but not finding him, was come to Charles Street resolved, whatever the cost, to speak with Mrs Murray about Jenny. It looked, however, as though the opportunity would not present itself, for other callers appeared, and the conversation became general. In a little while Basil was announced, and Frank saw Mrs Murray's hurried, anxious glance. With one sweep of her eyes she took in his whole person, his harassed air, his stern pallor and deep depression. She spoke laughingly, but he scarcely smiled, gazing at her with such an expression of anguish that her heart was horribly troubled. It was very painful to see his utter wretchedness. At length Frank found himself with Hilda out of earshot of the others.

'Basil looks very ill, doesn't he? His wife came to see me this morning. I dare say you remember that he was married about a year ago.'

Mrs Murray coloured, and stared at Frank with cold suspicion. She tightened her lips, wondering what he had in mind.

'I went down to see her,' she answered frigidly. 'She seemed to me vulgar and pretentious. I'm afraid I can take no great interest in her.'

'She loves Basil with all her heart, and she's desperately unhappy.' He looked steadily at Mrs Murray, and dropped his voice, so that it seemed no sound issued from his mouth; but Hilda heard every word so emphatically that it struck her heart as though with a hammer. 'She asked me to give you a message. She knows that Basil – loves you, and she begs you to have mercy on her.'

For a moment Hilda could not reply.

'Don't you think it's rather impertinent of you to say such things to me?' she returned, uttering the words disjointedly, as though she forced them out one by one.

'Excessively,' he answered. 'And I wouldn't have ventured

only she told me her love was like music in her heart, and something prevented it from ever coming out. It seemed to me that for a rather stupid, narrow, common woman to have got hold of a thought like that she must have gone through a perfect hell of suffering. And I was sorry.'

'And d'you think I've not suffered?'

Hilda could not preserve that mask of cold decorum. The question thrilled from her, and she had no power to leave it unasked.

'Are you very fond of him?'

'No, I'm not fond of him. I worship the very ground he treads on.'

Frank held out his hand to say good-bye.

'Then you must do as you think fit. You're playing the most dangerous game in the world; you're playing with human hearts. . . . Forgive me for what I've said.'

'I'm very glad – for now I know better what to do. I'd forgotten his wife.'

Frank went away, and presently Mr Farley, despairing to stay the others out, rose also. Shaking hands with Hilda, he asked when he might come again. In the agitation of her talk with Frank she had completely forgotten his proposal; but now, with a sudden passion for self-sacrifice, it seemed neither grotesque nor impossible. Indeed, if she accepted, it would solve many difficulties, and she determined not to put aside the offer, as at first she intended, but to think it over. At least, she must do nothing rashly.

'I will write to you tomorrow,' she answered gravely.

He smiled and pressed her hand affectionately, already with somewhat the fervour of an accepted lover. Mrs Murray was left alone with Basil. He turned over the pages of a book, and the trivial action, indicating to her excited temper a callousness which was not his, filled her with anger, so that for an instant, on account of all the pain he caused her, she hated him furiously.

'Is that a very interesting work?' she asked coldly.

He flung it aside with impatience.

'I thought that man was never going. It makes me angry

305

each time I see him here. Are you very much attached to him?'

'What an extraordinary question!' she answered coolly. 'I wonder why on earth you ask it?'

'Because I love you,' he burst out impulsively, 'and I hate anyone else to be with you.'

She stared at him with the utmost calm, and some icy power seized her, so that she felt absolutely no emotion.

'It may interest you to know that Mr Farley has asked me to marry him.'

'And what are you going to say?'

His face had suddenly fallen ashen grey, and his voice was hoarse.

'I don't know – perhaps yes.'

'I thought you loved me, Hilda.'

'It's because I love you that I shall marry Mr Farley.'

He sprang forward passionately and seized her hands.

'Oh, but you can't, Hilda. It's absurd. You don't know what you're doing. Oh, don't do that, for God's sake! You'll make both of us utterly miserable. Hilda, I love you; I can't live without you. You don't know how unhappy I've been. For months I've dreaded going home. When I saw my house as I walked along, I almost turned sick. You don't know how fervently I wished that I'd got killed in the war. I can't go on.'

'But you must,' she said; 'it's your duty.'

'Oh, I think I've had enough of duty and honour. I've used up all my principles in the last year. I know I brought the whole thing on myself. I was weak and stupid, and I must take the consequences. But I haven't the strength; I don't love – my wife.'

'Then, don't let her ever find it out. Be kind to her, and gentle, and forbearing.'

'I can't be kind and gentle and forbearing day after day for weeks and months and years. And the worst of it is there's no hope for me. I've tried honestly to make the best of things, but it's no good. We're too different, and it's impossible that we should continue to live together. Everything she says, everything she does, jars upon me so frightfully. A man, when he

306

marries a woman like that, thinks he's going to lift her up to his own station. The fool! It's she who drags him down to hers.'

She walked from end to end of the room distracted, and mingled feelings tore her breast. She knew how overwhelming was her own love, and knew that his was no less; she could not bear to think that he was unhappy. She stopped, and looked at him with tear-filled eyes.

'If it weren't for you I couldn't have lived,' he was saying, and his voice played upon her heart-strings as though they were some strange living instrument. 'It was only by seeing you that I gathered courage to go on with it. And each time I came here I loved you more passionately.'

'Why did you come?' she whispered.

'I couldn't help it. I knew it was poison, but I loved the poison. I would give my whole soul for one look of your eyes.'

It was the first time he had said such things to her, and they were very, very sweet; but she tried to be strong.

'If you care for me at all, do your duty like a brave man, and let me respect you. You're only making our friendship impossible. Don't you see that you're preventing me from ever having you here again?'

'I can't help it. Even if I see you never again, I must tell you now that I love you. For months it's been burning my tongue, and I've scarcely known sometimes how to prevent myself. I made you suffer, I was blind; but I love you with all my heart, Hilda. I can't live without you.'

He stepped forward, but quickly, with a cry of anguish, she sprang back.

'For God's sake, don't say such things! I can't bear them. Don't you see how weak I am? Have mercy on me.'

'You don't love me.'

'You know I love you,' she cried vehemently, angrily; 'but because of my great love I beseech you to do your duty.'

'My duty is to be happy. Let us go where we can love one another – away from England, to some place where love isn't sinful and ugly.'

'Oh, Basil,' she cried earnestly, stronger now because she

307

had thrown herself on his charity; 'oh, Basil, let us try to walk straight. Think of your wife, who loves you also – as much as I do. You're all in the world to her; you can't treat her so shamefully.'

She sank in a chair and dried her eyes. Her agony had calmed the man's ardent passion, and it wrung his heart that she should weep.

'Don't cry, Hilda; I can't bear it.'

He was standing over her, and very gently she took his hand.

'Don't you understand that we could never respect ourselves again if we did that poor creature such a fearful wrong? She would always be between us with her tears and her sorrows. I tell you I couldn't bear it. Have mercy on me – if you love me at all.'

He did not answer, and very brokenly she went on.

'I know it's better to do our duty. For my sake, dearest, go back to your wife, and don't let her ever know that you love me. It's because we're stronger than she that we must sacrifice ourselves.'

A profound discouragement seized him, and silence fell upon them both. At last he released her hand.

'I don't know any longer what's right and what's wrong. It all seems confused. It's very hard.'

'It's just as hard for me, Basil.'

'Good-bye, then,' he said broken-heartedly. 'I dare say you're right, and perhaps I should only make you very unhappy.'

'Good-bye, my dearest.'

She got up and gave him both her hands, and he bent down and kissed them. She could hardly stand the pain, and when he turned away and walked towards the door all resolution left her. She could not bear him to go – at all event, not thus coldly, not yet. She thought that perhaps this was the last time she would ever see him, and her passion, so long restrained, rose up and overpowered her, and it seemed that nothing mattered but love.

'Don't go, Basil,' she cried. 'Don't go!'

With a cry of joy he turned, and she found herself in his

arms; he kissed her violently, he kissed her mouth and her eyes and her hair; and she wept with the extremity of her desire. She cared now for nothing. All might go, and the very heavens fall; nothing in the world signified but this divine madness.

'Oh, I can't bear it,' she moaned. 'I won't lose you. Basil, say you love me.'

'Yes, yes: I love you with all my heart and soul.'

He sought her lips again, and she nearly fainted with the rapture; she yielded herself to his strong, encircling arms, and felt that there she could happily die.

'Oh, Basil, I want your love – I want your love so badly.'

'Now nothing can separate us. You belong to me for ever.'

He passed his hands over her face, and his eyes were flaming. She exulted in his ardent passion, proud that a man on her account should be thus frenzied.

'Say again that you love me,' she whispered.

'Oh, Hilda, Hilda, at last! We'll go to a land where the whole earth speaks only of love, and where only love and youth and beauty matter.'

'Let's go where we can be together always. We have so short a time; let's snatch all the happiness we can.'

He kissed her again, and in her ecstasy she burst into tears. They talked madly of their love and past anguish, making venturesome plans for the future, forgetting all but the passion that devoured them. At that moment only the present existed, and they wondered how it had been possible to live so long apart. She pressed his hands joyfully when he said that nothing now could separate them, for they belonged to one another for ever and always; and it signified not if they lost their souls, for they gained the whole world. But suddenly Hilda sprang up.

'Take care! There's somebody coming.'

And the words were scarcely out of her mouth when the butler came in, followed immediately by Jenny. Basil gave a cry of surprise. The servant closed the door, and for one moment, embarrassed, Hilda did not know what to say. Basil recovered himself first.

309

'I think you know my wife, Mrs Murray.'

'Oh yes, I know her; you needn't introduce me,' Jenny burst out with a loud and angry voice. She went up quickly to Hilda. 'I've come for my husband.'

'Jenny, what are you saying?' cried Basil, foreseeing a hideous scene. He turned to Hilda. 'Would you mind leaving us alone?'

'No, I want to speak to you,' interrupted Jenny. 'I don't want any of your society shams. I've come here to speak out. I've caught you at last. You're trying to get my husband from me.'

'Be quiet, Jenny. Are you mad? For God's sake, leave us, Mrs Murray; she'll insult you.'

'You think of her – you don't think of me. You don't care how much I suffer.'

Basil took his wife's arm, trying to get her away, but vehemently she shook him off. And Hilda stood before her pale and conscience-stricken; that sudden irruption showed her the sordid ugliness of what she had meant to do, and she was horrified. She motioned to Basil that he was to allow his wife to say what she would.

'You're stealing my husband from me!' exclaimed Jenny threateningly. 'Oh, you ...' She was at a loss for words violent enough, and she trembled with impotent rage. 'You wicked woman!'

Hilda forced herself to speak.

'I don't want to make you unhappy, Mrs Kent. If you like, I'll promise never to see your husband again.'

'Much good your promises will do me. I wouldn't believe a word you said. I know what society ladies are. We know all about them in the City.'

Basil stepped forward, and again begged Hilda to leave them. He opened the door, and his glance was so appealing that she could not stay; but though keeping her eyes averted, she felt that his besought her not to be angry for the hateful, odious scene to which she had been exposed.

'She's frightened of me,' Jenny hissed savagely. 'She daren't stand up to me.'

He closed the door, and then turned to his wife. He was pale with rage, but she heeded not.

'What d'you mean by coming here and behaving like this?' he said violently. 'You had no right to come at all. What d'you want?'

'I want you. D'you think I didn't guess what was going on? I've been waiting here for hours. I saw people come in, and I saw them go out, and at last I knew you were alone with her.'

'How did you know?'

'I gave the butler a sovereign, and he told me.'

An icy shiver of disgust passed through Basil, and she laughed bitterly when she saw his profound scorn. Then she caught sight of a photograph of Basil which stood on a table near the window, and before he could prevent her, seized it and flung it on the floor, and viciously dug her heel into it.

'She's got no right to have your photo here. Oh, I hate her, I hate her!'

'You drive me perfectly mad. For God's sake go.'

'I shan't go till you come with me.'

He watched her for a moment, trying to command the hatred, the passionate vindictive hatred, which now welled up uncontrollably within him. He strode up to her and seized her arm.

'Look here, until today I swear to you before God that I've never done anything or said anything that you couldn't have known. I've tried to do my duty, and I've done my best to make you happy. I've struggled with all my might to love you. And now I don't wish to deceive you. It's best that you should know exactly what has happened. This afternoon I told Hilda that I loved her. . . . And she loves me, too.'

Jenny gave a cry of rage, and impulsively with her umbrella gave him a swinging blow on the face. He snatched it from her, and in blind anger broke it across his knee and threw it aside.

'You've brought it on yourself,' he said. 'You made me too unhappy.'

He looked at Jenny as he might at some strange woman

311

whom he saw for the first time. She stood before him, panting and bewildered, trying to control herself.

'And now it's the end,' he went on coldly. 'The life we led was impossible. I tried to do something that was beyond my power. I'm going away. I can't and I won't live with you any longer.'

'Basil, you don't mean that,' she cried, feeling suddenly that he spoke in deadly earnest. Before she had fancied that he threatened only what he did not mean to perform. 'You've got me to count with. I won't let you go.'

'What more d'you want?' he asked bitterly. 'Isn't it enough that you've ruined my whole life?'

'You don't love me?'

'I never loved you.'

'Why did you marry me?'

'Because you made me.'

'You never loved me?' she repeated, entirely crushed now, trembling and faint with fear. 'Even at the beginning?'

'Never. It's too late now to keep it in. I must tell you and have done with it. You've been having it out for months – now it's my turn.'

'But I love you, Basil,' she cried passionately, going to him to put her arms round his neck. 'I'll make you love me.'

But he shrank away.

'For God's sake, don't touch me! ... Oh, Jenny, let us finish with it. I'm very sorry. I don't wish to be unkind to you, but you must have seen that – that I didn't care for you. What's the good of going on humbugging and pretending and making ourselves utterly miserable?'

She faced him, humbled, shaken with sobs which she would not allow to come, and stared at Basil with eyes preternaturally large.

'Yes, I've seen it,' she cried hoarsely. 'But I wouldn't believe it. When I've put my hand on your shoulder I've seen that you could hardly help shuddering; and sometimes when I've kissed you I've seen you put out all your strength to prevent yourself from pushing me away.'

After all, he was tender-hearted, and now that his first anger

312

was gone could not help being touched by the dreadful anguish of her tone.

'Jenny, I can't help it if I don't love you. I can't help it if I – if I love someone else.'

'What are you going to do?' she asked, dazed and cowed.

'I'm going away.'

'Where?'

'God knows!'

They stood for a while in silence, while Jenny sought to collect and order her thoughts, which throbbed horribly in her brain, like raving maniacs dancing some tumultuous, distracted measure. The butler came in softly and handed a note to Basil, saying that Mrs Murray had ordered him to bring it. Basil did not open this till the servant was gone, and then, having read, gave it without a word to Jenny.

You may tell your wife that I've made up my mind to marry Mr Farley. I will never see you again. – H.M.

'What does it mean?' asked Jenny.

'Isn't it clear? Someone has asked her to marry him, and she means to accept.'

'But you said she loved you.'

He shrugged his shoulders and did not answer. Then a ray of hope shot through Jenny's heart, and with outstretched hands, tenderly, anxiously, she went to him.

'Oh, Basil, if it's true, give me another chance. She doesn't love you as I love you. I've been selfish and quarrelsome and exacting, but I've always loved you. Oh, don't leave me, Basil. Let me try once more if I can't make you care for me.'

'I'm very sorry,' he returned, looking down. 'It's too late.'

'Oh God! what shall I do?' she cried. 'And even though she's going to marry somebody else, you care for her better than anyone else in the world?'

He nodded.

'And even if she does marry that other man, she'll love you still. There's no room for me between you, and I can go away like a discharged servant. Oh God, oh God! what have I done to deserve it?'

313

'I'm very sorry to make you so unhappy,' he whispered, deeply moved by her utter misery.

'Oh, don't pity me! D'you think I want your pity now?'

'You'd better come away, Jenny,' he said gently.

'No. You've told me you don't want me any more. I shall go my own way.'

He looked at her, hesitating, and shrugged his shoulders.

'Then good-bye.'

He went out, and Jenny followed him with her eyes. At first she could hardly believe that he was gone. It seemed that he must turn back and take her in his arms; it seemed that he must come up the stairs again and say that he loved her still. But he did not come, and from the window she watched him walk down the street.

'He's so glad to go,' she whispered.

Then, heart-broken, she sank to the floor, and burying her face in her hands, broke into a passion of tears.

14

BUT presently she got up and walked downstairs. She let herself out quietly into the street. Though much exhausted, Jenny's instinctive economy prevented her from taking a cab, and with heavy steps she set out on foot to Waterloo. The night was cold and dark, and the November drizzle soaked her clothes, but in extreme distress of mind she noticed nothing. She went, staring straight in front of her, a set despair upon her face, and her eyes saw neither houses nor people: she walked through the crowd of Piccadilly as though through an empty street. Muffled, with umbrellas up, folk hurried to their homes, or, notwithstanding the inclement weather, aimlessly sauntered. Sometimes she sobbed brokenly, and then on a sudden scalding, painful tears ran down her cheeks. The way seemed endless, and her strength rapidly failed; her limbs, heavier than lead, ached terribly; but she would not drive, for the pain of motion was less than the pain of immobility. She crossed Westminster Bridge, and at length, scarcely realizing it, found herself at Waterloo. In so dazed a manner that the porter thought she had been drinking, Jenny asked when there would be a train, and sat down to wait. The glitter of electricity difficultly pierced the humid night, and the spaces of the station in that uncertain light seemed vast and cavernous. It was a mysterious place, sordid and horrible, which stretched weirdly to an infinite distance: people came and went, porters passed with luggage, trains arrived and departed; and the whole scene impressed itself on her tortured brain with a hideous, cruel intensity.

Having reached Barnes at length, Jenny felt no relief, but if possible, a greater wretchedness, for she remembered how often in summer, under soft blue skies, she had wandered across the common, clinging to Basil's arm; and now it was dark and ugly, and the broom, all charred and bedraggled, even under cover of night had a dismal, squalid look. She came to the little poky villa, let herself in, and went upstairs, vaguely hoping that Basil, after all, had come back, for it seemed impossible that she would never see him again. But he was nowhere. Now her agony grew too great for tears, and she walked through the house like one demented, mechanically setting straight things which were not in their usual place. In her bedroom she looked in the glass, comparing herself with Mrs Murray, and noted with a certain bitter pride the splendour of her hair, the brilliancy of her eyes, the dazzling perfection of her skin: notwithstanding all she had gone through, Jenny was conscious of a beauty greater than Mrs Murray's. She was younger, too, and when she recalled the admiration which in the old days at the *Golden Crown* had been hers, could not understand how it was that with Basil she was so powerless. Other men had cared for her passionately, other men had been willing humbly to do her bidding; some, devouring her with their eyes, had trembled when they touched her hand; others turned pale with desire when she smiled upon them. Her beauty had been dinned into her ears, and Basil alone was insensible to it. Then, confusedly, with somewhat of that puritanic instinct which is ever in English blood, Jenny asked herself how she had merited such bitter punishment. She had done her best: she had been a good and faithful wife to Basil, and sought in every way to please him; and yet he loathed her. It seemed that God Almighty was against her, and she stood helpless before a vindictive power.

Still hoping against hope, she waited, and knowing at what hour each train was due, spent in agonized expectation the time which must elapse between its arrival and the walk of a passenger from station to house. The evening passed, and one train came after another, but Basil never; and then the last train was gone, and despair seized her, for he would not come that night. She understood that this was really the end, and abandoned utterly that shred of hope which alone had upborne her. She saw again the look of hatred with which he had flung at her the bitter words of scorn; his passion, long pent up, burst forth in that moment of uncontrollable irritation, and when she thought of it she quailed still. With all her heart Jenny wished she had closed her eyes to his doings, for now she would be thankful to keep him even without his love; she would have given worlds not to have forced from him the avowal of his passion for Mrs Murray; the suspicion which had tortured her before was infinitely preferable to this horrible certainty. She would have borne anything rather than lose him altogether; she would have been grateful even for a look now and then; but never to see him at all! She would far sooner die.

Her heart gave a sudden throb. She would far sooner die. ... That was the solution of it all. It was impossible to live with this aching pain; the unhappiness was too frightful — how much better it would be to be dead, to feel nothing!

'They've got no room for me,' she repeated. 'I'm only in the way.'

Perhaps by dying she would do Basil a last service, and he might be sorry for her. He might regret what he had said, and wish he had been kinder and more forbearing. Living, she knew it was impossible to regain his love, but who could tell what miracle her death might work? The temptation seized her, and possessed her, and mastered her. A great excitement filled the wretched woman, and gathering together the remains of her strength, without hesitation, she got up, put on her hat, and went out. She went swiftly, upborne strangely by this resolve which attracted her with an intense fascination, for she expected peace from all trouble and safety from this anguish which rent her heart as no physical pain had ever done. She came to the river which flowed silent and dark in the dark and silent night, with heavy flood, menacing and chill; but in her it inspired no terror: if her heart beat quickly, it was with fearful joy because she was about to end her torment. She was glad that the night was sombre, and thanked God for the rain that kept loiterers away. She walked along the towpath to a place she knew — the year before a woman had there thrown herself in because it was deep and the bank shelved suddenly, and Jenny had often passed the spot with a little shudder: once, half laughing, she said she was walking

317

over her grave. A man came towards her, and she hid in the shadow of the wall, so that he went by without noticing that anyone was there; the trees in the garden above dripped heavily. She came to the spot she sought, and looked about to see that none was near; she took off her hat and laid it on the ground under the wall, so that it should get as little wet as possible; then, without hesitation, went to the river-bank. She felt no fear at all. For one moment she looked at the torpid, unmerciful water, and then boldly flung herself in.

Basil, on leaving Mrs Murray's, went to Harley Street, but finding Frank out, proceeded to his club, where he spent the evening in morose despair, heart-rent because Hilda had signified her intention to marry the Vicar of All Souls, and repentant already of the pain he had caused his wife. At first he meant to pass the night in town, but the more he thought of it, the more necessary it seemed to return to Barnes; for though fully minded to part from Jenny, on account of all that had gone before, he could not part in anger. But he felt it impossible to see her again immediately, and determined to get home so late that she would be in bed. There was in him an absolute impossibility of sleep, and he so dreaded the long wakefulness that, thinking to tire himself out, he set out to walk. It was nearly two when he came to his little house in River Gardens, and when he turned to enter Basil was much surprised to see a policeman ringing the bell.

'What d'you want, constable?' he asked.

'Are you Mr Basil Kent? Will you come down to the station? There's been an accident to your wife.'

Basil gave a cry, and with horror already upon him, asked the man what he meant. But the policeman simply repeated that he was to come at once, and together with haste they strode off. An inspector broke the news to him.

'You're wanted to identify your wife. A man saw her walk along the tow-path and throw herself in. She was drowned before help could be got.'

Unable to understand the full meaning of those words, Basil stared stupidly, aghast and terror-struck. He opened his mouth

318

to speak, but only gasped unintelligibly. He looked from one to another of those men, who watched him with indifference. The whole room turned round, and he could not see; he felt horribly faint, and then it seemed as though someone cruelly tore apart the sutures of his skull. He stretched out his hands aimlessly, and the inspector, understanding, led him to where Jenny lay. A doctor was still with her, but it seemed all efforts to restore life had been stopped.

'This is the husband,' said Basil's guide.

'We could do nothing,' murmured the doctor. 'She was quite dead when she was got out.'

Basil looked at her and hid his face. He felt inclined suddenly to scream at the top of his voice. It seemed too ghastly, too impossible.

'D'you know at all why she did it?' asked the doctor.

Basil did not answer, but gazed distraught at the closed eyes and the lovely hair disarranged and soaking wet.

'Oh, God! what shall I do? Can nothing be done at all?'

The doctor looked at him, and told a constable to bring some brandy; but Basil pushed it aside with distaste.

'What do you want me to do now?'

'You'd better go home. I'll walk along with you,' said the doctor.

Basil stared at him with abject fear, and his eyes had an inhuman blackness, shining horribly out of the death-pale face.

'Go home? Can't I stay here?'

The other took his arm and led him away. There was not far to go, and at the door the doctor asked if he could manage by himself.

'Yes. I shall be all right. Don't trouble.'

He let himself in and went upstairs, and somehow a terror had seized him, so that when he stumbled against a chair he cried out in sheer fright. He sat down trying to gather his thoughts, but his mind seethed, so that he feared he would go mad, and ever there continued that appalling torture in his head which seemed to combine the two agonies of physical and of mental pain. Then there fell upon his consciousness the scene at the police-station, which before had been confused

319

and dim. Now strangely, with keen minuteness, he saw each detail – the bare stone walls of the mortuary, the glaring light with its violent shadows, the countenances of those men in uniform (every feature, the play of expression, was immensely distinct), and the body! That sight tore into the inmost recesses of his soul, so that he nearly fainted with horror and with remorse. He groaned in his anguish. He never knew it was possible to suffer so dreadfully.

'Oh, if she'd only waited a little longer! If I'd only come back sooner, I might have saved her.'

With the same unnatural clearness he remembered the events of the afternoon, and he was absolutely aghast at his own cruelty. He repeated his words and hers, and saw the pitiful look on her face when she begged him to give her one more chance. Her voice trembled still in his ears, and the dreadful pain of her eyes daunted him. It was his fault, all his fault.

'I killed her as surely as though I'd strangled her with my own hands.'

His imagination violently excited, he saw the scene at the riverside, the dread of the murky heavy stream, the pitiless cold of it. He heard the splash and the scream of terror. He saw the struggle as the desire of life grew for one moment all-powerful. His head reeled with the woman's agony of fear as the water seized on her, and he felt the horrible choking, the vain effort for breath. He burst into hysterical tears.

Then he remembered the love which she had lavished upon him, and his own ingratitude. He could only reproach himself bitterly because he had never really tried to make the best of things. The first obstacles had discouraged him, so that he forgot his duty. She had surrendered herself trustfully, and he had given sorrow instead of the happiness for which she was so brightly born, a dreadful death instead of the life which for his sake she loved so wonderfully. And at last it seemed that he could not go on living, for he despised himself. He could not look forward to the coming day and the day after. His life was finished now, finished in misery and utter despair. How could he continue, with the recollection of those reproachful eyes searing his very soul, so that he felt he could never sleep again? And the desire came strongly upon him to finish with existence as she had finished, thus offering in some sort reparation for her death, and at the same time gaining the peace for which she had given so much. A hideous fascination urged him, so that like a man hypnotized he went downstairs, out into the street, along the tow-path, and stood at the very place where Jenny had thrown herself in. He knew it well. And notwithstanding the darkness of the night, he could see that something had happened there; the bank was beaten and trodden down. But looking at the water, he shuddered with dismay. It was too bitterly cold, and he could not bear the long agony of drowning. Yet she had done it so easily. It appeared that she flung herself in quite boldly, without hesitating for a moment. Sick with terror, loathing himself for this cowardice, Basil turned away and walked quickly from that dreadful spot. Presently he broke into a run, and reached home trembling in every limb. That way, at all events, he could not face death.

But still he felt it impossible to continue with life, and he took from the drawer of his writing-desk a revolver, and loaded it. It needed but a slight pressure of the trigger, and there would be an end to the intolerable shame, to the remorse, and to all his difficulties. He stared at the little weapon, so daintily fashioned, and fingered it curiously, as though he were bewitched, but then, with vehement passion, flung it from him. He could not finish with the life which, after all, he loved still and he shuddered with horror of himself because he was afraid. Yet he knew that the pain of a wound was small. During the war he had been hurt, and at the moment scarcely felt the tearing, burning bullet. The clock struck three. He did not know how to bear the rest of that unendurable night. Nearly five hours must pass before it was light, and the darkness terrified him. He tried to read, but his brain was in such a turmoil that he could make no sense of the words. He lay down on the sofa and closed his eyes to sleep, but then with vivid and ghastly distinctness saw Jenny's pale face, her clenched hands and dripping hair. The silence of that room was inhuman. His eye caught some work of Jenny's on a little table, left carelessly when she went out, and he appeared to see her, seated, as was her habit, over her sewing. His anguish was insufferable, and springing up, he took his hat and went out. He must have someone with whom to speak, someone to whom he could tell his bitter, bitter sorrow. He forgot the hour, and walked rapidly towards Hammersmith. The road was very lonely, so dark in that cold, starless night that he could not see a step before him; and never a human soul passed by, so that he might have traversed desert places. At length, crossing the bridge, he came to houses. He walked on pavements, and the recollection of the crowds which in the daytime thronged those streets eased him a little of that panic fear which drove him on. His steps, which had been directed without aim, now more consciously took him to Frank. From someone he must get help and advice how to bear himself. In his exhaustion he went more slowly, and the way seemed endless. There were signs at last that the City was awaking. Now and again a cart trundled heavily by with produce for Covent Garden; here and there a milk-shop blazed with light. His heart went out to those early toilers whose busy activity seemed to unite him once more with human kind. He stood for a moment in front of a butcher's, where brawny fellows, silhouetted by the flaring gas, scrubbed the floor lustily.

At last – it seemed hours since he left Barnes – Basil found himself in Harley Street, and staggered up the steps. He rang the night-bell and waited. No answer came, and with anguish it crossed his mind that Frank might have been called out. Where could he go, for he was exhausted and faint, so that he could not walk another step? Since midnight he had trudged a good sixteen miles. He rang again, and presently heard a sound. The electric light was put on in the hall, and the door opened.

'Frank, Frank, for God's sake, take me in! I feel as if I were dying.'

With amazement Frank saw his friend, dishevelled, without a great-coat, wet, splashed with mud; his face was ghastly pale, drawn and affrighted, and his eyes stared with the unnatural fixedness of a maniac. He asked no questions, but took

322

Basil's arm and led him into the room. Then the remains of his strength gave way, and sinking into a chair, he fainted.

'Idiot!' muttered Frank.

He seized him by the scruff of the neck and bent his head firmly till he forced it between the knees; and presently Basil regained consciousness.

'Keep your head down till I get you some brandy.'

Frank was not a man to be disconcerted by an unexpected occurrence, and methodically poured out a sufficient quantity of neat spirit, which he made Basil drink. He told him to sit still for a moment and hold his tongue; then took his own pipe, filled and lit it, sat down quietly, wrapping himself up as best he could, and began to smoke. The nonchalance of his movements had a marvellous effect on Basil, for it was impossible to remain in that strained atmosphere of unearthliness when Frank, apparently not in the least surprised by his strange irruption, went about things in so stolid and unemotional a way. This unconcern exerted a kind of hypnotic influence, so that he felt oddly relieved. At last the doctor turned to him.

'I think you'd better take those things off. I can let you have some pyjamas.'

The sound of his voice suddenly called Basil back to the horrible events of his life, and with staring eyes and hoarse voice, cut by little gasps of anguish, he poured out incoherently the whole dreadful story. And then, breaking down again, he hid his face and sobbed.

'Oh, I can't bear it – I can't bear it!'

Frank looked at him thoughtfully, wondering what he had better do.

'I tried to kill myself in the night.'

'D'you think that would have done anyone much good?'

'I despise myself. I feel I haven't the right to live; but I hadn't the pluck to do it. People say it's cowardly to destroy one's self: they don't know what courage it wants. I couldn't face the pain. And yet she did it so easily – she just walked along the tow-path and threw herself in. And then, I don't know what's on the other side. After all, it may be true that

323

there's a cruel avenging God who will punish us to all eternity if we break His laws.'

'I wouldn't high-falute if I were you, Basil. Supposing you came into the next room and went to bed. You'd be all the better for a few hours' sleep.'

'D'you think I could sleep?' cried Basil.

'Come on,' said Frank, taking his arm.

He led him into the bedroom, and, Basil unresisting, took off his clothes and made him lie down. Then he got his hypodermic syringe.

'Now give me your arm and stop still. I'm only going to prick you – it won't hurt.'

He injected a little morphia, and after a while had the satisfaction of seeing Basil fall comfortably asleep.

Frank put away his syringe with a meditative smile.

'It's rather funny,' he muttered, 'that the most tempestuous and tragic of human emotions are no match against a full dose of *morphinæ hydrochlor*.'

That tiny instrument could allay the troubled mind; grief and remorse lost their vehemence under its action, the pangs of conscience were stilled, and pain, the great enemy of man, was effectually vanquished. It emphasized the fact that the finest-strung emotions of the human race depended on the matter which fools have stigmatized as gross. Frank, in one wide-embracing curse, expressed his whole-hearted abhorrence of dualists, spiritualists, Christian Scientists, quacks, and popularizers of science; then, enveloped in a rug, settled down comfortably in an arm-chair to await the tardy dawn.

Two hours later he found himself at Barnes, gathering at the police-station more precise details of Jenny's tragic death than Basil had been able to give him. Frank told the inspector that Kent was in a condition of absolute collapse and able personally to attend to nothing, then gave his own address, and placed himself for all needful business at the disposal of the authorities. He discovered that the inquest would probably be held two days later, and guaranteed that Basil would then be well enough to attend. After this he went to the house and found the servant amazed because neither master nor mistress had slept in bed, told her what had happened, and then wrote to James Bush some account of the facts. He promised the maid to return next morning, and went back to Harley Street.

Basil was up, but terribly depressed. All day he would not speak, and Frank could only divine the frightful agony he suffered. He went over in his mind eternally that scene with Hilda and his bitter words to his wife; and always he saw her in two ways: appealing for one last chance, and then – dead. Sometimes he felt he could scream with anguish when he recalled those passionate words of his to Hilda, for it seemed that final surrender was the cause of the whole catastrophe.

Next day, when Frank was about to go out, he turned to Basil, who was looking moodily into the fire.

'I'm going to Barnes, old chap. Is there anything you want?'

Basil began to tremble violently, and his pallor grew still more ghastly.

'What about the inquest? Have I got to go through that?'

'I'm afraid so.'

'And the whole story will come out. They'll know it was my fault, and I shall never be able to hold up my head again. Oh, Frank, is there no way out of it?'

Frank shook his head, and Basil's mouth was drawn to an expression of hopeless despair. He said nothing more till the other was on the point of leaving the room; then he jumped up.

'Frank, there's one thing you must do for me. I suppose you think me a cad and a brute. Heaven knows I despise myself as much as anyone else can do – but because we've been friends for such ages do one thing more for me. I don't know what Jenny said to her people, and they'll welcome a chance of hitting me now I'm down – Mrs Murray's name must be kept out of it at any cost.'

Frank stopped and meditated for a moment.

'I'll see what I can do,' he replied.

On his way to Waterloo the doctor went round to Old Queen Street and found Miss Ley breakfasting.

'How is Basil this morning?' she asked.

'Poor devil! he's in rather a bad way. I scarcely know what

325

to do with him. I think as soon as the inquest is over he'd better go abroad.'

'Why don't you let him stay here till then? I'll feed him up.'

'You'd only fuss. He's much better by himself. He'll just brood over it till his mind is exhausted, and then things will get better.'

Miss Ley smiled at the scorn with which he refused her suggestion, and waited for him to go on.

'Look here, I want you to lend me some money. Will you pay two hundred and fifty pounds into my bank this morning?'

'Of course I will,' she answered, delighted to be asked.

She went to her desk to get a cheque-book, while Frank looked at her with a little smile.

'Don't you want to know what it's for?'

'Not unless you wish to tell me.'

'You brick!'

He shook her hand warmly, and glancing at his watch, bolted off to Waterloo. When he arrived at River Gardens, Fanny, the servant, who opened the door, told him that James Bush was waiting to see him. She said he had been telling her all he meant to do to ruin Basil, and had been through the house to find papers and letters. Frank congratulated himself on the caution with which he had locked up everything. He walked upstairs softly, and opening the door, found James trying various keys on the writing-table. He started away when Frank entered, but quickly recovered his coolness.

'Why are all these drawers locked up?' he asked impudently.

'Presumably so that curious persons should not examine their contents,' answered Frank, with great amiability.

'Where's that man? He's murdered my sister. He's a blackguard and a murderer, and I'll tell him so to his face.'

'I was hoping to find you here, Mr Bush. I wanted to have a talk with you. Won't you sit down?'

'No, I won't sit down,' he answered aggressively. 'This ain't the 'ouse that a gentleman would sit down in. I'll be even with 'im yet. I'll tell the jury a pretty story. He deserves to be strung up, he does.'

Frank looked sharply at the auctioneer's clerk, noting the keen suspicious eyes, the thin lips, and the expression of low cunning. Wishing to prevent a scandalous scene at the inquest, for Basil was ill enough and wretched enough without having to submit to cross-examination on his domestic affairs, Frank thought it would not be difficult to bring James Bush to the frame of mind he desired; but the distaste with which this person inspired him led the doctor to use a very brutal frankness. He felt with such a man it was better not to mince matters, and unnecessary to clothe his meaning with flattering euphemisms.

'What d'you think you'll get out of making a row at the inquiry?' he said, looking fixedly into the other's eyes.

'Oh, you've thought of that, 'ave you? Did Master Basil send you to get round me? It won't work, young feller. I mean to make it as 'ot for Basil as I can. I've 'ad something to put up with, I 'ave. He's simply treated me like dirt. I wasn't good enough for 'im, if you please.'

He hissed the words with the utmost malevolence, and it was possible to imagine that he cared little for his sister's death, except that it gave opportunity for paying off the score which had so long rankled with him.

'Supposing you sat down quietly and listened to me without interruption for five minutes.'

'You're trying to bamboozle me, but you won't. I can see through you as if you was a pane of glass. You people in the West End – you think you know everything!'

Frank waited calmly till James Bush held his offensive tongue.

'What d'you think the furniture of this house is worth?' he asked deliberately.

The question surprised James, but in a moment he replied.

'It's a very different thing what a thing's worth and what it'll fetch. If it was sold by a man as knew his business, it might fetch – a hundred pounds.'

'Basil thought of giving it to your mother and sister – on the condition, of course, that nothing is said at the inquest.'

James burst into a shout of ironical laughter.

327

'You make me laugh. D'you think you can gag me by giving a houseful of furniture to my mother and sister? '

'I had no such exalted opinion of your disinterestedness,' smiled Frank icily. 'I come to you now. It appears that you owe Basil a good deal of money. Can you pay it?'

'No.'

'Also it appears there was some difficulty with your accounts in your last place.'

'That's a lie,' James interrupted hotly.

'Possibly,' retorted Frank, with the utmost calm. 'I merely mention it to suggest to your acute intelligence that we could make it uncommonly nasty for you if you made a fuss. If dirty linen is going to be washed in public, there's generally a good deal to be said on both sides.'

'I don't care,' cried the other vindictively; 'I mean to get my own back. If I can get my knife into that man, I'll take the consequences.'

'I understand it is your intention to unfold to a delighted jury the whole story of Basil's married life.' Frank paused and looked at the other. 'I'll give you fifty pounds to hold your tongue.'

The offer was made cynically, and James actually coloured. He jumped up indignantly, and went over to Frank, who remained seated, watching with somewhat amused indifference.

'Are you trying to bribe me? I would 'ave you know that I'm a gentleman; and, what's more, I'm an Englishman, and I'm proud of it. I've never had anyone try and bribe me before.'

'Otherwise you would doubtless have accepted,' murmured Frank gently.

The doctor's coolness greatly disconcerted the little clerk. He felt vaguely that high-flown protestations were absurd, for Frank had somehow taken his measure so accurately that it was no use to make any false pretences.

'Come, come, Mr Bush, don't be ridiculous. The money will doubtless be very useful to you, and you're far too clever to allow private considerations to have any effect on you where business is concerned.'

328

'What d'you think fifty pounds is to me?' cried James, a little uncertainly.

'You must have mistaken me,' said Frank, after a quick look. 'The sum I mentioned was a hundred and fifty.'

'Oh!' He coloured again, and a curious look came over his face. 'That's a very different pair of shoes.'

'Well?'

Frank observed the struggle in the man's mind, and it interested him to see some glimmering of shame. James hesitated, and then forced himself to speak; but it was not with his usual self-assurance – it was almost in a whisper.

'Look 'ere, make it two hundred and I'll say done.'

'No,' answered Frank firmly. 'You can take one fifty or go to the devil.'

James made no reply, but seeing that he agreed, Frank took a cheque from his pocket, wrote it out at the desk, and handed it.

'I'll give you fifty now, and the rest after the inquest.'

James nodded, but did not answer. He was curiously humbled. He looked at the door, and then glanced at Frank, who understood.

'There's nothing you need stay for. If you're wanted for anything, I'll let you know.'

'Well, so long.'

James Bush walked out with somewhat the air of a whipped cur. In a moment the servant passed through the room.

'Has Mr Bush gone?' asked Frank.

'Yes. And good riddance to bad rubbish.'

Frank looked at her reflectively.

'Ah, Fanny, if there were no rogues in the world, life would really be too difficult for honest men.'

15

Six months went by, and again the gracious airs of summer blew into Miss Ley's dining-room in Old Queen Street. She sat at luncheon with Mrs Castillyon, wonderfully rejuvenated by a winter in the East, for Paul, characteristically anxious to combine self-improvement with pleasure, had suggested that they should mark their reconciliation by a journey to India, where they might enjoy a second, pleasanter honeymoon, and he at the same time study various questions which would be to him of much political value. Mrs Castillyon, in a summer frock, had all her old daintiness of a figure in Dresden china, and her former vivacity was more charming by reason of an added tenderness. She emphasized her change of mind by allowing her hair to regain its natural colour.

'D'you like it, Mary?' she asked. 'Paul says it makes me look ten years younger. And I've stopped slapping up.'

'Entirely?' asked Miss Ley, with a smile.

'Of course, I powder a little, but that doesn't count; and you know, I never use a puff now – only a leather. You can't think how we enjoyed ourselves in India, and Paul's a perfect duck. He's been quite awfully good to me. I'm simply devoted to him, and I think we shall get a baronetcy at the next Birthday honours.'

'The reward of virtue.'

Mrs Castillyon coloured and laughed.

'You know, I'm afraid I shall become a most awful prig, but the fact is it's so comfortable to be good and to have nothing to reproach one's self with. ... Now tell me about everyone. Where did you pass the winter?'

'I went to Italy as usual, and my cousin Algernon with his daughter spent a month with me at Christmas.'

'Was she awfully cut up at the death of her husband?'

There was really a note of genuine sympathy in Mrs Castillyon's voice, so that Miss Ley realized how sincere was the change in her.

'She bore it very wonderfully, and I think she's curiously happy. She tells me that she feels constantly the presence of Herbert.' Miss Ley paused. 'Bella has collected her husband's verses and wishes to publish them, and she's written a very touching account of his life and death by way of preface.'

'No; that's just the tragedy of the whole thing. I never knew a man whose nature was so entirely poetical, and yet he never wrote a line which is other than mediocre. If he'd only written his own feelings, his little hopes and disappointments, he might have done something good; but he's only produced pale imitations of Swinburne and Tennyson and Shelley. I can't understand how Herbert Field, who was so simple and upright, should never have turned out a single stanza which wasn't stilted and forced. I think in his heart he felt that he hadn't the gift of literary expression, which has nothing to do with high ideals, personal sincerity, or the seven deadly virtues, for he was not sorry to die. He only lived to be a great poet, and before the end realized that he would never have become one.'

Miss Ley saw already the pretty little book which Bella would publish at her own expense, the neat type and wide margin, the dainty binding; she saw the scornful neglect of reviewers, and the pile of copies which eventually Bella would take back and give one by one as presents to her friends, who would thank her warmly, but never trouble to read ten lines.

'And what has happened to Reggie Bassett?' asked Grace suddenly.

Miss Ley gave her a quick glance, but the steadiness of Mrs Castillyon's eyes told her that she asked the question indifferently, perhaps to show how entirely her infatuation was overcome.

'You heard that he married?'

'I saw it in the *Morning Post*.'

'His mother was very indignant, and for three months refused to speak to him. But at last I was able to tell her that an heir was expected; so she made up her mind to swallow her pride, and become reconciled with her daughter-in-law, who is a very nice, sensible woman.'

'Pretty?' asked Grace.

'Not at all, but eminently capable. Already she has made Reggie into quite a decent member of society. Mrs Bassett has now gone down to Bournemouth, where the young folks have taken a house, to be at hand when the baby appears.'

'It's reassuring to think that the ancient race of the Barlow-Bassetts will not be extinguished,' murmured Grace ironically. 'I gathered that your young friend was settling down, because one day he returned every penny I had – lent him.'

'And what did you do with it?' asked Miss Ley.

Grace flushed and smiled whimsically.

'Well, it happened to reach me just before our wedding-day, so I spent it all on a gorgeous pearl pin for Paul. He was simply delighted.'

Mrs Castillyon got up, and when she was gone Miss Ley took a letter that had come before luncheon, but which her guest's arrival had prevented her from opening. It was from Basil, who had spent the whole winter, on Miss Ley's recommendation, in Seville. She opened it curiously, for it was the first time he had written to her since, after the inquest, he left England.

My dear Miss Ley,

Don't think me ungrateful if I have left you without news of me, but at first I felt I could not write to people in England. Whenever I thought of them everything came back, and it was only by a desperate effort that I could forget. For some time it seemed to me that I could never face the world again, and I was tormented by self-reproach; I vowed to give up my whole life to the expression of my deep regret, and fancied I could never again have a peaceful moment or anything approaching happiness. But presently I was ashamed to find that I began to regain my old temper; I caught myself at times laughing contentedly, amused and full of spirits; and I upbraided myself bitterly because only a few weeks after the poor girl's death I could actually be entertained by trivial things. And then I don't know what came over me, for I could not help the thought that my prison door was opened; though I called myself brutal and callous, deep down in my soul arose the idea that the

332

Fates had given me another chance. The slate was wiped clean, and I could start fresh. I pretended even to myself that I wanted to die, but it was sheer hypocrisy – I wanted to live and to take life by both hands and enjoy it. I have such a desire for happiness, such an eager yearning for life in its fullness and glory. I made a ghastly mistake, and I suffered for it: Heaven knows how terribly I suffered, and how hard I tried to make the best of it. And perhaps it wasn't all my fault – even to you I feel ashamed of saying this; I ought to go on posing decently to the end – in this world we're made to act and think things because others have thought them good; we never have a chance of going our own way; we're bound down by the prejudices and the morals of all and sundry. For God's sake let us be free. Let us do this and that because we want to and because we must, not because other people think we ought. And d'you know the worst of the whole thing? If I'd acted like a blackguard and let Jenny go to the dogs, I should have remained happy and contented and prosperous, and she, I dare say, wouldn't have died. It's because I tried to do my duty that all this misery came about. The world held up an ideal, and I thought they meant one to act up to it; it never occurred to me that they would only sneer.

Don't think too badly of me because I say these things; they have come to me here, and it was you who sent me to Seville; you must have known what effect it would have on my mind, tortured and sick. It is a land of freedom, and at last I have become conscious of my youth. How can I forget the delight of wandering in the Sierpes, released from all imprisoning ties, watching the various movement as though it were a stage-play, yet half afraid that a falling curtain would bring back the unendurable reality? The songs, the dances, the happy idleness of orange-gardens by the Guadalquivir, the gay turbulence of Seville by night: I could not long resist it, and at last forgot everything but that time was short and the world was to the living.

By the time you get this letter I shall be on my way home.

Yours ever,
BASIL KENT

Miss Ley read this letter with a smile and gave a little sigh.

'I suppose at that age one can afford to have no very conspicuous sense of humour,' she murmured.

But she sent Basil a telegram asking him to stay, with the

result that three days later the young man arrived, very brown after his winter in the sunshine, healthy and better-looking than ever. Miss Ley had invited Frank to meet him at dinner, and the pair of them, with the cold unconcern of anatomists, observed what changes the intervening time had wrought on that impressionable nature. Basil was in high spirits, delighted to come back to his friends; but a discreet soberness, underlying his vivacity, suggested a more composed temperament. What he had gone through had given him, perhaps, a solid store of experience on which he could rest himself. He was less emotional and more mature. Miss Ley summed up her impressions next time she was alone with Frank.

'Every Englishman has a churchwarden shut away in his bosom, an old man of the sea whom it is next to impossible to shake off. Sometimes you think he's asleep or dead, but he's wonderfully tenacious of life, and sooner or later you find him enthroned in full possession of the soul.'

'I don't know what you mean by the word *soul*,' interrupted Frank, 'but if you do, pray go on.'

'The churchwarden is waking up in Basil, and I feel sure he will have a very successful career. But I shall warn him not to let that ecclesiastical functionary get the upper hand.'

Miss Ley waited for Basil to speak of Mrs Murray, but after two days her patience was exhausted, and she attacked him point-blank. At the mention of the name his cheeks flamed.

'I daren't go and see her. After what happened, I can never see her again. I am steeling myself to forget.'

'And are you succeeding?' she asked dryly.

'No, no – I shall never succeed. I'm more desperately in love with her than ever I was. But I couldn't marry her now. The recollection of poor Jenny would be continually between us; for it was we, Hilda and I, who drove her to her death.'

'Don't be a melodramatic idiot,' answered Miss Ley sharply. 'You talk like the persecuted hero of a penny novelette. Hilda's very fond of you, and she has the feminine common sense which alone counterbalances in the world the romantic folly of men. What on earth do you imagine is the use of making yourselves wretched so that you may cut a picturesque figure? I should have thought you were cured of heroics. You wrote and told me that the world was for the living – an idea which has truth rather than novelty to recommend it – and do you think there is any sense in posturing absurdly to impress an inattentive gallery?'

'How do I know that Hilda cares for me still? She may hate me because I brought on her humiliation and shame.'

'If I were you I'd go and ask her,' laughed Miss Ley. 'And go with good heart, for she cared for you for your physical attractiveness rather than for your character. And that, I may tell you, whatever moralists say, is infinitely more reliable, since you may easily be mistaken in a person's character, but his good looks are obvious and visible. You're handsomer than ever you were.'

When Basil set out to call on Mrs Murray, Miss Ley amused herself with conjecturing ironically the scene of their meeting. With curling lips she noted in her mind's eye the embarrassed handshake, the trivial conversation, the disconcerting silence, and without sympathy imagined the gradual warmth and the passionate declaration that followed. She moralized.

'A common mistake of writers is to make their characters in moments of great emotion express themselves with good taste. Nothing could be more false, for at such times people, however refined, use precisely the terms of the *Family Herald*. The utterance of violent passion is never artistic, but trite, ridiculous and grotesque, vulgar often and silly.' Miss Ley smiled. 'Probably novelists alone make love in a truly romantic manner, but then, it's ten to one they're quoting from some unpublished work, or are listening to themselves in admiration of their glowing and polished phraseology.'

At all events, the interview between Hilda and Basil was eminently satisfactory, as may be seen by the following letter, which some days later the young man received:

MON CHER ENFANT,

It is with the greatest surprise and delight that I read in this morning's *Post* of your engagement to Mrs Murray. You have fallen on your feet, *mon ami*, and I congratulate you. Don't you remem-

335

ber that Becky Sharp said she could be very good on five thousand a year, and the longer I live the more convinced I am that this is a *vraie vérité*. With a house in Charles Street and *le reste* you will find the world a very different place to live in. You will grow more human, dress better, and be less censorious. Do come to luncheon tomorrow, and bring Mrs Murray. There will be a few people, and I hope it will be amusing – one o'clock. I'm afraid it's an extraordinary hour to lunch, but I'm going to be received into the Catholic Church in the morning, and we're all coming on here afterwards. I mean to assume the names of the two saints whose example has most assisted me in my conversion, and henceforth shall sign myself,

> Your affectionate mother,
> MARGUERITE ELIZABETH CLAIRE VIZARD

P.S. – The Duke of St Olpherts is going to be my sponsor.

A month later Hilda Murray and Basil were married in All Souls by the Rev. Collinson Farley. Miss Ley gave away the bride, and in the church besides were only the verger and Frank Hurrell. Afterwards in the vestry Miss Ley shook the Vicar's hand.

'I think it went off very nicely. It was charming of you to offer to marry them.'

'The bride is a very dear friend of mine. I was anxious to give her this proof of my goodwill at the beginning of her new life.' He paused and smiled benignly, so that Miss Ley, who knew something of his old attachment to Hilda, wondered at his good spirits. She had never seen him more trim and imposing; he looked already every inch a Bishop. 'Shall I tell you a great secret?' he added blandly. 'I am about to contract an alliance with Florence, Lady Newhaven. We shall be married at the end of the season.'

'My dear Mr Farley, I congratulate you with all my heart. I see already these shapely calves encased in the gaiters episcopal.'

Mr Farley smiled pleasantly, for he made a practice of appreciating the jests of elderly maiden ladies with ample means, and he could boast that to his sense of humour was due the luxurious appointing of his church; for no place of

336

worship in the West End had more beautiful altar-cloths and handsomer ornaments, nowhere could be seen smarter hassocks for the knees of the devout or hymn-books in a more excellent state of preservation.

The newly-married couple meant to spend their honeymoon on the river, and having lunched in Charles Street, started immediately.

'I'm thankful they don't want us to see them off at Paddington,' said Frank, when he walked with Miss Ley towards the Park.

'Why are you in such an abominable temper?' she asked, smiling. 'During luncheon I was twice on the point of reminding you that marriage is an event at which a certain degree of hilarity is not indecorous.'

Frank did not answer, and now they turned in at one of the Park gates. In that gay June weather the place was crowded; though the hour was early still, motors tore along with hurried panting, carriages passed tranquil and dignified; the well-dressed London throng sat about idly on chairs, or lounged up and down looking at their neighbours, talking light-heartedly of the topics of the hour. Frank's eyes travelled over them slowly, and shuddering a little, his brow grew strangely dark.

'During that ceremony and afterwards I could think of nothing but Jenny. It's only eighteen months since I signed my name for Basil's first marriage in a dingy registry office. You don't know how beautiful the girl was on that day, full of love and gratitude and happiness. She looked forward to the future with such eager longing! And now she's rotting underground, and the woman she hated and the man she adored are married, and they haven't a thought for all her misery. I hated Basil in his new frock-coat, and Hilda Murray, and you. I can't imagine why a sensible woman like you should overdress ridiculously for such a function.'

Miss Ley, conscious of the entire success of her costume, could afford to smile at this.

'I have observed that whenever you're out of humour with yourself you insult me,' she murmured.

Frank went on, his face hard and set, his dark eyes glowering fiercely.

'It all seemed so useless. It seemed that the wretched girl had to undergo such frightful torture merely to bring these two commonplace creatures together. They must have no imagination, or no shame – how could they marry with that unhappy death between them? For, after all, it was they who killed her. And d'you think Basil is grateful because Jenny gave him her youth and her love, her wonderful beauty, and at last her life? He doesn't think of her. And you, too, because she was a barmaid are convinced that it's a very good thing she's out of the way. The only excuse I can see for them is that they're blind instruments of fate: Nature was working through them, obscurely, working to join them together for her own purposes, and because Jenny came between she crushed her ruthlessly.'

'I can find a better excuse for them than that,' answered Miss Ley, looking gravely at Frank. 'I forgive them because they're human and weak. The longer I live, the more I am overwhelmed by the utter, utter weakness of men; they do try to do their duty, they do their best honestly, they seek straight ways, but they're dreadfully weak. And so I think one ought to be sorry for them and make all possible allowances. I'm afraid it sounds rather idiotic, but I find the words now most frequently on my lips are: "Forgive them, for they know not what they do."'

They walked silently, and after a while Frank stopped on a sudden and faced Miss Ley. He pulled out his watch.

'It's quite early yet, and we have the afternoon before us. Will you come with me to the cemetery where Jenny is buried?'

'Why not let the dead lie? Let us think of life rather than of death.'

Frank shook his head.

'I must go. I couldn't rest otherwise. I can't bear that on this day she should be entirely forgotten.'

'Very well. I will come with you.'

They turned round and came out of the Park. Frank hailed a cab, and they started. They passed the pompous mansions of the great, sedate and magnificent, and driving north, traversed long streets of smaller dwellings, dingy and grey notwithstanding the brightness of the sky; they went on, it seemed interminably, and each street strangely, awfully, resembled its predecessor. They came to roads where each house was separate and had its garden, and there were trees and flowers. They were the habitations of merchants and stockbrokers, and had a trim, respectable look, self-satisfied and smug; but these they left behind for more crowded parts. And now it seemed a different London, more vivacious, more noisy. The way was thronged with trams and 'buses, and there were coster-barrows along the pavements; the shops were gaudy and cheap, and the houses mean. They drove through slums, with children playing merrily on the curb and women in dirty aprons, blowzy and dishevelled, lounging about their doorsteps. At length they reached a broad straight road, white and dusty and unshaded, and knew their destination was at hand, for occasionally they passed a shop where gravestones were made; and an empty hearse trundled by, the mutes huddled on the box, laughing loudly, smoking after the fatigue of their accustomed work. The cemetery came in sight, and they stopped at iron gates and walked in. It was a vast place, crowded with every imaginable kind of funeral ornament, which glistened white and cold in the sun. It was hideous, vulgar, and sordid, and one shuddered to think of the rude material minds of those who could bury folk they loved in that restless ground, wherein was neither peace nor silence. They might prate of the soul's immortality, but surely in their hearts they looked upon the dead as common clay, or they would never have borne that they should lie till the Day of Judgement in that unhallowed spot. There was about it a gross, business-like air that was infinitely depressing. Frank and Miss Ley walked through, passing a knot of persons, black-robed, about an open grave, where a curate uttered hastily, with the boredom of long habit, the most solemn words that man has ever penned:

Man that is born of a woman hath but a short time to live, and is full of misery. He cometh up, and is cut down, like a flower; he fleeth as it were a shadow, and never continueth in one stay.

Miss Ley, pale of face, took Frank's arm and hurried on. Here and there dead flowers were piled upon new graves; here and there the earth was but freshly turned. They came at last to where Jenny lay, an oblong stone of granite whereon was cut a simple cross; and Frank gave a sudden cry, for it was covered at that moment, so that only the cross was outlined, with red roses. For a while they stared in silence, amazed.

'They're quite fresh,' said Miss Ley. 'They were put here this morning.' She turned to Frank, and looked at him slowly. 'You said they'd forgotten, and they came on their wedding-day and laid roses on her grave.'

'D'you think she came, too?'

'I'm sure of it. Ah, Frank, I think one should forgive them a good deal for that. I told you that they did strive to do right, and if they fell it was only because they were human and very weak. Don't you think it's better for us to be charitable? I wonder if we should have surmounted any better than they did their great difficulties and their great temptations?'

Frank made no reply, and for a long time they contemplated those rich red roses, and thought of Hilda's tender hands laying them gently on the poor woman's cold gravestone.

'You're right,' he said at last. 'I can forgive them a good deal because they had this thought. I hope they will be very happy.'

'I think it's a good omen.' She laid her hand on Frank's arm. 'And now let us go away, for we are living, and the dead have nothing to say to us. You brought me here, and now I want to take you on farther – to show you something more.'

He did not understand, but followed obediently till they came to the cab. Miss Ley told the driver to go straight on, away from London, till she bade him stop. And then, leaving behind them that sad place of death, they came suddenly into the open. The highway had the pleasant brown hardness of a country road, and it was bordered by a hawthorn hedge. Green fields stretched widely on either side, and they might have been a hundred miles from London town. Miss Ley stopped the cab, and told the man to wait whilst she and her friend walked on.

340

'Don't look back,' she said to Frank, 'only look forward. Look at the trees and the meadows.'

The sky was singularly blue, and the dulcet breeze bore gracious odours of the country. There was a suave limpidity of the air which chased away all ugly thoughts. Both of them, walking quickly, breathed with wide lungs, inspiring eagerly the radiance of that summer afternoon. On a turn of the road Miss Ley gave a quick cry of delight, for she saw the hedge suddenly ablaze with wild roses.

'Have you a knife?' she said. 'Do cut some.'

And she stood while he gathered a great bunch of the simple fresh flowers. He gave them to her, and she held them with both hands.

'I love them because they're the same roses as grow in Rome from the sarcophagi in the gardens. They grow out of those old coffins to show us that life always triumphs over death. What do I care for illness and old age and disease! The world may be full of misery and disillusion, it may not give a tithe of what we ask, it may offer hatred instead of love – disappointment, wretchedness, triviality, and heaven knows what; but there is one thing that compensates for all the rest, that takes away the merry-go-round from a sordid show, and gives it a meaning, a solemnity, and a magnificence, which make it worth while to live. And for that one thing all we suffer is richly overpaid.'

'And what the dickens is that?' asked Frank, smiling.

Miss Ley looked at him with laughing eyes, holding out the roses, her cheeks flushed.

'Why, beauty, you dolt!' she cried gaily. 'Beauty.'

THE HISTORY OF VINTAGE

The famous American publisher Alfred A. Knopf (1892–1984) founded Vintage Books in the United States in 1954 as a paperback home for the authors published by his company. Vintage was launched in the United Kingdom in 1990 and works independently from the American imprint although both are part of the international publishing group, Random House.

Vintage in the United Kingdom was initially created to publish paperback editions of books acquired by the prestigious hardback imprints in the Random House Group such as Jonathan Cape, Chatto & Windus, Hutchinson and later William Heinemann, Secker & Warburg and The Harvill Press. There are many Booker and Nobel Prize-winning authors on the Vintage list and the imprint publishes a huge variety of fiction and non-fiction. Over the years Vintage has expanded and the list now includes both great authors of the past – who are published under the Vintage Classics imprint – as well as many of the most influential authors of the present.

For a full list of the books Vintage publishes, please visit our website
www.vintage-books.co.uk

For book details and other information about the classic authors we publish, please visit the Vintage Classics website
www.vintage-classics.info

www.vintage-classics.info